Elsa

The Secret Heritage
Book 1

Allison Bruning

Marfa House
Marfa, Texas

Published by Marfa House

ISBN: 978-1-940022-82-6

REVIEWS

Must Read Historical Romance!

Elsa is the first book in the Heritage Series. It is the tale of a woman in love with a man with high-functioning autism. Of course, the condition was never given a name in the book because at that time it didn't have one, but looking back now with our knowledge of the condition it's easy to tell that's what it was. This book was a refreshing look at the unconditional love and acceptance of an individual of a person with special needs.

Elsa is jam-packed with family drama. With the male-centred society at that time women tended to be more like chattel and had to do what their husbands told them. If their husbands did not provide enough for them to take care of them after they died, then the wives would lose their homes and end up relying on other family or out on the street. Women did what their husbands told them to do or they could be "disciplined" by their husbands.

The story of Elsa and Franklin is a beautiful one and full of unconditional love. Two people who want nothing more than to be husband and wife are met with an enormous number of obstacles. The twists and turns in the plot lines of this book brought insight into the main protagonist's characters as well as the way of life for women in that era.

– Kathryn Svendsen

Great Story! Just What I Needed.

Elsa, is a strong woman who is willing to fight for what is right, her struggles feel very real and are placed appropriately for the time line of the story. Franklin (The man Elsa wants to marry) is well developed as a character with a quite believable life. The drama that the reader experiences throughout the book is quite intriguing and keeps the reader's mind grasping for more.

Franklin, really seems to have no place in society, Elsa sees him differently and quite interestingly this makes her character even more powerful and creates a strong reason for the reader to continue reading just to try and understand her desires.

The sexual scenes are well written, explorative but still leaves something to the imagination of the reader to develop for themselves. There are many twists and turns and events that I do not want to ruin for the perspective reader, but I must admit there is something here for everyone and you will not be disappointed.

-JesterDev

Great Read!

All Elsa Garrett wants in life is to be Franklin's wife. He's asked her father for her hand and knows he has permission to ask her. Yet when and how would her boyfriend with Aspergers Syndrome ask the question?

When Franklin has a diabetic seizure all hope seems lost once Elsa learns Franklin can no longer marry her due to an obscure law in Ohio relating to his seizure. With the help of Franklin's parents, Elsa has a plan. But will it work?

Lost in a society that doesn't understand Franklin or why she would ever choose to be with him, Elsa comes face to face with death, destruction, and misfortune as she tries to clear her boyfriend's name. With each step towards progress Elsa falls two steps behind. One simple task shifts her entire life towards a direction she could have never imagined. Alone, pregnant, and without her Franklin, is despair all she has to look forward to in her new life, or will fate finally bring them together?

This book was very well-written.. characters in this book all very strong..this book was very caring and all emotions there as well..
I also have some dislikes about this book even how good it was.. i found myself skipping parts to get to the good stuff because some parts just little boring i hate saying that but would i read book 2 when it comes out that be big YES.

- Theresa F.

By Allison Bruning

<u>Novels</u>
Calico (Children of the Shawnee)
Elsa (The Secret Heritage)
Bailey's Revenge (Irish Twist of Fate)

<u>Poems</u>
Reflections: Poems and Essays

<u>Short Stories</u>
Who is the Real John Wilkes Booth?
(Non-fiction)
The Lady of Wild Rose Pass
(Paranormal)
The Legacy (Christian Fiction)
The Lost Camper

Acknowledgements

This book and the rest of the books in the series are loosely based on the actual events of one of my ancestor's lives. The names and some of the circumstances have been changed to maintain their privacy.

As of May 2012, the DSM-5 no longer used the term Asperger's Syndrome to diagnosis someone who exhibited impairment in social interaction; stereotyped patterned or repetitive behaviors, activities, and interests; or who did not have a significant delay in language or cognitive development. The new term to use is Autistic Spectrum Disorder.

DEDICATION

This book is dedicated to Jeff and Kate Carr, a wonderful, sweet couple who taught me what it means to love someone unconditionally.

My husband, Delfin Espinosa, who kept encouraging me to chase after my literary dreams.

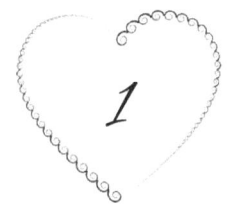

The warm spring sun shone over the flat north-central Ohio farmlands. Sweat soaked Franklin Thaddeus Raymond's short-sleeve undershirt as he stood on the front porch of his parents' two-story farmhouse. He watched his thirteen-year-old brother, Abraham, eagerly plow the last of the fields. His black suspenders gripped against his machine-made, white, silk-cotton undershirt. Franklin picked up the metal canteen in the porch chair. Exhausted, he sat in the chair with the canteen, leaned his head back, and closed his weary eyes. Moments of blissful silence filled his mind. He took several deep breaths then lifted the canteen to his mouth. The cool refreshing water soothed his parched throat and dry mouth. He emptied the canteen, wanting more. Nothing could satisfy his thirst. His stomach growled for food while his throat begged for more water. He looked into the dry canteen with disappointment. He had worked hard all day. He needed more water but couldn't find the strength to rise from his chair. Since daybreak he had plowed his father's fields with few breaks in between. With ten acres of land to plow, the task took days to complete. As the eldest son, he had done the work by himself plenty of times when his father was ill or injured. The work took a toll on his body and he couldn't afford to miss the church social tonight. Desperate for relief he had asked his father, Gideon, to allow Abraham to help him with the fields three days ago. Gideon granted Abraham permission to help Franklin.

Franklin's head pounded. He scrunched his head with a long groan. A wet towel slapped across his face. Franklin opened his eyes, grabbed the towel then jerked his face to the left. His sixteen-year-old sister, Cora, stood over him with her hands on her hip. "What?" he grunted to her.

"Pa said you were to share the work with Abraham, not let him do all of it."

"He's not doing all of it. I have a headache and he has a field to finish."

"You'll have more than that if Pa comes home to find brother did all the work."

"Go away, Cora. Pa left me in charge not you."

"Uh huh, Pa didn't trust you alone with Abraham. That's why I'm here," she teased.

"You're here to finish the chores inside the house while we plow the fields! I'm the eldest son, Cora. I know what I'm doing."

"Right, and that's why you're here and Abraham's out there."

"I'll have you know, it takes five hours to plow one field. We have ten. Do the math, Cora. I have ten fields to plow, two teams of horses, and two plows. That means if I had done the work by myself, letting each team rest while the other worked, I could push out two maybe three fields per day. But if Abraham and I split the teams we could save the time, assuming we don't push both teams too hard. I had already finished six fields before I asked Pa for Abraham's help today. That left four fields. I've been out here since five this morning. According to the sun it's already three. I skipped lunch and pushed my team hard so I could finish in time to get ready for tonight. Which means, dear sister, my horses are in the back pasture and my work's done."

"And how much more does Abraham have to finish?"

"He just started his last field."

"Franklin, help him finish it."

"No."

"Abraham's done more work than you have. He cleaned the barn, milked the cows, fed the chickens, and now he's plowing two acres by himself. What have you done?"

"Helped."

"More like daydreaming of Elsa Beatrice Garrett."

Franklin growled deep in his throat. "You best be glad your boyfriend isn't around to hear this conversation."

"Oh, do you have something against my manners?"

"Yes, you don't have any."

Cora gasped, "Franklin Thaddeus Raymond, how dare you insult me?!"

"A proper woman of society does not inquire or comment on

someone's private affairs in conversations," he stated as a matter of fact.

"I don't have to listen to you, Frank. You're only my brother."

Franklin glared at her with a smug look on his face but he knew his blonde sister spoke truth. Thoughts of Elsa had captured his thoughts. For nine years, Elsa's older brother Henry had lived on the small farm south of their home with his wife, the once widowed Portia Bradley, and her son, Sam. The widow had been the talk of the county for years until she had married Henry. Before their marriage, there wasn't any man who wanted to be associated with her. Who would want a woman in her late thirties as a wife? Especially one who already had a son. Franklin had felt bad for the widow. Mrs. Bradley didn't have a dime to her name after the creditors took what her husband had owed. She and her son had returned to her parents' home in Wyandot County, Ohio. A year later her mother died of old age. Six months after that her father had a heart attack and joined his wife in heaven. When the creditors came she had no more money to give them. The creditors had threatened to auction off her house and farm in order to pay the debts. Everyone in the county had felt bad for the old widow.

On the day of the auction, the community had made certain no outsiders could attend the auction, then they had all gathered around Portia's house, where they bought everything the creditors sold. Afterwards, the creditors left town with their money and the community sold everything back to widow Bradley for a penny. Portia had been speechless with gratitude. That night, Franklin's father offered Mrs. Bradley a position in the factory while Sam attended school. After school, Franklin, Sam, and other boys from the community would help the old widow with the farm work. For eight years, the widow worked in their factory and on her farm.

Then four years ago, Henry Garrett mysteriously arrived, married her, and they settled down. Many had questioned where he had come from. The only reply from Mrs. Bradley was that she had met him in Marion. Franklin often wondered when she had the time and where she met this mysterious man. No one saw or heard of his family until last April when Henry grew ill with tuberculosis. Elsa had arrived with her parents and older brother, Nathan. One Sunday afternoon, Franklin's family had visited the

Garrett family. There Elsa had instantly caught his attention. Armed with any excuse he could think of, Franklin had made extra trips to Henry's farm just to see the brown-eyed girl who had stolen his heart. Several times, he spoke to Elsa only to be interrupted by Nathan. He could hear the female members of her family gossiping: "Oh, I think that boy has an eye for our Elsa Bea." Annoyed, he tried to ignore them all. Every night he dreamed of her and each day made him think of her even more. Her brown hair and eyes, the way her dress highlighted the S-shaped curve of her body, and her sweet smile.

"Miss Elsa Beatrice Garrett is a good person," Franklin interrupted the silence.

"Are you balmy on the crumpet?"

"I'm not insane! Pa said I don't belong in a mental hospital! I'm just different. Not insane. Different."

"You're different all right, Frank," she muttered.

"What?"

Cora ignored him. "Frank, Elsa's an outcast, an absent-minded beggar on the doss."

"She is not a vagabond. She has a home."

"That home belongs to her brother, not her parents."

"She's not homeless. There's a roof over her head. If she was homeless she wouldn't have a home to stay in therefore she is not homeless," he argued.

"No she's poor. Poor people should never associate with the middle class."

"Cora, that's petty."

"Have you seen how dirty and baggy her clothes are? No respectable woman should be seen in public with clothes like hers. A fashionable woman should look like the Gibson girl. A tight waist, an emphasis on the hips and big bosoms," she replied showing off her curves as she spoke.

"Miss Elsa doesn't have the financial resources you do. Your boyfriend has more than enough money to buy you what you want."

"Money is no excuse to not ascribe to the current fashions. Mr. Garrett could afford to clothe his daughter in better attire."

"Mr. Garrett does the best he can do with what he has to

offer. He served the Ohio 1st Heavy Artillery Regiment during the Civil War. He lost most of his hearing working the mortars, and his knees are bad from marching. He depends on his pension and farming to feed his family."

"That's not an excuse. Our family served in that war too."

"Our Pa was twelve when Ohio entered the war. His father served in the war and lost his life. Pa suffered. Grandma Raymond had to move into her parents' home to raise Pa, his brother, and his sisters while she worried about her eldest son in the war."

"Uncle Vernon survived the war."

"Cora, Uncle Vernon was shot in the knee in the same battle that Grandpa Raymond was shot in the chest. He was seventeen. When the doctors came they tried to save Grandpa first but Grandpa Raymond told them to help his son first. The doctor prepared to cut Uncle Vernon's leg. Grandpa Raymond held Uncle Vernon's hand and told him when the doctor takes his leg he was to fight the urge to die. Uncle Vernon was sedated. He never heard his father's last breath. The military brought Grandpa's body home when Uncle Vernon was dismissed from the army. After Uncle Vernon returned home he suffered from terrible nightmares, then an infection. Pa had to help Uncle Vernon a lot. A month later he found his brother dead in the bed. Cora, that war affected a lot of families, including our own. It took Pa years to get over the loss of his brother and father."

"Pa survived that and Grandma remarried. Everything turned out alright."

"Pa didn't suffer like Mr. Garrett did. Most of the soldiers who returned home had a harder time providing an income for their families. They were either physically disabled and depended on their pensions or suffered mentally. The men who stayed home fared better financially than the men who fought in the war."

"It's still not an excuse. Besides, does Miss Elsa even know how to speak? I went to school with her last year. She just sat there, did her work, and never participated when the teacher asked."

"She's worried about Mr. Henry. He has days when he doesn't tire or cough blood; then there are days he does. It's the bad days that are worse for Miss Elsa. She's only known death, illness, and tragedy. The threat of Mr. Henry's imminent demise only brings forth the pain she's hidden for years. She's not a bad person, just a person with horrible circumstances."

"And when you asked Mr. Garrett for her hand did you think how it might affect members of our family?"

"What is it between you and Miss Elsa Garrett?" Franklin yelled, exhausted from his sister's constant belittling of his beloved.

"I only care for your welfare."

"You have never cared for my welfare."

"That's not true. I love all my brothers, including you. It's just sometimes you act without thinking about the consequences. If you marry Elsa, there will be consequences."

"Consequences?"

"Frank, she can never make you as happy as Rebekah Webster does. Elsa is only an infatuation. You've had them before."

"I love Elsa."

"You think you do. But sometimes what you think is not always what you feel. You have problems with relationships and lord knows a fly has better social skills than you do."

"A fly doesn't have social skills. It's an insect."

"Exactly. Frank. Rebekah's a better match for you."

"Cora, let me set something straight for you. No matter how you may feel, I know the woman I love and my heart no longer beats for Miss Rebekah Grace Webster. Tonight, Pa will present Miss Elsa and me in front of the entire county. I need to know my sister, my only sister, accepts the woman I love."

"I'll support you but never her."

"That's not fair."

"That's a consequence you have to think about. You know the woman I'll support and it's not Miss Elsa Beatrice Garrett. She…" Franklin turned his eyes towards the field, ignoring his sister's constant pleas for him to drop Elsa out of his life.

Abraham sang while he led the team of horses down another row with the reigns around his neck. Abraham tripped over something and fell to the ground with the reins twisted around his neck. Mindlessly, the horses picked up speed, dragging Abraham behind them. Abraham screamed, "Frank!" Franklin jumped from his chair quickly. "Abraham," he screamed with a clumsy sprint towards the plow. Franklin's heart pounded fiercely with each leap he took towards the runaway plow. The muscles of his legs burned as he ran. He tripped over his own feet several times between sprints. His brother's body bounced on the hard ground. "Let go of the reins," Franklin yelled, rising from the ground where he had tripped and fell.

"I can't!"

"Do it before you choke! I can't run any faster!" Abraham sobbed as he moved his hands towards the reigns. Franklin tried to run faster as the horses picked up speed. He peered towards the horses. Side to side, the horses wove Abraham and the plow uncontrollably down the acre. Abraham screamed then fell silent. His limp body bounced up and down. "No," Franklin whispered to himself. "Abraham," he yelled after him. His brother never responded. Franklin stared down at his feet as he ran. All his life his legs and feet had given him problems. Uncoordinated, he could never run, skip, or hop like the other boys his age. Even when he walked he was different. His gait was noticeably different when he walked, even more so when he ran.

"Abraham," Cora cried nearby. Franklin turned his head to the right. Cora ran a few paces behind him. "Do something, they'll kill him before they ever stop from exhaustion," she pleaded to her older brother.

Franklin glanced across the plow then turned to Cora. "Stay with him."

"What are you going to do?"

"Don't worry about me, worry about Abraham. Can you run any faster?"

"Yes."

"Good, catch up to Abraham while I stop the horses."

"Frank," she yelled as Franklin sprinted towards the brown mares. He ignored his sister's pleas. Cora had every right to be scared. At the speed the horses were travelling if he made the wrong move Abraham wouldn't be the only one to die. At 1,000 pounds each, cantering at twenty miles per hour, one slip of his foot and the four-year-old mares could stampede him to death. Franklin lunged towards the larger horse and grabbed her by the bridle. The panicked horse protested. With gusto, Franklin tried to pull himself onto the horse's back. The mare shook her body, his foot slipped and his leg slid back to the side. The horse gained more speed. Franklin began to lose his grip. His feet hit the hard ground.

"Franklin!" Cora yelled.

"Shut up," he yelled with annoyance as he regained control of his limbs. The last thing he needed was Cora's screaming. His fingers began to loosen their grip on the bridle. Franklin grasped it tighter, inhaled a deep breath, and gathered what little strength he possessed. With a loud grunt he lifted his leg over the mare's large back and settled onto her back. Franklin sighed in relief. He looked behind him at Cora then to Abraham. He didn't have much time until the reins around his brother's neck suffocated him. Franklin quickly leaned over the mare's long neck with his hand on the left reign. He leaned across the second horse, grabbed the other reign then pulled. "Whoa," he ordered several times, pulling with all his might.

"Hurry, Frank. The plow pulled him under! He struggles to breathe! The blades hit his legs! He's not reacting to it," Cora protested with a sprint beside the horse.

Franklin jerked harder on the reigns and pulled himself back. "Whoa, Bess. Whoa, Sally." The mares finally submitted under his familiar command. With a long sigh of relief Franklin tapped Bess on the neck. "Good girl." Franklin lowered himself off the horse and ran towards the back. Abraham lay behind the harrow with blood down his torn pants. Cora untangled the reins from Abraham's neck and threw them to the side. Abraham gasped with his eyes bulged then coughed. Deep red marks circled his throat. Franklin rubbed his brother's chest. He scanned with his eyes then ran his hand down Abraham's long, thin legs. Abraham screamed at his touch. He peered up at Cora, "The leg's broken. I can see the bone. We need Doctor Riley."

"The telephone's broke. Pa tried to fix it but said he needed a new piece. We can't use it until he returns," Cora replied.

"I'll ride to Marion."

"Doctor Riley's at least an hour ride to Marion on a good horse and Pa took those with him to Upper Sandusky."

Franklin lifted his eyes towards the road with frustration. Cora was right. Without the good horses on the farm his trip would take too long. He thought about the options he had. They could wait for their parents to arrive home but how long would that take? He could run to the nearest farm for help but that was at least two miles away and the neighbors couldn't afford a telephone let alone a car. He turned his eyes towards Abraham. Abraham sobbed while Cora applied pressure to the bleeding. "We can take you to the house and wait."

Abraham shook his head, "No."

"I won't leave you and Cora alone."

"Pa has the carriage. I can't ride. Go to Marion. Get the doctor."

Franklin ran to Bess, untied her from Sally, jumped on her back, and slipped off. "Franklin, maybe I should go instead," Cora protested as he tried to climb on the horse's back and fell again.

"I can do it," he yelled, grapping tighter on the harness. He grunted as he pulled himself up on her back. He turned back to his sister and brother. "Stay with him. I'll be back with the doctor as soon as I can."

"Alright, Frank," she said as she watched him turn around and ride quickly off the farm.

Doctor Jebadiah Riley's Office
Marion, Ohio

Car horns mixed with the sounds of carriages and horses outside the doctor's small office along Marion's busy Main Street. Elsa paced inside the front waiting area of Dr. Riley's office, periodically glancing at the closed door along the back wall that hid the only examination room. How much she wanted to be in there. The wooden clock chimed three times. She lifted her gaze to the grandfather clock in the back left-hand corner behind the doctor's desk. Three o'clock already? Where had the time gone by so quickly? Henry had been in the examination room for an hour and a half! What was going on in there? Her mind filled with concern for her eldest brother. Henry's deep coughs echoed in the examination room before her. She cast her eyes back towards the closed door and listened carefully to the conversation behind the door.

"Lie down, Mr. Garrett," Dr. Riley's medium-toned voice bellowed. A tear fell from Elsa's eye as she listened to her brother move. Elsa felt a tender touch along her back. She wiped her tear then turned. Her mother, Margaret, stood beside her.

"His cough's worse," Elsa whispered to her.

"Henry's lived longer than most with tuberculosis."

"Ma, maybe I shouldn't go to the dance tonight."

Margaret placed her hands on her daughter's shoulders. She wiped them up and down her daughter's thin arms. "Attend the dance. Wear the dress Portia made you. I'm quite certain you'll appease Mr. Franklin Raymond's eyes."

"My beau loves me. He will understand if I miss the Annual Marion County Barn Dance to be with my dying brother."

"Elsa, go to the dance."

"But ma! Henry's dying."

"He's not dying. It's only another fit of the tuberculosis and it will leave him just as it has before."

"You're lying!"

Margaret slapped her hand across her daughter's cheek. The sharp sting of pain radiated through the right side of Elsa's face while a tear fell from her eye. "You will not disrespect me, Elsa. I am your mother. I only want the best for you and the best thing for you to do is go to the dance and think not of Henry's ailment."

"Yes, ma'am," she huffed, rubbing her hand on her face. Elsa stared at her mother's stern face with shock. Rarely had her mother ever struck her. How could her mother be so unreasonable and why was she insisting that she go to a dance when Henry was dying? If anything, she should be telling her to stay home tonight. Her parents held a tight rein of control on her and her brother, Nathan, especially when something went wrong in the family. Elsa crossed her arms across her chest and glared towards her. "Is there something I don't know, Ma?"

Margaret turned her eyes from the door to her daughter. "Elsa, go to the dance and do not ask any me any more questions," Margaret ordered, emphasizing every word.

"Yes, ma'am." Elsa stepped away from her mother. Deep in her heart she wanted to spend time with Franklin. Franklin was the sweetest man she had even known, aside from Henry. Franklin's presence always brought relief to her worried mind. He had a way of dissolving all her cares until nothing came to her mind except him. She wished Franklin was here to support her. No one other than him understood her.

The bell over the front door jingled. Elsa turned her eyes towards it. Her father, Oren Garrett, stepped inside the door with a brown paper-wrapped bundle under his left arm as he leaned upon his simple wooden cane in his right hand. Thick rope surrounded the package. He stepped towards Margaret and handed it to her. "It arrived today." Margaret took it from him then secretly looked into the package.

"Good, this will do just fine. It is absolutely beautiful. I was beginning to worry it wouldn't arrive in time."

Elsa watched her mother peer into the package with curiosity. "Can I see," she asked, stepping towards her mother.

Margaret clutched the package tightly against her chest with both arms. "No," she answered.

Elsa stepped back. It wasn't like her mother to refuse her

request to glance upon any packages she received, especially fabric or store-bought clothes. Fabric and clothes were a luxury to her family.

"Who is it from?" Elsa asked.

"None of your business, Elsa." Margaret turned to her husband. "The boys?" Margaret asked him.

Oren looked at his wife with a shake of his head. "Eh," he said holding his hand behind his ear.

"The boys!"

"Nathan took Sam to the feed store to gather items we need for the livestock. How's our boy?"

Margaret yelled, "No word, yet. Portia went inside with him and the doctor. He…" Henry's loud groans erupted from behind the examination room door, followed by unending deep coughs.

"Sit him forward, Mrs. Garrett," Dr. Riley's voice bellowed. Elsa clutched her heart with worry at each sound of movement. The coughs suddenly ended. "Mr. Garrett!"

Elsa turned to face her parents with a tear in her eye. "Ma?"

Oren tapped Margaret on the arm. She turned from Elsa towards him. "What's wrong, Margaret?"

Portia's voice lifted behind the door, "Breathe!" Thump. Elsa jumped with a jerk of her head towards the door. "Breathe, my love! Breathe," she yelled louder. Another thump then the sound of many feet moving around the room. "Henry! Don't do this to me! Think of our children! You can fight this," she screamed. More movement then another thump. A sudden gasp. Cough.

"Hank," the doctor called to him with his nickname. Cough. "Mr. Henry Garrett, speak to me!"

A tense moment passed through the doctor's office as mother, father, and daughter glared at the door, never taking their eyes off of it. Elsa held her breath, desperately hoping her brother would respond. Maybe this was the end for her brother. Maybe all her fears had come true. Henry had finally died.

"Huh, Portia," Henry gasped then coughed.

Elsa exhaled with a long sigh of relief. Her eldest brother was still alive. She felt conflicted with that sense of relief. Henry's life was full of suffering and hardships due to the tuberculosis. She hated that he had to live like that but his death wouldn't be of any benefit to her. She needed him just as Portia and their children did. Yet deep in her heart she felt the deepest of sorrows for Henry. If he had died he would have found peace and restoration in heaven with Jesus. Why was she being so greedy to think of only herself when he was in agony on a daily basis?

"Portia," Henry gasped from behind the door in between coughs. "Huh, Portia."

"Shh, I'm here, my love. Breathe deep and slow," Portia answered.

Margaret leaned closer to Oren. With a tap of her hand on his chest she said to him loudly, "Hank struggles in the doctor's office. I think it's time."

Elsa stared at her parents with confusion. Time for what, she wondered to herself. "I'm not calling him," Oren yelled.

"He should know. Oren, please, don't let your hate for your brother stop you from doing what you know is the right thing to do. Moses deserves to know about Henry."

"Moses deserves nothing," he growled then walked over to Elsa.

"Pa, who's Moses?" she asked as he stepped towards her.

Her father placed his left hand on his daughter's cheek. "He's nobody to concern yourself with, little girl."

"But Ma said he's your brother. I thought Uncle Jesse and Uncle Carlisle are your brothers."

"They are."

"Then who is Moses? Why did mother call him your brother and why are you upset with him?"

"This has nothing to do with you, Elsa. When the boys return I want you to go home."

"No, Pa."

"Don't argue with me. You don't need to be here if your brother dies."

"She's been disrespectful and argumentative even after you disciplined her in the store, Oren," Margaret yelled.

Oren turned to his wife then to his daughter. He sternly glared at his youngest daughter with a fierce look only a father can give his child. Elsa took a step back. "What's with the attitude, young lady?" he yelled.

"Aren't you going to tell me I can't go to the dance because I have been disrespectful to my mother?"

"Is that what you want?" Margaret asked.

"Henry almost died in there," Elsa yelled pointing to the door. "And you want me to go to some stupid dance!"

"You're going to that dance whether you like it or not," Oren bellowed.

"Why?"

"Don't ask me why. You will do what your mother and I tell you to do! Do you understand me?" Oren yelled, grabbing her by the wrist and pulling her close to him.

"Yes, sir," she spit out in defiance.

Oren grabbed her by the edge of her jacket and pulled her even closer to him. "Elsa, enough with the attitude. I understand you care deeply for Hank. We all do. But that is not an excuse for the disrespectful behavior you have had towards your mother and me ever since we picked Henry up from work! You will honor your mother and me. It's one of God's commandments, or so help me child after the dance is over I will tan your hide so hard you won't be able to sit for a week! Do you understand me?!"

"Yes, sir," she yelled as if she was in the military.

"Good, at ease," he replied lowering his hand from her bodice. "Mr. Raymond said he'd pick you up at six and take you to dinner at the diner before the dance. It is now four. You still need to get ready."

"Yes, Pa."

The bell over the door chimed again. Elsa and Margaret cast their eyes towards the door. Oren turned in response. Gasping for breath, Franklin stumbled inside the doctor's office, staggered forward, then fell to his hands and knees. Franklin lowered his head. His short jet-black hair was matted to his scalp. His lean body soaked with sweat. He trembled as he tried to pull himself off the ground. Franklin's arms gave way. He fell to his stomach with a loud groan. "Franklin," Elsa yelled and ran to his side. She rubbed his back, lifted her hand, and stared at the moisture. "Your undershirt is soaked with sweat. Did you run here?" Franklin stared at the wall. He could hear his beloved's voice but what was she saying? Every sound was slurred. "Franklin," Elsa yelled as she shook his back. He moved his mouth to speak but nothing came out. What did she want, again? "Franklin, answer me!"

"Elsa," he pushed out with slurred speech.

"Lie still. I'll get Doctor Riley," She said as she began to rise.

"No you won't, little girl," Oren yelled. He grabbed her by her arm and pulled his daughter away from Franklin.

"But Pa, he's sick," Elsa protested.

Her father gripped her tighter and pushed her towards Margaret. "Stay with your mother. It's improper for a man to be seen in public without his shirt and waistcoat. He's intoxicated and I won't have you near him."

"Hel…," Franklin swallowed hard then tried to push the words out again. "H…p."

Oren turned his attention towards the young man. "Sir, did you speak?"

"H..el…ugh," Franklin turned his head then fell still.

"Franklin," Elsa yelled in his direction then turned to her father. "Do something, Pa! He's so sick he can't ask for help."

"He's not sick, Elsa. He's drunk." Oren proclaimed as he stepped closer to Franklin. Oren tapped Franklin's side with his cane. "Get up, boy," he ordered. Franklin slowly opened his eyes and peered at the middle-aged man beside him.

"Hmm,"

"I said get up!"

Franklin gathered his strength and rose from the ground. The chair fell over as he pushed himself forward. "Oh," he breathed through his teeth with his hand on his forehead. Franklin pressed his right hand along the wall and moved forward. Oren pushed Elsa behind his back and slowly walked towards his wife. Elsa cautiously kept her eyes on Franklin. A tear strolled down her cheek with each struggling step he took.

"Mr. Raymond?" Oren asked the young man with a deep authoritative voice.

Franklin stumbled to the left. He grabbed another chair for support then turned his head towards Oren. Elsa gasped as she saw his pale face and dry lips. Oren cast his eyes up and down the boy's body then asked, "Where is your shirt?" Franklin stared at Elsa's father without comprehension. Why was his mouth moving but he couldn't hear any tangible words? "Your shirt," Oren yelled.

Franklin shook his head. He pushed his hand down, turned, and then started back to the examination room. He swayed side to side as he made his way to the door. Franklin pounded on the examination room door. Elsa's heart jumped with each pound of his fist. Sympathy filled her. Franklin had always been the strong one in their relationship yet she knew something drastic must have happened for him to present himself without decorum. She wondered what ailed him. Franklin leaned on the door as he pounded. The door opened. Franklin fell forward. Doctor Riley suddenly caught the young man in his arms. "Help, dizzy," Franklin pushed out of his mouth. Finally he was able to say the words.

The middle-aged doctor led Franklin over to his desk and sat him in his chair. Franklin began to close his eyes and slumped in the chair. "Mr. Raymond!" Doctor Riley yelled with a pat to Franklin's face. Elsa grasped her father's arm.

Franklin opened his eyes. He whispered with a heave of his chest, "Help." The grey-haired doctor with metal glasses began to examine Franklin.

"Symptoms?"

Franklin protested with a shake of his head. He opened his mouth to speak but once again the words stayed deep within the recess of his mind, refusing to spill from his lips. "Ugh," he grunted, pressing his hands to his forehead. He leaned his head back and heaved. Why did it have to be so hard to say his brother was in trouble? What he wouldn't give to be able to tell the doctor what needed to be said! He twitched, feeling someone touch his hands.

"Frank, shh, lower your hands, Son. I'm not going to hurt you. I need to examine you," Doctor Riley said gently, guiding Franklin's hands downward. Franklin groaned in agitation. Every touch felt like a thousand tiny needles pricking his skin all over his hands. He couldn't stand it! Why was the doctor touching him! Nobody touched him. Doctor Riley lowered Franklin's hands then began to examine Franklin's face. Franklin arched his head back and tapped his foot in agitation. He moved his head side to side, grunting, trying to detour the doctor.

"He doesn't like to be touched," Elsa proclaimed.

"He hasn't liked to be touched since the day he was born, Miss. Garrett," Doctor Riley answered.

"I can help."

Doctor Riley chuckled, "Young lady, there is nothing you can do for the boy. He's problematic."

"That's because you don't see him."

"Elsa, hush," Oren ordered.

"But Pa."

Doctor Riley turned on his heel and glared at Elsa. Her heart skipped a beat as the three adults glared at her. "You have a better idea, Miss Garrett?"

"There are only two people in this world who can calm him. His father and I. Please let me help you."

"Absolutely not! He's a drunkard," Oren protested.

"I can assure you, Mr. Garrett, Franklin is not a drunk. He's an idiot."

"No, he's not," Elsa protested. "He's the most intelligent, loving, kind man in the world. How can you be his doctor but not see the man before you?"

"Elsa," Margaret disciplined, grabbing her by the arm.

Elsa jerked away from her mother's grip and walked towards the physician. "Please Doctor Riley. He's very ill and obviously been trying to tell you something. I can help."

Doctor Riley peered up at Oren. "Oren?" he questioned.

"Please Pa, think of what Jesus would do in this situation. Franklin's sick and Doctor Riley can't examine him if Franklin won't let him. Please, Pa, please. I love him," Elsa begged her father. Oren glanced over to his wife then back to his daughter. He nodded coldly with a stern eye on Franklin. "Thank you," Elsa proclaimed, leaned up on tiptoes, and kissed her father on the cheek. She ran to Franklin's side.

"Humph," Oren huffed. "If he hurts her…"

"I have never known Franklin to hurt anyone," Doctor Riley interrupted then turned back to Elsa and Franklin. Elsa placed her hand on the side of Franklin's face. He grunted and heaved with his eyes closed.

"Frank," she said, rubbing her thumb along his cheekbone.

"Franklin, listen to my voice. It's me…"

"Elsa," he whispered with a parched throat.

"Yes, shh. Listen to my voice."

"Headache," he muttered.

Elsa turned her attention to Doctor Riley. "He says he has a headache. I can feel the sweat pouring from his face and his hands are trembling."

"Trembling hands? I need to see his eyes," Doctor Riley said from behind her.

Elsa turned back to Franklin. She gently wiped her hand across his brow. "Frank?"

"Hmm," he moaned.

"Open your eyes." Franklin slowly opened his eyes and stared at Elsa. He gulped at the blurry vision of his beloved.

"Elsa?"

"Frank?"

"Am I moving?"

"No, why?"

"Room spins. I'm moving in a circle. Oh, my stomach." He pressed his arm across his stomach and leaned over.

Elsa turned to Doctor Riley. "He's dizzy and has a stomachache."

"Franklin," Doctor Riley stepping toward him.

"Ugh," Franklin moaned.

"Anyone else at home ill?"

Franklin shook his head. "Abraham. Hurt bad."

"What happened?"

Franklin raised his body and stared at the doctor with confusion. The room spun. His body sat still but it felt as if it was turning. He placed his hands to his face and leaned over his lap, clutching his black hair. If only he could stop the movement. He closed his weary eyes. His body felt as if it continued to spin, only slower this time. Franklin felt Elsa place her hand on his back.

"Franklin," Elsa asked.

"Hmm."

"You said Abe is hurt."

"Who?"

"Your younger brother, Abraham. He's hurt. What happened

to him? Tell me what you want to say." Franklin lifted his head and slouched back in the chair. "Franklin, where's Abraham?"

"Hurt bad."

"What happened?"

"Ugh. Elsa. Feel sick. So sick."

"I know you do. Doctor Riley and I are going to help you but we need to know about Abraham. Is he with you?"

"No. Farm."

"He's on the farm?" Franklin nodded. "Did you run here?" Franklin shook his head. "Horse."

"You rode a horse to Marion?" He nodded. "Okay, Abraham is hurt on the farm. You are ill and you rode one of the horses to Doctor Riley's office for help? Is that correct?"

"Yes."

"Good. What happened to Abraham?"

"I had to finish the fields before the dance tonight. I skipped breakfast and lunch. I worked all day but then had a headache. I sat on the porch after I finished the last of my fields. I was so thirsty. Nothing could quench my thirst. My stomach ached. Abe had just started the last acre. He screams. Horses drag him. He had the reins around his neck. I ran to the team and stopped them. Cora pulls reins from his neck. He can breathe. Leg's broken. We saw the bone and there's blood."

"How long have you gone without food?" Doctor Riley asked.

Franklin stared at Elsa. "Answer him, Frank. How long has it been since you ate anything? Elsa asked.

"I," he swallowed hard then shook his head.

"Franklin, how long?" Elsa asked.

Franklin glanced up at Doctor Riley at the sound of the doctor's voice. "Mr. Raymond, for you to have skipped two meals does wear upon the body, yet based on your condition I can't believe you've gone with only one meal today."

"I can't think." Franklin exhaled a deep breath then closed his eyes.

Doctor Riley instructed Elsa, "Inside the examination room is a clear jar with peppermint sticks. Bring me one and hurry child!" Elsa ran into the examination room. Margaret and Oren watched as Doctor Riley tried to wake Franklin. He tapped Franklin on the cheek. Franklin never moved. "Open your eyes, Frank. Come on boy, open your eyes, fidget, do something!"

"Doctor?" Margaret asked, clutching Oren's arm.

"I can't be certain until your daughter returns with the candy and he sucks on it, but he's acting like he's having an attack of the diabetes," Doctor Riley informed as he continued to try to coax Franklin.

"Is he a diabetic?" Oren asked.

"Not that I am aware of, but I wouldn't put it past his parents to keep something like that away from me. His father and I do not see eye to eye on what should be done with Franklin. If he is diabetic then I'm not the physician he is seeing. Gideon and Juliette Raymond are originally from Upper Sandusky. They could have taken Franklin to see a physician up there, but I doubt that."

"When you say you do not see eye to eye with his parents concerning what should be done with the boy, what do you mean by that?"

"I believe Franklin needs to be committed to an asylum. I've stood that ground since he was only a few weeks old, but his parents refuse to do so."

"Is he insane?" Oren asked.

"I believe so, but Gideon won't allow his son to be admitted. The boy is more trouble than he's worth. When he was a baby he would cry for no reason. If you held or touched him it would make his fits even worse. There was nothing his mother could do to calm him down but just leave him alone."

"He was colic?" Margaret asked.

"At first I had thought so but the fits lasted longer than they should have. Franklin had problems learning how to walk and speak. When he was two and a half, Juliette delivered Cora. I told Gideon and Juliette they should focus all their attention on Cora and not Franklin. But they never listened to me. She was determined to care for both her children. When Franklin entered school he had a hard time socializing and still does to this day. If you ask me, poor Cora has been the victim of it all. Her parents give Franklin more attention than her or her brothers."

Franklin moaned then fidgeted. "Frank," Doctor Riley yelled, grabbing Franklin's face with both hands. Franklin heaved. "Calm down, Frank, and stay awake."

Franklin glanced across the doctor's left shoulder. "Elsa," he muttered.

"She'll be back, Frank. She went to get you something."

"Elsa!"

"I'm here, Franklin," Elsa said, running towards the two of them with a peppermint stick. She held Franklin's hand as she gave the piece of candy to Doctor Riley. Franklin stared at her without expression. She was all he needed right now. He tightened his grip. "You're going to be alright, Frank. Do what Doctor Riley asks of you. I'm right here. I won't let go."

"Okay," he mumbled.

Elsa smiled then kissed him on the back of his hand. Doctor Riley tore apart the top of the stick. He leaned Franklin back. Franklin wandered in and out of consciousness. Doctor Riley pushed the piece of candy into Franklin's mouth. "Suck on it until it's gone," the doctor ordered. Franklin obeyed as he looked at Elsa. He could feel the sugary mint travel down his parched throat.

Oren watched Doctor Riley and Elsa interact, ignoring the conversation between them. Conflicting thoughts entered his mind. The young man before him was nothing like the man he thought Franklin to be. The Franklin he knew was shy, quiet, and very intelligent. He felt confident Franklin could not only care for Elsa but also whatever children God had granted the two of them. Yet this Franklin—this idiotic, weak, and pathetic Franklin—was not someone he wanted to marry his daughter. Elsa needed a strong man. One that would be a strong provider and would be the head of the family. The man before him depended on his parents and Elsa to care for him. What kind of man did that? He wasn't certain Franklin would be a good husband for his little girl, but there were also the practical reasons to grant Franklin permission to marry Elsa. As much as he had wanted to keep his little girl to himself, Oren knew he didn't have financial resources to always provide for her. Money was scarce. His farm in Marion County had lain barren for years while they lived with Henry and Portia, who did the best they could to ensure he and his family had food and lodging. But when Henry dies that sustainable income will go away. He'd be left with seven mouths to feed, and when Portia gave birth that would rise to eight. Nathan and Sam would have to quit school and find work to help support them all. He would do as much as he could with Henry's farm, but Oren knew it just wasn't enough. One less mouth to feed would help a little. The sooner Franklin married Elsa the better.

"Ugh, doc," Franklin called.

"How do you feel, Frank?"

"Tired. My head hurts," Franklin groaned as he pressed his hand into his forehead and leaned over. Doctor Riley supported Franklin. He lifted Franklin's right hand and studied the younger man's shaking hand.

"Do you always shake when you don't eat?" Franklin nodded. "When did this begin?"

"I don't know."

"Think Frank. It's important. When did you notice your hands shake?"

"A few months ago."

"The headaches, how long after you have missed a meal do they come?"

"I don't know."

"Do you have a headache at certain times of the day?" Franklin nodded. "When?"

"Between meals. Sometimes if I wait too long for a meal my stomach aches and I vomit. I'm always hungry and thirsty."

"When did you notice the change in appetite?"

Franklin scrunched his face as he thought about the doctor's question. He looked to Elsa.

"When Frank?" she asked.

His head pounded fiercer the more he tried to push through his clouded mind. When was the first time he noticed his hands shaking? How many headaches had he experienced? He swallowed hard as the answers slowly came to the front of his mind. "Four months ago," he mouthed.

"Four months ago," Elsa told Doctor Riley.

"And your parents never noticed?" Doctor Riley asked.

Franklin shook his head, "I never eat a meal with them. I've been working extra hours at the factory, taking odd jobs on the side, and working part time delivering hardware. The only day off

I have is Sunday. I'm so tired I wake up, get dressed, attend services, eat lunch, and then go back to bed. I usually sleep until early Monday morning, do my chores, eat a piece of toast, and then start my week over again."

"I know your mother wouldn't leave for the day without making a meal in advance."

"She left us ham, sweet potato pie, and corn."

"When we get back to your house, I want you to eat a portion of everything you mentioned."

"Yes, sir."

"Swallow the last of that mint."

"Yes, sir." Doctor Riley watched Franklin obey.

"You said Abraham's bone is sticking out of his leg?" Franklin nodded his head. "Any other injuries you noticed?"

"Rope burns around his neck."

"Keep sucking on that candy, Frank. I need to get my supplies." He rose from over Franklin and walked into his examination room. Franklin cast his eyes upon Elsa. A tear fell down her cheek.

"Who's in the room?" Franklin whispered to her.

"Henry," she sniffed.

Franklin nodded. He turned his gaze to her parents. Oren stared him down with a stern look of disapproval. Franklin swallowed hard. He had been drunk before. He couldn't blame Elsa's father for thinking he was drunk. If he didn't know better he'd think he was too. Doctor Riley exited the examination room with his black medical bag. The doctor turned to Oren while Margaret stepped beside her husband. He spoke to Margaret with his eyes on Oren. "Your son may return home. He's not to leave his bed until the cough goes away."

"Doctor, how close to death is he?" Margaret asked.

"That I can't tell you."

"But only a moment ago, those sounds?"

"I tried to lay Mr. Henry on the table, but when I did so he couldn't lie down for a few moments without aggravation to the lungs. I sat him upright but he's so weak he fell forward. That is when he stopped breathing. He fell off the table. Your son's lungs have deteriorated to the point he can't breathe unless he lies in a certain position. I don't recommend he stand for long moments of time or he'll once again fall as he did at the store. He's to be confined to his bed until full recovery from this attack or his death, whichever comes first."

"Thank you, doctor."

"You're welcome. Mrs. Garrett, I suggest you let your husband rest his legs until your son and grandson arrive with the wagon. His knees are shaking."

"I will."

"I'll stop by tonight after my visit with the Raymond family." Doctor Riley grabbed Franklin by the arm and pulled him out the door. "Get in my car. I'll bring your horse to your family tomorrow."

"May I accompany you?" Elsa asked, walking swiftly towards them.

Doctor Riley paused and turned his view to her. "I don't mind. It's up to your pa."

Elsa turned to her father. "Please, Pa. I want to be with him."

"Go, but I will expect you home for dinner."

"Yes, sir," she beamed then went with Doctor Riley and Frankli

April 25, 1904
Raymond Farm
Wyandot County, Ohio

Franklin rolled onto his back in his simple wooden bed with a long groan, opened his weary eyes, and stared at the black suit hanging on the back of his bedroom door. The red rose his mother had placed on his left lapel had already begun to wither. He studied the rose's deep red color fading into a lighter, crisper brown on the edges of the flower's petals. He saw every fine detail most people would have missed. All his life, Franklin had been sensitive to the visual world around him. He could see patterns everywhere. All the colors were brighter, more vibrant and magnificent for him than his peers. Some days it was as if he lived in his own little secret world. He had tried to describe how he saw the world to his peers and family, but no one understood him. He'd rather live in that world than ever be bothered by people.

Franklin moved his eyes towards his oak desk along the wall. His black hat sat on top of his desk with an open ledger beside it. Papers scattered on the other side of his hat with an ink pen on top. He thought about the love letter he had started to write Elsa. He had wanted to say just the right words, yet every time he wrote about his love the words had sounded stupid. He had never been good at expressing his feelings. His entire childhood he had always had a hard time developing and maintaining relationships. Most days he found more comfort tinkering with his machines than interacting with people. Sometimes he would say or do something that would make one of his peers upset. He could never understand what he had done to hurt them. The harder he tried to mend the relationship the more problems he caused. It seemed to Franklin, life was easier with his little mechanical trinkets than with other humans. At least the machines didn't talk back.

Franklin thought about Elsa. He loved Elsa more than any other woman he had ever known. Yet he had a hard time expressing that love. "I love you" were hard words for him to say. Not because he didn't love her but because sometimes he couldn't bring his thoughts out of his mouth. The more he stressed the less he could speak. Stress was all he had had since the day he asked Oren Garrett for his daughter's hand in marriage. He could still recall that day. As he stood in the parlor of Henry's house, alone with Oren, he could barely speak. His hands had shook. He had tried to ask that simple enough question several times. All he had to ask was "Mr. Garrett, I love your daughter. Would you consent to our marriage?" Instead he had said, "I want your daughter." Oren had laughed hard then told him he knew what Franklin meant. He had been expecting him for days to ask that question. Franklin was overcome with relief when Oren had consented to the proposal.

Franklin could have told Elsa the following day but he wanted to make it a surprise. He couldn't afford to say the wrong words to his beloved. He needed it to be perfect—the perfect setting, the perfect question, and in front of everyone. Elsa deserved nothing less than perfection. It had taken him a long time to plan it all. When the time came for him to think of the perfect words to say he couldn't express them. It had only infuriated him more.

His mother had suggested instead of saying or writing his feelings he should present them in a bouquet of flowers. Juliette had lent him her copy of the *Language of Flowers* book by Kate Greenaway. She had explained that flowers held more meaning to a woman than adding color to a room or enjoying their perfumes. Every flower had a special meaning. Women could pass secret messages to their lovers and friends using a special code. The book was the code breaker. Franklin had loved the idea! He could put together a bouquet of flowers for Elsa then present them to her at the dance. For days, he studied the 88-page book. He memorized every definition and detail of the flowers then composed the perfect message. Juliette had helped him to gather all the supplies. He wrapped the edges of the basket with ivy to mean marriage and fidelity. He mixed red roses with orange blossoms in the middle to signify the passionate love he held for her and the bridal celebrations she would encounter. He declared his love for her with a red tulip towards the front of the bouquet. A peach blossom sat next to it to signify she had captured his heart. The bouquet of flowers had declared his love and intentions for his beloved Elsa. All he had to do was present the flowers to her in the perfect setting. Franklin had meticulously planned his presentation to occur at the Annual Marion County Spring Barn Dance. He would dance with his beloved then halfway through the dance the music would stop, he would hand her the bouquet with his mother's book, drop to his knee, pull out the ring and propose.

Franklin could feel the warm morning sun shine through his window. It couldn't be morning. It had been late afternoon by the time they had returned to the farm. He could vaguely recall his mother screaming his name as he fell unconscious before them. Franklin focused on the bright sunlight that illuminated his room. The warmth of the sun had given way to the time. It was early afternoon. Franklin closed his eyes and shook his head with disappointment. Clearly, a day had passed. He had missed his opportunity to propose to Elsa at the dance. How could he have been so stupid! Everything he had worked for had disappeared like water vapor. There was no going back. Now she couldn't be his wife!

He opened his eyes and looked around the small bedroom. It was times like these he was grateful he had a bedroom to himself. Most boys his age had to share their room with their brothers. But not him. He had always had his own room. When his brothers had grown old enough to share a room with him, Franklin wouldn't have it. He needed his own space. His brothers didn't understand how Franklin felt. Besides, there was only one person he wanted to see now. The woman he wanted to see didn't have a clue how much that dance had meant to him. His entire life revolved around her.

Franklin looked at the coat on the back of the door. His black pants draped across the back of his chair. "Oh Elsa," he whispered. His heart broke. A small piece of silver caught his peripheral view. He lowered his eyes towards his nightstand. An open ring box containing a ring with a pearl surrounded by five diamonds sat before him. Franklin picked up the ring box and held it. He smiled at the small, delicate fixture. For half a year he had saved his earnings just to pay for the engagement ring. Most days he worked before sunrise until after sunset, only to return to his share of the work on the family farm. Exhausted, he had pushed his body beyond the limits for his beloved. But Elsa was worth the suffering.

The round, white, metal door handle to his room twisted. Franklin closed the box then watched the door open. His heart lifted at the sight of his beloved. Her chestnut hair sat perfectly in a bun atop her head. The light twinkled in her deep-set brown eyes. Her white shirtwaist blouse and purple walking skirt clung to her slender S-frame body, the collar of her shirtwaist blouse wrapped around her thin neck. She was beautiful. No, she was more than beautiful. What was the word he was looking for? Gorgeous. Yes, that was it. Gorgeous. Elsa Beatrice Garrett was gorgeous. No other woman in the world made his heart jump the way she did. "Miss Elsa," he whispered with a hint of a smile as she walked into his room with a tray of food.

"You're awake," she replied to him.

"I just woke up."

"How do you feel?"

"I have a headache."

"You must be starving."

"I am hungry."

"Good. I brought you sausage, mashed potatoes, corn, and some buns."

"Sounds delicious. Did you make it?"

Elsa shrugged her shoulders. "Your ma made the sausage and I did the rest."

"Then it has to be delicious," Franklin replied.

Elsa smiled towards her beau. She cast her eyes to his right hand. "What's in your hand?"

"Nothing important anymore."

"If it once was it must still be."

"I don't know," he whispered with a disconnected look.

Elsa placed the tray of food on the nightstand. She sat beside him then stared at the box in his hand. "Frank," she addressed him as she placed her left hand on the right side of his face. Franklin turned his eyes to hers. She smiled at him then leaned her mouth close to his. Franklin lifted his chin and kissed her. Her sweet kisses brought relief from his ongoing thoughts. He dropped the ring box to the floor, wrapped his arms around her, and pulled her closer. Elsa crawled on top of the bed and held him. His heart beat faster for her touch. Never before, except with Rebekah Grace Webster, had he wanted a woman to touch him! The couple rolled in the bed kissing and embracing one another with his white quilt between them. He could feel his excitement level rise. How much he wanted to make her his wife! He pushed Elsa underneath him. She smelled of honeysuckle, vanilla, and brown sugar. The world disappeared from around them. He may have missed his opportunity to propose but he could still make her his wife. At least under God's eyes, if he had relations with her they would be bonded for life. Wasn't that the way they did it in the Old Testament times? Franklin traced his mouth along Elsa's jaw line, making certain to kiss every inch of her skin. He slid his mouth upwards and kissed her. Elsa pulled his head closer to hers. The couple nibbled on each other's lips.

"I missed you," he whispered to her.

"And I you. I thought you would die."

"Shh," he whispered as he pushed back a strand of her hair. "I'll never leave you, Elsa. Never."

Franklin kissed her more deeply. The white blanket wrapped them as the couple rolled on the bed. Franklin put his hand underneath Elsa's ankle-length skirt. He gently traced his hand up her leg along her stocking to her knee. Suddenly, Elsa rolled him underneath her and sat upright.

"What are you doing?" she asked as she composed herself.

"I love you," he proclaimed.

"I love you too, Frank, but why is your hand under my skirt?"

"I want to be with you."

"We can't do this. It's not proper. I'm not your wife." Elsa corrected him with a disciplined tone. Franklin stared at her with a confused look. Why was she rejecting him? Didn't she understand he loved her?

"I don't understand. You kissed me."

"I wanted to hold and kiss you but not go farther than that."

"Elsa, what's the difference? We've lain together in my bed before."

"With our clothes on! We hold each other, kiss, talk, and nothing more. You've never touched me beneath my clothes."

"Are you saying you don't want to be with me?"

"No. I'm saying this was a mistake. I'm sorry. I should have never kissed you like that," Elsa apologized.

"What's the difference if I want to touch your skin? We love each other."

"I can't give you what you want from me." Franklin watched her rise from the bed. Elsa had said she loved him but didn't want to proceed any farther. That didn't make sense. If she loved him then why didn't she want to bond under God? Didn't she feel the same way about him? He could have sworn he felt her hand on top of his drawers. Didn't she understand how hard it was for him to act as he did with her? He had reached out to show her how much he loved her and now she dismissed him! His chest and head began to ache with thoughts of her rejection. He rolled onto his stomach with a long groan. Elsa sat on the bed beside him. He could feel her hand lightly touch the middle of his back. He always hated a tender touch. Franklin shivered. She moved her hand up and down in a long fluid motion. She slid her hands up his back and massaged his tense shoulders.

"Hmm," Franklin groaned.

"Relax, you're very tense."

"I have a right to be tense. You rejected me."

Elsa paused her hands on his shoulders and stared at him. "Frank, what you want from me you know you can't have until I'm your wife. If you want that from me, then propose. I know you have spoken to my father," she stated frankly.

"You do?"

"Nathan overheard you asking father for my hand. He told me about it. When are you going to ask me?"

"I can't."

"Then you can't have what we both want."

Franklin rolled onto his back with a confused look on his face. "You want to be my wife under God?" he asked.

"Yes."

"But you don't want me to touch your skin?"

"I want that just not yet."

"Elsa, I'm confused."

"I can't make the mistake my sister made. Deborah had relations with Liberty before they married and Pa disowned her. I don't want to lose my family. They're all I have."

"My family will be your family."

"Frank, the Bible states in Genesis 2:24 'Therefore a man leaves his father and his mother and cleaves to his wife, and they become one flesh.' You can't remain with your parents. It's not biblical."

"Where else do you expect us to live?"

"Pa's not using our farm in Marion County. I'm certain if we ask him he would allow us to stay there until we can get a place of our own."

"I'm not moving thirty miles away from my parents."

"We're not moving anywhere until after the wedding. A wedding we won't have because you won't ask me to marry you."

"I can't. Ugh, Elsa, you're making this harder than it has to be."

"I love you, Frank. I truly do. Telling you no just now was as hard for me as hearing my rejection was for you. There are certain biblical rules we must adhere to. I won't disobey them." Elsa rose from the bed, crouched to the floor, and handed the ring box to him. "You dropped this," she said, handing it to him.

Franklin stared at the box. Rules. Expectations. Why did everything have to be so complicated? He traced his fingers along the smooth silver side. He wanted to scream and cry all at the same time. He could feel himself detach from his surroundings. The darkness of feeling nothing beckoned him to retreat from his body. Elsa touched his hand. "Frank," she whispered. He jumped at the sound of his name, his brown eyes locking his gaze with hers. He opened his mouth to speak then closed it. Normally he would scream for his father but Elsa was by his side. She was comfort enough. "Frank, I'm here. I'm right here," she whispered.

"I don't know what to do," he cried, clutching the ring box.

"What do you want to do?"

Franklin shook his head. "Can't," he muttered. He turned his head to the wall. His mind couldn't stop thinking about Elsa and his situation. It was never his intention to harm her. Had he harmed her? Was she playing games with him? So many questions rolled in his mind it overwhelmed him. All he had to do was propose to her, but how? How was he to do that? What he wouldn't give for his father at this precise moment. He lifted his eyes to the bouquet of flowers across from him. "Elsa," he whispered.

"Yes."

Franklin opened his mouth to speak. He knew what he wanted to say—Will you marry me? It seemed like a perfect question. He tried to push the words out but nothing came. What he wouldn't give for his father to interpret for him now! Why wouldn't the words push out of his mouth? He could feel his heart beat hard against his chest with aching pain. He breathed quick, shallow breaths. The more he thought about his proposal to Elsa the more his chest and head hurt. He couldn't have what he wanted the most. It had taken every ounce of strength he had just to think of a way to propose to her properly. Now he had lost it all. He had missed his opportunity to propose! The dance was over and the plan forfeited. She could never become his wife the way she wanted and she wasn't willing to be his wife without a wedding. What was he supposed to do?! There was no solution.

"Frank!" Elsa yelled. Franklin turned his attention to her. "Take deep breaths. Whatever you are thinking about, stop."

"I can't."

"Yes you can. Breathe." Franklin closed his eyes and breathed under her constant guidance. He began to sob. "Franklin, what's wrong?" she asked.

What's wrong?! Everything was wrong! How he wished he could tell her what was in the depths of his mind. He sniffed his nose and shook his head.

"Frank, tell me," she beckoned.

"Do you know what this box is?" he asked, lifting his eyes to hers.

"No, I've never seen anything like it before."

Franklin slammed the silver ring box onto the nightstand with a loud grunt of frustration. Elsa jumped back at his abrupt action. He grabbed his face with both his hands, sat up, and leaned his head back. Why didn't Elsa understand what he was trying to say?

"Frank," she whispered.

"Just leave me alone," he yelled. If only the entire world would disappear!

"Let me help you."

He lowered his hands, turned his head, and yelled at her, "You want to help! Then do what I ask of you! I only want what's best for the both of us."

"Fornication is not what's best for the both of us. It's not biblical!"

"Stop hurting me!"

"Hurt you? How am I hurting you?"

Franklin heaved his chest as he stared at her in disbelief. Why didn't she understand? It was like a dog talking to a canary. Elsa sat on the edge of the bed and took his hand into her own. He inhaled deeply at her simple touch. "Frank, I want to help you. If I have done anything to offend you, tell me." He stared in silence at her. Were they even in the same room together? Hadn't she been here when she rejected him? "Franklin, please," she pleaded. "What have I done to you?"

"What didn't you do?"

Elsa's face fell. "Frank, we can't do that. The bible states in 1 Corinthians 6:18-20 and 1 Corinthians 7:1-2 'Flee from sexual immorality. Every other sin a person commits is outside the body, but the sexually immoral person sins against his own body. Or do you not know that your body is a temple of the Holy Spirit within you, whom you have from God? You are not your own, for you were bought with a price. So glorify God in your body. Now concerning the things about which you wrote, it is good for a man not to touch a woman. But because of immoralities, each man is to have his own wife, and each woman is to have her own husband.' We must be married before we touch each other in that manner. It is God's commandment."

"I want you," he struggled to push out.

"You can't always have what you desire. Ask me the question you want to ask."

Franklin inhaled with a shake of his head. "Can't."

"Can't or won't"

"I can't," he yelled.

A moment of tense silence filled the room. "Why can't you?" Elsa whispered.

Franklin stared into her beautiful oval face. Why can't he propose? It wasn't as if he wasn't trying to propose. He thought by seducing her he was trying to show her he was proposing. She didn't understand what the silver ring box held. "Flowers," he pushed out.

"You can't propose to me because of flowers?" Franklin shook his head. "Franklin, I don't understand."

"Sometimes, my brother has a hard time saying what he means. He's so stupid he can't even budget his own ledger," Cora's voice lifted from behind them. Elsa and Franklin turned their attention to the door. Franklin's sister entered the room and stood beside Elsa.

"What do you want?" Franklin demanded.

She crossed her arms as she greeted him, "Well, it's good to see you awake."

"Cora, I'm not in the mood."

"You're never in the mood, bonehead."

"I'm not a bonehead. My head has my skull, a brain, muscles, blood, eyes, nose, mouth, ears, and hair, not bones."

"I believe she called you stupid," Elsa corrected him with a glare towards Cora.

"See Elsa, he's so stupid he doesn't even know when someone calls him stupid," Cora said.

"He's not stupid. How can you treat your brother with such contempt? Don't you love him?" Elsa asked her.

Franklin tightened his jaw with a stern look. A tension headache began to throb. He didn't know how to react to the girls. Elsa had rejected him and Cora—well he wasn't certain what Cora was doing in his room at all. Although only a couple of years apart in age, he and his sister rarely saw eye to eye on anything. Most days, Cora annoyed him. She was self-centered and jealous of all the attention their parents gave him. Many times she had advocated that their parents should commit him into the Central Ohio Psychiatric Hospital. Thank heavens, their parents never enacted her suggestions. He wasn't an idiot, just too smart for his own good. At least that's what his mother had said. Franklin disconnected from his surroundings as the two girls argued over his intelligence or lack thereof. His heart beat hard on the inside of his chest. The pain in his chest grew stronger. He began to gasp for breath as he struggled to breathe. This was the end! He was going to die. It was a heart attack! He was too young to die! The more he thought about his impending death the more pain he felt. It was hard to breath. The room spun. Help. Oh, God, please someone help!

"Frank!" Franklin turned at the sound of Elsa's voice. She held his face.

"You have to calm him down. It's a panic attack. He gets them sometimes," Cora informed as she sat beside Elsa.

"Breathe, my love," Elsa instructed.

"Dark," he pushed out.

"What's dark?"

"I'm dying."

"You're not dying. Take slow, deep breaths." Franklin pressed his hand against his chest with a grimace of pain. "Slow and deep breaths, Frank."

"Heart. Dying."

"Stop that! You're not dying."

Franklin moved his eyes to Cora. Sharper pain filled his chest. He groaned loudly as he lifted his left knee and arched his head back, "Frank, I won't argue with Elsa anymore. I promise. Obey her, please, it's for the best. We both care about you. Remember what father taught you to say?" Cora said.

"I'm not dying. This will pass," he answered.

"Keep saying it until you believe it."

Franklin repeated the two phrases over and over again to himself. Elsa and Cora watched him as his lips moved without sound. Elsa's heart fell for her boyfriend. Poor Franklin. Never before had she seen him in such agony. Cora had said he had had these panic attacks before. She wondered when they had begun and how she could help him to overcome them. There was no need for Franklin to suffer. "Hmm," Franklin moaned as he lowered his leg and turned his head towards her.

"Frank," Elsa replied.

"Tired," Franklin said as he began to close his eyes.

"You can't sleep. Doctor Riley wants you to eat. You said you were hungry earlier."

"Famished. Too tired to eat."

"Sit up. I'll help you."

Franklin nodded. Elsa helped Franklin sit upright while Cora cut the sausage into small bite-size pieces. He watched the two girls work together in perfect harmony. Cora would hand Elsa a small piece of food, Elsa would feed him, he'd chew and swallow then the cycle repeated. The taste and texture of each scrumptious morsel felt like heaven to his taste buds. How long had it been since he last ate a full meal? He couldn't remember. His stomach ached as if it had never had food before. He wanted more but his body began to protest. He grabbed the spoon of corn, pushed Elsa back, leaned over the side, and vomited. Franklin stared at the pile of stomach acid mixed with potatoes, corn, and sausage. His head pounded with fury. "Oh, Elsa, I'm so sorry," he whispered with disappointment.

She put her arm around his waist and lowered him back to his bed. "Don't worry. We'll try something else," she replied as she placed another pillow under his head. "If you're too weak for solid food then we'll try the bread." Elsa took the cup of water on his nightstand and held it next to his mouth. "Drink," she ordered. Franklin obeyed. She lowered the half-empty cup.

Franklin whispered, "Cora."

"Eat first, talk later."

"No."

"Frank, this isn't the time for an argument."

"I don't want to argue. I want to talk to my sister!"

"Frank," Elsa said tenderly, placing her hand along the side of his face. Franklin swallowed hard.

"Leave me," he whispered.

"No, you're too frail to be left by yourself. Doctor Riley said as soon as you awaken you were to eat something. I've been checking on you every hour or so waiting for you to open your eyes."

"Why?"

"Why?"

Franklin nodded, "Why wait for me?"

"Because I love you. Please Franklin, stop being so pig-headed."

"I don't have the head of a pig."

"Oh, Frank. I meant you are being stubborn. Now, try to eat.

36

Do it for me, please."

Cora huffed, "See, Elsa, he's too stupid to be with anyone."

"Shut up, Cora," Franklin yelled.

"He's mean too."

"I said shut up," Franklin yelled louder.

"He's not mean or stupid," Elsa argued. She gingerly stroked her hand down the side of Franklin's face. Franklin breathed with staggered breaths through his mouth with each touch of her fingers. He turned his head away from Elsa's hand with a low moan.

"He's weak, Elsa. Don't you want a man you can touch?" Cora goaded.

Franklin grabbed his extra pillow and threw it at his sister. "Leave her alone," he yelled. Cora caught the pillow and in one fluid motion flung the feather-downed pillow into her brother's face.

"You are a complete moron," she yelled, walking towards the bed. "Do you know how close to death you came yesterday? Huh? Knowing you, probably not! You never think of anyone other than yourself!" She shoved the bun into Elsa's hand. "Here I'm done helping my brother. If you want a child for a husband then so be it, Elsa. But let this to be a warning to you, he is a complete imbecile!"

Cora glared at Franklin, huffed, and then turned to leave. Franklin reached across with his right hand and grabbed her left wrist. She jerked her arm. "Stop it," Franklin said calmly.

Cora relaxed. "I hate you," she snarled at him with tears slowly cascading down her rosy cheeks.

"Cora, please. What's wrong with me?" he asked.

She smiled, sniffed her nose, and answered, "You're stupid, now let me go."

"There's more than that. I know you, Cora. If my intelligence and the selection of whom I want to marry is all you can insult me with then there is something more wrong with me than I can imagine."

"Don't be so conceited, Frank," she whispered to him. "If I had wanted to make fun of you because of your physical ailments then I would," she gloated.

"You're scared."

"Me, scared? It's your life not mine."

"Then tell me what the doctor said," he said, lowering his grip from her wrist.

Cora rubbed her wrist, exchanged glances with Elsa, then turned to Franklin. "Elsa was right in thinking you were dying."

Franklin swallowed hard as he looked to Elsa. Elsa spoke, "Doctor Riley said the longer you slept the more likely you were never to wake again. He said you suffered from exhaustion and dehydration but the longer you went without food the more dangers your body faces from the diabetes."

"I'm not diabetic."

"You are," Cora retorted. Frank turned his eyes on Cora. Diabetes? That was the worst fate any person could face. He could die! He wasn't ready to die, yet. Cora sat on the bed next to Elsa. He paid close attention as she continued. "Doctor Riley said with the symptoms you exhibit from the lack of nourishment he's certain you have it, too."

"Too?"

"Mother said Grandma Maxim died from complications of diabetes the year before I was born. Mother's sister has diabetes. Father told Doctor Riley that Uncle Vernon had it."

"He did?"

"Yeah, he claims the complications Uncle Vernon had after he served in the Civil War came from diabetes, something called gangrene killed him. Father also said Grandpa Garrett had the diabetes before he was killed in the Civil War. Doctor Riley claims with so many in our family with diabetes it doesn't surprise him you would have it too. He's been asking our parents all kinds of question about you. Mother told him she had seen your hands shake sometimes but she didn't think anything of it."

"It's not serious."

"Frank, your hands shake so bad sometimes your food falls off your fork or spoon. You can't deny that."

"What else did she tell him?"

"She told him that you have excessive thirst and appetite, fatigue, nausea, slow-healing cuts, and she's noticed recently that you've had some unusual weight loss."

"I've been working more than usual."

"Pa told him that too. Doctor Riley says it doesn't matter if you worked that hard or not you shouldn't have lost that much weight. He's prescribing a treatment for you with mother and father. You're supposed to follow it as soon as you awaken."

"What kind of treatment?"

"Six small meals a day and plenty of rest and exercise. No more sweets."

Franklin lifted his trembling hand towards Elsa's left hand. "Frank," Elsa gasped as she clutched it. Elsa withdrew her hand and handed him a piece of the roll. "Eat this," she said as she wrapped her hands around his. "Small pieces and eat slowly," she pleaded as she lowered her hands.

Franklin sat up in bed. He tore the bun apart and obeyed. "I love you," he whispered towards her.

"I love you too." Elsa stroked the side of his face with her hand. He lowered the bun, placed his hand around the back of her head and leaned towards her. Franklin gently kissed her on the lips. Her sweet kisses felt like honey upon his lips. He nibbled on her lower lip. The couple kissed deeper. If only he could make her his wife right now!

"Frank," Cora tried to get her brother's attention. Franklin ignored his sister. Nothing mattered in the world except for Elsa. Oh, how he had missed her! He kissed Elsa with more passion. "Franklin!"

The couple continued to kiss slowly and deeply. They held each other tighter. Franklin pulled away from Elsa with a swallow. He turned his eyes towards Cora. "Cora. I forgot you were here."

"Obviously," she huffed.

Elsa grabbed the roll from between Franklin's legs and handed it to him. "Eat," Elsa instructed.

He took the roll with a smile and obeyed. He peered up at Cora as he chewed. "How much trouble am I in?" he asked Cora as Elsa placed her hand on his upper left thigh.

"A lot. Pa blames you for the accident," Cora answered.

"That plow should've never pulled Abraham under."

"Pa says the plow broke when the team took off and that's why Abraham was pulled under. He's really upset with you."

"Ma?"

"She's more concerned about your health than the accident. Doc Riley upset her with his diagnosis."

"I can imagine," he replied as he took another piece of the roll and ate. His stomach turned as the bread went down. He pushed Elsa aside, leaned over, and vomited. Cora reached under the wooden bed, pulled out an empty chamber pot, and handed it to Elsa. Elsa held the pot underneath Franklin's face. He continued to spit pieces of bread mixed with stomach acid into the pot. Franklin's head spun. He pressed the palm of his hand against his pounding forehead. "Ugh," he groaned as he closed his eyes. Elsa placed her hands around his face. "Help," he whispered.

"We should try to feed you something simpler. Perhaps soup. Mrs. Raymond is making chicken for dinner. There's plenty of broth. If you're too frail for bread then crackers and soup will do." Franklin nodded. "Lie down," she said as she guided him down on his back. She pulled his white quilt over his body, kissed him on the forehead, then said, "I'll be back with soup soon enough. In the meantime, rest." Elsa rose from beside the bed and grabbed the tray of food. He watched her exit the room.

The door closed behind her. He held his upset stomach then stared at his sister. "Am I going to die?" he asked with a flat tone.

"No. Doc said as long as you awoke from your sleep you'd live."

"I've heard of people diagnosed with diabetes dying within a few years from when they were diagnosed."

"Don't concern yourself about that. Frank, you have matters to concern yourself with other than your demise."

"Other matters?"

Cora reached over to the nightstand, grabbed the ring box, and shoved it on her brother's chest. "This." Her hand clutched the box as she yelled into his face.

"Put Elsa's ring back, Cora."

Cora leaned over her brother and snarled, "That ring doesn't belong to Elsa. You had it made for Rebekah last year. The box is new but the ring is not."

"I don't want to marry Rebekah Grace Webster anymore. I'm done with her."

"Rebekah isn't one of your fixations that once you're done with it, you throw it away. She's a human being."

"I'm not throwing her in the trash. She's with her family in Indiana."

"Frank, it was a figure of speech! You cannot treat Rebekah the way you are treating her."

"I've done nothing wrong to her."

"You promised your devotions to Rebekah Grace Webster not Elsa. Have you forgotten Elsa is the mistress, Rebekah is the fiancée?"

"Elsa means more to me than Rebekah."

"That's not true!"

"Yes it is."

"Frank, you had a mental breakdown last year after Rebekah was gone for two months. You've never been away from her for so long. You can't live your life with Elsa."

"That's not true. I told Pa how I felt. He told me I was developing feelings for Elsa and I should act on them. I have done what he wanted. Rebekah's nothing to me but my past."

"I can't believe that. You have done this before, Frank. You're obsessed with Rebekah. She likes the attentions you give her but sometimes you are too intense. Whenever she needs time apart from you, she tells our father. Father finds a girl for you to be with. Rebekah is always within your eyesight when you court another girl. Every girl in Marion and the surrounding counties knows the truth about you Frank. You can't be away from Rebekah! You'll go insane."

"I will not."

"Yes you will. You're so fixated on Rebekah you can't see how much you harass her."

"I'm not trying to hurt her. When she returns I'll prove it to everyone. I won't be anywhere near her. I want Elsa in my life, not Rebekah Grace Webster."

"Ha, I don't believe that. You'll do what you do every time Rebekah's ready for your full attentions. You'll dump Elsa and go back to Rebekah. You're too predictable, Franklin."

"I haven't asked to go back to Rebekah."

"Only because Rebekah hasn't attended school with us this

year. She's in Indiana. Frank, as soon as she returns home you'll beg for her forgiveness. This relationship between you and Elsa has gone on for too long."

"Elsa and I belong together."

"You say that about all the girls you've been with."

"This time it's true. With Rebekah gone, I can see the truth. We weren't meant to be together."

"How can you say that? Everyone can see the attractions you two have for each other."

"I'm not attracted to her."

"Liar. Every time you're around her you can't stop touching her. Isn't that why you wanted to marry Rebekah in the first place? You told me you wanted to obey what the bible teaches about marriage but the thoughts you have about Rebekah tempt you. There was a time, Franklin, you wouldn't touch any female. Then one kiss from Rebekah led to another. You got comfortable with touching her. Then your kiss led to touching and you wanted more than that. You're unstoppable around her. But Rebekah feels the same way. She's told me several times she doesn't know how much longer she can wait to be your wife. Frank, she wants to carry your child."

"I don't want her, Cora. I want Elsa."

"Elsa's only a distraction. Wait until Rebekah returns then you'll see. You two will be embracing, kissing, and fondling once again as if she never left."

"It won't happen. I don't have the same feelings for her like I do for Elsa. I won't change my mind!"

"You have an obligation to both her family and ours."

"I want to marry for love not out of obligations."

"You'll learn to love her."

"Cora, it's a new century! Things have to change. We can no longer live the way our parents did. I believe a man should marry for love not out of obligation. A marriage stands stronger for it. I mean my words, Cora. I don't love Rebekah Grace Webster. I love Elsa Beatrice Garrett."

"If you didn't love Rebekah then why did you seek her hand from her father last year?"

"I thought I loved her then I met Elsa. That ring belongs to

Elsa. Give it back to me." He grabbed the box under his sister's grip. Cora clasped it tighter. Brother and sister struggled to win the box free from the other's grip. "Let go!"

"No. It belongs to Rebekah! I won't let you give her ring to Elsa!"

"Leave the ring alone!"

"You can't give her something that belongs to another girl."

"Give it back!"

"No, Frank, this is for your own good." Franklin paused with his hand on the ring. The room began to blur. He stared at his sister with a blank look in his eyes. "Frank?" she questioned. Franklin lowered his hands and fell unconscious. Cora stared at her brother. "Franklin," she whispered. Franklin didn't respond. She inhaled a deep breath with shock. Franklin couldn't be dead! Cora threw the ring box to the floor, grabbed him by the arms, and shook him. "Franklin Thaddeus Raymond, answer me!" He didn't respond. "Oh, God, Frank, please. Please, please, my dear brother, answer me!"

4

The delicious smell of boiling chicken filled the large kitchen. Isaiah sat at the round table with his school book open. He tapped his pencil with frustration. He couldn't think about math right now. Franklin was sick in bed with diabetes and Abraham had almost lost his leg. All he could think about was them. He turned his head towards the L-shaped kitchen counters. Juliette stood talking to Doctor Riley about dietary precautions for Franklin. He dropped his pencil and turned his gaze towards the metal stove. Elsa poured a ladle full of broth into a bowl. He watched her with curiosity. Franklin had courted Elsa for a long time, long enough she had become a fixture in his family's life. When Elsa wasn't at school and Franklin wasn't at work they were always together. Isaiah had begun to see Elsa not as just his schoolmate but as another older sister. Cora was a good older sister but she could be overly demanding at times. Elsa had patience, humility, and understanding. He could talk to Elsa more than he could with Cora. He liked that. It wasn't hard to see why Franklin had fallen in love with Elsa. But there weren't too many people who wanted to be Franklin's friend.

Isaiah's face fell as his thoughts turned to his eldest brother. The day since Franklin had fallen unconscious had been the worst day of his life. Gideon had taken to sleeping in Isaiah's bed so he could be closer to Abraham. His parents had always had separate bedrooms with a door connecting the two rooms. Gideon had ordered Abraham to stay in his bedroom while Cora took their mother's room. Juliette had charged Cora with taking care of him so they could be free to care for Franklin and Abraham. Cora and Juliette had exchanged rooms. No one was allowed upstairs without permission. His parents never told him how his brothers fared, nor did they allow him to visit. Isaiah had begun to feel neglected. He had taken matters into his own hands. Today in school, he had gotten into a fist fight with one of the boys. Mrs. Webster had spanked him ten times with the back of her ruler. It had hurt a lot but he didn't care. He was angry, confused, and hurt. Why wouldn't his parents tell him anything?! Franklin and Abraham were his brothers. At lunchtime, he had stolen a sandwich from a five-year-old boy and started a fight with a nine-year-old girl. It had felt good to get the anger out of him. But Mrs. Webster hadn't been too happy about it. She had immediately removed him from the playground and sent Cora to her husband at the *Raymond and Son Emporium.* Hayden Webster had arrived with Cora soon enough. His wife wrote a letter to Gideon and Juliette then sent it with Isaiah. Hayden took Isaiah home. After Gideon had read the note, he tanned Isaiah's hide well with his belt then locked him in the bedroom until Cora arrived home from school. Cora had brought plenty of schoolwork for Isaiah to do. But he didn't care. He had thrown the work on the floor in a fit, yelled at his sister, and then pushed her to the ground. That had earned him another spanking. Gideon had pulled him out of bed and ordered him to do the work at the kitchen table under Juliette's careful eye. Gideon had warned his young son if he disrespected his mother he would not be able to sit for a week. Isaiah knew his father had meant his words.

Isaiah rested his face on his hand and studied the next row of triple-digit subtraction. He crossed out the 0 and wrote 10 on top. The chair across from him suddenly moved. He lifted his eyes to his visitor. Elsa sat across from him. "What are you working on?" she asked.

"Math."

Elsa took his workbook and turned it to face her. She peered at the fifteen rows of triple digit subtraction. "When did you start this page?"

"While you were upstairs with Franklin."

"You should be done already. You're quick with your numbers like Frank," she said as she turned it then pushed the workbook towards him.

"He's smarter than me."

"He should be. Frank's older than you."

Isaiah asked after a moment of silence, "How is Frank?"

"He's awake and can't stomach solid foods."

"Do you know what's wrong with him?"

"Yes but I think you should hear that from Mr. and Mrs. Raymond."

"Uh huh, they think I'm too young to understand. Please, Elsa, tell me what you know."

Elsa exhaled a deep breath then peered at Doctor Riley and Juliette. The adults spoke amongst themselves on the other side of the kitchen. She turned back to Isaiah. "Franklin has diabetes. Your folks claim they both have had family members die from complications of it."

"Is Franklin dying?"

"No, but he could have. Doctor Riley said Franklin's pancreas stopped working properly. It made him very ill. When I saw Franklin enter Doctor Riley's office he acted like he was drunk. My pa was very upset with him for his behavior."

"Did Doctor Riley think he was drunk? He's seen him drunk before."

"Really?"

"Uh huh, Frank got drunk in Marion one time."

Elsa's face fell. Franklin had never told her of his escapade in the bar. If her father knew of his adventures he would never let her be alone with Franklin. Oren was very conservative and supported the temperance movement. "One drink is too much for any decent man to take. No daughter of mine will marry a drunkard nor shall any son of mine become one," he would quote almost on a daily basis. "Does he do that often?" she whispered.

"Get drunk?"

"Yes."

"No."

"How do you know about it?"

"I overheard him talking to Hayden one time about it. One time, Franklin had passed out in the bar and Hayden took him to Doctor Riley's office."

"When was this?"

"Last year. Hayden and Franklin were celebrating Franklin's engage…" Isaiah stopped in mid- sentence, grabbed his glass of water and drank.

"Engagement," Elsa offered with a lift of her eyebrow.

"What?" Isaiah asked, putting the glass down.

"You said Franklin and Hayden were celebrating Franklin's engagement?"

"No, not engagement … his eighteenth birthday," Isaiah recovered.

"Oh, ok." Elsa smiled with a huff. "I don't know why I thought you said engagement. Franklin would have told me about that. Go on with your story."

"Hayden decided to take him to a bar to get his first drink. After a few drinks, Franklin passed out. He slept it off that night in Doctor Riley's office. The next morning, he awoke with a terrible headache. Doctor Riley told our father Franklin was sick with a head cold. Our father believed him. Hayden and Franklin promised they would never drink again if Doctor Riley would keep their secret."

"Who is Hayden?"

"Hayden Webster is Franklin's best friend. He works as father's accountant and is married to our teacher."

"Oh, the tall gentleman with sandy blonde hair and brown eyes that sometimes visits Mrs. Webster at lunch."

"That's him."

"They have a three-year-old daughter and a year-old son? Why would the school board hire a woman with a family?"

"They didn't."

"I don't understand. She's a new teacher isn't she? We had a different teacher last year."

"No, she has been our teacher for four years. The first time she was with child, she had quit her job to take care of her new baby. The teacher the school board hired to replace her was horrible. A lot of parents complained. The school board pleaded with Hayden to persuade his wife to return to teaching. She came back. Then a few years later, the same thing happened. The parents didn't want a repeat of what happened last time so they asked the school board to hire a substitute teacher from our community to finish out the year. That's why Mrs. Webster seemed new to you."

"It must be hard on her."

"It is but we help the Webster family a lot. Our family is very close to the Webster family. Hayden's father owns the bank we use and Hayden has been father's accountant for years. Last year

Franklin, uh, never mind."

"Frank what?"

"It's nothing, Elsa."

"No you were about to tell me something about Franklin. Finish your words, Isaiah." Isaiah stared at Elsa with regret. How could he tell Elsa the truth? It would break her heart to know Franklin's true intentions. He had seen girls come and go in Franklin's life yet there was one who always remained, Rebekah Grace Webster. Despite the three years difference in age, Franklin had his eyes set on Rebekah Grace since she had turned twelve years old four years ago. But a girl couldn't start courting until she had turned thirteen. Franklin had waited patiently for her to come of age. Then on her birthday, he asked her for a date. The couple became steady a year later. There were times Franklin grew bored with her and would seek other girls' attentions. Those relationships never lasted long. Elsa was just another girl for Franklin to be with while he and Rebekah were separated. Isaiah couldn't admit the truth to Elsa. It would only break her heart. Franklin had promised to marry Rebekah this summer.

"I was going to say, Franklin had once courted Hayden's sister. Rebekah Grace is Cora's best friend. Cora once had eyes on Hayden. Both Franklin and Cora thought it would be interesting to date each other's best friends. But Hayden didn't like Cora that way. He saw her more like a sister than a potential wife. He met his wife at college then they married."

"Why did Franklin break up with Rebekah? I know her from school. She's quite popular with the boys."

"Yes, but she's conceited too. Franklin hates that. He prefers an honest, humble woman like you."

"Oh."

"Elsa?"

"Yes."

"You said Franklin has diabetes but you never told me why he collapsed."

"Doctor Riley said Franklin slipped into a coma from the diabetes."

"But he's awake now?"

"Yes. Once we get some broth in him he should feel a little

better."

"That's good. What about Abraham? Have you seen him?"

"No but your pa told me about him. Nobody is allowed in his room. When did you see him last?"

"The last time I saw Abraham was three days ago when my parents and I came home. Cora was putting pressure on his wound. Franklin had disappeared. We all ran to Abraham's side. Abraham had stopped screaming by the time we arrived. His face was whiter than usual. He didn't look good, Elsa. A few moments later, Doctor Riley arrived with Franklin. Franklin had collapsed. Pa had told Cora and me to take Franklin upstairs then stay with him. We did. I never saw Abraham again after that. An hour and a half later, Doctor Riley came to Franklin's room. There was blood on his shirt. I asked about it but he wouldn't answer me. He told Cora and me we had to leave Franklin's room. We did. When we went downstairs, father told Cora to make supper and I was to do all the chores. I didn't see mother until the next morning."

"She was asleep in your bed."

"Why?"

"Mr. Raymond told me Doctor Riley had stabilized Abraham then performed surgery on his left leg. He set the bone then placed metal plates with screws to stabilize the bone. Once it heals he'll go back and remove the metal plates. Doctor Riley had to give a blood transfusion. Your mother volunteered. They moved her bed next to Abraham's and performed the transfusion. Your father helped Doctor Riley with all the procedures."

Abraham stared at Elsa with shock. "Does..." he swallowed hard trying to push out the words. "Will...will Abraham be a cripple?"

"I don't know, Isaiah. Doctor Riley said for your parents to watch for infection. He claims since Abraham's only thirteen he should heal faster than an adult. I sure hope so. Abraham's in tremendous pain."

"I want to visit him."

"You can't. Nobody can. Your parents want him to rest in peace and quiet. No homework, no siblings, no visitors, just rest."

"Does Franklin know?"

"Not yet."

"He'll ask."

"Yes, I know. I just don't know how I could tell him about Abraham when he's ill. Franklin probably blames himself."

"Don't tell him, Elsa, please don't tell him."

"Why not?"

"Franklin's not like Pa or any other man. He can't handle too much stress. You should let Franklin recuperate before he learns about Abraham."

"That's what your mother told me, too. Why do you all protect Franklin like he's a child?"

"He's different. Haven't you noticed that by now?"

"What I see in Franklin is the quiet, thoughtful, charming man I love. He doesn't speak often but when he does it comes from his heart."

"You haven't seen his dark moments. I have."

"We all have our dark moments, Isaiah." Elsa turned her gaze towards the stove. The chicken broth bubbled to the top. She looked back at Isaiah. "The broth is ready. Do your schoolwork."

Isaiah nodded. Elsa rose from the table. "Mother," Cora's voice echoed from the stairs behind him. Isaiah, Elsa, and the adults turned in her direction.

"What is it?" Juliette asked as she approached her daughter.

Cora landed on the floor and gasped. "Franklin and I were talking then he…he fell silent and still."

"That's nothing unusual with your brother."

"It's different. I called his name but he wouldn't respond. A few moments later his body shook. I tried to hold him down but his body shook faster."

Doctor Riley picked up his medical bag from the counter and ran up the stairs. "Doctor?" Juliette asked after him.

"It's a seizure caused by the diabetes, Mrs. Raymond. Get the food ready and bring it up to me as soon as possible. After the seizure he will be exhausted. We mustn't allow him to fall asleep before he consumes a good portion of soup. If we aren't successful, your son will die," he yelled as he turned the corner.

Elsa dropped the metal ladle with a gasp. Tears rolled down her cheeks. Franklin dying? She couldn't fathom a life without Franklin. She stared at the mahogany stairs in shock. Henry was dying of tuberculosis and Franklin was dying from the diabetes. It seemed God deemed to take the men she loved the most, excluding her father. Perhaps Oren was next. Maybe God wanted to take both men at once. What had she done to God that he would punish her so? Didn't he know they were the only men who understood her? If she could trade her life for one of theirs she would.

"Elsa," Juliette said as she picked up the ladle. Elsa ignored Franklin's mother and stared at the stairs. Franklin! Her poor Franklin. A tear streaked down her cheek. God can't call him home yet!

"Miss Elsa Beatrice Garrett," Juliette said firmly as she grasped Elsa's upper arms.

"What?" Elsa asked in a whisper towards Juliette.

"Did you hear me, child?"

"No, ma'am. I'm sorry."

"Go to him."

"Ma'am?"

"Go to my son."

"What about the broth?"

"I'll take care of the broth. You take care of my son."

"What about you?"

"What about me?"

"You're not upset. He's dying. Your son is dying!"

"He's not dead, yet. Doctor Riley's a good physician. He'll save my son. I have faith in that and the Good Lord's mercy."

"God's mercy doesn't exist for me."

"God's mercy is all around us. You just have to open your eyes. Go to Franklin. I'll be right behind you. Cora is telling her father what she told me and Isaiah went with her. Go."

"Yes, ma'am."

Elsa ran up the steep stairs and around the corner to Franklin's room. She paused in the doorway as Doctor Riley knelt on the floor next to Franklin's shaking body. She lifted her eyes to the bed. Franklin's bed covers trailed off the bed to the floor like a waterfall. Franklin must have fallen off the bed. She hoped he hadn't hurt himself. Doctor Riley pushed the sheets and quilt away from his patient. He backed away. Franklin thrashed up and down. He cried out loudly with incomprehensible guttural groans. Elsa's heart broke as Franklin fought for his life. She clutched her golden cross pendant Franklin had given her, recalling the story of Jesus miraculously healing the epileptic boy in Mark 9:14-29. If Jesus could heal that boy then why couldn't he heal Franklin too? Elsa closed her eyes, lowered her head, and prayed. "Oh, please, Lord don't take him away from me. Let him survive. Let him be whole again. Make him better than he was before the diabetes. Take it all away, oh Lord. Please take these afflictions from him. Your son, Jesus Christ, healed the boy with epilepsy. You are greater than he. Father, I plead with you, please heavenly father. Heal Franklin Thaddeus Raymond. Oh, heal him, holy one. In Jesus' name. Amen."

Elsa lifted her brown eyes in Franklin's direction. Franklin had stopped moving. She watched as Dr. Riley pulled out his stethoscope, placed the ends in his ears and listened to Franklin's chest. She held her breath. Franklin couldn't be dead. Why would God take an eighteen-year-old's life? He had a bright future ahead of him. Yet Elsa knew age didn't matter when God called one of his children home. She had lost six siblings ranging in ages four years to twenty-four years to influenza five years ago. God didn't care how old a person was. If he wanted the child he'd take the child no matter what.

"You can relax, Miss Elsa Garrett, he is alive," Doctor Riley proclaimed as he removed his stethoscope and laid it to the side. Elsa drew her attention to the doctor. "He's exhausted. He requires nourishment before he falls into a deep sleep. Where's the broth?"

"Right here," Juliette's voice rang behind Elsa. Elsa moved to the side. She watched Franklin's mother kneel on the other side of her son. Doctor Riley tapped Franklin's cheek. "Frank, wake up," he coaxed his unconscious patient. Doctor Riley grabbed Franklin's chin and moved his head. "Wake up, Franklin! I know you're tired but you must eat. Open your eyes, boy!"

Franklin slowly opened his eyes with a moan. "Pa," Franklin whispered.

"He'll be here shortly," Juliette answered.

"Pa," Franklin whispered as he turned his head and closed his eyes.

Juliette lowered the spoon, grabbed him by the chin and

instructed, "Open your eyes, Franklin Thaddeus!"

Elsa stared down at her beau. He never complied. The sound of someone ascending the wooden stairs caught Elsa's attention. Juliette and Doctor Riley tried to coax Franklin while she stepped to the door. Elsa peered out into the hall. Gideon ascended the wooden stairs in a rush. "Elsa," he greeted her from the landing.

"Mr. Raymond. Franklin's asking for you," she informed him.

Gideon nodded. He hurried into his son's bedroom. "Juliette?" he asked as he walked towards her.

"He won't obey me. Doctor Riley says he needs nourishment. I brought broth but he won't even acknowledge I'm here. He just cries for you," Juliette answered.

"Trade places with me. I'll feed him."

Juliette laid the bowl of chicken broth to the side, rose from the floor, and sat on the bed. Gideon sat where his wife once was. He tapped Franklin on the side of the cheek. "Frank," Gideon called to him with his deep voice.

"Pa," Franklin moaned with a turn of his face.

"Open your eyes and look at me, son." Franklin obeyed. "You will not rest until you finish this bowl of broth. Sit up and eat." Doctor Riley lifted Franklin into a sitting position. "Open your mouth." Gideon coaxed with a spoonful of broth while Franklin gazed into his father's eyes with a glassy look. Elsa gulped. That was Franklin's body but where was he? It was as if he was someone she had never known. Franklin opened his mouth. Gideon poured the spoonful of broth into his mouth. "Swallow," he instructed. Elsa watched as Gideon continued to feed his son like a baby. A tear fell down her cheek. A helpless child had replaced her vibrant, loving beau. She peered around the room. The adults seemed calmed as if this was normal for them. But this wasn't normal! This wasn't her Franklin!

Doctor Riley shifted his weight. A small silver box slid from under his foot. Elsa shifted her gaze to the box. She wondered why it was on the floor. Had Franklin knocked it off his nightstand when he fell? She peered up at the nightstand. Everything seemed in perfect order. Franklin was meticulous when it came to order. It wouldn't be like him to have it on the floor if it meant anything to him. And she knew it meant something to him. He had been holding the box when she had entered the room.

Elsa walked to the right and crouched before the small silver box with black etchings. On top of the square box, set in monochrome, were the initials EBG. Elsa peered at the initials with curiosity. EBG? Those were her initials. Why would Franklin have a box with her initials? She picked the case up and turned it in her hand. Little legs stood on the bottom of the deep box as if it was meant to stand. She flipped it to the side. A small drawer lay underneath a larger compartment. She pulled the small drawer open. Green leather encased the interior. A small slit lay between two rectangular pillows. Nothing. She pushed the drawer back then studied the larger compartment. A button of silver lay above the empty, closed drawer. She pushed the button. The lid on top of the box popped upright. Under the lid lay an inscription.

My darling Elsa Bea
Press the button on the right-hand side of the box.
Truly Yours Forever,
FTR

Elsa smiled. It wasn't uncommon for Franklin to give her something with a mystery attached to it. Franklin's mind was complex. He enjoyed cryptic puzzles, codes, and mathematical games. Sometimes he would give her a puzzle that to him seemed so simple to solve but only confused her. A lot of her peers didn't appreciate Franklin's mind games. Yet she had always admired the way his mind worked. "Oh, Frank," she whispered with a grin. Elsa felt the right side of the box with her tender fingers. She bit down on her lip with suspense as she pressed the tiny button inward. The sound of a crank erupted from deep within the box. Elsa watched as the empty green leather tray inside the box turned inward. The form of a silver ring began to make its way to the top. The tray clicked and pushed upwards until it locked into place at the top. There before her eyes lay a beautiful silver ring with a large pearl and five diamonds. She swallowed hard. Franklin had bought her an engagement ring! No wonder her mother had been so adamant she attends the dance. Franklin was going to propose! Elsa pulled the ring out of its tiny enclosure. She carefully placed the ring on her left ring finger. It easily slid down her thin finger. The band was too loose, as if it had been made for someone with larger fingers. She studied the ring as she twisted it back and forth. Franklin must have bought the ring without thought of her small frame. That was typical Franklin, always acting without thought of the consequences. He probably didn't think about ring size. It was common sense to find out the ring size. But Franklin didn't have common sense. She smiled at the thought of his gesture. She didn't mind that it didn't fit. It was the meaning behind the ring that mattered more; besides she could get it adjusted at a jewelry store.

"Elsa," Franklin moaned.

Elsa removed the ring, placed it back in the box and closed the lid. She returned to Doctor Riley's side. "I'm here Frank," Elsa said as she took his left hand into her own. Franklin squeezed her hand while his father continued to feed him. A long moment of silence passed between the two of them. Elsa looked into his face. His brown eyes scanned the room then turned back to Elsa. She smiled towards him. "I'll never leave your side, Frank. I promise. I'll always be here."

He swallowed then said to her, "Sorry."

"For what?"

"Dance."

"What about the dance?"

"I missed the dance."

"I don't care about that."

"No."

"It's just a dance. There will be more."

"It wasn't just a dance," he yelled with a slam of his fist. Elsa released her grip and scooted back. Franklin pushed the spoon away from his mouth, yelling repeatedly, "It wasn't just a dance!"

"Frank, calm down," Gideon instructed, grabbing Franklin by the arms.

Franklin sighed as he muttered, "It wasn't just a dance. It's over. I calculated the time lapse. It's over. I can't ask her. It's over."

"We'll figure this out, Frank," Gideon tried to calm him.

"There's nothing to figure out. It's over. I can't. We missed it. She's..."

"Elsa is still by your side. Look, son. She hasn't left your side."

Franklin turned his head to the right. Elsa stared at her boyfriend with shock. She peered into his deep brown eyes. His angelic eyes immolated childlike innocence that melted her fears. Elsa wondered how much Franklin comprehended what was going on around him. Franklin turned his eyes to his father. "Tired," he yawned, laying against Doctor Riley's chest.

"One last bite," Gideon coaxed as he lifted the last spoonful from the bowl and fed his son the last of the broth. He lowered the spoon to the bowl as Franklin swallowed. "Now you may rest."

Franklin nodded. He closed his eyes and fell limp. Gideon lowered the almost empty bowl to the floor. Doctor Riley lifted Franklin into his arms, rose from the floor, and placed him on the bed. Juliette rose from the bedside. She pulled the white quilt over Franklin's body. Gideon rose from the floor with the bowl and spoon. He handed the items to his wife then turned back to Doctor Riley. Doctor Riley began to gather his items into his large black medical bag. "Jebadiah?" Gideon asked.

"Franklin requires more sleep, Gideon. I suggest he remain in bed until he has gathered his strength. Be certain to wake him every three hours and feed him more broth."

"Yes, sir," Juliette answered. Elsa rose from the floor and sat next to Franklin on the bed. She stroked her finger down his long arm then held his hand. She watched him sleep as the adults conversed.

"Jeb," Gideon said, taking the doctor by the arm. Doctor Riley lifted his gaze to meet Gideon's. "What do you plan to do about my son?"

"Meaning?"

"He's had a seizure."

"Yes."

"He's already fragile. Will the seizure make his condition worse?"

"Only time can tell." Gideon lowered his hand, turned his gaze to Franklin and stared. Doctor Riley stepped towards the brown-haired, green-eyed, English-descent man. "Gideon." Gideon turned his attention to the doctor. "Perhaps it would be best to…"

"…you can stop there, Jeb. Juliette and I told you years ago why we left Upper Sandusky. I will not have the same discussion with you about Franklin I had with both our families. He's an intelligent boy."

"I'm not suggesting he isn't."

"Franklin will do well to stay where he is. I've given him a place at the machine shop designing more inventions. He loves his new office and is doing well overseeing the workers on the floor."

"Gideon, when are you going to accept Franklin will never be able to run your store? He doesn't have the social skills to do so. He needs help."

"He has help," Juliette answered. The men looked to her. "Franklin has all the help he needs to be successful in life. He doesn't belong behind an institution's wall. He's a mechanical genius, Jeb. He loves tinkering with machines and playing mathematical games. God created our son for a purpose. If we place him within the institution he cannot live a successful and productive life. You've been a good friend. I pray the trust we have placed in you will not be forfeited."

"I am your friend but first I am your doctor. As such you know my opinion concerning Franklin. How much longer do you think you two will be able to care for him? There will come a time when you are gone and he will have to depend on someone else in order to survive. Who will that be?"

"Me," Elsa answered.

The adults turned to face the young woman. Elsa stepped towards them. "You three are treating Franklin like he's a child. He may be different but he's no child."

"Elsa, you don't understand," Juliette replied.

"I understand perfectly, Mrs. Raymond. He's the eldest son. You want him to have a perfect life and be responsible for his own actions. You left him in charge of the farm and his siblings. Under his care, Abraham was severally injured. Franklin had become fixated on proposing to me…"

Gideon turned to Doctor Riley, "Jeb, can you leave us alone."

"Of course. When he has slept enough he will not remember anything from the time of the seizure to his full recuperation. He will be very sore. Draw him a bath of warm water and let sit in the water until his muscle aches cease."

"How long do you believe it will be until he recuperates?"

"Three, perhaps four days. It is hard to tell. Everyone is different. His lifestyle will have to change now that he has the diabetes."

"Thank you."

"You're welcome. I'll check on Abraham before I leave. Is there anything else I can do for you, Gideon?"

"No, thank you."

"Very well." He turned to Juliette and tipped his hat to her, "Mrs. Raymond." Doctor Riley grabbed his black bag, pivoted, and walked out the door.

Gideon groaned. "Elsa you weren't supposed to see that. He wanted it to be a surprise."

"It was on the floor. I simply picked it up to place it back on the end table so he wouldn't know it was missing."

"You can't let him know you found it," Juliette asked.

"Why not? I told him I knew he already asked my pa for my hand."

Gideon and Juliette exchanged glances. "Well let's pray he forgets that conversation," Gideon said.

"Hmm," Juliette replied with a nod of her head.

"I don't understand why you two are acting like this and why Cora says he's stupid. He's not stupid, he's wonderful," Elsa protested.

Gideon answered, "Elsa, Franklin has to do things a certain way. Every day of his life he has to follow a strict routine or he will not be able to concentrate on the task he's asked to do. When he plans to do something it is planned down to the tiniest of details. Sometimes one of those details is so peculiar you would miss it. Not Franklin. He has to complete each step of his plan in precise order."

"He was going to propose at the dance, wasn't he?"

"He was."

Juliette interrupted, "He had it all planned out. How did he react when you told him you knew his intentions?"

"He was upset. Cora said it was a panic attack."

Gideon shook his head, "It was too much for him. Elsa, you are right about my son's intelligence. He is very smart but there are just some things we don't tell him because we know it will upset him."

"I upset him?" she asked.

"Probably," Juliette answered walking towards the bed. She pulled the sheets higher over his body.

Elsa turned to face her, "So when he apologized for missing the dance? It wasn't the dance he was apologizing for, was it?"

"No," Juliette answered turning back to her.

"You said everything he does is planned down to the tiniest details and his life has to be in a strict order. So if he missed the dance then…he doesn't plan to ask me to marry him, does he?"

"It's not that he doesn't want to. In his mind he missed the opportunity to ask you," Gideon answered.

She turned to face him. "But he can still ask me."

"Elsa," Juliette answered. She stepped to her, placed her hands on Elsa's arms, and then turned Elsa to face her. "Sweetheart, it would take Franklin months to come up with a way to ask you to marry him."

"Why, all you need to do is have a dance."

"It's not that simple," Gideon replied.

"Yes, it is."

"Elsa, you don't understand. His seizure changes everything."

"He has to change the way he lives. I heard Doctor Riley."

"No, Franklin can't marry you."

Elsa stared silently towards Juliette in shock. Can't marry her? "Why would you forbid our union when you have welcomed me into your home and your family?"

Juliette answered, "If there were some other way I would not hesitate to support my son in his decision. I want you as my daughter. I already love you as if you were my own."

"Then why take this from him?"

"It's not me, Elsa. Ohio Law forbids any person who has epilepsy, is a drunkard, an imbecile, or insane from obtaining a marriage license or marrying."

"But Franklin is none of those."

"It doesn't matter, Elsa. When he applies for the marriage license the county clerk will ask him, under oath, to testify he does not suffer from epilepsy, is not a drunkard, imbecile, or insane. He can't lie to the courts about that."

"But he's not lying. He has diabetes not epilepsy."

"Doesn't matter. Franklin had a seizure. Marion's a small town. My husband's factory is well known throughout the county and Doctor Riley's a physician in Marion. If Franklin applies for a marriage license in Marion County the courts will know of the seizure. The law was created to protect future generations. It was created to ensure epileptics, drunkards, and lunatics don't pass their traits to the next generation."

"That's discrimination."

"Perhaps. Elsa, there isn't a judge in Marion County who doesn't respect the medical opinion of Doctor Riley. Franklin is very honest with anyone. He won't lie to the courts about his seizure. He can present the county clerk with medical records of his ailment but I don't think that will help. Most people when they hear seizure instantly think of epilepsy. If Franklin challenges the ruling I can't think of a single judge who will deem him competent enough to marry."

"I know one."

"Who?"

"My brother-in-law, Liberty. He's the family court judge for Marion County."

"Judge Liberty Watkins is married to your sister?"

"Yes, ma'am. Deborah and I have been close since my birth."

"I'm surprised to hear that. She is ten years older than you, is she not?"

"No, ma'am. Deborah and Franklin are the same age."

Juliette stared at Elsa in shock. She opened her mouth to speak then closed it with a perplexed look on her face. "That would mean she was thirteen when she married Judge Watkins," Gideon answered.

"Yes, sir. My sister was with his child when they wedded."

"But Judge Watkins is thirty-seven years old!"

"Liberty was running for county judge at the time when all this happened. His platform was to prohibit child workers, prostitution, and underage marriages. He decided it was best for all if he lied about Deborah's age. I had confided the truth to Franklin a few months ago. Other than that, my family and I have sworn to keep the truth a secret. That is why you never knew who my sister was married to, only that my father had disowned her."

Juliette answered, "If someone was to learn the truth of Judge Watkins' wife's age he could lose many supporters. He's a popular judge and there are some who want to run against him. That kind of information would hurt his career. It's no wonder she looks young for her age. Many women speak of her beauty. Mrs. Watkins is quite fashionable and well-known."

"She'll turn nineteen in July. Liberty was afraid others may claim he molested a child."

Gideon objected, "He did molest and rape a child if she was as young as you say."

"Yes, sir but it wasn't rape or molestation. Deborah wanted to lose her purity to him."

"It is what it is, Elsa. The man's a judge in the Marion County Family Courts. Before that he was a prosecuting attorney. He puts men in jail for what he did to your sister."

"My pa wanted to press charges on him for it, too, but didn't."

"Why not?"

"Pa said people like us don't go around claiming things like that to people like that. We're poor folk. Liberty has money, power, and a reputation. He knows what harms Liberty can harm us. Mr. Raymond, he's afraid that since we're poor Liberty could say my parents aren't good parents. Pa thinks Liberty would separate us if we do him any harm."

"I don't believe Judge Watkins would do that. He's a good judge."

"Yes, sir."

"Do you still speak with your sister?" Juliette asked.

"Yes, I call her when my pa ain't around. My ma doesn't agree with the way pa treats Deborah. Sometimes when we're in Marion and Pa ain't with us Ma lets me sneak over to Deborah's for the afternoon. I know if Deborah learns of my predicament she'll help me. After school tomorrow you can drop me off at her house and I'll speak to her about it."

Juliette looked at her eldest son. She wanted Franklin to live a happy, productive life. To be labeled a diabetic prone to seizures wasn't something she wanted for him. She turned to Elsa. "Say your family helps my son. If Franklin has another seizure, then if the courts learn of his deceit he could go to jail for lying. Judge Watkins could be punished for helping you."

"I know another doctor who can help him overcome the seizures."

"Who?"

"My aunt's a doctor in Wheelersburg, Ohio. I've only met her once. She cured the influenza my family had five years ago. I had never met her until then. Her name is Doctor Betsy Garrett. She's married to my father's older brother. My pa doesn't speak much to his side of the family. Once Franklin and I are married we can move to Wheelersburg for a time. I'm certain Aunt Betsy can cure him."

Gideon huffed, "Hump, a female physician. Women are incapable of logic and intelligence due to their emotions."

"My aunt's father is a doctor too," Elsa stated.

"What is his name?" Gideon asked

"Doctor Amos Summerland of Summerland Hospital and Clinic in Wheelersburg, Ohio."

Gideon paced back and forth in contemplation. A female physician! Women were emotional, unreliable, and dimwitted. He didn't know if he could trust a woman to treat his son. What if she couldn't control her emotions? If she gave into emotions without any logical thought she could do more harm than good to Franklin. He had lived with Juliette long enough to know when she was on her cycle because she was an emotional wreck. Cora had inherited her mother's monthly distasteful manners as well. But Elsa had said her aunt's father was a physician as well. At least there was a man who could oversee his son's treatments. That he would be willing to consent to. Gideon turned towards the women. "I want to speak to your aunt," he declared to Elsa.

"Does this mean you will help us?"

"Yes, but Franklin has to propose to you first. I won't have you two down there before you become his wife. Do you understand?"

"Yes, sir," Elsa beamed.

"Good, Juliette, tomorrow I will stay home with Franklin and Abraham. After you pick up the children from school take them to Judge Watkins' house. Elsa, you are certain you can gain Deborah

and Liberty's support?"
    "Yes, sir!"
    "Very well. Then it is settled."

5

April 26, 1904

The full moon hung high above the Raymond farm, illuminating everything in the moonlight's path. An eerie silence filled the farmhouse. Cora slowly slipped out of her mother's bed, grabbed her violet robe with peach flowers, and wrapped it around her body. Elsa moaned from her side of the bed they shared. Cora's heart jumped. She couldn't allow Elsa to know why she was up so late. No one could ever know. Cora turned to face her bed companion. Elsa pulled the blankets up, snuggled deep inside them, and then fell silent. Relieved, Cora grabbed the lantern from her mother's nightstand, lit it with the matches beside it, lowered the wick, and then lowered the globe. Slowly and cautiously, she began to tiptoe around the room.

"Where are you going?" Elsa asked.

Cora paused before the foot of the bed. "I have to use the outhouse."

"It's late."

"So? This is my house not yours, Elsa. I can go where I want, when I want, and however I want! Go to back to sleep! Jeez, the only reason I even allow you to share the bed with me is because of Franklin. But wait until the day he throws you away."

"What do you mean by that?" Elsa asked, sitting up.

Cora laughed as she walked around the bed, "Elsa, don't tell me you think you are the only girl my brother has been with."

"He's dated others?"

"Of course, he's dated others! My brother's a fool. He'll pick up any girl he finds, be with her awhile, then when's he's done he'll just forget about them." She scanned her eyes up and down Elsa's body. "Obviously, he dug into the trash to find you," she sneered then walked out of the room. Cora walked down the hall and paused at Abraham's room. She placed her hand on her brother's door and peered inward. Juliette lay asleep in Isaiah's bed. Poor Abraham laid asleep on his back with his broken leg propped upright with pillows and a board underneath. He was just another victim of Franklin's carelessness.

Her entire life her parents had given Franklin more attention than her and her brothers. She hated it. But most of all she loathed the way her father believed Franklin was capable of taking over the family business after he was dead. Gideon Alvin Raymond's mind dwelt in the archaic world of Victorian society. She didn't know how her mother could stand being married to him for the past twenty-one years. Gideon had treated both her and her mother with contempt, relegating them both to housework, childrearing, and other delicate matters of womanhood. The times had changed! This was the twentieth century! With the turn of the century came the progressive movement. Cora was proud to call herself a progressive. Progressives wanted to change the world for the better for women, children, and families. But there were others, such as her father, who stood firm in their old Victorian thinking. It was that thinking she hated the most. Under her father's will, he had deemed Franklin receive full control of all the family business and assets. Her brothers would divide the farm in half between them. By the time everything was said and done, nothing was left for Cora. Every time she spoke to her father about it he would just smile and say "Cora, my darling, you have nothing to fret about. Your husband will care for you." Why couldn't she care for herself? Her father infuriated her but Elsa infuriated her more! If Elsa became Franklin's wife she would gain everything that went to Franklin, but if Rebekah Grace was Franklin's wife then Cora could control not only her brother but his assets as well. Elsa had to be stopped before it was too late!

Cora closed the door and walked into the kitchen. She laid the lantern down, picked up the round receiver of her family's wooden wall-crank phone. Cora cranked the phone and waited for the switchboard operator. Anxious, she studied her surroundings for even the slightest of movement. She couldn't afford for anyone to catch her on the telephone. A door closed upstairs. She peered up at the staircase on her right. Footsteps. Oh, no, what time was it after all? Cora slammed the phone on the hook as someone started to descend the stairs. She ran to the counter, grabbed the lantern, and began to turn down the hall.

"Cora," Gideon said from behind her.

Cora turned with both her hands firmly clutched to the handle.

"Pa?" she asked.

"What are you doing out of bed?"

"I had to use the outhouse." She stared up at the top of the stairs then back to her father. "How is Franklin?"

"He's sleeping peacefully. I came to get him something to eat."

"Oh," she said softly.

"Go back to bed, Cora. You have school tomorrow."

"Yes, sir," she replied then turned down the hall. Cora opened her father's bedroom, stepped inside, and closed the door behind her. She heard Isaiah move in her father's bed then fall silent. Isaiah could sleep through anything. Cora lowered the wick. She had to get to that phone and make her call to Indiana. Somehow, someway she had to warn Rebekah that Elsa had thwarted their plans. She heard her father step down the hall. Cora opened the door slightly and peered through the crack. Gideon stepped into Abraham and Isaiah's room. He walked over to Juliette. Cora watched her parents interact.

"Jules," Gideon whispered.

Juliette stirred from her sleep. "Hmm, what time is it?" she yawned.

"Midnight. You said you wanted to change rooms at midnight. I can go back if you need more sleep. You need your rest so you can take the children to school in the morning and run some items to Hayden for me."

She yawned again while rising from the bed, "No, go to bed. I can sleep while the children are in school."

"There's a bowl of broth on the stove for Frank to sip," Gideon said, taking off his shoes. Juliette nodded then exited the room, closing the door behind her.

Cora closed the door and leaned her back against the wall. She heard her mother stop before the room. "Isaiah," her mother called out. Cora's heart raced with anticipation and fear. She glared down at the dimly lit light. Maybe her mother saw the light. If it moved then surely she would know someone was inside the room. Juliette tapped on the door and called out to her son again. Cora closed her eyes, desperately wanting her mother to go away. She heard a door open; someone walked to her mother then spoke.

"What's wrong?" Gideon's voice lifted from behind the door.

"I don't know. Look under the door, there's a light in your room."

"Maybe it's from the window. There is a full moon out."

"I closed the drapes so Isaiah could sleep. You know how much the light disturbs him."

Gideon knocked harder on the door, "Isaiah! Put that light out and go to bed! Now!" Cora heard Isaiah stir in their father's bed. She opened her eyes, peered at her brother, and then stared across the room. "I'm not going to tell you again, son," Gideon bellowed. Isaiah opened his eyes and stared at Cora.

"Cora?" he questioned.

"Shut up and agree with Pa."

"What for?"

"Just do it or I'll tell him you went swimming with a girl in the pond without clothes on."

"I never did that."

"Doesn't matter if you did or not. He'll believe me. You're the one causing all the trouble lately, not me," she grinned.

"Isaiah, I'm coming in there," Gideon yelled, turning the knob.

Cora rushed across the room, handed the lantern to Isaiah and dove under her father's bed as the door opened. He peered under his bed then lifted his gaze as his parents entered the room.

"Isaiah, give that to me before you burn the bed," Juliette said, approaching him. Isaiah handed the lantern to his mother. Gideon stared at his son with a stern look of disapproval.

"You want to tell me why you are up at this time of night with a lit lantern?" Gideon asked.

"Cora...uh," he grunted, feeling Cora thump the bottom of the mattress with her knee.

"Cora?" Gideon asked.

"I heard a noise in my room and lit the lantern to see who was in here with me. Cora had come into my bedroom by mistake. She told me to go back to bed then went to her room. I was about to turn off the lantern when you pounded on the door."

"Why didn't you answer me?"

"Sorry, Pa, I was distracted. Cora was talking to me."

"I didn't hear any voices. Are you lying to me?"

"No, Pa, honest," Isaiah shook his head.

Juliette grabbed Gideon by the arm and looked at him. "It's getting late. Franklin needs food and you need your sleep. Perhaps we should discuss this in the morning."

"Go to bed, Isaiah. You have school tomorrow."

"Yes, sir," Isaiah answered then lay back down. Cora watched their mother extinguish the lantern then walk out the room with Gideon. Cora lowered her head with a sigh of relief in unison with the door closing. So close. She was so close to getting caught, especially with Isaiah's big mouth. She jabbed her fist hard into the mattress.

"Cora," Isaiah complained.

Cora slid out from under the bed and rose beside him. She grabbed his blankets and pushed her ten-year-old brother. "Ever do that again and I'll hurt you even more," she growled as she shoved him. She walked to her bedroom, opened the door, and slammed it behind her. She glared at Elsa. Someway, somehow she was going to get rid of Elsa Beatrice Garrett!

Home of
Judge Liberty and Deborah Watkins
Marion, Ohio

Liberty leaned against the doorframe that separated his bedroom from Deborah's. He watched the grey-haired, plump, Doctor Betsy Garrett examine Deborah on the queen-size four-poster bed. Three days ago, he and Deborah had attended Saint Mark's Catholic Church in Marion, Ohio with his parents and five children. Thirty-three weeks into her pregnancy, this was to be Deborah's last mass she could attend before being placed on bed rest. During the sermon, Deborah had fallen forward in the pew with tremendous abdominal pain. Her screams had lifted high in the sanctuary. The priest had stopped his message. "Liberty. Help," had been the only words his wife could push out of her labored breaths. Everyone had gathered around them, including the priest. Doctor Riley had rushed up the aisle to Deborah's side. Liberty's parents had gathered the children then left the sanctuary with them. Doctor Riley had asked everyone to clear the room then he examined her. The baby was in distress and Deborah was in labor. Liberty had helped the doctor by administering chloroform to Deborah to ease her suffering. Later Deborah had given birth to their stillborn son. Deborah's grief had overwhelmed her. Liberty had to control her as the doctor wrapped their dead son in his coat and walked outside with the bundle.

The congregation and priest had acted quickly to arrange a burial. The following day, he and Deborah attended the funeral at Marion Cemetery along with their family. Deborah's grief had been evident. She could barely stand. Liberty's mother had supported her throughout the service. The women had surrounded her but she refused to be consoled. Liberty had feared he had lost the sweet, cheerful young woman he had married five years ago. After the funeral, Deborah had locked herself away in her bedroom. He could hear her continual sobs through his bedroom door. Many times he had tried to comfort her, but she would only yell at him to get out of her room and leave her alone. Their children had tried to speak to their mother but she would yell at them also. Chaos had erupted in his home. His parents aided him with the children. As Deborah grew deeper in her depression he realized there was nothing he could do to help her. She needed a woman to confide in and a doctor. There had only been one woman he could think of who met both those qualifications— Deborah's estranged aunt. He called Doctor Betsy Garrett of Wheelersburg, Ohio, introduced himself as Deborah's husband, and then pleaded for her to visit Deborah. This morning Liberty found Deborah on the floor with a high fever, vomit beside her, and moaning in pain with her arm across her lower stomach. Moments later, Betsy had arrived with her husband, Jesse, and their seventeen-year-old daughter, Victoria.

Deborah fidgeted as Victoria replaced the dry cloths on Deborah's forehead and neck with wet ones. "Liberty," Deborah whispered repeatedly.

Liberty walked to the left side of her bed, sat beside her, and took her warm hand. "I'm here, Debs."

"So cold," she whispered with an arch of her neck. Deborah lifted her right hand to her forehead. She pressed the dry cloth and tried to lean forward.

Victoria placed her hands on Deborah's shoulders and guided her down. "Be still, Deborah. You're too frail to move."

"Who are you?" Deborah asked into her cousin's thin face.

"I'm your cousin, Victoria Letha Garrett."

"Letha? You have Grandmother Garrett's first name?"

"Yes, father said he wanted to honor his mother by giving me her name but mother liked the name Victoria. So they compromised. It's a shame Grandmother Garrett died in childbirth when your father was nine. He mustn't remember much about her. My father was ten when she died. He doesn't recall much about her except that she was a loving woman full of grace and beauty."

Deborah exhaled a deep breath. "My pa thought the same of her. He gave me the middle name of Grace in honor of his mother. Ugh," Deborah protested to the throbbing headache. She clutched Liberty's hand and leaned forwards. Liberty rubbed her slender back. "It feels like someone is hitting me with a hammer."

"Lie down," Liberty instructed.

"No," she cried. Deborah pressed her hand tighter.

"You should listen to your husband, cousin Deborah," Victoria said with a hint of a southern accent.

Deborah turned her eyes to Victoria, scoffed, and then turned them back to her husband. "Libby," she whispered with a parched throat.

"Lie down, Debs," he answered.

"No. What is she doing here?"

"She's helping her mother."

Deborah shook her head. "Mother?" she mouthed.

Liberty lifted his eyes to the end of the bed. "Aunt Betsy."

Deborah followed his gaze. "Aunt Betsy," Deborah yelled at the image of the plump, grey-haired woman with thin-wired eyeglasses. Deborah pivoted her hip and glared at her husband with anger. "What is she doing here?"

"Saving you."

"I don't need help, Liberty. I need them gone."

"No."

"My father told me never to communicate with any member of his family!"

"He also told you not to marry me nor claim my child. You didn't listen to him then. What makes you think I would believe you would obey him now? Besides, I know you have been in communication with Aunt Betsy, but what I don't understand is why you told them you were my servant and that you've been working in my home for five years?"

"You haven't told them the truth, have you?"

"Lie down, Debs. We'll speak of this when you're well enough for an argument."

"Oh, God, you did, didn't you?" she panicked.

Sharp pain filled her stomach. She leaned over her stomach with a loud cry. A wave of nausea overwhelmed her. Betsy lowered the medical chart and addressed Deborah. "Deborah, lie down."

Deborah lowered her head. Her long, brown, wavy hair covered the sides of her face. Tears fell down her cheeks. "Debs, do what Aunt Betsy tells you to do," Liberty coaxed as he put his arms around her back. She leaned into him.

"Uncle Jesse. Did he come too?" she asked as she pressed her head into his shoulder.

"Yes, he is speaking to my father."

"Liberty, Uncle Jesse is stricter than my father. You thought pa disapproved of our marriage, wait until you meet Uncle Jesse."

"Shh, Debs, I'm not worried about that. I'm more concerned about you."

"Ugh," she groaned loudly then leaned further over her legs.

"Debs," Liberty whispered as he rubbed her back.

"Oh, it hurts! It hurts, Liberty. My head hurts. I want to vomit. My throat's on fire and my stomach hurts. I'm so cold."

"Sweetheart, lean back. Let Aunt Betsy treat you."

Liberty grabbed Deborah by her forearms and guided her onto her back. He tenderly stroked the left side of her face. "Close your eyes and rest."

"I'm thirsty," she replied with her eyes fixed on him.

Liberty looked up at Deborah's raven-haired cousin. The slender young woman lowered the last of the dry clothes into a bucket of water. "Victoria," Liberty addressed her. Victoria rose from over the bucket. "The maid brought Deborah a pitcher of water and a glass. It's behind you on the vanity. She's thirsty."

Deborah moaned loudly and clutched his hand as Victoria turned to get the water. Liberty lowered his eyes to his wife. Betsy moved her hands to Deborah's lower abdomen. With each of the older woman's touches Deborah groaned. "When did she lose the child?" Betsy asked.

"Three days ago. She has bled since then and refused to leave her bedroom. This morning, I found her on the floor with this fever, there was blood between her legs, and vomit beside her."

Betsy opened Deborah's legs. Deborah moaned and fidgeted while Betsy examined her. She turned her face towards him, cried and winced in pain. Betsy closed Deborah's legs and rose. She lowered Deborah's legs then addressed Liberty. "I am not worried about the blood loss. That is to be expected from a woman who has given birth. It should decrease within the next six weeks. Some women who have placental abruptions do tend to lose a lot of blood. The blood loss causes the woman to go into maternal shock and ultimately kills her. If that was the case, Deborah would have died the same day she gave birth."

"What about the fever? She never had a fever after she gave birth to our children," Liberty asked.

"It's Childbed Fever. Her womb is infected, I can smell it. Your doctor caused it."

"How?"

"He didn't wash his hand before he delivered the baby."

"He didn't have time. Deborah and the child were in distress."

Betsy raised her hand to silence him. "Liberty, I'm not blaming him. He did everything he could to save your wife. This fever can kill Deborah. How many hours has it been since you found her?"

Liberty peered up at the clock on the mantle. "It's ten right now. It's been an hour and half. Why?"

"Her fever has risen since I arrived and will continue to do so. By the end of the day, it will be so high she will become confused and debilitated. That is the most dangerous part of this disease. The fever can last up to ten days. After the tenth day, the fever will lower."

"She can survive this, then?"

"Her chances for a full recovery are slim. Most women don't make it that long. Once the womb is infected the disease will spread to her blood and she will die."

"But Deborah's not like most women. She has survived influenza, hunger, and three miscarriages. My Debs is strong. She'll survive this too."

"Liberty, you need to prepare yourself for the worst. The fever will be persistent and aggressive."

"Then do something to stop it!"

Betsy stared at Deborah then back at Liberty. "There is something I can do but it is risky. She already has a fever and I wouldn't offer it to any of my patients with a fever."

"What is it?"

"Liberty, it's not something I would offer lightly."

"Name it!"

Betsy swallowed hard, looked into Deborah's eyes, and then turned to her nephew. "I can remove the womb. But that would mean…"

"…she couldn't have any more children," Liberty finished. Betsy nodded. "And if you don't operate?"

"We could lose her either way. But it is for certain she will die if I don't operate."

Liberty looked over at his wife. Victoria sat on the end of the bed with a glass of water held to Deborah's lips. Deborah slowly sipped on the water. He played with Deborah's white gold wedding band. She turned her eyes to face him. He huffed with a smile, kissed her on her forehead, and then whispered in her ear, "I love you."

Deborah swallowed then whispered, "I love you too. Forgive me. I don't want to die."

"You won't. Deborah," he took a deep breath, sniffed his nose, then opened his mouth to speak. He closed it, unable to bring himself to tell her what Betsy had offered. Deborah continued to focus on sipping the water her cousin offered her. He peered up at Victoria then looked into Deborah's eyes. "Did you hear my conversation with your aunt just now," he asked his wife.

"No, too tired and thirsty."

"Debs, I have to make a decision. It's a decision I don't want to make without you."

"I trust you," she whispered then sipped the water. Liberty pressed his forehead against hers as Victoria backed away with the empty cup.

"Liberty, I need a decision. The longer we wait the less of a chance I have to save her, surgery or not," Betsy said.

Deborah cringed with a low moan. "What?" he asked. She pushed him to the side, leaned over the edge and vomited into the chamber pot. Liberty held her long hair as he rubbed her back. She suddenly fell limp. "Debs," he said. Nothing. He placed his hand on the back of her neck. He could feel the warmth of her skin without a touch. "Deborah," he yelled. Liberty quickly lowered her back on the bed. Her head flopped to the side. Betsy knelt beside her and felt for a pulse on Deborah's neck. "Her heart rate has risen." Betsy grabbed her stethoscope, placed it then listened to Deborah's chest. "Breathing is fast and shallow." She turned to Liberty. "Her fever is too high to operate. If I can lower it there may still be hope left but I need your decision, Liberty!"

Liberty nodded. "Take it out of her," he reluctantly granted permission.

Betsy raised her head to her daughter and barked orders, "I need more water and clothes. Bring me a bottle of whiskey. Hurry!" Victoria ran to the door. Betsy yelled after her, "Tell your father Deborah's dying and to call her parents then send for the butler. Tell Deborah's maid to draw a cold bath. After you've done all return to me immediately!"

Victoria held the rim of the door and peered at her mother. "But you just told Liberty, Deborah could survive this with the operation."

"Go and do what I told you to do! The longer you wait the more danger she is in of dying. I need to lower her temperature and I can't do that without the butler to carry Deborah and the maid to prepare the bath! Water, cloths, whiskey, now!"

"Yes, ma'am," said Victoria.

Liberty couldn't believe he had granted permission for Betsy to operate. The decision, as hard as it had been for him to make, was a no brainer. Deborah's life was in danger no matter how he had decided. At least this way, Deborah had a fighting chance before the disease went into her bloodstream. But he knew Deborah would be upset with him for that decision. All she ever wanted was to be the mother of his children. He swallowed hard as he looked at Deborah's still body. Liberty stared into his beautiful wife's face. He lowered his head with tears streaking his cheeks. "Oh, please Lord, don't take her away from me. Haven't I lost enough?" he prayed. Liberty closed his eyes as the memory of his previous wife's death came to the forefront of his mind. Nellie had died in childbirth. He could still hear her torturous screams of pain and labored breath. He could smell the foul stench of blood pouring out from her as their twin daughters, Tabitha and Zipporah, were born nine years ago. Nellie had died and now Deborah's life was threatened. It seemed to him having children only caused death and agony to the women he loved the most. He swore to himself if Deborah died he would never take another woman to his bed. Their deaths were on his hands.

"Liberty?" Betsy asked with a sharp tone.

Liberty raised his head sharply. "What?" he asked with a

shake of his head.

"I asked how long has it been since you slept?"

"It doesn't matter."

"Yes, it does. You have been through much. The circles under your eyes give away your lack of sleep. You can't sit still without fidgeting, you're constantly yawning, and have a delay in reaction. You require sleep."

"I can't. Debs needs me."

"There's nothing you can do for her now. I suspect her fever was higher than you believed it to be this morning for her to fall ill this fast. Victoria and I need to lower her temperature enough so I can operate."

"Shouldn't you have suspected that earlier? Deborah never pays attention to her own health! What kind of doctor are you? I told you when you came into her room she won't think of herself. Deborah's used to placing the needs of others before her own. Her parents raised her to be like that. She's never been a child," Liberty sighed at Deborah. Tears fell down his cheeks. He tenderly stroked his thumb across her right cheekbone. "You don't know what they did to her."

"My husband's brother is a good man. I'm certain Oren took care of his children the best he knew how."

Liberty shook his head as he sobbed. "She told me of the struggles her family went through."

"Liberty, you are fortunate enough to have been born into money. You don't know how horrible life can be to middle and poor classes."

"My Deborah missed more school days caring for her family than any child should."

"Life wasn't perfect for Deborah because life was never perfect for her father. I'm certain Oren tried his best to provide a decent life for Deborah despite the complications of his disability. Liberty, you have to leave Deborah and get some rest."

"I don't want to leave her side. "

"I won't have you in this room as I operate on her."

"She's my wife."

"I only need a nurse in the room while I conduct the procedure."

"I can help."

"Victoria is enough help for me."

"What if Deborah dies and I'm not here?"

"If it should come to her death I will be certain to wake you."

"I can't leave her."

"You are of no use to her without sleep. Go to bed, Judge Watkins."

"Yes, ma'am." He rose from beside the bed, kissed Deborah on the forehead, and then stepped away.

Liberty turned into his bedroom and closed the door behind him. He leaned his back against the door and peered at his four-poster bed. He watched the memory of him and Deborah last July in his bedroom.

Deborah answered the bedroom door dressed in Liberty's long-sleeved white nightshirt trimmed on the collar and pocket with gold thread. Deborah's thick, long, chestnut hair cascaded down her back with elegant waves. Liberty pulled his black stocking over his left calf and strapped it to his black garter. He lifted his eyes towards his wife. The hem of his nightshirt lifted just above her knee as Deborah clung to the side of the door. She cheerfully spoke to someone in the hallway. He glared down at the back of her knee. He loved her slender frame. He moved his eyes to her bottom. The white fabric gently hung off her perfectly round ass. His heart skipped a beat. Liberty pushed his trousers aside, rose from the bed, and walked to Deborah. He wrapped his arms around her slender waist, pressed his waist into her, and pulled her against him. "I love you," he whispered in her ear. He cast his eyes to his eight-year-old twin daughters. "Zipporah and Tabitha, don't you have something to do?" he instructed them.

"We wanted to wish mother a happy birthday. It's July 17th*, father. Mother turns eighteen today," Zipporah answered with her hands clutched around a golden frame.*

"The girls made a cross stitch sampling for me," Deborah said with a turn of her head to Liberty.

"Ah, I see," Liberty said.

Zipporah continued, "We had the cook prepare mother's favorite breakfast. We thought she might want breakfast in bed. We knocked on her bedroom door but she didn't answer."

"*Your mother and I...*"

"*We had a long discussion last night and I never made it back to my bed,*" *Deborah interrupted.*

"*Are we going to have a new baby sister or brother?*" *Tabitha asked.*

Liberty chuckled, "Tabitha, why would you ask that?"

Tabitha shrugged her shoulders then answered, "Every time Deborah spends more time in your bedroom than her own you two make a lot of noise. Then a few months later she's sick with a child."

"*You are too observant for your own good.*"

"*Much like her father,*" *Deborah teased, turning to face him.*

"*Well are you?*" *Zipporah asked with a smile. Deborah turned her attention to her stepdaughter. "God took the last baby from your stomach. Are you going to ask him for another?*"

"*That's enough,*" *Liberty disciplined her as Deborah's face fell. He turned to his wife. A tear fell down her cheek. "Are you alright? We don't have...*" *she placed her finger on his lips, sniffed her nose then answered. "Zipporah's right. We should ask God to grant us another.*"

"*Are you ready for that?*"

"*Was I ready last night?*"

"*Oh, I can't deny you were,*" *he grinned. They turned back to their daughters.*

Zipporah grinned, "What are you going to ask for? A boy or a girl?"

"*You have to allow your mother and me to be alone with God before you ask that question.*"

"*Oh.*"

"*Do you want us to bring your breakfast up here as well, father?*" *Tabitha offered as Liberty kissed Deborah's neck.*

"*I think...,*" *Deborah smiled from his kiss beneath her ear. She giggled, and then controlled herself. Deborah continued, "I think your father has other plans for the moment. We will join you downstairs later. Perhaps we should celebrate today with a picnic at the park for lunch?*"

"*Oh, yes, that would be splendid. Wouldn't it, Tabitha?*" *Zipporah suggested.*

"Girls, go away. God can't give us another child with you standing here," Liberty ordered as he continued to seduce his wife.

"Yes, sir," Tabitha answered. She tapped her sister on the arm.

Deborah closed the door while the girls ran down the hall. She leaned her back against the door with a grin, "Another child?"

Liberty pulled away from her. "You said last night you were ready. But if you're not then we won't try again."

"No, no. You have needs and I shouldn't take that away from you. I...," she swallowed hard then looked to the side.

Liberty gently placed his hand on the side of her cheek, turned her to face him, then said, "Deborah, I truly enjoyed you last night. I know you enjoyed it as well. But if it is too soon..."

She leaned into him and kissed him deeply on the mouth. Liberty wrapped his arms around his wife. The couple passionately kissed each other. Deborah moved her hands up and down his silk undershirt and pulled away from him. "I'm not a stranger to death. You know that," Deborah whispered. "I can handle the pain as long as you are by my side."

Liberty pressed his forearm against the green wooden door and stared down the front of her body. Her slender, youthful body always intoxicated him. Deborah had given him three beautiful children, yet the only portions of her body to tell the tale were her large bosoms. He stared at the round pink nipples pushing against the light white silk fabric of his shirt. He had suckled on those beautiful mounds last night. What he wouldn't give to suck on them again. The light fabric rose up and down her chest with every breath she took. He bore his gaze on her flat stomach. Last night, he had tapped into her secret garden, hoping his seed would produce another child. Maybe this time God would see fit to leave the child in her womb.

"Liberty," Deborah whispered. Liberty lifted his brown eyes to meet hers.

"Deborah, I love my nightshirt on you but I think I prefer it off of your body."

Deborah grinned. She grabbed the lip of his underpants and pulled him forward. Her slender fingers played with the top button of his cotton drawers over his stomach. *"I thought you had to work this morning,"* she whispered with her lips next to his.

"Work can wait."

"Are you certain?"

"Hmm, I find myself a bit too distracted for boring legal papers."

Deborah grinned. With one move of her slender finger she unbuttoned the top button. Liberty peered down as her fingers trailed down to the second button. *"I wouldn't know why you would find me such a distraction,"* she teased, popping the second button loose. Her hand slid inside his drawers. Liberty pinned her between his body and the door. Deborah grinned. She moved her hand up and down his already rising penis.

"Oh, you shouldn't tempt me like this Debs."

"You don't like it?"

"I like it! But I'm more concerned about you than me."

"I'm ready, Liberty, and by the feel of it you are too."

"It's your birthday not mine," he grunted.

"Who said I didn't want you for my birthday?" Deborah unbuttoned the last button and pulled his drawers down. Liberty passionately kissed her on the lips as he stepped out of them. He grabbed the edges of her nightshirt, pulled it off her body and dropped the shirt to the floor. In one swift move, he picked her up by her bottom and inserted his penis into her. Deborah wrapped her legs around his waist. He pushed her back against the door. Quick and hard, he thrust himself deep inside her. Her seductive groans encouraged him even more. Her large breasts bounced up and down with every rocking motion of their hips, tempting him. He moved his hands around her chest. Deborah glanced down, breathing through her open mouth. She clawed at the back of his skin-tight, machine-knitted undershirt. Deborah arched her head back and groaned. With an insatiable hunger for her, he quickly lowered his mouth to her breasts. Deborah's moans intensified. Empowered, he embraced Deborah tighter, walked over to the bed, and laid her down. He stood beside the bed, pulled her towards him, and pushed himself inside her once again as he groped her breasts. Deborah smiled between her groans of delight. *"Oh,"* she moaned, grabbing her head.

"You alright?" he asked between thrusts.

Deborah clutched his quilt and screamed, "Keep pushing. Oh, don't stop."

Liberty grinned. Her nipples were hard and she felt good. He knew this was it. If ever a time came for God to give them another child then this would have to be it. She gripped her head, screaming and groaning from deep within her. She pounded her hand against the wooden footboard.

"I can stop if I'm hurting you."

"You're not hurting me! A woman isn't supposed to enjoy it but I have more than once gleaned enjoyment from this encounter."

Liberty grinned. He crawled on top of Deborah and pushed even harder. They grabbed each other. Something wonderful was happening inside her. He could feel it. God was going to bless them! There was something special about this child. Never before had they ever experienced this much passion together. It was almost as if God was reminding them of the deep love they shared for each other. The overwhelming tension filled Liberty. He pressed his hand on the bed beside Deborah's head and grunted. Deborah gasped between her deep groans. With one quick thrust, the two of them screamed as he released inside her.

Liberty swiped his hand across the fireplace mantle with a yell of frustration. His wooden mantle clock fell to the ground with trinkets of glass and metal. He pounded his open hand into the lip of the black mantle. Liberty bent an arm and leaned his forehead on it. He stared at the interior of his fireplace. If only he hadn't granted Deborah her desire! Now she was dying! He pounded his left hand on the mantle several times. Liberty sobbed. "Why! Oh, God, just tell me why. Why do you want to ruin my life? You give my wife and me the most pleasurable moment together we have ever faced! You allow the child to grow inside her, only to take the child at birth, and now you threaten to take my wife from me! You granted us hope only to steal it away from me? Tell how that is supposed to be fair," he pleaded between his tears. He listened for an answer. He had been a good Catholic boy. Went to church, obeyed the sacraments, confessed his sins every Thursday, and prayed his rosary. What else did God want from him? He knew it was wrong to question God but somebody had to. You don't give a gift only to take it back two fold! God had given them a life then had stolen it. Now God wanted his wife too. He heard Deborah scream his name. Liberty turned, opened the door, and stepped into Deborah's bedroom. Betsy quickly rung more clothes from the half-filled bucket and placed them on the base of Deborah's neck. She continued to replace dry clothes with wet ones as they spoke.

"Nephew," she addressed him.

"I heard Deborah scream."

"She's asleep, as you should be."

Liberty released his grip on the metal door handle. He turned to his wife. "I don't understand. I heard her scream my name," he replied with a shake of his head.

"Liberty, she was asleep when you left her room and hasn't awakened since."

"Asleep? How can that be? She yelled for me."

"You're exhausted. I can give you something to help you rest."

Liberty turned his head to the older woman. "I don't need anything."

"Go to bed and sleep." Liberty glanced at Deborah. "She'll be alright. I promise to take good care of her. Victoria hasn't arrived with the supplies yet. When she does we'll lower her fever and I'll conduct the hysterectomy."

"You don't know her like I do. She's not a deep sleeper. She hears everything. She won't rest if she believes someone needs help. She'd sacrifice everything for the sake of another human being."

"Liberty, you're panicking."

"No, you don't know her! You only know the lies she told you. She's an excellent liar too. She has to be to live the life I require her to live."

"I know Deborah more than you think I do. I may have not known your true relationship with her but I got to know the sweet, charming, loving woman she has grown up to become. I know deep in my heart she'd want you to find rest."

"Yes. Yes she would."

"Go to bed."

"Ok, sorry for the intrusion," he whispered.

"Don't be. It only shows me how much you care for her."

"I care a lot."

"I can tell."

"Do you believe I am a horrible man for making her my wife?"

"May I be honest with you?"

"Yes, please." Liberty nodded.

"When you called yesterday and told me who you were to Deborah I was shocked. I know who your father is. He was my husband's commanding officer in the Civil War. Jesse told me your father is a strict Catholic man."

"He is."

"I thought he would raise his son to be the same. When you told me you had married Deborah five years ago, had three children with her, she miscarried three times since, and she was pregnant again, I did not approve. Victoria is a year younger than Deborah. I have another daughter who is fourteen and my youngest daughter is thirteen. If there was ever a man who sought to take any of my girls as his wife I can assure you Jesse would kill that man before he ever had a chance to lay hands upon her."

Liberty gulped. "Do you believe your husband thinks the same of me?"

"He was quite angry on the train ride up here. Usually I don't take him with me whenever I'm treating someone for an infection or disease. He never came with me when I treated his brother's family for the influenza. Jesse has a delicate immune system. He becomes ill quickly. But he insisted on the journey to help his brother remedy the situation. I asked him instead of killing you that he would persuade you to divorce her."

"I don't believe in divorce."

"I wouldn't ask that from you anymore. Liberty, I know you love Deborah. It's very evident she loves you as well. You're the first person she cries out for. No woman would do that if she didn't love the man. Love aside you can't deny the truth. Deborah was just a baby when you married her. You should have known better than to take her to your bed."

Liberty turned his gaze to his wife. "I never meant to fall in love with her. It just happened." He turned back to Betsy. "I'm not the soldier my father is but I am a good man."

"You don't have to convince me of that."

"But I do your husband."

"You let me worry about Jesse Garrett. Get some rest, Liberty."

"Yes, ma'am."

"Goodnight."

"Goodnight, Aunt Betsy."

He turned back to the door, opened it, and entered his bedroom. Liberty walked to his bed and sat on the edge. He pulled off his black, machine-made, leather shoes, and stared at the round mirror across from him. He was a mess. His short, black hair was uncombed, bags threatened to form under his eyes, and his body ached all over. He heard the sound of children laughing outside his bedroom window. Liberty rose, walked to the left, and peered out of the six-foot-tall window. He watched his three-year-old identical twin daughters chase their four-year-old brother through the garden. Liberty sighed. They were so young. He wondered just how much they understood their mother was dying. He leaned his arm on the windowpane, thinking about Deborah's children. Unlike her pregnancy with the twins, when Deborah was pregnant with their son they had followed the strict Victorian guidelines. Deborah had been secluded from society during her entire pregnancy. Victorian society had never allowed a woman to be seen large with child. He could have waited until three months before his son's birth to seclude her but he wasn't ready to present Deborah to his social circle. There were strict guidelines Deborah had to adhere to if she was to be his wife. Deborah had come from poverty. She didn't know the codes of conduct expected from a woman of the upper classes. He and his parents had spent the time educating her. Deborah had been a quick student. Three months after his son's birth Liberty introduced his wife and infant son to society. Everyone believed Deborah came from an upper-class family in England and he had married her in London. It would have been easier to falsify documents for that than to say she came from the upper-class circles of the East Coast. Too many upper-class families knew each other no matter what state they lived in.

He had told everyone that he and Deborah had quickly conceived. She had wanted to deliver the child in England then they came to the United States. Deborah had even been able to pull off an English accent. His brilliant Deborah had fooled everyone for years.

Liberty's smile fell as he caught a glimpse of Tabitha on the bench. Tabitha stared into the bushes while the nanny chased her younger siblings. Tears streamed down her cheeks. His mother knelt before his eight-year-old daughter, took her hands, and spoke to her. Liberty wondered what she was telling her. For the first four years of their lives the only mother they knew was the nanny, aided by his mother. After he married Deborah, she had tried to become their mother but the twins hated her. It had taken the twins three years to accept Deborah and their siblings into their lives. The last two years had been full of bliss between mother and stepdaughters. He knew his daughters understood how ill Deborah was. He could see it on their faces. Tabitha raised her head in his direction. His mother followed Tabitha's gaze to the window. Liberty stared at his daughter's face. He had never noticed how much she looked like her mother at that age. His heart broke. He reminded himself Nellie didn't have to die. If he hadn't been with her she would still be alive. But then he wouldn't have Deborah or any of his children. He sighed and lowered the dark burgundy curtains and walked away from the window.

Liberty sat on the edge of the bed. His eye caught something silver on the nightstand. Liberty peered at the object. He picked up Deborah's silver hair comb with pearl inlays. Tears formed in his eyes as he examined the piece she had left behind. It was his fault entirely that she was dying. Deborah had miscarried three times in the past two years. What made him think this child would be any different? If she had struggled before then why did the death of his child shock him? He couldn't endure watching Deborah lose her life to the fever if it came to that. He fell to his knees and sobbed. Liberty grabbed the back of his head, rocked, and sobbed even harder. Why! Why was this happening to her? What kind of monster was he?

Someone knocked loudly on his bedroom door. Liberty lifted his head towards it.

"Father," a young girl's voice came from the behind the door.

"I said no visitors, Zipporah. Turn the calling card over and hand it back to whoever desires your mother's or my appearance."

"It's not a visitor, father. Grandfather Watkins and Uncle Jesse want to speak to you."

Liberty wiped away his tears and rose from the floor. He gathered himself then went to the hallway door. Liberty opened the door. His brunette, blue-eyed, nine-year-old daughter stood in front of a grey-haired gentleman who was missing a right leg. An older man dressed in a military uniform stood beside the other man. Liberty swallowed hard at the sight of his daughter. Identical to Tabitha, it didn't seem fair he should see the youthful image of his dead wife, let alone in duplicate. He stared at Zipporah with sorrow. The laughter of her mother at their age filled his ears.

"Father?" Zipporah asked.

"Nellie?" Liberty replied to her.

"I'm not Nellie. That was my mother," she whined.

"What?" Liberty asked, shaking his head.

"You called me Nellie."

Liberty smiled with a slight huff. "Zipporah, I know the difference between you and your mother."

"But you called me Nellie. Father, are you ill too?"

Liberty swallowed hard at his daughter's question. Was he ill? Ever since he found Deborah this morning all he could think about was her and their dead child. Now he was haunted with the memoires of his dead wife. He couldn't breathe without thinking about her. What was it with Nellie? It had been nine years since she had died. Why was he still grieving over her when his current wife was about to join her? He exchanged glances with his father then knelt before Zipporah. A tear fell down her cheeks as she looked into her father's eyes. He tenderly wiped the tears away. "I am not ill."

"But you called me by mother's name. You said when you married Deborah we weren't ever to speak her name to you again. Mother needed to rest in peace and you needed to start a new life with our new mother."

"That's true. I meant those words."

"You said her name. You never say her name."

86

Liberty placed his hands around her arms. "I hurt a lot right now. Deborah is very ill and I haven't had enough time to grieve the loss of the baby."

"Victoria said mother is dying. Is that true?" Liberty placed his hand on the side of her face. He stroked along her cheekbone with a slight nod. "How long does she have?"

"I don't know. Your Aunt Betsy and I are doing everything we can to save your mother from the fever. The best thing you can do right now is to pray. Pray with all your heart that God doesn't call your mother to heaven."

"Tabitha and I can pray for her."

"That would be appreciated."

"We can pray for you too."

"Oh?"

"To heal your broken heart, father."

Liberty leaned close to his daughter and kissed her on the forehead. "You are as sweet as your mother ever was. I love you," he whispered.

"I love you too, father."

Liberty released his grip and rose over her. He reached into his pocket, pulled out a few coins, and then placed them in her hand. "Stay here."

"Yes, sir."

Liberty walked to the other side of his bedroom to his desk. He pulled out pen and paper from the right-hand drawer then wrote a note. Liberty lowered the pen. He folded the note in three and walked back to the door. "Give this note to your nanny. It has instructions in it for her to take you to the Catholic Church then downtown to the candy store."

"Yes, sir. Thank you."

"You're welcome. Remember Zipporah, everyone gets a piece of candy. I gave you enough change for that. No more coming home with a bag of candy and finding half of them have been eaten on the way home. You understand me, young lady?"

"Yes, sir."

"Good.

Liberty watched his daughter walk down the hall then descend the twenty-foot staircase until she disappeared. He lifted his eyes to his father. The tall, grey-haired general looked sternly towards his son with a look of concern. "You look horrible, Liberty. Where are your shoes?" the general asked.

"By my bed. I was about to go to sleep. I do not feel well."

"You don't feel well, or do you regret marrying my niece?" Jesse asked.

Liberty turned his head sharply in his direction. "Sir," he reacted harshly.

"You just called your daughter by the name of your dead wife. Why would the memory of your dead wife be on your mind when your current wife is dying?"

"I am greatly offended by that question."

"Why would you be offended? It is merely an observation. By your reaction I have to question whether or not my niece is just some young girl to warm your bed."

"Sir, you think I'm a child molester! Do you know whom you are talking too?" he yelled, stepping in front of Jesse. Liberty's face turned red with anger. How dare this man accuse him of molesting the woman he loved!

"I know the man you present yourself to be in public but I want to know who the real Liberty Watkins is. Who's the man behind the robe?"

Liberty grabbed Jesse by the vest and pulled him forward. One-legged or not, this man was getting on his last nerve. He snarled in the older man's face, "You have no right to enter my house and accuse me of abusing your niece."

"I never said abuse. I said molested."

"That sir is a serious charge to place upon someone with as much power, finances, and resources as I have at my disposal. Are you certain you want to accuse me of molestation?"

"Liberty," his father said, separating the two men with his arms. He pushed his son against the hallway wall with a thump.

"Father?" Zipporah asked from downstairs. She stared up at the three men.

"Do what your father asked of you," General Watkins yelled over his shoulder.

"Yes, sir," she replied then disappeared towards the back of the house. General Watkins pressed his son against the wall with his forearm.

"Calm down," the general ordered.

"He called me a child molester and you want me to calm down!"

"Liberty, think this through. Deborah was thirteen when you made her your wife without consent or marriage. I can see where he might think you molested and raped her."

"Rape! It wasn't rape!"

"Perhaps we should have this discussion inside your room away from where small ears, servants, or your mother may hear."

"Agreed." Liberty snarled towards Jesse. General Watkins released his grip. Liberty stepped to the side and extended his arm towards his bedroom. Jesse hobbled on his crutches into the room behind the general. Liberty closed the bedroom door then walked to a table on the far side of the room. General Watkins exchanged glances with Jesse then turned back to Liberty. Liberty grabbed a bottle of whiskey and poured himself a drink with his back turned to them. "Mr. Garrett has concerns he wishes to discuss with you. I believe his concerns are justifiable," his father stated after closing the bedroom door.

"Concerns, father, or insults? The only reason I called him yesterday was for Deborah to speak to a woman. A woman she could trust. I figured whom better to trust than a female physician. There are not many female physicians in Ohio that are creditable."

"Judge Watkins, I did not come to your home to insult you," Jesse said.

"You could have fooled me, Mr. Garrett. You called me a child molester! If you are anything like your brother you have already judged me without cause."

"Liberty Watkins, that is enough from you," the general scolded his son. General Watkins turned to Jesse. "Please excuse his behavior. He is usually not this inhospitable. I quite assure you, I did not raise my son to have such ill manners."

Liberty drank a glass of whiskey then lowered the crystal to the table. He swallowed. "I love her," he said with his back turned.

"Which one?" Jesse asked.

"Both," Liberty said as he closed his eyes. His head pounded with each sound in the room. If only he could drown away his sorrows. He opened his eyes and poured three glasses of whiskey.

Jesse turned his gaze at the two large oval portraits of women over the fireplace. Deborah's light chestnut hair flowed gently around her face with tender curls. Ruffles of lace covered the scoop at the top of her blouse. She smiled an angelic smile while she held a bouquet of rich-colored flowers. Jesse looked at the woman on the right. The black-haired green-eyed woman stared back at him with a stern look on her face. Dressed in a chocolate-brown gown, her eyes demanded your attention. If one didn't know any better, the two women could be mother and daughter. "She was quite beautiful," Jesse said.

"Who?" Liberty asked.

"Your first wife."

Liberty dropped the whiskey bottle and stared into the mirror before him. An image of him and Nellie dancing at a ball filled the mirror. He could hear the sweet music. They spun around the floor with laughter. Nellie had been gorgeous that night. The way her dark purple dress had highlighted her raven-black hair, and her sparkling green eyes had twinkled under the candlelight. The image faded from the mirror. Liberty pivoted with a glass of whiskey in his hand. "Nellie."

Jesse asked, "Nellie?"

"Her name was Nellie Fitzpatrick," he replied as he walked to Jesse then handed him the glass. He turned to the portrait. "Her father owned the largest bank in Marion. We grew up together."

"What happened to her?"

"You don't have to answer that," the general protested.

Liberty turned to his father. "I'll answer him, father. It's time I speak about her. The twins have asked several times about their mother. One of these days, I will have to sit down and tell them about her. Nellie would have wanted that." He turned back to Jesse. "When Nellie turned sixteen, she was introduced to society at her debutante ball. I had attended all the balls that season. I hadn't been interested in any of the girls until Nellie's ball. The moment I first laid eyes on her I became smitten. I couldn't believe my eyes. Nellie and I had always been friends. I was an only child and she was the only daughter of six children. She loved to fish, swim, hunt, and play games. She was a boy's best friend. But that night she had transformed into the most beautiful princess you could ever lay your eyes upon." Liberty turned back to the table with a grin, grabbed two glasses of whiskey, then turned back to the men. He handed his father a glass.

"Did she notice you in the same manner?" Jesse asked.

"No. I had tried several times to catch her attentions but she was more interested in other men. I finally gave up and courted several young ladies. I never felt for them the way I felt for Nellie, though. In December of 1888, I decided once again to try to woo her. That night I completely filled Nellie's dance card with my name so no other man could dance with her."

"Was she upset?"

"No, she told me she had hoped I would dance with her. It had taken her five years to realize the only man she had feelings for was I. That night we danced every dance together. Nellie and I courted publically for a year then married. We were quite happy. There was tremendous pressure for us to have children right away. We tried for six years but Nellie never conceived until the night of our six-year wedding anniversary." Liberty grinned, "That night was magnificent. Nellie was, well, Mr. Garrett. Nellie was everything I dreamed of and more that night. We had always been happy together but that night we were…"

"Liberty," the general scolded. Liberty turned to his father. "Remember your manners. You should respect your dead wife and not speak of intimate matters you two shared."

"Yes, sir." Liberty turned to Jesse. "Forgive me. A few months later Nellie had the morning sickness. She continued with her societal functions until the morning sickness placed too much demand on her. It wasn't long after the morning sickness grew worse before she began to experience complications. Doctor Riley confined her to bed for the entire duration of her childbearing. We didn't want to be apart so I gave her my bed and slept on the couch you are sitting on. I spent many days by her side when I wasn't at work. She found comfort in my bedroom. We would talk, embrace, and share our hopes for the future. As the months passed Nellie had grown larger and everything seemed well. We were excited at the prospect of becoming parents. When the time drew close for her to deliver, she complained of pain in her lower stomach. My mother said it was probably early contractions. Later that day the pain grew more intense. My father sent for Doctor Riley. When the doctor arrived blood had already begun to trickle down my wife's legs. She was in agony. Doctor Riley said the twins were in distress then Nellie's water broke. He delivered Tabitha but when Zipporah was being delivered my wife began to lose her strength. My father sent for the priest. By the time Father McNally arrived, Nellie was struggling to push Zipporah out of her body. She pushed our daughter out then fell silent. Doctor Riley informed me Nellie had suffered from a hemorrhage caused by the placental abruption. She had lost too much blood and would die. He couldn't save her life if he had tried. Father McNally performed the last rights on my wife. Nellie breathed her last as Zipporah took her first breath."

"I am sorry for your loss."

"Thank you."

"I lost my mother in childbirth."

"And your father?"

"Six months prior to her death he was on top of our roof fixing a hole when he suffered from a heart attack. He fell to his death. My mother depended on my older brothers after that to care for her, my siblings, and me. I never saw her cry but I heard her sobs late at night. When she gave birth to our sister, she hemorrhaged. My mother died just as your wife died, one life given and another one taken at the same time. My eldest brother, Lucas, had just turned twenty. My four older sisters were married with families of their own. The trustees of their township wanted to take all the children ages seventeen years or younger and make them indentured servants to families who would provide for them. But Lucas wouldn't have it. He vowed he would provide for all his siblings if they wouldn't split his family apart. My other older brother, Carlisle, was old enough to work. So Lucas and he worked while I, Oren, and Moses went to school with our sisters. We four boys raised our newborn sister and young siblings as our own with help from our older sisters. I was only ten when my mother died. I mourned for her as any child would when a parent dies. As a boy, I didn't understand the love a man has for his woman but when I met Betsy that all changed. I have been married only once in my life. Betsy has given me twelve beautiful children. Childbirth is painful and dangerous to any woman no matter what class they come from. I cannot imagine what my life would be like without my wife. How did you grieve the loss of your first wife, or have you?"

General Watkins looked to Liberty. Liberty turned, walked toward the back of the room, picked up his whiskey, and sat down in a green-padded velvet armchair next to the fireplace. General Watkins answered Jesse's question, "My son grieved tremendously. He refused to acknowledge his daughters. He grew angry, bitter, and cold-hearted. I never saw my son shed a tear. I feared I had lost Liberty to his mind. I could do nothing to console him and I had my own obligations in Washington to fulfill."

"What did you do?" Jesse asked.

"I decided to move my family to Washington, D.C, hoping the change would do Liberty well. I ordered the nanny to stay behind with Zipporah and Tabitha. When Liberty was well enough to be a father I would allow him to return to Marion. A few weeks after we arrived, Liberty emotionally broke down and sobbed in my arms. Afterwards, he admitted his feelings to me. A few days later I was able to secure him a position as a prosecuting attorney in Washington, D.C. For two years he served as prosecuting attorney. His reputation grew fast. Powerful men in politics began to take notice of him. At the same time, my good friend Theodore Roosevelt asked me to join him in the 1st U.S. Volunteer Calvary Regiment. I agreed."

Liberty concluded, "My father said my mother and I could stay in Washington while he served as a rough rider with Teddy Roosevelt, but I refused his offer."

"Why would you do that? You had a promising career in Washington," Jesse asked.

"My daughters needed their father. My mother and I returned to Marion. I took a position as Assistant District Attorney for Marion County, Ohio and became the father my toddler daughters needed. Every day I would walk with them in the park, attend social engagements with them, and take them to church functions. I adore my daughters. I can see little pieces of Nellie in their personalities and appearance. I was happy being a single father until the day I saw Deborah."

Jesse swirled the golden brown liquid in the glass then asked, "Did you know how young Deborah was six years ago?"

"Yes, sir. Deborah was twelve and I was thirty-two. She was a mere child, but there was something about her that attracted me to her."

"That attraction was unnatural," Jesse growled with a swig of his glass.

"I tried to dismiss it. There wasn't a day or night I didn't think about her."

"How did you meet my brother's family?"

"When Mr. Henry Garrett married the widow Portia Bradley, he did so with the Marion County Justice of the Peace. Deborah, Elsa, and their sisters stood by her side while Nathan, his brothers and parents stood by him. I served as a court witness. When I heard the last name Garrett I was intrigued. I had heard my father speak of the infamous five Garrett brothers who served together and were inseparable. It was rare to hear of any family staying together and supporting the same side. I spoke to Mr. Oren Garrett about it. He said he was indeed one of the brothers. I informed him of whom my father was. Once I did so he no longer spoke to me and he told his family to stay well away from me. I never understood why he reacted the way he did."

"He's upset at your father."

General Watkins shifted on the couch and looked at Jesse. "Why is he upset with me?" the general asked.

"He blames you for all the suffering we endured."

"The loss of your leg?" Liberty asked with a shift of his eyes towards Jesse missing right leg.

Jesse stared down at his stumped limb then raised his eyes to Liberty. "That and more. "

"I don't mean to be rude, Mr. Garrett, but how did you lose your leg."

"Liberty," the general scolded.

Jesse raised his hand, "No, no, sir. It's quite alright. I'll answer your son's question." Jesse lowered his hand and turned his attention to Liberty. "Your father had ordered my brothers and me to eliminate the bridge at Strawberry Plains in Tennessee. Oren and Moses had begun to set the dynamite while Carlisle, Lucas, and I guarded them with other men. The rebels came out of nowhere. A skirmish began that turned into a battle. I was separated from my brothers. Then I saw the four rebels overtake Carlisle. I ran to aide him but one of the rebels shot my knee and shin. They captured my brother then disappeared. Lucas and your father took off after them while Oren tended to me. I lay on the battlefield for an hour until the medics arrived."

"An hour is a long time to wait."

"He was fortunate it was only an hour," his father added. "Earlier in the war it was common to wait longer than an hour to receive medical care. I lost more men on the battlefield from shock and blood loss than in the camp from disease."

"So you followed after the rebels and left a wounded soldier behind?" Liberty questioned his father.

"He wasn't the only wounded soldier that day, just one of five."

"You left him to die, father."

"No, he didn't. Quite the opposite," Jesse replied.

Liberty shook his head. "I don't understand."

"The rebels had taken my brother. Your father couldn't attend his wounded men and give chase. He sent Moses to the camp for the doctor then led the rescue team. He did what any commander should have done. But Oren never understood that and I doubt he does today. That battle turned Oren into a man I hardly recognize."

"Was he shot?"

"No, his mind was wounded. After I was shot, Oren cradled me until Moses and the doctor came. I don't remember much except for the pain. What little I know comes from Moses. When the doctor arrived at the battlefield, the doctor assessed all the wounded. He decided I was the most severe. They laid me on the ground, gave me ether, and I lost consciousness. Oren and Moses held me down as the doctor took my leg. Moses said Oren screamed the entire time. When I awoke I was in our tent back at our camp in Knoxville, Tennessee, without my right leg and knee."

Liberty's father continued, "When I arrived to Knoxville, Lucas asked if he could inform his brothers we couldn't locate Carlisle. I agreed. I gave Lucas, Jesse, Oren, and Moses time to themselves."

"You allowed Lucas to be alone with his brothers because you understood they were closely bonded?" Liberty asked.

"Yes, and I knew they wouldn't trust anyone to solve their problems unless they carried the last name of Garrett. When they had enlisted, the boys had told the army they wouldn't serve unless they were all in the same unit with Lucas and shared the same tent. I thought it would be best for the eldest brother to confront the clan with the truth."

"But Oren didn't understand that either," Jesse interjected. The men turned to Jesse. Jesse continued, "I don't remember much about when Lucas arrived. When I awoke, Oren sent for the doctor. The doctor checked my bandage, gave me a morphine pill, then left. I wanted to hear what happened to Carlisle but Lucas had insisted I take the morphine pill. We argued. Oren yelled at me, 'Just take the God damn pill, Jesse!' That was the first time I ever heard him swear. And you have to realize, I am only a year older than Oren."

"So you two were close?"

"Not as close as he was to Moses, but yes. Lucas was ten years older than I. Carlisle eight. I idolized my older brothers whereas Oren and Moses saw Lucas more like a father. After Oren yelled, Lucas insisted I take the morphine for Oren's sake. I withdrew my argument and obeyed. It sedated me. I have no recollection of what happened in the tent after that. When I awoke I was in a hospital transport to West Virginia. That was the last time I ever saw Lucas."

The general stated, "In December of 1864, Lucas was killed at the Battle of Saltville. Oren did not take his death well."

"Did you know?" Liberty asked Jesse.

"At that time, no. During the war it was hard to pass information along to family members. In December of 1864 I was lying in the hospital recovering from my amputation. It had been four months since my amputation had occurred. I was struggling. Betsy's father was my physician. I never knew Doctor Summerland was Betsy's father until years later when I met her. In the spring of 1865 I was transferred to Camp Dennison where I was placed in the recovery unit that Margaret worked in."

"You knew Oren's wife?"

"Oh, she wasn't his wife then. During the war she was a nurse at the unit for amputees. By the time I reached Ohio I was struggling mentally and physically. Without my brothers around, I had become an angry man. I refused treatment and was screaming for Carlisle. I blamed myself for his capture. Margaret was the only nurse that could calm me down. The doctors increased my morphine dosage, gave me a wooden leg, taught me how to use it, and then sent word to my sisters I could be released. My twin sister and her husband came for me. I stayed with them while I recuperated. A few months after that we received word from Margaret, Carlisle had been traded in a prisoner exchange from Andersonville Prison. I went to Camp Dennison with my twin sister, Hannah, and her husband, Elijah, to retrieve him. We were appalled at the condition the rebels had left him in. Carlisle was blind, malnourished, and had several broken bones. The deplorable state he was in broke me mentally. I couldn't be strong for him and my family knew it. I sobbed so hard I fell to the floor. Hannah took Carlisle and me home and cared for us. Three months later, Oren and Moses returned home with news of Lucas' death. He had been buried in Tennessee. Oren, Moses, Carlisle, and I tried to regain our lives the way they were before the war but it was impossible. We all had the night terrors. Oren was screaming from the dismemberment of my leg. Moses was screaming about Lucas' death. I was screaming about my guilt of losing Carlisle. Carlisle was screaming of his capture and his imprisonment at Andersonville. There wasn't a night one or more of us didn't wake from our sleep in sheer terror. Hannah tried to care for us but couldn't endure it. We have always felt each other's pains and emotions. She even felt the pain of my amputation. I had severe stomachaches when she gave birth to her children during my tour of duty in the war. Our sisters understood her torment. They took turns caring for my brothers and me when she was unable to do so. Even when we were awake, we couldn't be the men our sisters needed us to be."

"Why not?"

"Carlisle suffered mentally with an inability to concentrate, mood swings, failing memory, sense of helplessness, nervousness, irritability, intense fear, paranoia, aggression, frustration, and anxiety. Physically he suffered from hypertension, headaches, sleeplessness, and coronary heart disease. I tried to help my sisters but my mind had worked against me. I had phantom pains. The morphine helped with the pain and sedated me. I became dependent on it. When the morphine began to leave my body I became restless, irritable, suffered from diarrhea, and was drenched in sweat. I craved the morphine. Oren and Moses had taken the responsibility of helping to provide for our family. They worked odd jobs around Vernon Township, Ohio while Elijah tended to the farm. It was good for my brothers to be away from the house for a while. Everything went well until the winter of 1867."

"What happened?"

"That winter was cold. Oren awoke one morning with tremendous pain in his knees. He had tried to ignore the pain and rise from his bed. When he did, he fell. His knees were useless. One of our sisters heard his cries. When they came to his room, he was in the fetal position crying from the pain. She sent off the younger sisters for the doctor. After the doctor examined him, he found Oren suffered from arthritis in his knees. He told Oren he couldn't work anymore and to apply for his pension. Oren didn't want to bother Hannah and her husband with another bed-bound brother so he and Moses moved into our parents' cabin with our youngest sisters. The youngest one stayed with Oren until he married Margaret. We were never apart even though we lived in separate houses. Every Sunday the entire family would attend church in Mount Sinai Methodist Church where Elijah preached. Afterwards we would all eat together at one of our homes. I am one of sixteen children."

"Sixteen children!"

"My mother gave birth to four sets of twins. My sister and I are one of those sets. Multiple births are common for our family. As I was saying, we spent most of the Sundays together. Oren once said at one of those dinners, the worst mistake we ever made was enlisting into the Union army. Oren believes all our trouble started under General Watkins' command."

"My father didn't take your leg, kill your brother, or maim

your other brother."

"No, but Oren doesn't understand that. He believes to be an effective leader you have to be a strong man who looks after the welfare of all his men. With each tragic event that transpired in our family, it seemed to him your father meant us more harm than good."

"But according to your story my father did everything possible to give your family aide and respect."

"Liberty, the leader of our family was killed. Carlisle had disappeared and I was lying wounded in a hospital. Every man who ever meant something to Oren had disappeared out of his life by the time the war ended. Then when he came home he was faced with the reality that he and Moses had to be the strong ones. They were the youngest sons. I was addicted to morphine and Carlisle was useless. Surely you can understand why Oren is bitter."

"If your family is as close-knit as you claim then why did Oren leave his family, settle in Marion County, and tell his children never to contact his side of the family?"

"That is another story."

"I have time," Liberty said then sipped his whiskey.

"I would rather speak of how you came to be with my niece."

Liberty sighed as he lowered of his glass. "Of course you would," he muttered.

"Liberty," General Watkins scolded. Father and son exchanged glances. "You will show Mr. Garrett respect. He is a guest in this house."

"Yes, sir." Liberty turned back to Jesse. "The more I saw Deborah in town the more I wanted to get to know her."

"She was a child," Jesse yelled as he slammed the glass on the end table.

"Yes, sir. I understand why you and your brother would be upset with me. The harder I tried to ignore my feelings the more intense I found them to be. I began to take notice when Mr. Garrett would come to town for supplies, when the children were at Linn School, and when they attended church."

"You stalked them?"

"No, sir, I had no intention of harming anyone. I needed to see Deborah and hear her voice. Deborah and I had spoken several times when she was in town. I could tell she liked the attentions I gave her. I found myself buying her little presents. We would meet in secret and no one learned of our relationship."

Jesse groaned, "If I had been in my brother's life I would have made certain you never came close to her. You were a grown man with children of your own preying on a child. My brother isn't an ignorant man. I cannot believe he would not have noticed your attractions to his little girl. How did she come to be your wife without his consent?"

Liberty answered, "The following fall I waited close to the general store to give Deborah a present for her thirteenth birthday. I waited all day. The Garrett's never came into town. I thought perhaps they were delayed. I knew they would need winter supplies so every morning for two weeks I waited. Still, no one came into town for church or supplies. I concluded something had to be wrong so I went to their farm. Deborah answered the door. I'll never forget the look on her face. She was white as snow, weak with fever, and couldn't speak without coughing. She had begun to fall. I rushed into the house and caught her. When I sat her on the couch she told me her parents and siblings had all fallen ill with influenza. They couldn't afford a doctor. They had nothing to barter with. I asked to speak to her father. She took me to his bedside and I offered to pay for medical supplies, food, and a doctor for his entire family. He refused me."

"Oren probably didn't trust you. He won't accept help from strangers, especially ones that stalk his children. What did you do after that?"

"I left. When I came home I locked myself away in my room and grieved. I had to accept the inevitable fact Deborah would die. A few days later Elsa came to our home with Deborah in the back of the wagon. My father had just arrived from Washington D.C. that morning. He helped me carry Deborah into the house then Elsa disappeared."

"Why would Elsa bring her sister to you?"

"Elsa knew Deborah and I had feelings for each other. She never agreed with her father's decision to turn my offer away. I offered for her to stay but Elsa wouldn't have it. She said 'Deborah had given her entire life for the betterment of her family. It was

time Deborah had something she had wanted.' I never understood
what she meant by that until now. My wife has never been a child,
Mr. Garrett. Her parents depended a lot on her. She made sacrifices
so her siblings would not go without. When Deborah came to me
she was close to death. I think in a way, Elsa wanted Deborah to
die in my arms because I was the only person Deborah trusted
more than her." Liberty stared into his whiskey. "Two weeks later
Deborah fully recuperated. I spent much of the time from when she
was ill to then pacing the floor."

General Watkins continued, "My son told me of his feelings
for your niece. I urged him to stay away from her. He was running
for Marion County Family Court Judge on the platform to end
underage marriage. If he acted upon his desires he was no better
than a child molester. Unfortunately my son didn't heed my
warning. A few days later, while I was in the parlor with his
mother the maid ran into the room frantic. She told me she could
hear noises coming from Deborah's bedroom that were not natural
for a girl to make. Liberty had disappeared. I had immediately run
to Deborah's room. I found the doors locked, the sound of the bed
shaking, and inappropriate noises. I busted into the room. I found
Liberty on top of Deborah just as he released his seed inside her."

"You raped her," Jesse accused.

"No, sir," Liberty rebuked.

"Then how do you explain yourself?" Jesse asked.

"Deborah and I shared the same feelings for each other. The
day before she had risen from her bed and knocked on my
bedroom door. I allowed her entrance into my bedroom. She had
thanked me for the hospitality then we spoke much of that
morning. We kissed. One thing had lead to another. I found myself
on top of her with my coat, tie, shoes, and vest on the floor. She
had her hand on the lip of my pants. I told her we couldn't go any
farther. I wouldn't take her innocence from her, but Deborah said
we should act upon our desires."

"She was thirteen! The female persuasion acts upon emotions
not logical thought. That's why they depend upon a man to direct
them."

"How can you support that claim when your wife is a doctor?
Surely a man with those beliefs wouldn't allow his wife or

daughters to pursue a man's occupation."

"Betsy is a different matter. What you did with Deborah is what we should be discussing. Deborah was a girl. If she had suggested acting on her feelings then you should have said no. That is what any good Christian man should have done. She was not your responsibility. Deborah belonged to Oren and you should have honored my brother's position as head of her household."

"For all I knew he was dead."

"Doesn't matter, Liberty. You should have returned her to her father's household; instead you made her your wife under God without consent. You stole her from Oren."

"That wasn't my intent. Deborah's words made sense to me."

"What words?"

"She claimed her father would never approve of a marriage between us."

"I would have never, either. You are twenty years older than her!"

"It had nothing to do with age. She claimed Mr. Garrett doesn't approve of our union because of my last name."

"That is understandable coming from my brother."

"But that's prejudice. I'm not my father. Deborah had pleaded her cause to me. She said if she carried my child her father would have to approve of the marriage to save her honor. It made perfect sense. I granted her request. We bonded on the same bed that Nellie lost her life upon."

Jesse looked to Liberty's bed. "This bed?"

"Yes, sir. We became husband and wife, talked for a bit under the blankets, and then I got dressed, went down for lunch, and went to work. We bonded again after supper and that night after everyone went to bed. We couldn't keep our hands off one another. It felt natural. The following morning, we rose early and bonded again. I told her to rest in her room then went to breakfast. I took my daughters for a walk in the garden then ate lunch with my family. After lunch I went to her room and bonded. That's when my father found us. What we did, we both wanted."

"She was a child making an adult decision."

"Deborah has never been a child. By your own admission, her father is consumed with bitterness and hatred towards my father.

That kind of bitterness leads a man to illogical conclusions based on emotions and not facts!" He continued to yell as he rose from the chair. "Do I admit I made an underage woman my wife without consent of her father? Yes. I am guilty! Am I a danger to society! No, on the contrary, I am a progressive judge who betters society by the decisions I make in the courts!" He walked towards Jesse and glared down at the older man's face. "I will have you know, Mr. Garrett, Deborah is the best thing that has happened to my life. She's a sweet, charming woman whose behavior and intellect is well beyond her years. She loves me for who I am and not for my money, my power, or my last name. Don't sit there and tell me I'm not good enough for her. If anyone tries to hurt her or take her away from her home I will come after him or her. I know what we did and I know the repercussions of that act. I know very well that she's lying on her deathbed because of me! She's my wife! My responsibility! No one else's! I don't care what you, your brothers, or anyone else has to say about that!" Liberty sighed with a face of anger. He grunted, turned, and then walked towards his bed. The older men stared at him with shock. Liberty peered out the window beside his bed. He watched Deborah's children swing on the wooden tree swings he had built for them.

"Please accept my son's apology. He has had a rough couple of days," the general said.

"No apology necessary. Please accept mine. The truth has become clearer to me in our discussions. I knew Deborah loved Liberty but I wasn't certain if your son loved her," Jesse said.

"And now?"

"He loves her. That is obvious."

"Wonderful, can you make that obvious to her father without the argument?" Liberty scoffed.

"Liberty, you are in a foul mood today. Rid yourself of that attitude," the general ordered.

"Father, I have the worst headache you can imagine possible. Doctor Garrett ordered me to bed," Liberty said as he leaned on the window casing.

"You must obey the doctor. Go to bed."

"I wish that I may. I could sleep for days but if Deborah turns for the worst I want to be there. I don't know what to do."

"My wife will come for you," Jesse offered.

"Liberty, get the rest your body requires. You are of no use to anyone without sleep," General Watkins suggested.

"Rest is easier said than done, father. If Deborah doesn't die she won't be happy with the decision I had to make."

"That being?"

"I just granted Doctor Garrett permission to ensure Deborah never has children again. I didn't want to do it, father, but Doctor Garrett said it could save her life. You taught me it was against God to practice birth control, but isn't that what I just did? If Deborah survives this then I have doomed us to go against God's will!"

"Liberty, I'm certain my wife would not have offered that solution to you unless there was no other choice," Jesse declared.

Liberty wiped his hands down his face. "Go to bed, son. I'll call a priest to the house to pray over these matters," General Watkins said.

"Yes, sir," Liberty answered. He finished his drink, laid the empty glass on top of his dresser, sat on the edge of his bed, and then rubbed his hands up and down his face with a long yawn. Liberty closed his eyes. His aching body felt numb against the firm mattress. He moaned, pulled his feet up, rolled on his right side, and then fell into a deep sleep.

Warm sunlight filled the rolling countryside the little one-room schoolhouse sat upon. Children ran around, laughing and playing. Somewhere down the Columbus, Delaware, and Marion (CD&M) railroad line that passed the back of the schoolhouse, a train blew its horn. The younger children gawked at the large train coming down the track. Mrs. Webster quickly guided them away as the passenger train from Bucyrus rolled past the schoolhouse towards the depot in Marion. Elsa ignored all the commotion. She walked to her familiar spot along the right side of the wall of the red brick schoolhouse, sat on the ground, and peered out at the group of girls in the yard eating their lunch together. Cora laughed with her friends. It didn't take a fool to know whom they were cackling about. Elsa hadn't been well liked since the first day she and Nathan arrived at Linn School last year.

Although her family had lived in the same county as the school, Elsa had never attended a public school before. Before the influenza hit, Margaret had homeschooled all ten of her children. Her ma had been an excellent teacher. While Elsa excelled academically, she had a harder time finding friends than Nathan ever did. Only a few months older than Sam, Sam's friends had been quick to accept Nathan into their lot. Elsa envied her brother. The only girls Elsa's age were Cora and Rebekah. Those two girls had made it their sole duty to ensure no girl ever made friends with Elsa, and it had worked too. She dreaded the day Nathan graduated from school this year. Without him, there wouldn't be anyone to eat lunch with, do homework with, or talk to. What she wouldn't give for this to be her last year too. If all went well with her plans to marry Franklin then this would be her last year. Married girls don't go to school. Life would be perfect. She'd have the man of her dreams, a home of her own, and a business that would bring more money than her pa made now. Middle class. The sound of it both excited and frightened her. All her life she had been poor. It would be hard to adjust to Franklin's standards of living but if Deborah could adjust to upper class from poverty she could adjust to middle class.

Elsa laid her metal lunch bucket to her right, pulled out the plain calling card from her coat pocket, and stared at it. She had never had calling cards before. There was no need. Impoverished families couldn't afford the cards let alone follow the rigorous societal customs of the middle and upper classes. At first Deborah had allowed for her to visit without using calling cards but Elsa had always had to enter through the servant's entrance at the back of the house like a common servant. That hadn't bothered Elsa. She could understand why Liberty had insisted her visits not be made known to the public. Every time someone called upon him or Deborah their calling card would be placed on display in the hallway so everyone knew with whom they were associated. Deborah could never be known to associate with her family or everyone would know the truth about who she really was. In the close knit upper class society that knowledge could destroy everything Liberty and Deborah enjoyed in life.

A month ago, Deborah had given Elsa a stack of calling cards. Elsa was confused and had tried to give them back to Deborah saying she was fine using the servant's entrance to the mansion. Yet Deborah had insisted. She explained that after Elsa had told her she had overheard Franklin ask their father permission to marry her, she knew Elsa's life would change drastically. Middle and upper classes both used calling cards and it would be expected of Elsa to do so as well. Franklin could never teach her about calling card etiquette because he didn't understand social rules. Deborah had taught Elsa everything she knew about calling cards and the expectations that went with them.

Elsa traced her embossed cursive, handwritten name beneath Juliette's name, *Miss Elsa Beatrice Garrett.* Deborah had explained that an unmarried woman's name usually went beneath her mother's name, but she couldn't allow Elsa's name to be below their mother's name. Their mother was unknown to the upper and middle classes. Elsa needed a prominent middle-class woman to act as her guardian whenever they visited. Whose name would be better to use than Franklin's mother?

Every sound around Elsa disappeared as she focused on her name. What a life Deborah had! Travel, fashion, jewels, acquaintances with important people, and anything else her heart desired. Deborah had become a real life Cinderella! Life at home had always been hard for Deborah, Elsa, and their siblings. In a household of twelve, it had always been vital for everyone to help out with the chores. Although three years older than Elsa, most of the time Deborah had acted as if she was older than that. Always cheerful, she dutifully cared for all members of the family whenever their ma needed the extra help. There wasn't a day Deborah wasn't cleaning or caring for children. But she never complained until the day she fell in love with Liberty and their father told her not to pursue her heart. Deborah knew love. If anyone understood her predicament it would be Deborah. She couldn't wait to see her sister after school! The more she thought about her secret mission, the more slowly the morning passed her by. A horrible thought crossed Elsa's mind. What if her father ever learned she had asked Deborah for her help, let alone sought out Doctor Betsy Garrett's expertise? If she married Franklin, only to go back on her promise to stay clear of her father's family, would he disown her too?

"What you have there?" her eighteen-year-old brother, Nathan, asked sitting in front of her on the grass.

Elsa lifted her head at his question and quickly placed the calling card inside her coat pocket. "What?" she asked.

Nathan huffed with a smile. "If I didn't know better, I would think you didn't sleep enough last night. What were you doing at the Raymond house?"

"I slept enough."

"Then what are you planning?"

"Planning? What makes you think I'm planning anything?"

"Oh, because you were looking at something from your pocket," he teased, reaching for her pocket. Elsa pushed him back. "You're hiding something, Elsa. I can see it in your eyes."

"I wasn't hiding anything, just thinking," she sighed, and then turned back to the half-eaten lunch in her pail.

"How is Franklin?" Nathan asked, placing his hand on her left hand.

Elsa turned to her brother and changed the subject. "What did Ma pack for you?"

Nathan removed his hand, turned to his pail, and opened it. "Ham sandwich and an apple."

"I'll trade you."

Nathan looked up at her with curiosity. "Why?"

"You don't like ham and I love Ma's ham sandwiches."

"What did Mrs. Raymond give you?"

"Fried chicken, carrots, and cornbread."

Nathan and Elsa looked at each other for a brief moment then swapped lunch pails. Brother and sister ate in silence. Elsa periodically looked up at her brother. She knew Nathan meant well with his question about Franklin's wellbeing but she didn't want to go into detail with him. It wasn't as if they couldn't trust each other. Hadn't they overcome the hardships of their lives together? They had after all been through much together. Yet Nathan had always idolized their father. No matter how much she had wanted to trust him with all the details of her plans to save Franklin, she couldn't. She couldn't run the risk of Nathan running to their father.

"Aunt Elsa! Uncle Nathan!" Elsa and Nathan lifted their heads in unison to the sound of their seventeen-year-old step-nephew, Sam. They had rarely heard him call them uncle and aunt unless there was a family emergency. Nathan rose from the ground as Samuel ran around the corner of the schoolhouse. The tall teenager breathed heavily in front of Nathan.

"What's wrong?" Elsa asked.

"Uncle Oren's here," he gasped.

"What for?"

"He's checking you, me, and Nathan out of school. He told me he's going to drop me off at Doc's then when Doc goes to check on my pa he'll take me home."

"Why?" Nathan asked him.

"He wouldn't say much, just that you two need to hurry, grab your items, and we need to leave."

"Where are we going?" Elsa asked, gathering her belongings.

"He said a woman by the name of Deborah is dying and he

doesn't know when you will be back." Elsa froze in place. Had she heard Sam correctly? Deborah was dying? Deborah couldn't die. Without Deborah her plans to marry Franklin wouldn't come to fruition. Without Deborah, the woman she looked up to for sisterly advice and companionship would be no more. Without Deborah, every hope she held would wither away. Every important person in her life, with the exception of her parents, God had threatened their lives! Who would be next? She turned to Nathan with a stoic look on her face. Maybe God was waiting to inflect Nathan with something! Maybe God was going to kill Deborah, Nathan, Franklin, and Henry all at the same time! She couldn't take that! Why would God want to take away everyone who was in her support system? What had she done to curse her family?

"Elsa?" Nathan asked taking a step towards her.

Elsa stepped backwards, whispering through her tears, shaking her head, "This has happened before."

"What has?"

Elsa sniffed her nose. She wiped away her tears with her hands. She stared over Nathan's shoulder. The images of her deceased siblings playing in the yard came before her. Singing and laughing with the joy they shared before the influenza came to their farm. Deborah helping their mother hang the laundry, Elsa's younger sisters playing with her in the front yard, her brothers helping their pa mend the fence while some of the older ones fed the animals. All had been perfect. "Elsa," Nathan yelled, grabbing her by the arms. The image dissipated.

"What?" she asked, staring at her brother.

"You're not making sense."

"Deborah's dying. Franklin's ill with diabetes. He could die and Henry's dying from the tuberculosis. It's happening all over again, Nathan. Can't you see? God hates me. What did I do to deserve the deaths of our siblings and now this too?"

Nathan embraced his sister and pressed Elsa's head into his shoulder. He turned to Sam as she sobbed and instructed, "Gather our belongings and tell my pa we'll meet him join shortly."

"Will she be alright?" Sam asked.

Nathan nodded. "Go, please, leave us alone." Sam quietly packed Nathan and Elsa's lunches, picked up their pails, and disappeared around the corner. Nathan pulled Elsa away from him. "When were you going to tell me about Franklin's diabetes?"

Elsa lifted her eyes to his. She inhaled a deep breath, sniffed her nose, and replied, "Never."

"Elsa, diabetes is serious. I know pa wouldn't want you to become a widow at a young age only to turn into a spinster."

"That's exactly why I didn't tell you," she yelled, shoving him.

Nathan stumbled backwards, regained control of his footing, and then asked, "Has he asked you yet?"

"No."

"Does he plan to?"

"Of course he plans to! Why else would he ask Pa for my hand?"

"Don't yell at me, Elsa." Elsa took a deep breath, glared at Nathan, wiped her nose with her sleeve, and then began to walk away. It was futile to tell Nathan her true feelings. What she needed now was a female to confide in, not her nosey older brother snooping around her business.

"Elsa, wait," Nathan, said grabbing her by her right forearm. She spun around to face him. "Look, I overheard Cora talking to some of the girls before school this morning. I know about Franklin's seizure. How long do you think it would take for Pa to learn the truth? Cora made certain everyone around her heard about Franklin. How long do you think it will take until the entire county knows Franklin's not eligible for marriage? Rumors spread fast in Marion County."

"You can't tell Pa," Elsa yelled, jerking her arm away from him. He held a tighter grip on her forearm and pressed her towards him.

"I don't want to but if you marry him, Elsa, you're breaking the law."

"It's a stupid law!"

"It's a law to protect future generations from having children who are drunkards, idiots, or epileptics."

"He's neither!"

"Oh, come on, Elsa! I'm not the only one to notice Franklin's not exactly the most social guy there is. There's something off about him. You can do better."

Elsa clenched her teeth. She balled up her left fist, and slammed a left cross into his nose. Nathan fell to the ground. Thick blood poured down from his broken nose. He tapped the blood with his right hand, held it out, and stared up at her. "Fine. Two can play this game. I'm not supposed to hit a girl but you're not a girl. You're just my stubborn sister," he growled, leapt to his feet, and pushed her to the ground. Brother and sister wrestled each other on the ground. Their arms and legs embraced, they rolled back and forth tearing each other's clothes, insulting each other. Knees and elbows jabbed one another. Pain filled Elsa's body. Never before had she fought so hard for her love. The more Nathan insulted Franklin the more she wanted to rip him from limb to limb. If Nathan was going to be hardheaded about her relationship with Franklin then she was going to show him a thing or two. Nathan pulled her head back by her hair then hit her in the jaw with his fist. She kneed him in the crotch, shoved him on his back, raised her right fist, and then felt someone grab her arm. "Enough! Both of you," Oren yelled. Elsa tried to jerk her arm away from her father's grip but it was no use. The more she struggled the tighter he held her.

"Elsa, enough, you're a girl not a boy," her mother instructed from beside Mrs. Webster. Elsa lifted her head towards the women. The complete ensemble of students stood in a horseshoe formation around them behind her mother and teacher. The children stared back at her with the mixed emotions of shock and disgust. The boys were laughing, pointing at Nathan. She knew they were talking about him. Nathan had been beaten up by a girl, his younger sister no less. That was the worst thing any boy could hear. Her heart fell for Nathan. As self-righteous as he was he never deserved that kind of treatment from his peers. She looked over at the girls. Cora and her ten friends snickered, pointing to Elsa's torn dress and disheveled appearance. It was bad enough the girls made her feel unwelcome but to be ridiculed by them for her behavior was even worse. She had given then fuel to torment her even more. Cora grinned from ear to ear, leaned over to her classmates, and whispered something in their ears. Elsa released her fist. She wasn't going to satisfy Cora's hunger. Her father lowered his grip. She sobbed, rose from over her brother, and stumbled backwards. A surge of pain shot from her right shoulder throughout her body, almost taking her breath away. Every sound disappeared behind her as if they were far off in the distance. She took a step forward. Lightheaded and dizzy, her stomach turned. Her arm hung limp. She lifted her eyes at the sound of her name.

"Elsa! Stop screaming and let me have a look," her mother yelled.

Screaming? Was she screaming? Elsa closed her mouth. The overwhelming pain cascaded throughout her body. She gasped, pushed her mother aside, stumbled to her father's wagon, and began to climb into the back. Her body weak with pain, she tripped on the edge and fell onto the wagon bed. Elsa sobbed on her stomach. She clawed at the boards with her good hand and pulled herself forward, grunting from the pain. Exhausted, Elsa lowered her forehead to the wood, closing her eyes. Tears flowed down her eyes. Oh, what she wouldn't give for the pain to end.

Elsa felt the bed of the wagon move. Every jerk vibrated more pain into her body. "Ma," she cried as she rolled on her back.

Cora stomped her foot onto Elsa's dislocated shoulder, grinned, and said, "Not quite." Elsa screamed. She thrashed her legs.

"Get off, oh Cora, please get off!"

"Oh, does this hurt?" Cora asked, applying more pressure.

Elsa's screams lifted higher. "Stop," Elsa pleaded several times behind her tears. Cora grinned with delight at Elsa's suffering. Elsa knew Cora hated her but to torment her when she was in physical pain? "Cora, stop, please. Franklin wouldn't like this."

"Oh, yes, Franklin. He's too stupid to know the truth about you." Cora crouched over Elsa, releasing some of the pressure from her foot. She grabbed Elsa by the chin and snarled, "I know what kind of girl you truly are, Elsa. You don't love my brother. All you want is his money."

"That's not true. I love him."

"I doubt that. Listen to me and you listen well, you good-for-nothing piece of trash. I have plans for Franklin, plans that you aren't going to disrupt. I heard your pa say his daughter, Deborah, is dying. Now, I'm not a stupid girl, Elsa. If Deborah dies, she can't get word to her husband to help you, but if you're in the same house as they are you can!" She released her foot, grabbed Elsa by her blouse and pulled Elsa's torso closer to her. Elsa cringed as the nauseating pain continued to throb.

"Let me go, Cora."

Cora removed her grip. Elsa's torso dropped to the wagon bed with a thump. She gasped from the pain and sobbed. The bitter taste of vomit entered the back of her throat. She turned to the side and vomited, making certain some of the foul mixture landed on Cora's shoes.

"Why you little worthless filth," Cora growled, stomping her foot on Elsa's upper arm. Cora whispered in Elsa's ear, "You're like a snake in the garden, weaving in and out of my brother's life, threatening to devour all that I have planted. Well, Elsa, I can't have you ruining every seed that I've sown. Live in my garden and I'll chop your head off. Do we understand each other?" Cora threatened with a smile.

Elsa peered up into Cora's eyes. "Why are you doing this?"

"Doesn't matter why I'm doing this, what does matter is what you are going to do about it."

"What do you want?"

"Break my brother's heart. Tell him you don't love him anymore."

"No," she cried. Cora stomped on Elsa's shoulder. Elsa gasped. Cora was certifiably insane! "Remember that pain, Elsa. You either break up with my brother or next time I'll make certain you won't be around to ruin my plans."

"You're a monster," Elsa declared.

Cora chuckled, "No, Elsa, you are. It would be in your best interest to leave my family alone. Break my brother's heart or I'll break you. Have a nice trip," she said cheerfully, then dismounted from the back of the wagon and then walked back to the girls as if nothing had happened.

Elsa stared at the back of the wagon. Cora had always been cruel to her but this was farther than she thought Cora would ever go. What exactly did Cora mean when she said she had plans for Franklin? What little interaction she had seen between Franklin and Cora, Cora had always belittled her older brother. Whatever Cora had planned couldn't be good. Her mind stirred with the worst scenarios she could imagine. The more she thought, the more her heart beat with fear for her beloved. Determination stirred within her. She wasn't about to let Cora do anything to her Franklin! But what could she do? Elsa tried to raise her body. Lightheaded, her world spun around her. She gasped, lay back down, and closed her eyes. She had to get back to Franklin! She had to stay at school so Mrs. Raymond could pick her up. How was she ever going to convince her parents to leave her there if she couldn't move? But if she went with her parents, she could talk to Deborah about her situation. But wasn't Deborah dying? Ugh! The situation seemed hopeless.

"Elsa," her mother's voice beckoned from in front of her. Elsa opened her eyes. Margaret quickly crawled into the back of the wagon. Elsa cried in pain with every bounce. She closed her eyes, succumbing to the lightheadedness. "No, Elsa, sweetheart wake up," Margaret coaxed with a pat of her hand on Elsa's cheek. Elsa never moved. Margaret glanced upward. Oren stood talking to Nathan, Sam, and Mrs. Webster. "Oren," she yelled loudly, hoping her voice would carry over the noisy school children. Elsa moaned. Desperate, Margaret glanced down at her daughter. She could tell by Elsa's reaction on the playground she was fighting immense pain. But where? "Oren," Margaret yelled louder as she worked to remove Elsa's coat. "Oren, please, hurry," Margaret, muttered, pulling the coat down Elsa's right arm. Elsa whimpered and fidgeted her legs as the coat moved down her arm. Margaret stopped. Her eyes paused at the squared-off look of Elsa's right shoulder. "Dislocated. I should have suspected that by the limp in her arm and the pain," she whispered. She leaned over Elsa. "I have to take the coat off. It will hurt." Margaret peered up from the wagon. "Or...," she began to yell then paused as her husband ran towards the wagon.

"What's wrong?" he yelled.

"Her shoulder's dislocated and she's unconscious from the pain. I need Nathan and Sam to hold her down while you pop it back."

"Get back there and do what she says," he barked to Nathan

and Sam. The teenage boys jumped into the back and ran to Elsa's body. Oren crawled into the back of the wagon as Margaret directed Samuel and Nathan. He glared at Nathan, shook his head, and then knelt by his daughter's side.

"I didn't mean to hurt her, Pa," Nathan protested.

Oren glanced up at his wife. "What do I do?" he asked as Margaret stabilized Elsa's arm.

"Rotate the shoulder until you can feel it lock into its proper place." Margaret looked up at the boys. "Hold her down tight, boys. She will fight you."

Nathan and Samuel pressed all of their weight on Elsa. Oren looked at Margaret. "Ready?" he asked. Margaret nodded. Oren grabbed his daughter's shoulder and began to rotate it. Elsa opened her eyes, screamed, and tried to fidget. The more Sam and Nathan held her down the more she struggled. She turned her head towards her father. Why was he hurting her? She pleaded in agony for him to stop but he wouldn't listen. "Stay strong, Elsa," Oren guided. He rotated her shoulder. Elsa gasped as she felt the shoulder fall back into place. Relief filled her. Although it still hurt, it was more manageable now. "Elsa?" Oren asked his daughter.

Elsa sniffed her nose. She turned her head towards him. Weak from her ordeal, she just stared at her father. Margaret lifted the bottom of her dress, tore off a long piece from her petticoat, and then handed it to Oren. "We have to keep her shoulder immobilized or it will dislocate again. She's going to need a sling but for now use this," Margaret said, handing the cloth to Oren. Oren bent Elsa's arm and laid it over her chest as Nathan moved away from her. Elsa and Nathan stared at one another.

"I'm sorry," Nathan apologized.

Elsa nodded as she closed her eyes. "Margaret?" Oren asked, tying both ends.

Margaret checked Elsa's pulse on her neck. She lowered her ear over Elsa' nose. She rose and said, "She's alive, just exhausted. I'll stay in the back of the wagon and make certain she remains safe. When we drop off Sam with Doctor Riley, Elsa should go with him. She needs her rest."

8

April 28, 1904
Home of
Henry and Portia Garrett
Harpster,
Wyandot County, Ohio

Sunlight trickled through the slightly opened window of Elsa's second story bedroom. A gentle spring morning breeze lightly pushed through the white curtains. Elsa slowly opened her eyes. She moaned with disappointment. Why was she in her bed? Deborah was dying. Isn't that what Sam had told her? She needed to be at Deborah's bedside, not sleeping in her own bed, especially if she was going to save her relationship with Franklin. Franklin! Cora had plans for Franklin. The longer Elsa was away from Franklin the more dangerous Cora was to their relationship. What rumors was she spreading about them? What lies has she told Franklin and his parents? It wouldn't take long for rumors to spread about the fight she had had with Nathan. She knew Cora would use that information to discredit her with Juliette and Gideon. Cora could spin a tale to get whatever she wanted and that made her a threat.

The only way to save her relationship with Franklin was to fight for it and then manipulate him with his parents' help. She had to proceed with the plan she and Juliette had concocted. That meant she needed to talk to Liberty and Deborah. But if Deborah was dying she doubted Liberty would aid her unless Deborah asked him to as a final request. She hated to approach her sister on her deathbed. What kind of person tries to glean something from a dying person? But Deborah was all she had. She knew her sister wouldn't want her to be unhappy. Surely, Deborah would understand. Elsa pressed her left hand on her bed and pushed herself upright. Pain vibrated throughout her right shoulder. She peered over at the white sling holding her arm tight against her chest then cast her eyes down her body. Someone had taken her shirtwaist and skirt off, leaving her corset cover and petticoats exposed. Her sling looked new. Elsa pushed the blankets off, rose from the bed, and paused at her vanity. A piece of black fabric draped over her vanity mirror. Elsa swallowed hard. If black was draped over the mirror it only meant one thing. Someone had died. Whenever someone died in the house all the mirrors were to be covered by black so that the deceased person's soul wouldn't become trapped in the mirror. Worse yet, if a mirror in the same room where the person had died was left uncovered and someone looked into it then that person would soon die too. Elsa's heart sank. There was only one person in her home she knew to be dying—Henry.

Elsa walked to the dresser. A stack of black clothes lay neatly piled on top with a handwritten note folded in half like a tent. Her name was elegantly written on the end facing her in Franklin's handwriting. She bit her lower lip as she peered at it. Her beloved was here! The only person she wanted to see the most was here! She pressed the note against her chest, grinned, and pivoted as she called to him, "Frank." The rocking chair next to her armoire sat empty. Where was he? Maybe he went to the outhouse. Elsa walked around her four-poster bed to the window and peered outward. Nobody. Her heart fell. Franklin had to be here. It was his handwriting on the note, wasn't it? She lowered the note from her chest, opened it, and then read.

My dearest Elsa,

I have been by your side since yesterday morning. And before you wonder as to my condition, let me place your mind at ease. I am well rested, regaining my strength, and ascribing to Doctor Riley's orders. I regret that I have to inform you of this in a letter. It should not be so. Yesterday morning when I came to visit you, I found your front door open. Upon entering, I learned Henry had died that night in his sleep. Portia had awakened at dawn to find her husband dead beside her. I am so sorry for the loss of your brother. Henry was a good man. I shall miss our conversations.

Your mother is here with Portia but both women have secluded themselves. Your father is still at Deborah's house. Deborah is alive. Your aunt was able to save your sister with a surgery but Deborah will never be able to bear children again. Liberty is by her side constantly. Nathan has returned home and he is the reason I am able to give the update on Deborah and Liberty. He claims Deborah's fever has begun to lower but it will take time for her to fully recuperate. She does not know of Henry's death.

*Nathan and Sam are grieving but are trying to be strong for both
their mothers. They have returned to school. I have offered to pay
for all the funeral arrangements. If you are awake and I am not in
your room, then put on your robe and walk downstairs. Do not try
to dress yourself. Doctor Riley says you will need to keep your arm
immobilized for a week. Even after that, you will need to be careful
with that arm or it will dislocate again. It will be quite painful for
a while. Please, my love, heed the doctor's advice and be careful.
No more fighting with your brother, at least for the time being.*

*It has been a full day and a half since Henry's passing. My
mother is here to help you and your family. My mother has found
all the mourning clothes your family had from five years ago. She
has given Nathan Henry's old mourning clothes and had a new
dress ordered for you. They arrived this morning. You will find it
beneath this note. I have gone with my father to finalize the plans
with the undertaker. Henry's body has already been placed in a
temporary casket. He lies in the parlor. The funeral is scheduled
for noon on Monday. Your mother and Portia are writing the
invitations as you read this. They will need your help arranging the
seating plan for the funeral and organizing the carriages for the
ride to Oak Lawn Cemetery in Upper Sandusky. I love you dearly,
my brown-eyed girl. I shall return to your side soon enough.*

Yours dearly forever,

Franklin

Elsa lowered the letter and cried. Her worst fears had come
true. Henry was dead. The rock of their family, the firstborn, was
dead! A part of her told her she should have expected his death.
How many times had Doctor Riley informed them there was no
cure for tuberculosis? But somewhere deep in her heart, she had
believed his death would never come. Henry had survived the
influenza! He was stronger than to let anyone or anything destroy
him. Yet the tuberculosis had done just that. Even as Henry had
suffered he had never allowed his affliction to take life away from
him. Four months ago, Henry's tuberculosis had gone into
remission. At first, Henry had been careful not to exert himself, but
as time went by it looked to everyone as if the tuberculosis had
finally disappeared for good. Henry returned to his work at the
grocery shop, worked on the farm, and became the man of the

house he had been before the tuberculosis had ever afflicted him. Everyone had been happy, everyone, that is, except Doctor Riley.

Doctor Riley had warned them. This was only a phase, a very dangerous phase. Most patients with life-threatening illnesses usually get better before the disease killed them. If Henry was showing signs of improvement, his death was near. But no one in the family, not even Elsa, had wanted to accept that fact. Doctor Riley had warned Henry not to exert himself physically, including having sexual relations with Portia. Henry had ignored the doctor's advice. He and Portia had wanted another child together, especially since she was ten years older than him and he had only given her a son. Although Sam was a good older brother, Walter needed a brother or sister around his own age. Henry and Portia had tried every day and night to conceive while Oren managed the farm and Margaret took care of Walter.

Last month, Portia had announced she carried Henry's child. In a time of celebration, the family's hopes had once again been dashed. Portia had gone to share the news with Henry but couldn't find him anywhere. She had gone to the fields behind her house and there she had found Henry's unconscious body with a pool of bloody phlegm beside him. Sam and Nathan had carried him to his bed. Henry awoke as Doctor Riley was examining him. Doctor Riley had confirmed their worst suspicions. The tuberculosis had returned with a vengeance. He was to remain in bed. A week later, Henry had begun to feel better. He rose from his bed and went back to work with more determination now than ever. He had a new baby on the way. Then last week, Henry had fallen at work and they were back in Doctor Riley's office. Now her beloved brother was dead. His forty-seven-year-old pregnant wife was left a widow and his children were fatherless.

Elsa crumbled the note in her hand and cried, "Why, Henry?! Why did you have to be so stupid?!" She sat on the edge of her bed and sobbed. Her life shattered before her eyes. Henry, her rock, was dead. Twenty years older than her, Henry had been more than a brother. He was more of a father than Oren ever was to her. Now whom could she confide in? Nathan? Absolutely not! Although brothers, Nathan never cared for Henry after the influenza hit. Henry had abandoned the family to marry Portia. To Nathan, the greatest insult Henry had ever done to Oren was to leave the family. Their father had depended on Henry. With Henry's absence, Nathan tried to fill the void Henry had left behind. The more Henry was away the more empowered Nathan felt to become just like their father. He would stop at nothing to make certain Elsa never followed in Deborah or Henry's footsteps. Elsa wiped the tears from her eyes. The situation looked hopeless. Nathan didn't want her to marry Franklin, nor did Cora. Nathan was a popular boy at school and Cora was popular as well. The two of them got along quite well. Who was to say her brother and Cora wouldn't conspire together to break her and Franklin apart? She sobbed harder and she leaned over. Elsa rocked back and forth crying out, "Oh, God, Henry I need you! I need you now more than ever! I love Franklin. I need Franklin! Please, oh, please I don't know what to do without you!" Elsa rocked in silence. She sniffed her nose. Maybe this horrible nightmare was just a dream.

She opened her hand, unfolded the note, and read it again. Her heart sank. It wasn't a dream. Franklin would have never told her that Henry was dead unless it was true. He knew how much she had adored her eldest brother. She stared out the window. The world around her melted away from her mind as images of Henry's life passed swiftly before her as if they were a part of a motion picture. She'd miss his sandy-brown hair, chestnut-brown eyes, dimples, contagious laughter, and endless stories. Henry would want her to focus on Franklin. She knew that.

Elsa wiped the tears from her eyes, rose from her bed, grabbed her dark brown robe from the back of a chair, and carefully put it on with her sling underneath. She exited her bedroom and walked down the stairs to the dark, somber entryway. The front door stood slightly ajar with black crepe over the doorknob tied with a white ribbon. Elsa stared at the telltale sign proclaiming to everyone the unwelcomed visitor called death had claimed another victim. Elsa walked to the door. She gingerly stroked the dark black fabric between her fingers. Her mind turned back to the last time death had visited her home. She would never forget the time death had snuck into her home through influenza in 1896. She had lost six sisters ranging from ages twenty-six to four years of age. Now death had taken her eldest brother and had threatened to take

Deborah too. It wasn't right! It wasn't fair! Weren't the parents supposed to die before their children? Why was this happening?

The sound of horses caught her attention. Elsa peered outward. Two wagons full of visitors were pulling up to the house. Elsa peered down at her robe. She couldn't be seen in her robe. It wasn't proper. She lowered the black crepe back in place then walked inside. Voices came from the parlor on her left. Elsa walked towards the half-opened door, looked in, and glanced towards Henry's simple, wooden, open coffin. The floral scent from the bouquet of flowers around the coffin hid the smell of his decaying body. A thin pole with a tiny bell on top and a long string connecting Henry's wrist to the bell towered over her brother's coffin. Two deacons from their church and their wives stood talking about Henry. She turned away from the somber room. Elsa walked further down the dark long hallway as it T'd. She turned to her right then paused at Henry and Portia's door.

Elsa peeked between the crack left open between the door and doorway. Dressed in all black with a widow's cap, Portia leaned over her husband's desk, sobbing as she wrote the funeral invitations. She placed her hand on the small bump of her belly. Portia turned her head in Elsa's direction. Elsa quickly closed the door. She braced the door closed with her left hand and exhaled a deep breath. How many times she had seen death's effect upon those she loved! Yet never before had she ever faced the prospect of widowhood. It was a scary thought. She thought about her and Franklin. Franklin had diabetes. It wasn't unheard of for people to die soon after they were diagnosed. If she married Franklin and he died, then she would be a widow too. Maybe Nathan was right. If Franklin died, no one would want her. To be honest, she wouldn't want anyone besides him, either. Elsa laid her forehead on Portia's door. She closed her eyes with regret and fear. Widowhood. Widows had nothing in this world. The reality of her situation flooded before her very eyes. If Franklin dies first, which was a very real possibility, she wouldn't just inherit his assets but his debts too. After the debt collectors took their portions, how much would be left for her? Then there was the company he owned with his father. No man would ever listen to a woman. She couldn't run the company by herself let alone manage the farm. What if they had children? How would she support them? Widows and orphans usually ended up working in factories if they didn't have enough of an inheritance to live on. If Franklin's parents didn't support her then that was the life she would have to accept unless she remarried. And then there was always the social stigma attached to widowhood. A wife who lost her husband has to be in mourning for two full years. That meant she had to wear black woolen with crape. She couldn't attend social functions nor receive visitors or visit anyone. It would be a dull life, indeed.

Elsa felt Portia tug at the door. She released her grip, pushed her thoughts aside, and stepped back. "Elsa?" Portia asked softly behind her tears as she pulled opened the door.

"I'm so sorry, Portia. Franklin told me in a note."

Portia sniffed her nose and nodded. "He's a good man. His family's been very helpful. I couldn't ask for better friends."

"I'm sorry to disturb you. I...," she started to say then stopped as Portia cried. "Never mind. Portia, what can I do to help you and the children?"

"I need help with the...," Portia cried into her hands. Elsa embraced her sister-in-law. Portia cried on Elsa's left shoulder. "Oh, I can't believe he's dead."

"Me neither."

Portia lifted her head. "I keep thinking about how I found him. Maybe if I had stayed awake all night I would have noticed him dying. I could have done something to save him."

"We were on borrowed time with Henry. I think we all knew that but didn't want to admit it."

Portia placed her hand on her stomach, looked down, then peered back up into Elsa's eyes. "I have something for you."

"Me?"

Portia opened the door wider and invited Elsa in. Elsa stepped into the large bedroom. She froze in place as she stared at Henry's side of the bed. There her brother had not only created a family but breathed his last. She wondered how Portia could ever sleep peacefully in that bed again. If the roles had been reversed and it was she and Franklin, Elsa doubted she would ever have the strength Portia possessed now. Perhaps, since this was the second time Portia was a widow she was used to it all. Used to it. Elsa wasn't certain you could get used to death. Death's sting wasn't as painful once you got used to it but it still hurt, nonetheless.

"Elsa," Portia said loudly.

Elsa turned at the sound of her name. Portia walked away from the armoire across from the bed with a black ring box in her hand. She placed the ring box in Elsa's hand. Portia gently stroked Elsa's cheek with her left hand, sniffed, and smiled. "He cherished you. You know that?" Elsa nodded. "He used to tell me how much you reminded him of your mother before the influenza. He said she had your cheerfulness, faith, and determination."

"I loved to hear his stories of his childhood. It almost seemed as if we were born of different parents in a different time. I can't remember a day Henry wasn't helping pa with something. He was more than an older brother to me. He was someone I could look up to for advice. Someone I could trust with all my secrets, even if it meant keeping them away from Pa. Portia, you're without a husband and his children without a father. Why should you concern yourself with me when you have three children to raise by yourself?" Elsa wiped a tear from her eyes.

"Because you're his sister. I not only mourn his passing for the children's sake or me but for his family as well. I had hoped I would have had him as long as your family did but God deemed it not. Thank you for sharing him with me," she said, clasping her hands around Elsa's left hand and the ring box.

"You're welcome. He loved you. Whenever he spoke of you and the children, he couldn't stop smiling."

Portia smiled then sniffed her nose. She glanced across the room to a crib beside the bed. Walter slept peacefully under the blankets. "Henry was not only a good husband but an excellent father and my best friend," she said, turning her gaze back to Elsa. She exhaled a deep breath and peered down at Elsa's hand. "Take it. Henry wanted you to have it."

"What is it?

"His wedding band."

"No, I can't," Elsa cried, pushing the box towards Portia. "He was your husband."

"Elsa, all Henry could talk about was your wedding. I know you don't have a ring on your finger yet because of Franklin's accident but all Henry wanted from you was for you to leave this family and start a new life for yourself just as Deborah did."

"All the good it did for her. Look at what Pa did to her. I don't want that!"

"Your pa accepts Franklin, as did Henry. Frank's a good man. You deserve a better life than you have now. When Franklin asks for your hand, accept it. Move out of this house! Get as far away from the curse that plaque your parents as you can, and have a better life for yourself. Henry sacrificed his entire life to help his parents raise you and your siblings. He was thirty-two when he married me. He should have begun his own household long before that. But he didn't and do you know why?"

"Pa and Henry were always close."

"No, Elsa, they weren't. Henry resented the way your father treated him. Oren was very overprotective of him, more so than any of his other sons."

"Why?"

"That is a question that plagued Henry his entire life. I don't even know the answer to that. Henry stayed in that house in order to protect all his siblings from your father."

"But Pa never beat us."

"No, but he did seclude you from the outside world."

"Pa said family should stick together no matter how hard the circumstances are. He was trying to protect us, not harm us."

"From what?"

Elsa thought long and hard about Portia's question. Her entire life had revolved around her family, the farm, and church. Her closest friends had been her siblings. Sure, there were children at church but rarely did her family ever attend a social engagement. Her life had always centered on a strict routine. If there were ever a threat she didn't know what that would be. "I don't know," she said, shaking her head.

"That's the answer Henry gave me when I asked him the same question. What do you recall from your life before the influenza killed your siblings?"

"We rarely went into town except to buy supplies. When we did go to town, Pa never allowed anyone to go anywhere but the store."

"Why?"

"I don't know. I remember my older sister was engaged to a boy who worked there. She was supposed to marry him but three days before the wedding she died."

"Henry remembered her well. She was a twin."

"A twin?"

"Her sister died in a house fire when they were seven. Henry remembered that fire very well. Your mother had given birth to a son five months prior and was with child again. Life was great for your parents at that time. They had four children and family all around them. One of your father's sisters was the schoolteacher. Margaret was home with the children. Henry used to say that was the best time in his life because he went to school with his cousins. You pa used to take his children into Wheelersburg to look at the stores, go to the park, and whatever else they could find to do. Every Sunday, your father and his siblings would gather for a large family dinner. The day of the fire changed all that."

"What fire?"

"Henry was out in the fields with your father and his uncles when it happened. They noticed the fire and ran to help your mother. Margaret was able to get two of the children out of the house by the time Oren and the men arrived. They could hear their baby son cry from within. The fire was raging fast. Henry said the brownish-yellow smoke had lifted from the house in puffs and the windows had begun to be stained with black. Your uncles went to fetch water while Oren took care of his family. Margaret had wanted to go inside to save her child but Oren pulled her back. As they were arguing, the twin of the sister you spoke of went back inside to fetch her brother. Oren ran after her. Just as soon as she had entered the house the entire structure exploded. Oren had been blown backwards. He had hit the ground so hard he lost consciousness. Margaret had feared she had not only lost two of her children but her husband as well. When your uncles had returned with the water there was nothing they could do to stop the fire, so they let the house burn to the ground. They took your father to Jesse's house and called the doctor. It was one of the worst moments of Henry's life. Your father suffered from minor burns, a concussion, and broke his back. The doctor had warned the family it could have lead to paralysis."

"But it didn't."

"No, Oren was fortunate. He stayed in bed and obeyed the doctor's orders. As soon as the fire happened there was family surrounding your family. They arranged the funeral, helped Margaret with the surviving children, visited Oren, and did whatever else was needed. After the fire, the sister you recall suffered from the greatest of depressions. The family moved in and tried to console her. Then a few months later Margaret almost died in childbirth. The family dug deep to support your entire family. Margaret suffered from depression and wouldn't bond with her new daughter so one of Oren's sisters nursed the baby. Two years later, Oren moved his family up here, cut all contact with his family, and secluded himself from the outside world, along with his wife and children. A year later in 1881, your mother gave birth to another girl."

"It all doesn't make sense."

"What doesn't?"

"Why would Pa seclude us from our family when they showed only love and mercy to him?"

"I don't know. That was one of the questions that plagued your brother."

"If my parents don't want anything to do with their families then why does Ma write letters to them? I've seen her do that."

"She and your father periodically send letters to their family but always on the letters is the phrase, 'don't contact us or our children.'"

"But then how did Aunt Betsy come to save us from the influenza?"

"Henry had contacted her."

"How?"

"While you took Deborah to Liberty's house, Henry ran to one of the neighbors and asked them to send a telegram to your aunt and uncle. He knew your father would be upset but it didn't matter to Henry. His family was dying. He was an adult. There was nothing your parents could do to punish him for it. If he hadn't done that, none of you would have survived. After your family recuperated your aunt had suggested to your father to have a mass funeral with the family there to support him. She also suggested he move back to Vernon Township. But your father had rejected her ideas, thanked her, then sent her home to her husband."

"Vernon Township?" Elsa questioned.

"It's where your father is from. It's a small farming community in southern Ohio."

"Is my ma from there too?"

"No. She's from Jackson, Ohio. It's still in Southern Ohio, just farther north than Vernon Township." Portia walked over to Henry's desk, sat on the chair, and opened a secret compartment underneath. She pulled out a long green journal bound with a black ribbon around it, then turned to Elsa. "After Henry married me I urged him to reconnect with his family."

"Why?"

Portia rose from the desk and walked towards Elsa. "Elsa, you cannot imagine the pain Henry had—to be ripped away from a family he had loved only to move where he had no one. The strong man you remember was very insecure on the inside."

"Henry, insecure?" Elsa huffed. "Never."

"Your father took everything from Henry. By the time Henry was old enough to marry, your father had convinced him the only people in this world who cared about him were his parents and siblings. Henry struggled deeply when he courted me."

"Why?"

"Because in his mind, he didn't believe he could leave your parents and start a new life with me away from them."

"But he did."

"Yes, it took some time for him to work through the insecurities that your father had built up in him before he could do so. That's why we waited a year before we married. After we married, we told everyone we were going to honeymoon in Columbus, but that was just a ruse."

"Where did you go?"

"Wheelersburg."

"Wheelersburg?" Elsa asked.

"We went to share the news of our nuptials with the entire Garrett family. It was the best idea we ever had. That trip helped Henry in more ways than I ever could. He recorded what he learned in this journal and there are some pictures in there as well of the family. Take it," she said, handing the book to Elsa. "Throughout the years, we continued to re-establish connections between your father's side of the family and our own. When possible we traveled down there and they came up here to visit. Henry recorded everything."

"When you gave birth to Walter you said you were in the hospital at Upper Sandusky."

"Another lie. Henry took me to Wheelersburg a few months before I delivered. Your Aunt Betsy delivered our son."

"Does Sam know?"

"He does. We took him several times to Wheelersburg."

"But he's best friends with Nathan. Does Nathan know the truth?"

"No, my son and your brother are not as close as you believe them to be. Henry told Sam to be nice to Nathan but to never reveal the truth. Sam agreed."

"Why?"

"Elsa, my family can't be there for my son. We live too far away from them. Whatever interaction he has with my side of the family and his father's side are only through letters and telegrams. When Sam had the chance to bond with the Garrett family, it meant the world to him. He understands that if Nathan ever knew the truth, Nathan would tell his father and there would be more harm than good from that. Henry never wanted his parents involved in our lives."

"Then why did he ask for our help?"

"He had suffered from the tuberculosis long before he informed you of it. Henry waited to ask his parents to move in until he knew he was going to need help. His greatest fear was that his father would treat him as a child. But he knew I needed a man around the house to help me when he could not."

"Why didn't you move to Wheelersburg and ask Aunt Betsy for help?"

"He wanted to. I begged him to act upon those thoughts but he wasn't strong enough to move that far away from your parents. Elsa, take Henry's ring and his journal. Remember the devotion he had for his family. If you will excuse me, I have to finish the invitations."

"Thank you, Portia."

Portia smiled then kissed Elsa on the forehead. "You are such a sweet child. I only hope if I have a daughter she will be as sweet as you." Elsa smiled. Portia placed her hand on the small mound of her stomach, walked to the desk, and went back to writing her invitations. Tears flowed steadily down her cheeks. Elsa quietly walked out of Portia's bedroom, gently closed the door behind her, and stepped towards the kitchen door in the middle. Margaret's voice echoed from the kitchen. Elsa opened the door and began to step inside then paused as she overheard her mother's conversation on the wall-mounted telephone.

"Oren doesn't know… Of course I know what he will say but this is important…yes…Ruth, please…no, I'm not… Aren't you the one who told me Moses wanted to meet his son…? Please, this is hard on all of us…I know… Oren won't… I know what I did to Moses was wrong… That was thirty-eight years ago… Oh, I'm not the only one at fault. You saw how he treated Emma! I was ready to start a family with Moses… I didn't have a choice! I was with child…! Oh, you know that's a lie… Henry is Moses's son! I only slept with Oren after I gave birth to Henry…! Because Moses wanted me to abandon my daughter. I couldn't do that. You know how much I loved her father. At the end of the Civil War I was a widow left with a six-year-old daughter to raise by myself. I would have never abandoned Emma for a man… Never! At least Oren understood that… Ruth, please, just tell Moses his son is dead. Missouri is a long way from here. Board the next train to Marion. I will pick you, Moses, and your children up from the station… The funeral's at noon on Monday… Yes, I think that is an excellent idea… Portia has given Moses a grandson and carries another…"

Elsa stepped back into the hallway and closed the door with confusion. Why was her mother saying Henry wasn't her father's son? And who was the mysterious daughter, Emma? She had never heard of her before and as far as she knew Henry was Margaret's eldest child. She peered down at the journal under her arm. Henry's death had revealed more secrets than truths about her family. She placed the book and ring box on the side table. Elsa slowly opened the ring box and stared at Henry's ring. Henry had left their family to start a new life for himself. Deborah had done the same. Now it was her turn. But was she ready to face that reality? How could she start a new life for herself when she didn't even know whom she was or where her family had come from? She needed to be a strong wife for Franklin. She traced her finger around Henry's ring. An overwhelming urge to forget her desires and stay with her parents clung to the deepest part of her soul. Was that ingrained desire carved by her father the same thing Henry had felt? She would always be Oren and Margaret Garrett's daughter. But at what cost would her marriage to Franklin affect her relationship with them?

Elsa slammed the lid of the ring box down. It didn't matter. Nothing her parents had told her was ever the truth. They either hid her away from their family or lied to her. A deep pain seared through her heart. She closed her fist, leaned her forehead on it and sobbed. Lies, destruction, and despair. That was her life since the day Margaret had borne her. A part of her felt sorry for her parents but another part of her wanted answers, answers only the Garretts could grant her. Maybe, just as Henry had found hope and healing, she too could find it with them. But how? How was she to contact them? Her eyes glanced at the letter between the ring box and Henry's journal. She pushed the box aside, unfolded the letter, and reread it. Franklin had mentioned her aunt had saved Deborah's life. She laid the letter down then tapped her fingers on the book. Her aunt? As far as she knew the only aunt she had was in Wheelersburg, Ohio. Could her Aunt Betsy be the woman who saved Deborah's life? If so, then maybe God had used Deborah's tragedy to help her with Franklin. She needed to speak to Betsy.

"Elsa," Juliette's voice called out to her. Elsa turned to her right. Juliette stood before her with an empty wicker laundry basket in her hand. "Elsa, how long have you been down here?"

"Not long. I just woke up a few moments ago."

"Are you in pain?"

"A little. It's more of a discomfort than pain."

Juliette lowered the basket to the floor, walked over to Elsa, and examined her sling. She spoke as she adjusted it. "Doctor Riley said it needed to stay tight so your arm remains immobilized. I have some pain medication he left for you. You'll have to eat something with it and it will make you drowsy. I can get you some if you want."

"No," Elsa replied, casting her eyes towards Henry's book. "Franklin wrote me a letter and told me what happened."

"I'm so sorry, Elsa."

"Thank you. He said I should help with the funeral arrangements," she whispered, casting her eyes back at Juliette. "How's my ma?"

"She's grieving. It's hard for any parent to lose a child."

"When the influenza took my sisters from me she grieved so hard Doctor Riley wanted to commit her to an institution."

"Oh?"

"It was a bad year for my family. The winter of 1895 came and we barely had enough food then the influenza struck. We were starving, ill, and desperate. It was all too much for my ma to handle, especially when my sisters died. After the influenza, Henry left us to marry Portia and Deborah had run away with Liberty. I think that was the final nail in my mother's coffin. She wore her mourning clothes, refused to eat much food, and cried all the time. A few months after everything happened she tried to drown herself in the pond. Pa rescued her. He took her to Doctor Riley and Doctor Riley told Pa he should commit my mother to the Central Ohio Psychiatric Hospital. But my pa said he knew what kind of doctors worked there and he wasn't about to send the love of his life to no quack. When Henry called and asked us to move here, my mother changed for the better. It was as if Henry had come back from the dead or something. Pa had tried to tell her Henry was ill. I don't think my ma ever accepted that was the reason Henry asked us to be here. Once we moved, it was as if Nathan and I never existed. She only cared about him."

"Oh, Elsa, that's not true. She loves you."

"Henry was her favorite."

Juliette exhaled a deep breath then replied, "Every parent has a tendency to favor one child over another. If Margaret favored Henry over you I'm certain she didn't mean to leave you feeling neglected."

"Do you think you favor Franklin over the rest of your children?"

"I think some days it may seem as if Gideon and I favor him more. But that is never our intention. Franklin's a special boy. He has needs that require us to give him constant care."

"But he's a man not a child."

"Elsa, the man you love is only a dream that you want to see. You love him so you don't allow yourself to see the ugliness inside him."

"Such as?"

"He will always need you to help him survive."

"Because of the diabetes? I can do that. He loves my cooking."

"That and more, Elsa. Doctor Riley, Gideon, and I have tried for years to figure out why Franklin does what he does. He has his good days and then there are those days when he is so agitated it takes a long time to calm him down."

"I've never seen him act like that."

"Gideon and I have made certain to shield you from it. Sometimes, Elsa, I think my son is too smart for his own good." Juliette turned her eyes to the book and changed the subject, "Is that yours?"

Elsa nodded. "Portia gave it to me. She said Henry would want me to have it."

"What is it?"

"Henry's journal and his wedding band. I was going to take it up to my room."

"Oh, let me carry that for you," Juliette offered, picking up the basket and extending it toward Elsa, who gently placed the items inside the basket. A black and white picture poked out of the book. Elsa pulled the portrait from under the pages and stared at it. Three Union soldiers stood in a perfect row behind two seated Union soldiers. All the soldiers sat in perfect formation with their rifles at ease. Elsa studied the picture carefully. She smiled at the man sitting on the left. "Who is that?" Juliette asked.

"It looks like my pa. He was nineteen when he entered the war with his brothers."

"The man beside him looks a lot like Henry did."

Elsa traced her finger over the mysterious man's image. "He does. Do you know who he is?"

Juliette shook her head, "Your parents never talk much about their past."

"My pa said he had two older brothers. This man beside him looks younger but the three men behind him look older. I wonder who they are."

"Maybe there is writing on the back."

Elsa flipped the picture over. Written in her father's cursive hand were the words. *The inseparable five Garrett brothers! Lucas, Carlisle, Jesse, Oren, and Moses. Always together, never apart. We fight for our country with endless bravery and boundless courage in our hearts. October 15, 1862.*

"Moses," Elsa muttered. She flipped the picture several times, placed it back in the basket, and stared at the kitchen door.

"Something wrong?" Juliette asked.

"It's just that my pa always told me he only had two older brothers. He lied. Why would he lie to me?"

"Maybe he didn't lie. A lot of men died in the Civil War. Perhaps, he had four brothers and lost two in the war. It wouldn't be uncommon. What is remarkable is that your father and his brothers fought on the same side. Not many families can claim that. Too many fathers shot their own sons in that war. There are just some things men don't want to talk about that happened during that war."

"I don't think they're all dead," she admitted.

"Why do you think that?"

"I overheard my ma talking on the phone in the kitchen to a woman she called Ruth. I think Ruth is married to Moses. Moses is alive. They live in Missouri. She told Ruth Henry was Moses' son. If that were true then that would mean Henry's pa is my uncle. Why would my pa take my ma away from her husband and claim their son as his own?"

"I don't know, Elsa. Perhaps what you believe you heard is not what she actually said?"

Elsa stared down at the journal in Juliette's basket. Her heart had been shattered. Everything she thought she knew about her family was a lie and the one person who could tell her the truth was dead. How could she marry Franklin if she didn't even know who she was? But how could she not marry him? Franklin needed her and she needed him. He was the love of her life! Henry had wanted her to leave the family and start a better life for herself. But how could she do that? If her father had lied about being Henry's father, what other lies had he told her about her life? She reached into the basket, pulled out the ring box, and then opened it. Henry's solid white gold band sat nestled between the pillows. "Mrs. Raymond?" she questioned.

"Elsa."

"Franklin has bought me an engagement ring but has he bought our wedding set?" Elsa asked, lifting her eyes to the older woman.

"Not yet. Why do you ask?"

"I think Franklin should wear Henry's ring," she said, turning the open box to Juliette.

"Elsa, I don't know. What about Portia? Shouldn't she have that ring?"

"She gave it to me. She claims Henry would want me to have it because he wanted me to marry Franklin. I'm so confused though," she said, closing the box then laying it back in the basket.

"Why? I thought you had a plan. By what I hear Deborah isn't dying. You can still speak to your sister."

"I'm scared."

"Of what?"

Elsa swallowed hard. "I don't want to become like her," she claimed, pointing to Portia's room.

"You think by marrying my son he will make you a widow?"

"It's a possibility isn't it?"

"Yes, but you said you had an aunt in Southern Ohio that you thought could possibly cure him."

Elsa lowered her head with defeat. She was confused and scared. Her parents had lied to her, Henry was dead, Cora had threatened her life, and all she could think about was Franklin! She turned her eyes towards Portia's door. What kind of fool marries a man who has a debilitating condition? Tears flowed down her cheeks as the sorrows of her heart consumed her. Juliette lowered the basket on a side table and embraced Elsa. Elsa sobbed.

"What has stolen your ambitions to marry my son? Is it the grief of losing your brother?"

"No."

"Then what dear child?"

"I don't want to be a widow." Elsa lifted her head. "What if he leaves me alone to raise our children? I can't raise them by myself!"

Juliette grabbed Elsa's face and looked sternly into her eyes. "Stop it! Just stop thinking those kinds of thoughts. Do you love my son?"

"Yes, ma'am."

"Then follow your heart and not what you fear. Elsa, you're a strong young lady. Don't let the grief within this house consume you. Ask yourself this, if Henry was alive today what would he tell you to do?"

"Fight for my marriage."

"Then fight, child! Fight for Franklin. Do what you planned to do all along. Franklin will always be beside you. Once he is fixated on something he rarely lets the object of his fixations out of his eyes or mind. Elsa, my son loves you. He's already proven that time and time again. If you quit the fight for your marriage he won't marry you and it'll shatter his heart even if you never leave him."

"I don't want to lose him."

"Then don't, child. You have all the power in the world to make him marry you, even more so now than before."

"I don't understand."

"Elsa, didn't you grieve for your siblings when they died from the influenza?"

"Yes, ma'am."

"And how long was it before you could attend a social function?"

"Six months."

Juliette grinned, "In six months, the county will celebrate Harvest Fest. There will be another dance. Six months gives me plenty of time to convince Franklin to propose to you at that dance in the same manner he was going to at the last dance. But you must never let him know you know his intentions. What you should do is contact Liberty, Deborah, and your aunt about Franklin. Gideon had agreed for your aunt to examine him."

"Elsa," Franklin's voice beckoned from the hallway behind her. Juliette lowered her hands. Elsa turned as she heard her boyfriend call her name. Franklin walked swiftly down the hallway and kissed her. "I'm so glad to see you out of bed. I was worried," he said, pulling his lips away from her. "How do you feel?"

Elsa wrapped her arm around him and hugged him tight. "Frank, just hold me. Please, my love, just hold me."

Franklin clutched her tighter. She gasped.

"Frank, be careful with her arm. Don't hold her too tight. She's still in pain," Juliette warned.

"Sorry," he whispered in Elsa's ear then kissed her on the cheek.

"What did the undertaker say?" Juliette asked, shuffling the items in the basket.

Elsa clutched Franklin's vest and sobbed as Juliette and her son spoke. Franklin stood rigid. She lifted her eyes and studied his face. Emotionless and detached, Franklin was like a statue. He was serious and strong, just what she needed in her life at this very moment. She stared into his deep brown eyes. Perhaps Henry had been correct all along. Her only salvation was with the man she loved. She pressed her hand flat on Franklin's chest, lowered her gaze, and clung tighter to him. "Frank," she muttered.

Franklin stopped mid-sentence and looked down at her. "Elsa?" he asked.

"Can you help me put my dress on then take me to Deborah's?"

"But you're needed here."

"I want to see my sister. Please, Frank."

Franklin exchanged glances with his mother. Juliette nodded then replied, "Leave her door partially open when you're in her room."

"Yes, ma'am." Franklin lowered his arm around her waist and then led his beloved towards the bedroom.

9

Elsa stared at her half-opened bedroom door as she sat on her bed while Franklin silently gathered her clothes. She wondered what life would be like once she and Franklin married. Marriage. The sound of the word sounded as sweet as honey on her lips. Life with Franklin would be wonderful! Loyal and devoted to her alone, she felt confident Franklin would never cheat on her like her mother had done to Henry's father. Franklin had always been direct and honest with her. There wasn't a day that went by since they had begun their courtship that he hadn't supported her. She had looked forward to spending the rest of her life with this sweet and tender man. No matter how hard she tried to convince herself Franklin was just a normal young man, the more she only fooled herself.

There was something off about Franklin. His quirky disposition had been the talk of everyone around her, but she had never noticed it before. All she saw was a gentle, sweet, and tender man who truly cared about her. Yet, after Franklin's illness the reality of his quirkiness hit her hard. Common sense would say if this man truly loved her he would have asked her to marry him when she had seen the ring box in his hand. But he didn't. Most girls would have left him by now. You don't tease the woman you love by allowing her to see the ring box only to tell her it meant nothing. Nor do you say you want to be her husband but never ask her to marry you. She knew what Franklin wanted. She wanted it too. But how was she ever going to convince him to act upon those feelings, especially if her plan didn't come to fruition. What was it about Franklin that made him different? Why did his parents and Doctor Riley feel the need to treat him like a child?

"Elsa?" Franklin asked in front of her.

"Hmm," she answered, meeting his gaze.

"Sweetheart, are you alright?"

"I was just thinking."

"About?"

"The diabetes."

"Oh," he said then grew quiet.

"Are you scared of death?"

"I'm not dying."

"You could have."

"But I didn't"

"Oh, Frank, you were so close to death. And when you were awake, it was as if you weren't the man I knew but someone else. Your body was just a shell. My Franklin was gone," Elsa proclaimed.

Franklin lowered the clothes to the bed and knelt before her. "My body cannot be a shell. I am a human being. Humans don't have shells."

Elsa chuckled with the shake of her head. "Oh, Frank," she muttered as she looked at his solid expression. Franklin never moved. She tenderly placed her hand on the side of his face with a smile and stroked his cheekbone. Franklin jumped at her touch. He sighed as she stroked his face. Elsa pulled her hand away from his face with disappointment. "I'm sorry. I should have asked first," she apologized.

Franklin nodded. He silently rose, grabbed her clothes, and began to unfold them. Her heart sank. She knew better than to touch Franklin like that. While he enjoyed a firm touch, he couldn't stand a tender touch. He had come a long way from the beginning of their relationship. At first he wouldn't ever touch her. It had taken him a long time to be able to hold her hand, kiss her, and embrace her. She should be grateful for that at least. His lack of expression and touch would have turned many girls away from him but not her. She could see the wonderful man deep inside him. A pinch of pain soared down her right arm. She grunted as she cast her eyes to her left shoulder. Franklin untied the two cloth ends holding her sling in place. She gasped, feeling the pressure change.

"Don't move your arm," he advised, tossing the sling behind her. Elsa rose to her feet.

"Are you mad at me for touching you like that?" she asked, placing her arm into the sleeve.

"No. Let me help you put your right arm into the sleeve. Doctor Riley said we have to be careful." Franklin carefully helped her. She flinched with pain at every movement. Finally the front of her blouse was on! Now, they faced the hardest part—buttoning the back of her blouse without hurting her. Franklin moved behind her and tugged on the two ends. "Frank," she gasped.

He looked over her shoulder. "Elsa?" he asked as if nothing had happened. He pulled the ends of the fabric tighter so the tiny buttons and loops met.

"Hurts," she cried, closing her eyes and whimpering.

"I will try to be more careful. We don't have to go Deborah's house. If you want to remain here and relax in your bed…"

"Just get it on me," she snarled, emphasizing each word.

Franklin nodded then returned his attention to her back. He pressed his hand firmly over her shoulder, held it in place, and buttoned the tiny buttons. She leaned her head back with a moan of pain. Elsa closed her eyes and breathed through the radiating pain. "I'm almost done. Hold still," he instructed.

"Easier said than done, Frank."

"I do not think the expression of words can ever be compared to completing a task."

"Frank?"

"Yes?"

"It's an expression! You are hurting me!"

"I'm not trying to hurt you."

"Please, I beg of you. Just finish, please."

Silence passed between them as Franklin buttoned every button from her neck to her lower back. She felt his hands leave her body. Elsa opened her eyes. Franklin carefully placed the sling around her right arm then tied it tight to her left shoulder. Relief came as her arm was once again immobilized. "Ready for the skirt?" he asked.

"Yes." Franklin grabbed the floor-length, black walking skirt, lifted it above her head, then gently lowered it over the edges of her black shirtwaist. He gently hooked the top of the skirt together. "Is there a belt?" Elsa asked, peering down at her clothes. Franklin grabbed the solid black belt from the bed and placed it around her waist. "Thank you," she said to him.

"You're welcome. I'm sorry if I hurt you."

"Apology accepted. Franklin, do you think I'm a bad

person?" she asked, boring her eyes into his own.

Franklin stepped back with a confused look on his face. "No," he answered.

Elsa nodded her head then sat on the edge of the bed. She peered down at the floor thinking about Franklin's diabetes, Henry's death, Portia's widowhood, her father's family secrets, and her own future with Franklin. What kind of girl leaves her family to marry a man like Franklin? What kind of girl manipulates her way into marriage? Franklin wanted her to be his wife. She knew that. But he couldn't act on those desires without her manipulating him into doing so? Had they worked on their relationship so much only to come to this point? No woman should ever have to trick their man into marrying them even if he was as strange as Franklin.

"What's bothering you?" Franklin asked.

"Everything," she muttered.

"Are you upset because of the fight we had when I was sick?"

"No."

"Then what is it? I've never known you to have a physical altercation with Nathan. What would ever possess you to fight him? Did he hit you?"

"No, I hit him first."

"Why?"

"I...," she stared into his eyes. How much she wanted to tell him she knew about the ring! Doctor Riley had said Franklin wouldn't remember anything from after his seizure but he just asked her if she was upset about their fight. Shouldn't he have forgotten about the fight? She wondered what else he could recall. Did he know she already knew he planned to marry her? How she hoped so. If Franklin recalled why they fought then maybe she wouldn't have to wait for him to propose to her. Maybe he would ask her right here, right now. Oh, if only it could all be that simple. "Frank, what do you remember about our fight?"

"Nothing. All I remember is that you were by my side before I had the seizure then when I awoke you were gone."

"I'm sorry I wasn't there."

"I asked Cora where you were. She told me we had gotten into a serious argument and you left my house sobbing. She said you told her you never wanted to see me again. Then she told me about the fight you had with your brother. I couldn't stand the thought of losing you so I came here. I stayed by your side hoping we could work things out between us, but you never woke. My pa helped me to write the note you found then told me I had to leave you so we could talk to the undertaker. But now you are awake and we're alone, we can fix whatever stands between us."

"There's nothing you can do to change how I feel about you."

"Elsa, please. I cannot live my life without you."

"Frank, I'm not breaking up with you. Cora lied to you."

"I don't understand. Cora said we argued. Even my parents told me we had."

"We did argue but I never left your house sobbing or in anger. I had planned to return to your side but then I was injured."

"That's not what Cora told me."

"Why would you believe a word Cora says to you when you know she hates me?"

"She's my sister. She may have her flaws but I know she loves me. She only wants what is best for me."

"Frank, she's dangerous. You don't know what she did to me. I'm scared to be alone with her."

"I don't know why you would be. My sister can be mean but she would never hurt anyone. "

"That's not true!" Sharp pains radiated down her shoulder to her arm. Elsa inhaled a deep breath through her teeth. Franklin sat beside her and pulled her into his chest. She closed her eyes, allowing his strength to comfort her.

Franklin kissed the top of her head then asked, "What was the argument about?"

"With Nathan?"

"No, between us."

"It's not important."

"It is to me. I don't recall what happened from the time I awoke and saw you to the time I fell unconscious. If we fought I want to know why and if I hurt you then I want to remedy that situation."

"Cora was there. Why don't you ask her?"

Franklin held Elsa away from him. "I want to hear the story

from you, not her. "

"Why?"

"Because you're my girlfriend. I love you. Please Elsa, don't be like this."

"Your sister hates me and you are siding with her not me. How else am I supposed to feel, Franklin?"

"Are you asking me to choose the truth between you and her? She's my sister."

"And I'm your girlfriend. The bible says a man will leave his family and cleave to his w…" She swallowed hard.

"Wife," he finished.

"That's what our argument was about."

"Marrying you?"

"Yes. You said you wanted to marry me. Cora was there. She heard it and saw what you did to me."

"What did I do?"

"We kissed, held each other, then when I was underneath you, you placed your hand underneath my skirt. I pushed you off of me and stopped before things went too far between us. Cora was upset that you had done that to me. She taunted me endlessly after that."

"Cora has always taunted you. If she didn't taunt you then she wouldn't care about you."

"She doesn't want us together. She's mean, Franklin. Bitter and mean."

"Elsa, she was raised with three brothers. Sometimes, she can be a bit rough. You have to accept that."

"How can I when she threatened my life?"

"Threaten you? When was this?"

"After the fight with Nathan."

"How?"

"I was alone in the back of my pa's wagon. I was in agony. I thought I heard my ma but when I turned around it was Cora. She stepped on my dislocated shoulder then told me to remember that pain. She said if I didn't end my relationship with you she would kill me."

"Did she tell you why she wanted us apart?"

"She said she had plans for you and I was ruining them."

Franklin rose from the bed then silently walked to the door.

He leaned his side against the doorframe and looked out. Silent and still, her beau had once again turned into a statue. Elsa knew something bothered him. What dark secret had he kept from her? Did he know about the plans Cora had mentioned to her? Cora had made it sound like she was trying to control Franklin. Maybe Cora wasn't controlling Franklin as much as Franklin was allowing her to be involved in his love life. But why? Brother and sister had rarely seen eye to eye on anything let alone his involvement with her. "Frank?" she questioned, rising from the bed.

Franklin turned to face her with a serious look on his face. She sat back down on the bed. His flat, serious, commanding facial features spoke volumes to her. "I don't want to hurt you," he whispered.

"You are hurting me more by not telling me the truth. You've always been honest and blunt with me. Why aren't you now?"

"Because if I tell you the truth it will hurt you and I don't want to do that."

"Frank, are you breaking up with me?"

"No. I hate keeping secrets. I hate being dishonest but I don't know what to do."

"We've been together for a year. You know you can trust me with your secrets. All you have to do is confide them to me. If the secret is about something you are having trouble with then I will help you to overcome whatever problem you are facing. Be honest with me, Frank. It's all I have ever asked from you."

"I know the plan she spoke of," he admitted softly.

"And that is?"

"A childish plan that was made in our youth that has no bearing on how I feel about you."

"Then why keep it a secret from me?"

"Because you are not the only young woman involved. The other girl doesn't know the plan has changed, unless Cora has informed her."

"Franklin, you're not making any sense. Are you protecting this other girl?"

"I don't know what to do with her."

Elsa let out a long, drawn out sigh. "Franklin, what did you do?"

"It doesn't matter anymore. It was a long time ago. I don't love her, I love you."

Elsa's face fell with realization. "There's another woman!"

Franklin stepped towards her. "It's not what you think."

"You're seeing another woman behind my back!"

"No, Elsa. I'm not. I was but I am no longer."

Elsa rose from the bed, clenching her jaw. How dare he! Cora was right. She hadn't wanted to believe his sister's claim that Franklin shifted between girls. "Who is she?" she demanded.

"Elsa, she doesn't matter to me anymore. I only love you."

"Who is she?" she yelled in his face. Franklin took a step back. "Cora told me you see more than one girl at once but I didn't want to believe her," she began to cry. "How many others are you courting behind my back?"

"None. You are the only girl for me, Elsa."

Elsa huffed. "I've heard you say that many times. Yet Cora isn't the only one to tell me you have been with another girl. I thought they meant before you courted me but now I'm not too certain who to believe."

"Me."

"You can't even tell me the truth!"

"Elsa, if you would calm down I'll tell you everything."

"Why? Cora said I'm just another one of your girls you date then when you're done with me you'll throw me away like all the others."

"She's wrong. I am committed to you."

"How many other girls have you said that too?"

"Elsa!" Franklin wiped his hands down his face then paced. Elsa watched him silently pace between her north and south walls. He was clearly agitated but was that because she had caught him in a lie or because he had meant his words? She sat on the edge of her bed with the proverbial knife in her heart. She had given him everything. She had trusted him with her entire heart and soul. Franklin was the sweetest man she had ever known and she knew he had a hard time socializing with people. She had to face the truth. No matter how much he had hurt her, Franklin didn't understand why he had done so. She lifted her gaze towards him. "Tell me about the arrangement you have with Cora."

Franklin paused and glared back at her. "Why, so you can yell at me again?"

"No, Franklin. I want to know the truth. Cora doesn't like me and for some reason she believes the plans she has made with you will be better for you."

"The plans I have with her will not be better for me. You are better for me than Rebekah!"

Elsa gasped, widening her eyes. "Rebekah Grace Webster?"

"Yes."

"You courted her?"

"Yes."

"Did you touch her like you touch me?"

"Elsa," he moaned.

"Did you?"

"Yes! I kissed, hugged, and fondled her just as I have done with you. But only with you and her. No other woman has ever made me feel the way I do towards her and you." Elsa fell back on the bed with disappointment and closed her eyes. How could he? All this time she thought she had meant something more to him than any other girl in the county. "Elsa?" Franklin asked, sitting beside her. Tears rolled down her cheeks. The knife in her heart twisted and turned with each word he spoke. "Elsa, I'm sorry. I didn't know you back then. The feelings I had for Rebekah were strong but the feelings I have for you are stronger."

"Wh...ho...wha...how did it happen?"

Franklin swallowed hard. "When Cora and I were younger, we both had this plan to marry each other's best friends."

"Isaiah told me Cora had eyes on Hayden Webster but he broke her heart."

"True. Hayden has only seen Cora as a sister. How did you know Hayden and I are best friends?"

"Isaiah told me. My school teacher's husband is your best friend?"

"Yeah, we grew up together."

"Huh, and his wife?"

"She's from Upper Sandusky. He met her when he went to study accounting up there. When I was sixteen, I left school to help my pa with the farm but something else happened too. I began to have feelings for Hayden's sister. Rebekah was thirteen at the time. Cora and I believed the relationship would be beneficial for both our families. Our parents were close friends. The Webster's own a bank in Marion. Our marriage would merge both businesses. Our fathers decided to consent to our courtship. Our courtship has always been rocky. We have moments where we grow apart, I'd see other girls then we'd come back to each other. Last year, before I met you I asked Rebekah's father permission to marry her. He denied me and said I could ask again when she was eighteen. Rebekah left the state and I haven't spoken to her since."

"So am I one of those girls you date when you two aren't together?" Elsa asked in tears.

"You were but no longer. I don't love Rebekah, I love you."

"But you never broke it off with her?"

"Not yet but I plan to."

"You've been with Rebekah for three years and you never broke it off with her."

"I was waiting to do that."

"Waiting for what exactly?"

"I don't like change, Elsa."

"I know you panic when there is a change in your routine."

"It would be a big change for me to break off my relationship with her."

"How can you say I mean more to you than her if you won't break up with her?"

"I had a plan but that plan changed when I met you. I'm confused, Elsa. I know what I want but don't know how to achieve my desired results without hurting either you or Rebekah."

"Change is good, Franklin. You know what you must do. Why won't you act on that?"

"A year ago, you changed everything for me. Before I met you I had a plan that never included you. When you came into my life, you fascinated me. I became fixated on you but didn't know why. I had to be around you every moment of your life. There was only one other person I have felt like that with and my plan was to spend the rest of my life with her."

His harsh, direct words stung as if someone had stabbed her in the heart. A tear fell down her cheek. "Do you want a life with

Rebekah?" she whimpered.

"No. I no longer care for her that way. I want you. I always have."

"Then tell her."

"I can't. When my heart shifted to you, it was the worst feeling I had ever had in my life."

Elsa sobbed harder. She placed her left hand on her face and leaned over. His words had cut even deeper than before. A part of her wanted to remain strong. Franklin had always struggled with his words. Perhaps, he didn't realize how much he was hurting her. She hoped that was all it was; Franklin's lack of verbal skills hurt her and not the truth behind those words. Franklin continued to speak. "Cora knows the heartache and pain I faced when I decided to court you."

"Stop talking," Elsa yelled, rising to her feet.

"Cora knows the struggles I faced. When my heart shifted to you I struggled a lot with my decision to divert the plan I had for my life. Being with you would ruin everything I had worked so hard to accomplish."

"Shut up."

"Elsa I don't understand why you are upset. You told me…"

"Stop it! Stop talking! Shut up!" Elsa yelled then ran to the door. She slammed it closed behind her, leaned back, and cried. Why? Why was he doing this to her? She slid down the door to her knees, sobbing even harder. Her entire world had fallen apart all around her and now the one man whom she could lean upon was breaking her heart. She leaned over her knees as her tears cascaded down her cheeks. There had been another woman in Franklin's life! Why had he never told her about Rebekah? He had said he had planned to marry her. Her engagement ring had been too large for her finger. Franklin hadn't mistaken her finger size but originally had the ring made for Rebekah! What a fool she had been to trust him! She heard the sound of someone walking up the staircase. Elsa rose from the floor, sniffed her nose, wiped the tears from her eyes, and turned to face whoever approached her. A crowd of visitors peered up from the entranceway. How much had they heard? The last thing she ever wanted to do was to give anyone a reason to gossip. "Elsa?" Juliette asked, climbing a few more steps. Elsa shook her head with a sniff of her nose. "What's wrong?"

"He... Did you know?"

Juliette climbed to the landing, placed her hands on Elsa's forearms and looked deep into Elsa's eyes. "What happened?" she asked in a motherly tone.

"I don't know what happened between her and Franklin."

"Elsa, what are you talking about?"

"Rebekah!"

"Yes. We all knew of his plans to marry her."

"No one ever told me the truth."

"I had hoped Franklin would have told you."

"He didn't! He kept it from me. What other secrets is he keeping from me?"

"I promise you, Elsa, my son loves you and not her. Now what happened between you two?"

"I told him how Cora stepped on my shoulder at school."

"She did what?"

Elsa nodded. "After I fought with Nathan she came to our wagon while I was alone. She stepped on my shoulder and told me to remember that pain. If I didn't break up with Franklin she'd kill me. Franklin said he knew of the plans she spoke of then told me. He told me about Rebekah but that she didn't mean anything to him. He told me when he fell in love with me it was the worst feeling he ever had in his life. He keeps talking about it as if I'm a horrible person who made him fall in love with me and stole his heart away from her," she cried harder into Juliette's chest.

Juliette rubbed her hand along Elsa's back. "Shh, Elsa, I'm certain that's not the meaning he is trying to convey to you."

"He didn't even care that Cora threatened my life!"

"I'm certain if he understood she had done so he would have reacted. Franklin loves you."

"Then why is he doing this?"

"He's trying to be honest with you but you do not understand his words. Rebekah means nothing to him anymore." Juliette sighed, turning her gaze towards the group of visitors. Gideon mingled with several visitors. He glanced up at her. Husband and wife exchanged knowing glances. Gideon nodded his head, walked quickly through the crowd, and then ascended the stairs.

"How upset is he?" he asked them.

"I don't know," Elsa whined. "I told him to shut up but he wouldn't stop talking. I left him alone."

"Elsa claims Cora threatened her life," Juliette replied.

"What did Franklin do when he learned of it?"

"Nothing. I don't think he understood what she was trying to tell him."

"I'll speak to Cora when we return home. Right now, I'm more concerned about Elsa and Franklin. Let me enter the room, assess his behavior, and then you ladies may join us when he is calm. Get her something to eat in the meantime."

Juliette escorted Elsa down the stairs as Gideon entered Elsa's room. "Cora wants him to marry Rebekah and not me," Elsa said after a moment of silence passed.

"Yes, it would make sense my daughter would want that for him."

"Why?"

"Because Rebekah is her best friend. When the girls were younger Cora and Rebekah thought it would be a great idea if they married each other's brother. They vowed to each other they would do whatever possible to make certain their brothers married them. Hayden and Franklin thought it was a great idea. When Hayden came of age he courted my daughter one time then broke up with her. He said it felt as if he was dating his sister. It broke Cora's heart."

"But she has a boyfriend now. Isn't he a wealthy attorney in Cleveland?"

"Yes and he plans to marry her next spring."

"Then why would she be so preoccupied with Franklin?"

"Because before Rebekah left for Indiana Franklin had asked her father for permission to marry her."

"He told me Rebekah's father said he could propose to her in two more years."

"That is true. They are courting." Elsa stopped in the hallway and started at Juliette. "Franklin hasn't asked for her yet. He has her father's permission to do so in two years but hasn't asked her yet to marry him."

"He did the same thing to me," she sobbed.

"No, Elsa. He was going to ask you to marry him. My son has his heart set on making you his wife. That is what upsets Cora. Don't start to think my son does not love you more than he loves Rebekah. What Franklin and Rebekah have is a childish lust. I love the girl as if she was my own but Rebekah is not a good match for my son. You, my dear, are better suited for him. I feared the day he would marry Rebekah."

"Why?"

"Because Rebekah does not have the patience nor the consideration to deal with the many nuisances Franklin possesses. You would make Franklin a better wife because you have unconditional love for him. Do not worry about Rebekah, Elsa. My son loves you. What Cora wants and what Franklin needs are two completely different matters. Franklin knows this. You have nothing to fear."

Home of
Judge Liberty and Deborah
Watkins
Marion, Ohio

Oren sat quietly in the Queen Anne chair beside Deborah's bed and watched her sleep. For days he had sat by his daughter's side contemplating the words he had wanted to tell her. He loved her but couldn't support the decisions she had made for her own life. What Christian parent could? How could Deborah not understand how her decisions affected not only her life but the lives of her entire family as well, especially Margaret and Elsa?

His heart had broken when he learned of Deborah's failed pregnancies and the death of her baby, but he knew it had to be God's way of getting her attention. The bible had been explicit! Paul had stated in 1 Corinthians 6:18, "Flee fornication. Every sin that a man does is without the body, but he that commits fornication sins against his own body." Deborah and Liberty had both sinned against their bodies years ago. Oren had tried to save his daughter from the monster Liberty was but Satan had dug his claws deep into his daughter. Deborah had left to marry Liberty. It didn't matter if Deborah had married Liberty or not, a sin was still a sin. Worst yet, Deborah had left her Methodist faith to become Catholic. If God has seen fit to take life from Deborah's womb then so be it. Maybe that was the only way to get her attention. But for Liberty to consent to his wife never being able to bare children again. That was uncalled for! Who was he to have played God? Liberty's father had stolen life from his family in the Civil War, now his son had stolen Deborah's God-given right to bear children.

He thought about his daughter's condition. Although he had been by her side, Deborah's fever had been so high she never knew he had been there. The last time he had ever seen her with a fever this high was when the influenza had struck his home. Deborah had remained strong while he, Margaret, and her siblings had fallen weak from the illness. Deborah had ignored her bout of influenza and pushed herself to care for them all. She had always had the servant heart. Never looking out for own welfare, but for those whom she cared about instead. Determined and stubborn, it had been hard to reason with her some days, just like Henry. That was definitely a trait they got from their mother.

Oren rose from his chair and sat on the bed beside her. He replaced the dry cloth on his daughter's forehead with a wet one from the basin of water. She arched her neck, moaned, and then fell silent. Oren took her temperature with the back of his hand. Her high fever had broken late last night and had only begun to slowly fall this morning. Betsy had told him it was a good sign. Deborah would live as long as the fever continued to descend but if it ever raised again then Deborah's life would once again be in danger. Live. What kind of life was Deborah living away from her family? The anger and bitterness of her betrayal against the family had soured in his heart for years. The more children he had lost during the years the more he had tried to hold onto the ones he had left. Deborah was no exception. If she had never married Liberty she wouldn't be in this predicament in the first place!

"Lib," Deborah whispered with a parched throat, her eyes closed. Oren removed his hand. He thought he had seen her lips move. If she had spoken he had not heard it. Her chest rose and fell with every shallow, quick breath she took. "Liberty," she repeated, tossing her head from side to side.

"Deborah," he called to her, gently guiding her head to face him. Deborah slowly opened her eyes. She gasped at the blurry image of her father then cringed. "Pa? What are you doing here?"

"Jesse called and told me you were dying. Why wouldn't I be here? I may not agree with the way you conduct your life but you will always be my daughter," he stressed the last part.

"Hmm, you have three grandchildren too."

"Yes, I have yet to meet them."

"You don't accept them?"

"They are your children. That makes them my grandchildren. I accept them but I am more concerned about your fate at the moment than theirs." Deborah cringed again, holding her hands to her stomach. She arched her head back, breathing through the pain. "Deborah," he said, grabbing her hand.

"Pain. I feel different. Something is different with me," she said with a parched throat, turning to face him. Oren ignored his daughter as he poured a glass of water. He laid the pitcher down, grabbed two pills from the glass bottle of Aspirin, and then helped his daughter. "Take these," he said, handing her the two round white pills.

"What is it?"

"Aspirin. It's for the pain. Take them with the water. Betsy said you would feel pain and discomfort for a time."

Deborah placed the two pills in her mouth then sipped on the water. She swallowed the last of the water then laid her head down. "Thank you," she replied.

"You're welcome."

"Where's…?" Deborah closed her eyes then fell silent. A few moments of silence passed between them.

"Deborah," he called to her, putting the glass down.

No response. His heart skipped a beat. Had his daughter died too? Deborah couldn't die. Betsy had said as long as the fever continued to fall Deborah would be fine. What if she had been wrong? How many more times was he to witness the deaths of his own children? He tapped her on the cheek. "Deborah, wake up. Speak to me again."

Still she did not move or make a sound, at least none that he could hear. He stared at her weak body. The look of death came upon her. He had been partially deaf for years from his service in the Civil War, operating the cannons. Maybe she had said something to him but he didn't hear it. "Deborah," he shouted, grabbing the side of her face. She still did not reply. Oren placed his two fingers under her jaw and felt for a pulse. It beat fast. He breathed a sigh of relief. His daughter was alive, just overcome with fever.

A knock on the door startled him. He moaned with annoyance. Ever since he had arrived, Jesse had wanted an audience with him. He knew what his brother had wanted from him. How could he not? They had been together their entire lives until the day he had moved to Marion County with his wife and children. Oren loathed the thought of Jesse and Betsy being around his daughter. His children didn't need to know about his family. Oren had thought a lot about what little he had known about his parents and the stories his older siblings had told them. Oren's grandfather had been born and raised in the home of a Revolutionary War general. His grandfather had traversed throughout the wilderness west of the Appalachians, leaving his wife and children in New York State. The family had surrounded his grandfather's wife and children, yet the fact remained his mother and her siblings didn't have their father in their lives. When his mother came of age his father had proposed marriage to her. They wed then decided to leave New York in order to start a new life for themselves in Ohio. Oren's mother had refused to tell them much about both sides of the family. Perhaps it had been for the best. If his grandfather had abandoned his family to traverse around the wilderness, perhaps that was only a symptom of the dysfunctional environment his mother's people came from. Who knew what kind of people his father's family were. His parents had cut all ties from their family, raised a family of their own, only to leave their children stranded after their deaths. The sins of his forefathers had been upon them. Seemed to him, the sin just kept spreading to his generation, especially since the Civil War. That war had changed everything for the worst. His life and the lives of his siblings grew harder after the war. Why should he have to subject his children to the effects of his grandfather's sins?

"Oren," Jesse said from behind the door.

"Go away," Oren replied.

"We should talk."

"There's nothing to talk about."

"Oren, please, open this door. You and I need to talk brother to brother. We made a pact, remember. When ma died, we promised we would all stick together. You, me, Moses, Carlisle, and Lucas."

"Lucas is dead. And we made that pact so the town council wouldn't decide to split us apart from our sisters since we were orphans. As for Moses, he means nothing to me anymore. I meant my words to him," Oren exclaimed as thoughts of his younger sisters came to the forefront of his mind. Oren had to quickly become a man the day his mother died or risk the county taking away his sisters who were younger than sixteen. He and his brother knew nothing about raising a newborn, toddlers, and young girls.

Thankfully he and his brothers had their older sisters to help them.

"Oren, you're the one who stole Margaret from Moses, not the other way around. Please, open this door!"

Oren rose, walked to the door, and then swung it open. Jesse leaned on his crutches with a look of authority on his face. "Call him," he ordered his younger brother.

Oren slammed the door in Jesse's face then walked back to his chair. Jesse huffed. He opened the door and walked into the room. "Why does everyone act as if I am the guilty one when you know what Moses did to my wife," Oren asked, hearing his brother close the door behind him.

"That should have been between Moses and Margaret, not you. Call him and tell him his son is dead."

Oren huffed, "Don't need to. I told Margaret to call him when she visited this morning. Don't know why though. That man hasn't spent a day in Henry's life let alone help Margaret in any way. You would have thought Moses would be man enough to accept he had gotten Margaret pregnant before marriage! But no! He didn't want to marry Margaret as long as Margaret had a daughter to raise. Damn it, Jesse, the war made Margaret a widow and left her with a six-year-old daughter. Moses knew that when he started the relationship with her. I had no problem calling her daughter mine. Broke my heart when her daughter drowned in the lake on the day my twins were born."

Jesse nodded. "I know, Oren. No matter how you feel about what Moses did he was still Henry's father." He grabbed the edge of the footboard and peered at Deborah. "How is she?" he asked.

"She awoke a few moments ago then fell back to sleep. She's exhausted from the fever. I thought she was getting stronger but I think not anymore."

"Have you sent for my wife? She said if there were any changes in Deborah's condition to let her know."

"No, Deborah just needs her rest."

"Poor girl. Does she know you are here?"

"Yes, but she's too weak to argue with me."

"You want to argue with her?"

"No."

"Did you tell her about Henry?"

"No."

"Oren, have you ever thought to consider the feelings you have against Deborah and Liberty are not for them but for the anger you hold for Moses and General Watkins?"

"Humph, you have some nerve," Oren grunted, sitting in his chair then crossing his arms over his chest.

Jesse walked to the other side of the bed and sat down in a chair. He spoke as he lowered his crutches to the ground. "Your displaced anger is destroying your family."

"I'm not angry and you need to stop acting like the eldest brother! Lucas was that and he's dead because of General Watkins. Carlisle is older than you but we all had to treat him as the youngest because of the sufferings he had that occurred at Andersonville Prison," Oren yelled.

"Carlisle is blind from when the rebels tortured him and he has many health problems due to the starvation he endured while he was confined at Andersonville. He will always need our help, Oren, but he has not lost his senses. He still thinks and acts like an adult. He cares deeply for all his brothers, not just Moses or me. He loves you and still desires to protect his younger brothers even in his old age."

"Things changed between all of us. We are not the same boys who entered that war."

Jesse said, leaning over, "What happened to the bond we had?"

"Moses happened! And you weren't there to help me when I needed you the most. So I made the only decision I could without your advice."

"I can't deny I was not there for you when I should have been. I'm sorry."

"You were addicted to morphine until you replaced that addiction with cocaine. What does your wife have you on now for the pain?"

"I've been off the cocaine for a year and a half. She discovered marijuana is a safe alternative for pain relief. I will not lie to you, Oren. I was not a good brother to you after the war. I could not deal with the nightmares, pain, and addiction. But I am here now."

Oren leaned back in his chair and peered at his brother. Two years apart in age, he and Jesse had always been close as children. Jesse was ambitious. Their father had once said Jesse was born to be a leader of some sort. Jesse had always wanted to spend more time with their older brother instead of him and Moses. Ten years his elder, Carlisle had entertained his younger brother's ambitious desires to be a man among men. But Lucas never did. "Everyone misses you, Margaret, and the children. Whenever you wrote of a new child being born our sisters wanted to be with Margaret. You shouldn't have had to face the influenza and the death of your children alone. We had always been there for all of you before you left for Marion County."

Oren answered, "It was better this way. Margaret couldn't handle seeing the remains of the house, nor our children's graves. If we had been in Vernon Township when the influenza…" Deborah moaned, grabbing her stomach, and began to roll on her stomach. "Stop, lie still. Let the aspirin work," Oren gently guided her onto her back by her shoulders. Her head fell to the left with a cringe on her face. "Shh," he coaxed her as he stroked her head. "Lie still, Debs, go to sleep and the pain will go away." Deborah fell silent. Oren pulled the sheet up his daughter's chest.

"Elsa is a lovely girl," Jesse said, changing the subject.

Oren lifted his eyes at hearing Jesse's remark. He leaned back in his chair with a curious look on his face. "When did you meet her?" Oren asked his older brother.

"She's downstairs with her beau." Oren began to rise from his chair. "Oren, my wife is examining her shoulder."

"There's no need. It was dislocated. I put it back into its proper location under Margaret's guidance and Doctor Riley said she is to be careful with it."

"She was complaining of pain while I was speaking to her."

"You know Margaret was a nurse in the Civil War at the hospital at Camp Dennison. She was your nurse, after all! Then when you were discharged she was Carlisle's nurse. That woman has healed more people in this family than before you ever married Betsy!"

"I'm not saying she isn't an excellent caregiver. Elsa was in pain when she arrived. Betsy offered to help her. Please,

Margaret's a wonderful nurse. I don't mean any disrespect. Lord knows if that woman is strong enough to handle the horrors she saw in that war she was strong enough to learn from them too."

Oren nodded with a clenched jaw. He stared at the door then back to Jesse. "My little girl," he nodded towards the door.

"Betsy said the trip in the wagon probably aggravated her shoulder. Franklin had been trying to hold her still and gently guide the wagon towards the house but each bump in the road brought her pain. My wife wanted to ensure Elsa hadn't done more damage with the trip here."

"Why is she even here to begin with? She should be resting in her bed."

"Probably to visit her sister."

"I forbade her from ever doing so."

Jesse peered at Deborah, turned to his brother and arched an eyebrow. "Obviously your children don't listen well. Hmm, much like their father."

"Huh," Oren huffed, crossing his arms over his chest. "You should talk. I seem to recall you got into more trouble with Lucas than I ever did after father died."

"Eh, we were just boys. Oren, brother, please sit down and speak to me in a civilized manner. I no longer have the drug-induced outbursts. We can speak together as rational men."

Oren glared at his brother for a long moment. He lowered his arms and walked to his chair. "How are you and Betsy? I see you have a daughter close to my Elsa's age."

Jesse chuckled, "I have twelve children. She is one of my middle children. My son is attending medical college. Some of his brothers and sisters have gone with him to live with family in Pennsylvania."

"I thought you couldn't have children."

"So did we. We found out it was a side effect from the morphine and not a physical problem. I am very capable of having children."

"How did you come to figure that out?"

"A few months after I was on the cocaine my urges returned. Betsy and I weren't expecting it. I couldn't control myself, went to her office and took her as my wife in one of the examination rooms. Every day since my urges would return and we'd remedy the situation. Betsy began to notice my urges came only after I would reach a high on the cocaine. She knew what time I took my dosage so she would time how long it took for me to reach a high. Then she made certain to make herself available to me at those moments. We were together sometimes three, four times a day. I'd get her with child, she'd deliver then we'd conceive right away. I can't recall her not being with child for a good twelve years of our marriage. It's amazing she ever found the time to practice medicine. The hardest part of my addiction was when she was too pregnant to be with me. My excitement levels were higher than normal and I couldn't control them. I was anxious too. So my father-in-law and Betsy decided it was for the best if they hired prostitutes to ease my dilemma. I went right back into the habits you, me, and our brothers had established with the whores that entertained us during the war, even had Carlisle join in the fun with a girl and me just like old times. That just led me back to the addictions I had in the war with the orgies and pornography."

"And now?"

"I can no longer entertain those temptations. Betsy gave birth to our youngest son two years ago. After that we have not been able to conceive."

"I thought things were well."

"They were but after I withdrew from the cocaine we discovered the drug had an adverse effect. The marijuana increases my need to have relations but I can no longer finish what I begin. I often leave my wife wanting for more than I can give her."

"Oh, Jesse."

"It has caused some problems in my marriage but we are working on a solution. That is not something we should be discussing. As I said, I am not the man I was when you left the family. I want to be the brother you and your family need."

Oren nodded. Deborah cried in her sleep, clutching her stomach. She tossed and turned with agonizing pain. Oren rose from his chair and sat beside her.

He grabbed her by the shoulders and pulled her towards him. "Shh, Deborah," he coaxed as he tried to stop her from fidgeting.

"It hurts. Oh, God, it hurts," she panicked, opening her eyes.

"Where?" Jesse asked. Rising from his chair, he grabbed the side of the bed, lunged to it, and then sat beside her.

"Everywhere," she cried in his direction then froze.

"Deborah?" Jesse asked. She arched her neck back, pressed her hand to her forehead, clutched her stomach, rolled to the side of the bed with a long groan, and leaned over the side of the bed. Deborah hung over the side with her right arm hanging over. She stared at the floor with a grimace on her face. Sweat poured from her face.

"Pa, I..." her body went limp as it began to fall over the side of the bed.

"Deborah," Oren yelled, picking her up. He cradled his unconscious daughter's limp body. Oren tapped her on the cheek. "Deborah?" Nothing. The brothers exchanged glances. Oren grabbed her by the chin and lifted her face to meet his. "Deborah Grace Garrett Watkins, speak to me!" Still nothing. Oren lowered his daughter to her bed with tears forming in his eyes. "Baby girl, don't do this to your mother and me," he yelled, clutching the side of her face then lowering his ear to her nose and mouth.

"Anything?" Jesse asked.

Oren shook his head. "If she's breathing I can't tell."

"Check her pulse."

Oren placed his fingers underneath Deborah's jaw. He closed his eyes, paying close attention. "I can't feel a heartbeat nor hear her breath."

"Allow me," Jesse offered, moving towards Deborah. Oren moved away from his daughter, allowing his brother to lay his ear close to Deborah's nose. Oren rubbed his hands down his face. One child dead and now another? It was just like when the influenza had stricken his farm. When was all of this going to end?!

"Oren," Jesse called softly to him as he rose over her. Oren turned to face his brother. "I checked her pulse and her breath. I..."

"...she's dead?"

"Betsy will have to verify but I think so. I can't feel either. Oren, I am so sorry."

Oren rose from his chair and pounded his fist on the door that separated Liberty's room from Deborah's. "It's not your fault, it's his," he yelled, pointing towards Liberty's room. "Damn this family to hell! I tell you! They took Lucas from us and now they took my daughter. How many more lives from our family must they take from us?!"

"You need to calm down. "

"Calm down! My daughter just died because he got her with child!"

"What if we are mistaken? What if she is alive but we can't tell. Let me get Betsy to examine her to be certain," Jesse said, reaching for his crutches.

"No, you said she is with Elsa."

"Yes."

"Where?"

"In the front parlor."

"I'll go," Oren replied calmly, staring at his daughter's frozen expression. "I can get to her faster than you."

"Oren, you're in no position to be around people. Henry is dead and Deborah may be as well."

"You said you wanted to be the older brother I need?"

"Yes."

"Then stay with my daughter."

"Go."

Oren ran out of the bedroom.

11

Elsa sat on the Queen Anne sofa in the formal parlor holding a glass of water. She peered up at the grey-haired woman who was handing her two Aspirin. "These should help with the pain," Betsy said as Elsa placed them in her mouth.

Elsa stared at the closed door barring Franklin from entering the medium-sized room. She wondered what her beloved was doing while he was away from her. Franklin never liked being alone with strangers, especially in unfamiliar places. She thought about the trip to Marion. After his parents had calmed both of them down Franklin and Elsa had left for Deborah's house. The entire trip had been healing for both of them and had only reaffirmed to her that she needed to help Franklin even more. She could see the hurt and confusion in his eyes. It wasn't a matter of Franklin not wanting to break up with Rebekah. It was more a matter of him having to accept the change of feelings from Rebekah to her. No matter how much Franklin wanted to make Elsa his wife he was going to have to accept that his plans had changed. That was the hard part. She had no choice but to seek aid from Betsy and Liberty. It didn't matter which girl Franklin married, he would still be prohibited from marriage in Marion County as long as everyone believed he was either insane or had epilepsy. She had to proceed with her plans. Yet how could she have been so inconsiderate? Here she was keeping her plans a secret from him when he had done the same to her. But she had to keep it all to herself. Franklin couldn't handle the truth. "Elsa," Betsy called to her.

Elsa turned her attention to her aunt. "Aunt Betsy? May I call you that? Aunt Betsy?"

"Of course. I am Jesse's wife and he is your father's brother. That makes me your aunt."

Elsa smiled, handed the empty glass to Betsy, turned to her right side where Henry's journal lay beside her, and tried to reach for it. "Let me," Betsy said, lowering the glass to a table, and then she picked up the large book and began to hand it to Elsa.

"Open it," Elsa said.

"What is it?"

"Portia gave it to me today. She said Henry would want me to have it."

Betsy peered at her niece then complied. She flipped through the pages, paying particular attention to Henry's notes and the photographs in Henry's journal. She paused at the family photo of her, Jesse, their children, Henry, Portia and their sons. "I remember when this was taken. Have you seen it?"

Elsa peered over and stared at her brother. "No," she whispered. "I miss him. He was more than a big brother to me. It never mattered we were so far apart in age. Henry treated me as if I was his own daughter. Sometimes I'd forget he was my brother and go to him if I had a question I couldn't ask pa."

"Henry was a good man."

"I miss him."

Betsy nodded then continued to flip through the pages. She paused at a birth certificate with her signature on it. Betsy sighed then sat beside her. "It pained me greatly to learn of his death. Henry was a good man. Jesse and I had enjoyed getting to know him, his wife and stepson. We would do anything to help him."

"Would you do anything to help me?"

Betsy closed the journal and shifted so she faced Elsa. "Did you ask me to examine you because you were in pain or because you were afraid to ask me what you really want to ask?"

"How did you know?"

"Henry spoke a great deal about all his brothers and sisters when he visited us. He once told me you look and act like your father."

"I hope I don't. Father can be bitter and cold-hearted."

"His heart hurts, Elsa. The Civil War changed him and his brothers. Life only grew worse for them afterwards."

Elsa pulled the picture of her father and brothers in their Union Civil War uniforms from the journal. "I recognize my father and Uncle Jesse, but who are these other men?"

"May I?" Betsy asked extending her hand towards the picture. Elsa handed it to her.

"There are names on the back in my father's handwriting. He

claims they are his brothers but I don't know them."

Betsy flipped the photograph to the back, read the writing, and then turned it back to the front. She sat on the couch next to her niece and explained, "Your father and his brothers entered the Civil War as Union privates in the Ohio 117th Heavy Artillery Unit on September 14, 1862 at Camp Dennison. They were too poor to ever have a photograph taken."

"Then how did my father have this one?"

"The day they enrolled many of the soldiers had been talking about them. It wasn't unheard of for family members to enlist in the war. Many men left their homes to join in the fight. What was so unique was that your father and his brothers all served on the same side. Not only that, they had insisted they remain together and share the same tent. There was a photographer there that day to document the war efforts at Camp Dennison. When he heard about your father and his brothers he asked if he could photograph them. The brothers had agreed as long as he gave each of them a copy of the photograph. The boys sat in front of that camera for six hours."

"Six hours!"

"It takes an hour for a photograph to be made. You have to remain very still or the picture will be ruined. That's why no one ever smiles in a photograph. Could you imagine smiling for an hour?"

"No."

"Every brother has one of these. Jesse doesn't like for me to look at it in his presence."

"Why not?"

"He says it reminds him too much of the day he lost his leg, Carlisle's capture, and his brother's death."

"Who's Carlisle?"

"Ah, see this man here," she pointed to the man. Elsa stared at the unfamiliar man in the back row. "That's Carlisle Garrett. He's the oldest surviving brother. He was in his twenties when he joined the army. Carlisle was strong, vibrant, and stubborn. He kept all his brothers in line but when they had downtime he was the practical joker who enjoyed teasing his three younger brothers. He was quite handsome and charming. There wasn't a girl anywhere they went who didn't take notice of him. But the war changed all that."

"How?"

"He was captured by rebel soldiers at the Battle of Strawberry Plains in Tennessee. Jesse had tried to save him but as he ran towards his brother the rebels shot my husband in the leg."

"He lost his leg from that battle?"

"Yes. After the battle the surgeon had no choice but to amputate. He sedated my husband and removed his leg as your father held him down."

"My pa saw that?"

"He screamed the entire time too. That wasn't unusual though. Most of the time when you heard screaming it didn't come from the patients but the ones who were witnessing the amputations. The patients usually screamed after they woke up and took notice of their missing limbs."

"I never knew pa saw that."

"Your father saw more than that on the battlefield, as did his brothers. They just don't like to talk about it and you can't blame them for that."

"What happened to Uncle Jesse after the surgeon took his leg?"

"He was taken by the hospital wagon to the hospital in Knoxville, Tennessee. There wasn't a day that went by either your father, Lucas, or Moses wasn't by his side. A week later, he was transported to Wheeling Hospital in Wheeling, West Virginia and his brothers had to continue with the war without him. My father was stationed at Wheeling Hospital as a Union physician. There he met Jesse. A few months later, the army transferred my husband to the hospital at Camp Dennison where your mother was his nurse in the amputation unit."

"My mother was a nurse in the war?"

"You never knew?"

"No, my parents don't speak much about their past and we're never allowed to ask questions. My ma knows a lot about medicine and healing but it never had occurred to me she was a nurse."

"She's an excellent one."

"You said Carlisle is alive. Where does he live?"

"With Jesse, me, and our children."

"But you said he had been captured by the rebels. How did he return to Ohio?"

"Your father and the remaining boys searched everywhere for their brother during the war every chance they got. But the rebels kept Carlisle on the move, taking him from one prison camp to another. I don't know much about his experience. He rarely speaks of it. I do know at least one time he had escaped from his captors. There was a battle nearby and he thought he heard his brothers calling his name. Carlisle managed to free himself and ran towards the battlefield. Just before he could crest the rise separating him from his brothers one of the captors had managed to catch up with him. He tackled Carlisle. They skirmished, the rebel hit him in the head with his rifle and took him back to the camp."

"Then what happened?"

"I don't know. A year later, Carlisle was reunited with his brothers when he was part of a prisoner exchange. The rebels gave six of their weakest prisoners in exchange for one of their officers. When Carlisle was rescued he was so malnourished you could see his bones. His eyes had been gouged. He had burn marks on his feet and hands. The doctors took him immediately to the hospital in Knoxville. He was reunited with his brothers a months later at Camp Dennison's hospital. After the war he was still suffering mentally and physically. Your father and his brothers felt it was best if they committed him to the Athens Hospital for the Insane in Athens, Ohio. Four days a week, one of the brothers would be there to visit him. Every visit Carlisle would plead with them to free him. But your father and his brothers ignored his pleas. They began to notice new marks on Carlisle. They would ask the nurses about them but the nurses would only say Carlisle had been doing it to himself. The patients were responsible for all the manual labor on the grounds, including the gardening, farming, and household duties. They had tried to teach him how to care for himself but Carlisle wouldn't comply with their instructions. The doctors claimed Carlisle's mind had suffered severely not only from the blindness but also from his captivity in the war. They had tried to cure his mental ailment with hydrotherapy but it only made Carlisle worse. In his mind he was being tortured by the rebels and not being treated by doctors. After none of the treatments worked the doctors called your father and his brothers into his office to discuss performing a lobotomy on Carlisle."

"Lobotomy?"

"It means the doctor wanted to open up Carlisle's head and remove part of his brain. "

"And did they agree to it?"

"No, quite the opposite. They removed their brother from the hospital and brought him back to Vernon Township. Carlisle gave his younger brothers several harsh words on the way home. Jesse once told me that was when he knew Carlisle wasn't insane. He was treating them like the children he had always seen them as."

"Where was Lucas? His name is on the back of the photograph."

"Ah, Lucas is this man here. He was the eldest brother. He died in the Battle of Saltville and is buried in Tennessee. Jesse and Carlisle never knew of Lucas' fate until after the war. Oren and Moses thought it would be for the best if their brothers never knew the truth until they were home with their sisters."

"Is this Moses?" Elsa asked, pointing to the man beside her father.

"Yes. He and your father were very close until…"

"…Henry was born," Elsa finished. "Henry's Moses' son isn't he?"

"How did you know that?"

"I overheard my ma talking to someone on the phone about it. Is that why we aren't allowed to be near the family cause Pa stole Ma away from her husband?"

"I think that is a question you should ask your parents," Betsy replied, handing the photograph back to her. Elsa peered at it for several moments then looked up at her aunt. "They won't tell me anything. I was very close to Henry. Portia told me Henry had issues with Pa cause of the way Pa treated him. Why would Pa hold onto Henry so tight and keep us away from our family? It has to do with Moses and Ma, doesn't it?"

"Elsa, I can't tell you his reasoning."

"You can't or won't?"

"It's not my place to divulge the secrets you are after. If you want to know the truths then ask your mother."

"She won't tell me anything without talking to my pa first." Elsa sighed then changed the subject. "You said your father was in the army as one of the doctors. Did you know Uncle Jesse from the war?"

"I was too young to assist my father in the war. I only met your uncle in 1885. After his leg was removed the army gave him morphine for the pain. Jesse grew addicted to it and caused many problems for his family. Your father brought him to my father's clinic to purge him from the addiction. We used cocaine to cleanse the morphine from his body. I was attracted to Jesse the first time I saw him, as he was to me, but the morphine addiction did not allow him to act upon those feelings. After he was discharged from the clinic he returned a week later asking to court me. My father consented and I agreed. Jesse and I went for a walk in the park. It was very lovely until he collapsed."

"Why did that happen?"

"Jesse had inadvertently overdosed. When he awoke in the hospital bed he apologized. He told me he had taken more than his usual dosage because the dose we had given him wasn't alleviating the pain. He wanted to spend a day with me without having to suffer from the phantom pains. My father and I admitted him to our clinic and I oversaw his care until he was discharged. A month later we married."

"So soon?"

"We did not make our decision in haste. My father and I felt it would be better for Jesse if he were under constant care. His family did not have the funds for Jesse to be placed in our hospital for a long duration. My father wanted to offer him medical treatment, room and board pro bono, but he could not do so without the consent of the hospital board. He pleaded Jesse's case to them but they had denied my father's arguments, stating we had plenty of patients who would pay for the same services he had been trying to hand out. There was a waiting list for rooms and we could not deny anyone who had paid for treatment. So my father decided it would be in Jesse's best interest to marry me. We loved each other anyway. If Jesse married me then he could live in our home. Our clinic was downstairs and the hospital was a block away. Jesse would fare better if he were in our environment and not in the county. We married and I have always been by his side since."

Elsa lifted her eyes to the door, thinking about her aunt's story. Betsy had been attracted to Jesse despite the lack of a leg. Most women would take one look at a man without an arm or a leg only to dismiss them as potential husbands. Who wants a man who couldn't work? Sure, there was enough money on pension, but a woman wants a man who will be her provider. She knew what it felt like to love someone whom society had decided to throw away as useless. Many girls wouldn't give Franklin the time of day. Franklin could work. He was the heir of his father's business, but when it came to being around people, Franklin had no social skills whatsoever. Who would want a man who couldn't socialize? She did. He was her strong, silent, wonderful man. Like her aunt she had stayed by Franklin's side throughout his ups and downs because she loved him. If Betsy had done what she claimed then who better to help her? She turned her attention back to Betsy. "I do the same for Franklin."

"You do what?"

"Help Franklin with his problems."

"What kind of problems?"

"Franklin is special. He has a brilliant mind, a sweet disposition, but there are some things he does that, well…that don't make sense."

"Such as?" Betsy asked with the keen interest only a doctor could give. Elsa shrugged her shoulders then cringed. "Don't do that, Elsa," Betsy said, stopping her in mid–action then examining her. "You have to be extra careful with your shoulder."

"Yes, ma'am," Elsa replied.

"Good. You said he is different but you can't tell me how."

"It's kind of hard to describe. Didn't you notice when we arrived how different he is?"

"I was only paying attention to you."

"Oh, well, I'll show you." She rose from the sofa then walked to the door. Elsa opened it, approached Franklin in the hallway, and then led him into the parlor. She closed the door behind them. Franklin stood perfectly straight with an emotionless expression on his face. He gingerly held Elsa's hand. She smiled towards him then began to walk towards the couch. Franklin held her hand tighter then cast his eyes in her direction. She walked back to him and stood before him, laying her left hand on his chest. He gasped with her faint touch. "It's alright. She didn't hurt me," she coaxed him.

"I…I…I don't know her," he mumbled to her.

"She's nice. She gave me something for the pain."

"You said you wanted to see your sister. This is not your sister's room. I do not know why you are delaying what you came here to accomplish. Let's go and visit with Deborah then I can take you home."

"I want to change our plans."

"Elsa," he snarled.

She tapped his chest then rubbed it. "Frank, it's alright. I want my aunt to examine you."

"No. I have a doctor. He is the same doctor we have always used. I don't need a new doctor. I don't…"

"Alright, alright. I won't ask again. I promise. You can stay with your doctor." Franklin shifted his eyes towards the center of the room. Betsy slowly walked towards them. Franklin took a step back. Elsa turned, stepped forward and paused as she felt him grab her hand. She turned to him. "It's alright, Frank. She is not going to harm you or me. Release my hand."

Franklin nodded then complied. She turned back to Betsy, who asked, "Is he always like this?" as she stepped closer to Elsa.

"Only when we are around people he doesn't know. He doesn't like change or strangers. If you change too much at one time it will make him upset."

"Elsa, that is not normal."

"I know. He does stuff like that all the time. He won't make eye contact with you. Sometimes I feel like he is trying to say something to me but he doesn't. It's almost as if his mind can think it but his mouth can't speak it. When we're alone he's fine. He's very gentle, romantic, sensitive, sweet, and charming. He's strong, Aunt Betsy, and he's good to me."

Betsy stepped towards Franklin and extended her hand towards him. Franklin glanced at her hand then lifted his eyes to her. "He doesn't like to be touched," Elsa said, standing next to him.

Betsy lowered her hand. "Sorry. My name is Doctor Betsy Garrett. I'm Elsa's aunt."

Franklin stood silent. Elsa tapped him on his chest. "Tell her your name," she urged him.

"Franklin," he said to Betsy.

"Franklin, what is your last name?" Betsy asked.

"Raymond. My name is Franklin Thaddeus Raymond."

"It is a pleasure to meet you. What do you do for a living?"

"I design machines for my father's store."

"Ah, you're an inventor."

Elsa grinned, "He just designed a new type of sewing machine. His pa's store has been overrun with orders for it. Franklin can fix anything. Can't you, Frank?"

"Elsa, if we are not going to see your sister let's return home," Franklin interjected.

"Franklin?" Betsy asked. Franklin turned his attention to her. "Do you mind if I speak alone with Elsa. I promise I shall not take too long."

Franklin looked at Elsa then back to Betsy. He nodded then walked out of the room. Elsa waited for the door to close then asked Betsy. "See what I mean? There's something not right about him but I find him to be perfect."

"He should be in an asylum," Betsy said with her eyes on the door.

"He's not insane or feeble minded. He's just quiet."

"Elsa, has he ever been violent with you?"

"Never."

"He was clearly agitated when you brought him in here and I approached him."

"That's because he's in a strange place with people he doesn't know. It's worse today for him too because we had an argument before we came to Marion."

"What about?"

"It's nothing, Aunt Betsy. We talked the entire trip to Marion about our quarrel and we made amends with each other. It's been a very long day for both of us. Franklin's not insane, Aunt Betsy. People treat him as if he is a child but he's not. You should understand what it feels like when everyone is against your decision to be with a man when you know deep in your heart he's right for you."

"Elsa, I can tell something is not right in his mind. You can't compare my relationship with Jesse with the one you have with Franklin. Jesse's missing a leg. Franklin's missing social cues. That much is obvious. What concerns me is what is not obvious."

"How can you question our relationship when Uncle Jesse had been addicted to drugs and you wanted a relationship with him even though he was an addict?"

"An addiction is easier to cure than a mental deficiency."

"He's not deficient, Aunt Betsy. He's the most intelligent, caring man I have ever known. I need your help but if you can't see the man I see in Franklin then perhaps you will never grant my request."

Betsy glared at her with a serious look. "Oh, and what would that be?"

"Franklin wants to propose to me but can't do so."

"Why not?"

"He's…well…he's not like any other boy I have ever known. He was supposed to ask me to marry him at the dance but he fell unconscious."

"Unconscious?"

"Something called diabetes made him ill. Doctor Riley said he was also suffering from exhaustion. Franklin woke up but he was still very ill. Then he had a seizure. Doctor Riley claimed the diabetes caused it. Franklin doesn't remember anything that happened from the day he fell ill to when he awoke after the seizure. His pa tells me Frank's been distraught over not being able to ask me to marry him. He says even if Franklin does marry me there would be people who would question the validity of our marriage because people in Marion talk too much."

"And you want me to give an affidavit that he is not an epileptic, insane, or a drunkard?"

"Yes."

"Elsa, I can't do that."

"But why not?"

"First of all, I'm not convinced he isn't insane."

"But he's not!"

"Elsa, your love for him is blinding you from the truth. Even you have admitted there is something not right about him."

"What's the second reason?"

"I would have to examine him before I make that statement."

"Does this mean you will do it?"

"How old is your beau?"

"Eighteen."

"He's a legal adult which means I don't require his parent's permission. When you asked him to allow me to approach him it only agitated him. I don't know how you will convince him to allow me to examine him."

"His father."

"His father?"

"Yes, Franklin will do anything his father tells him to. I've seen it time and time again. Mr. Raymond knows I had wanted to speak to you about his son. He said he would give consent for the examination and any procedures you deem appropriate to help him. I told Franklin I had wanted to come here to visit Deborah but that was only a half-truth. I wanted to meet you. I figured if you could examine Franklin and give me the affidavit then if Deborah convinced Liberty to marry us then after the wedding we would move to Wheelersburg so you can treat Franklin for the diabetes."

"You said Franklin doesn't do well with change. Marriage and then a move, Elsa, that's a lot of changes."

"Franklin's pa said he would help us but only if Franklin and I marry. He doesn't want us to be alone down there unwed and all."

"Neither would I. Very well, how do we get a hold of Franklin's father?"

"Franklin's pa is over at our house helping out with the funeral arrangements. He has to return home today to stay with Abraham."

"Abraham?"

"Abraham is Franklin's younger brother. He had an accident with the harrow while Franklin was supposed to be watching him. The harrow broke, pulled Abraham under and broke his leg. Doctor Riley had to surgically place the broken bone back together again with metal plates. I don't believe Franklin's father would ever be able to leave his responsibilities to come and talk to you here, but I can call him."

"That sounds like a good idea."

"Then you will speak to him about the situation?"

"I will help you on one condition."

"That being?"

"Whatever I deem to be in the best interest of both you and Franklin you will comply with even if I determine he is not suitable for marriage."

"But..."

"Take it or leave it, Elsa. Those are my conditions."

"And you won't tell pa about any of this?"

"I take patient-doctor confidentially very seriously. If you don't want Oren and Margaret to know any of this, then so be it."

"And Nathan?"

"Nobody, Elsa. You have my word."

The door to the parlor opened quickly. Elsa and Betsy peered towards the door; both thinking Franklin had needed something else from them. Instead, Oren walked through the doors. He turned to Betsy then to Elsa. "What are you doing here?"

"I came to see Deborah."

"How did you know where she lives?"

"Pa?"

"Never mind," he shook his head then barked, "Go home."

"Pa?" she asked.

"Do as I say, Elsa. You and Franklin go home, now!"

Elsa peered over at Betsy, quickly grabbed her belongings, and then exited the parlor. She slowly closed the door then leaned her ear against it, listening to her father's conversation. She turned her eyes towards the left, hearing movement. Franklin silently approached her.

"What are you doing?" he asked.

"Something's wrong."

"What?"

"I don't know. Pa's upset. I thought he was upset cause I was here. He told me to go home."

"Then we will go home."

"No, I'm not the reason he's upset. I think it has to do with something else. I can hear him yelling at Aunt Betsy."

"Elsa, he told you to go home. You should obey your father."

"Sh, I want to know what's going on," she whispered to him. Elsa listened closely to the conversation behind the door. She gasped, pulled away from the door, and ran towards the stairs. "Elsa," Franklin yelled after her.

"It can't be," she cried, dropping the journal on the floor.

"Can't be what?" Franklin called from behind her.

"Pa said Deborah died a few moments ago. It can't be." She ran up the stairs, around the top hallway, and burst Deborah's door wide open. Jesse sat beside the bed as a white sheet covered Deborah's body.

"Elsa?" Jesse asked in her direction.

"No," she cried, running to Deborah's bed. She climbed on top of her sister's bed, pulled the white sheet down, and then stared at Deborah's pale face. "No, get up," she cried between her sobs, clutching Deborah's shirt. "Get up, Debs, get up!" Deborah never moved. Elsa sobbed, laying her head on Deborah's chest. She felt someone placing his or her hand on her back. Elsa turned to see Franklin standing over her.

"Come on, Elsa. There's nothing you can do for her. Deborah's dead."

"No," Elsa whined.

Franklin pulled Elsa away from her sister's body. She turned and cried into his strong chest. Franklin gently wrapped his arms around her, letting her cry in his arms.

12

May 10, 1904
Home of
Henry and Portia
Garrett
Harpster
Wyandot County, Ohio

Two funerals she had never wanted to have ever attended. In one solitary week her life had gone from bad to worse. Last Monday, Jesse and Betsy had accompanied her family to Henry's funeral in Upper Sandusky. The entire county had come out to pay their respects to Portia, the children, and her family. As strong as Portia had tried to remain during the entire ordeal, she could no longer contain herself as they lowered Henry's body into the ground. She had collapsed in Sam's arms, overcome with grief. When it had come time for Elsa to throw a fistful of dirt on top of her brother's grave she had just stood there staring at it. It had seemed so final. Once she released the dirt it would be done, gone forever, just like her brother and sister. She had stared at the dirt for what seemed an eternity until Franklin had placed his hand on top of hers. "We'll do it together," he had told her. With his unfailing support she emptied her hand then sobbed on his chest as he held her. The hour-long trip back to her house had been quiet and somber. She had laid her head on Franklin's chest, staring at the scenery as the carriage drove them south. No one wanted to say a word. Henry was gone.

The following day, she had attended Deborah's funeral at Marion City Cemetery with her parents and Franklin. Crowds of people had gathered around Deborah's grave. Elsa and her family had to stand at the very back of the crowd because no one could ever know Deborah wasn't who she had claimed to be. How much Elsa had wanted to be up front with Liberty and his family! She couldn't say her goodbyes before they laid her sister in the ground, let alone see what had been going on without standing on her tiptoes. She would try to peer through the spaces between people but it was hopeless. Not everything was hopeless though. Once again, Franklin had been by her side to show his unfailing support.

After the undertakers had placed the last shovel full of dirt over Deborah's grave, the crowd had made a long line to give their last respects to Liberty and his family. She had waited two hours in line before she was finally able to visit her sister's grave, Liberty, and his family. Full of anger, her father couldn't bare the sight of Liberty and his father. He had just sneered at the men, gathered his family, and then walked away without paying his respects.

The days had passed slowly after they returned to the farm. She had rarely seen Portia. The day after the funeral, her father had dismissed Doctor Riley and allowed Betsy to examine her shoulder. She had removed Elsa's sling and told everyone Elsa's shoulder had healed.

There were new people in her life as well. Carlisle and some of her father's sisters had made the trip north from Vernon Township to help Portia and her family around the house. In any other circumstances she would be elated to get to know her uncles, aunts, and cousins, but now wasn't the time. Thankfully, Jesse and Betsy oversaw all the affairs of the household. Life had returned to the farm, although the somber gloom of death had enveloped her family.

Elsa peered out her window holding one of the black curtains. She watched a carriage leave her driveway while another carriage came down the winding gravel road. Rain descended upon the flat land, adding more gloom to her life. Someone knocked on her door. She lowered the curtain and turned. "Who is it?" she asked.

"Frank." Elsa walked to her door then opened it. She leaned on the door, as it stood ajar. "Good morning," he said, handing her a bouquet of flowers.

She took them from his hands, smelled them, and then smiled. "Thank you."

"You're welcome. I'm sorry I have not been around much since Deborah's funeral. Pa needed me to help him at the warehouse and the farm."

"It's alright. You've done more for me than I could ever ask for."

"I wanted to ask if you wanted to go for a picnic but it's raining so I brought the picnic to you," he said, pulling out a basket full of food from behind his back.

Elsa grinned at the basket then cast her eyes towards him. "Franklin! You shouldn't have."

"I didn't mean to offend you. I'm sorry. I'll leave," he said, turning toward the hallway and beginning to walk away.

Elsa lowered the flowers onto her dresser then walked swiftly out of her room towards him. She placed her hand on his arm and stepped in front of him before he descended the stairs. "Franklin," she said, placing her hand on top of his as he held the basket. "I want to have a picnic with you."

"But you said I shouldn't have."

"I'm sorry. It was an expression. I forget sometimes you don't understand what I am trying to tell you. Please forgive me."

Franklin leaned down and kissed her on the lips. They held each other as they deeply kissed each other with a long, slow, passionate kiss. He pulled away, stroked her cheek with the crook of his finger, and then said. "I forgive you."

"I think I should ask for forgiveness more often if you are going to kiss me like that," she beamed.

He leaned his mouth close to hers and whispered, "You don't have to seek an apology for me to kiss you like…"

"Absolutely not," Oren's voice bellowed from the entranceway below them. Elsa and Franklin turned their attention to the scene downstairs. "Get out of my house," Oren yelled at a slender, salt-and-pepper-haired man who looked similar to him.

"Oren, he was my son. I only want to care for his wife and children," the man proclaimed.

Oren shoved the man into the grandfather clock and slammed his fist into the man's face. The clock shattered as the man lunged towards Oren and pulled him to the ground. A crowd began to gather around them. The women around them screamed. "Moses!" "Oren!" "Stop it!" The brothers didn't pay them any heed. Arms and legs entangled as they continued to wrestle each other. The women and children moved as the men rolled around the small space. Fists flew. Blood spilled. Bones broke. Never before had Elsa seen her father act in such an irresponsible manner.

"Enough," A man's deep voice echoed in the room as Jesse and his twin sister's husband pulled her father and the mysterious man apart. She wondered where they had come from.

"Let me go or I swear I'll knock that fake leg out from underneath you," Oren fought against his brother's grip.

Jesse held him tighter. "No, Carlisle's right. This feud between you two is going to end right here, right now!"

Moses spat blood on the floor and sneered at Oren, "I ain't been the one who started this fight!"

"Oh, you started this long ago, Moses Aaron Garrett," Oren yelled.

"Enough, both of you," Carlisle said in a disciplined tone as he wheeled his wheelchair towards the sound of his brothers' voices. He stopped in front of them, grabbed his cane from beside him, and then rose out of the chair. He walked towards them, moving his long cane side to side until he felt their feet. "Moses," he greeted to the right.

"Good to see you again, old man."

Carlisle chuckled. "And you my young whipper-snapper brother. Sorry to hear about your son."

"Oh shut up, Carlisle! Henry was more my son than his," Oren yelled.

Carlisle swung his cane and hit Oren on the side of the leg. "I don't care who raised Henry, Oren. The fact of the matter is he was and always will be Moses' son. Now do I agree on how he treated Margaret when we learned she carried his child? No! Never! He should have taken the responsibility and become the father Henry needed him to be. But that is in the past. We cannot fix what has been done in the past! Lord knows if we could I wouldn't have lost my sight. I would have run harder towards you that day I escaped and would have evaded that rebel unit I had run into."

The crowd grew silent with tension. "Care to elaborate?" Oren broke the silence.

"No! Leave the past alone, Oren. It's best that way. You two have got to work this out! We made a promise to each other. Look around you, Oren. Most of our sisters stand here to support you. Even the ones we raised on our own. Why bring such conflict into your household when you still have a daughter and a son who need their father?"

"Pa," Elsa said towards them. All eyes turned in her direction. Oren tried to take a step forward but Jesse held him back.

"Let him go, Jesse," Carlisle ordered.

Jesse complied. Oren stepped forward, turned, and then peered up at her. "Elsa, are you alright?" he asked.

"Yes, sir. Are you?"

"I will be. Come down here. I want you to meet your Uncle Moses. Bring Franklin."

"Yes, sir." Elsa turned to Franklin and paused before him. He stood rigid, staring into nothing towards the crowd. "Frank," she said, turning his face towards her as he dropped the basket to the floor.

"I can't," he whispered.

"They are my family."

"Yes and they are why I didn't come to you after Deborah's funeral."

"But you said your pa had work for you to do."

"He gave me extra work in order to keep me from coming here."

"You lied to me? I thought we promised we were not going to keep secrets from each other or lie."

"I didn't want you to know the truth because I was embarrassed."

"You don't need to be. I understand you."

"Elsa, you're not the only one going through a hard time. My father was only trying to protect me from you."

"But why? Your pa said I'm like another daughter to him."

"It has nothing to do with you. It's me. He said I've been exposed to too much in such a short amount of time. I'm having a hard time living with all the changes from day to day. I wanted to come see you but there are so many people around you now. Elsa, there's too many people in your house. It took me an entire day to gather the courage to come to you even now. There are too many strangers. Too many..."

She placed her finger on his lips. "Shh, go to my room. Stay there and prepare our picnic. I'll tell my father you came to surprise me and wanted to set up the picnic for us."

Franklin took her hand, kissed it then whispered, "I love you."

"I love you, too. Go."

Elsa watched her boyfriend pick up the basket, enter her room, descended the stairs, then walked to the brothers. "Uncle Carlisle," she greeted her blind uncle as she placed her hand on his shoulder.

"Elsa," he nodded to her.

Elsa greeted Jesse then turned to her father. "Pa," she said as her aunt's husband released Moses.

Oren placed his arm around Elsa's back then reluctantly presented her to his disheveled brother. "Moses, this is my youngest. Elsa Beatrice Garrett. The young man who was beside her is her boyfriend, Mr. Franklin Raymond. Where is Franklin?" Oren asked her.

"He brought a picnic basket to surprise me and wanted to set it up in my room."

"How romantic," Moses said.

Elsa smiled, "He is that and more, Uncle Moses."

"You are a very fortunate girl to have found a good man."

"Thank you," she replied. "It is a pleasure to meet you. I don't know much about my father's side of the family. I only wish we would have met under better circumstances."

"As I do, Elsa."

Oren guided Elsa away from them. "Go tell your mother Moses has arrived."

"Yes, sir," Elsa said then walked down the hallway. Moses stared at his niece as his sisters one by one came to greet him. He turned his attention to them, exchanged pleasantries, then the women and their husbands scattered, leaving the brothers alone.

"Ah, Oren, I see you still have a mean right cross," Moses said, rubbing his jaw.

"You alright?" Jesse asked his brother.

"Hmm, I will be. Oren?" Moses asked in the direction of Oren.

Oren grumbled as he walked towards the red Queen Ann sofa, held his hand across his chest, and grimaced. He leaned his head back as he closed his eyes. Jesse and Moses exchanged glances. "Oren?" Jesse asked, stepping towards him.

"I think he broke one of my ribs."

"Get Betsy," Carlisle ordered.

Jesse immediately left the room.

"Geez, Oren. Do you know how much Elsa looks like you?

How old is she?" Moses asked, changing the subject.

"Sixteen going on twenty-five. I can't keep up with her."

"Which brings us to another problem," Carlisle added as he sat back in his wheelchair with Moses' help.

"Problem? What problem?" Oren asked.

Carlisle moved his wheelchair closer to the sofa. "I won't discuss it until Jesse returns." Moses grunted. The two brothers glanced towards him. "Moses?"

"Damn, this wouldn't hurt as much if we were younger."

"Sit down," Carlisle ordered.

Moses complied. Sounds of a woman's heels echoed from the hallway. The men turned their attention to the noise. Betsy stopped with her bag in her hand in front of Carlisle. "You two should be ashamed of yourselves, acting like children," she scolded Owen and Moses as Jesse entered the room.

"Nice to see you again, Betsy," Moses grimaced.

Betsy glanced toward her husband then to her two patients. She pulled a white cloth from inside her bag then handed it to Jesse. "Use this to stop Moses' bloody nose while I tend to Oren."

"Yes, dear," Jesse replied, took the cloth, then tended to his brother. Betsy knelt before Oren. She glanced at his hand inside his coat, placed her hand on top of his, and then pushed. "Ugh, Betsy, I know it's broke! Just fix it!" he screamed.

"Just fix it indeed. Don't you think your household has gone through enough heartache and now you only add more by fighting with Moses? Take your coat, vest, and shirt off!"

The brothers chuckled as Oren complied with her desires. Betsy turned to the men. "Think it's funny, do you?"

"No ma'am," Carlisle, Moses, and Jesse replied together.

Betsy turned her attention back to her patient. She examined Oren, wrapped his chest, tended to his other wounds, and then rose. "Your rib is broken and you're quite fortunate that is the only break you have. You have some bruising but only time will tell the severity. I'll ask Margaret to watch over you for a few days and you will need to rest."

"Thank you, Betsy," Oren answered.

"You're welcome." She turned to Moses and began to examine him. Oren and Jesse exchanged glances.

"Oren," Jesse began.

"Don't. Just don't make this any worse than it already is," Oren replied, putting his shirt on.

"Your bitterness is not helping the matter at hand either," Carlisle answered.

Oren glared at his eldest brother. "Bitterness? Isn't that like the pot calling the kettle black? You've held onto much bitterness and regrets since you were rescued from Andersonville and yet you are the one calling me bitter?"

Carlisle clenched his jaw. "Oren, you have no idea the horrors I went through."

"I would like to know."

"So would I," Jesse said.

"I too," Moses said as Betsy worked on his mouth.

Carlisle nodded, "It is not that I do not want to tell you. It's that I don't want to recall and relive those moments."

"And has it ever occurred to you that perhaps by telling them the truth it would release those memories from your head?" Betsy said, lowering a bloody cloth into her bag. She rose from over Moses.

"What's wrong with him?" Carlisle deflected.

"A sprained elbow, broken wrist, and the blow to the jaw broke some of his teeth. They will both have some terrible bruises on their faces, maybe on their torsos as well. I'll want to monitor them for a couple days at least."

"Nothing severe?"

"Not that I can tell. Only time will tell that."

"Good. Leave us, Betsy," Carlisle ordered.

"Yes, Carlisle," she answered, grabbing her bag then exiting the room. Jesse, Oren, and Moses sat quietly, staring at Carlisle. A long moment of tension and silence passed through the room.

Carlisle broke the silence, "We have grown apart from each other ever since the feud between Oren and Moses began over thirty years ago. I don't have a family of my own so I don't know what it means to be a father, but you three do. How foolish were all of you to think that you could start your own families without the support of your brothers and sisters!"

"Now wait a moment, Carlisle. I have the support of our

sisters and you in my marriage with Betsy. I go to you with all my problems; if you can't answer them then I go to our sisters," Jesse answered.

"Forgive me, Jesse, I didn't mean you hadn't. These two bullheaded, prideful, sorry lot of brothers haven't done that."

"Oh, not you too," Moses objected. "I heard enough of this shit from Jesse," he protested as he began to rise.

"Sit down," Oren, Carlisle, and Jesse yelled at him all together.

Moses stared at them with a huff. "You know the only reason I moved to Missouri was to get away from him," he growled pointing to Oren.

"No you married Margaret's sister and moved away so you wouldn't have to face reality. You've always been a womanizing drunk," Oren rebutted.

"Weren't we all in the same war?" Carlisle asked.

"Yes, but we walked away from the life, he didn't!"

"I'm not a drunk any longer," Moses protested.

"So he's just a womanizer, huh," Jesse said.

"How dare you! Aren't you the man who couldn't control himself so you had to not only be with your wife but prostitutes too! How can you judge me when you do it too, Jesse? Huh?"

"We all have our faults, Moses. Sit down," Oren said calmly.

Moses grumbled then sat back beside him. "God I miss Lucas," he said, leaning over his legs with his hands on his face.

"Lucas wouldn't have put up with any of your arguments, addictions, or shenanigans! I miss him terribly too but that was over forty years ago and we all have learned to move on with our lives. The boys we were in the war have grown into men with families and responsibilities of our own. We cannot go back, only forward," Carlisle said in a flat tone.

Moses nodded. "What do you want from us, Carlisle?"

"I want to make certain the mistakes of our past do not continue with our children. Oren has lost eleven children to death and we cannot let this path continue. I think it is only fitting that we should protect Elsa and Nathan."

"I agree," Jesse answered.

"As do I," Moses said.

A long moment of silence passed between the brothers. Carlisle stared in the direction of Oren. "Oren?"

"I moved away from the family to protect my wife and children. The deaths of our children began while we were still among the family. I understand what you are asking from me but I don't understand how that will benefit my family. Margaret is very sensitive. If we return to the land where our children are buried or where our house once stood then it will only further break her heart. She's fragile enough as it is. Besides, I don't have the money to move back."

"We know this," Jesse said.

"How?"

Carlisle answered, "Henry stayed in communication with us even after Betsy saved your family from the influenza."

"He what?! I have told all my children never to contact my family! It was one thing to learn Deborah had done so, but Henry? I thought the only time he ever contacted the family was when the influenza came to our farm. What of Elsa and Nathan? Have they ever contacted any of you?"

"Never," Jesse answered. "Henry wanted to know the truth about why you disowned the family."

"And did you tell him Moses was his father?"

"Never. I told him there was a reason behind it but that needed to be something discussed between you and him. Oren, if you take Moses' offer then it will not only benefit Henry's family but also your own."

"He's right," Carlisle interrupted.

Oren turned his attention to his eldest brother. "What about Elsa? Franklin asked for her hand. If I sell my farm, move back to Vernon Township, Portia sells this farm and moves in with Moses and his family, then Franklin won't be able to marry Elsa."

"Has he asked her yet?" Carlisle asked.

"No, believe me when that boy does Elsa will be dancing around the house, all excited. She hasn't done that yet so that tells me he hasn't asked her."

"Then you can retract your permission."

"And for what reason would I do that?"

"Oren, do you want her to end up like Deborah?"

"Franklin is nothing like Liberty."

"No, he's worse," Jesse interrupted.

The brothers turned towards him. "Are you saying my judgment is off?" Oren accused him.

"It's always been off, Oren. You're idealistic and want to see the good in everyone. Why do you think it was hard for us to convince you to lose your virginity to a bunch of whores in the war…?"

"…oh God not this again," Moses muttered, shaking his head.

"Lucas bought those two women as your birthday present. You were supposed to share them with us and all you could think about that day was saving those poor souls," he sung. "They were whores, Oren. Nothing but whores! But no, you and your bible thumping beliefs ruined that night for all of us. I couldn't have been more grateful when Lucas stole your bible and told those girls to break that stern attitude out of you."

Moses chuckled, "Now that was a night, indeed! Damn best night of sex we ever had, especially when he discovered how much he liked giving into those temptations."

"What we did to those girls was an abomination," Oren growled.

"Ugh," Jesse and Moses groaned in unison.

"We aren't here to argue religion with you, Oren," Carlisle rebutted. "You have to decide. Do you want a better life for your children than the life you have now, or do you want to continue living this hell you have found yourself in? I don't know how much in debt Henry was but we all know the truth. The debt collectors will come. If Henry hasn't left enough money to pay them they will take the house, the household possessions, and the farm. Portia's a widow with a child on the way. She'll have four mouths to feed including her own. She's too old to get a job in the factory."

"Nathan and Samuel said they would work in the factory for her."

"And who is to run the farm?" Moses asked.

"I will."

"Ha, you're on a pension because you can't work with those knees. Admit it, Oren. You need our help and my money."

"I think, Moses, this has nothing to do with you. I would prefer if you would stay out of my children's lives! Better yet, stay out of my life. I've done well on my own since Margaret and I moved to Marion County."

"By what I hear you haven't done well at all," Jesse objected.

"What is that supposed to mean?" Oren questioned him.

"You're in serious debt. The bank is threatening to foreclose on the house in Marion County, and you have debt collectors coming after your farm."

"I can pay if off."

"How Oren?! Henry is dead! Elsa told me everything. Your hearing is worse. Your knees are so bad you can't work. Henry was supporting you and Margaret with the income he made from work. Your crops failed. You lost your money in the recession. You are in so much debt you can't afford any more bills but Henry's medical bills are adding up. Come back to Vernon Township and let us all help you. We have plenty of sisters who miss you, especially the ones we raised after mother died in childbirth. You remember our baby sisters. They used to call you Papa Oren?"

"I've done pretty well for myself in Missouri," Moses beamed.

"Then pay off the debts," Oren yelled at him.

"No."

"Typical, self-centered, egotistical waste of breathe! If you were half the man you say you are then you wouldn't have abandoned your son!"

"Oh, yeah! And if you were half the man you portray yourself to be behind that bible of yours you wouldn't have stolen Margaret from me. Which commandment is that again? 'Thou shall not covet a man's wife!'"

"She wasn't your wife. She was your whore and Margaret hasn't ever been a whore! She deserved better than the mistake she made in sleeping with you. Of course she found that out in our bed. I've had many children with her after those glorious nights she was screaming my name and not yours."

Moses lunged towards Oren. Jesse held his brother back. "Enough, both of you. Sit down, Moses and shut up, Oren," Carlisle yelled. The men grumbled. Moses punched the wall behind the sofa then lowered his fist. He lowered his head between his legs. Tears swelled in his eyes. No matter how much Oren ridiculed him, his brother was right. He had used and abused the women he had loved the most.

"Oren, you were right."

"Excuse me?"

Moses sat upright. "You were right. Okay, I admit it. I messed my life up. I have never been a father I should have been to Henry. I was cruel to Margaret. It took me years to realize the mistake I made in abandoning her and Henry. I know you are upset because you love her. I love her too."

"You married her sister!"

"Only because I couldn't have her. I'm still in love with Margaret. Nothing will ever change that. When my wife and I started making children I never saw her, I saw Margaret. I buried my disappointments with liquor, prostitutes, and gambling that I couldn't afford. No matter what I did nothing ever took away the guilt, hurt, and pain I bore. When Margaret called to inform us of Henry's death we were in the middle of signing our divorce papers."

"Divorce?"

"She left me, Oren. I guess I always knew my marriage would turn out like this. We were married for twenty years and had five children together. She waited until our last child left the house then left me. When she got off the phone with her sister she signed the papers, told me the news, and then my son took her to the train station. She's living in Jackson, Ohio with her parents. I still have my ranch but my children won't speak to me. I figure the least I could do is show mercy, love, and grace to Portia and her children. They are my grandchildren, after all. I'll have a family again."

"No, you'll have rumors running around that you have taken your bastard son's wife, married her, and have taken his children as your own," Oren said.

"He has a point," Carlisle said.

"Then what do you suggest I do?"

"Sell the ranch and buy a farm close to the family. Pay off Henry's debts…"

"And this house?"

"Give it to Franklin and Elsa," Oren answered.

The brothers stared at Oren in disbelief. "Oren?" Carlisle asked.

"That's my answer. I'll sell my farm in Marion County if this house and farm is deeded over to my daughter. She's done well since we moved here and she is very happy with Franklin. If I relocate her she will not do well. I want the best for my little girl."

"That boy is dangerous, Carlisle," Jesse objected.

"You don't know him," Oren objected.

"Do you?"

"He's a good boy, Jesse. He's treated my daughter with nothing but kindness and love."

"He's insane! Betsy told me he should be committed," he yelled, pointing to Elsa's room.

"On what grounds?!"

Jesse lowered his hand. "Oren, I know you want to believe Franklin is a good man to your daughter, but you can't look past your own need to find the best in people and see what is before your very eyes. The boy doesn't talk. He doesn't like to be touched or approached by strangers. He won't look you in the eye. His mannerisms are cold and indifferent. Besides that, Betsy claims Elsa told her he has diabetes. Diabetes, Oren! You've consented Elsa to marry a man who is either a raving lunatic, has a terminal illness, or both. Why, oh please tell me why, would you subject Elsa to a life with a man like him?"

"The boy is productive, smart, and is the heir of his father's business. Elsa has everything to gain and nothing to lose."

"She could lose her life if the boy ever strikes her out of anger," Moses replied.

"I would never consent to him marrying her if I thought he would hit her."

"Truth is, Oren, your children don't care whether you give them consent or not. Deborah and Henry married when you didn't agree with their choices. If Elsa is anything like them she will not listen to you. You need one of us to discipline your children. Jesse's children would never stand against Jesse if they knew we were in agreement over a matter," Carlisle instructed.

"And what would you have me do, beat my son and daughter

into complying with your will? They don't have respect for you because they don't know any of you," Oren said.

"We come at them just as we did to the rebels," Moses said.

"What do you mean by that?" Jesse asked.

"On all fronts," Carlisle answered.

"Exactly, we show Nathan and Elsa there is a new law in the household. If they ever disobey you they will have to answer to all of us. We discipline them as one body and not four separate men. And if Elsa wants to marry Franklin then Franklin needs to prove himself worthy to all brothers, not just you," Moses answered.

"They will rebel at the new rules," Oren said.

"Children always rebel to change. We just have to show Nathan and Elsa they cannot cross the boundaries. The first thing we need to do is get Franklin out of this house," Jesse said.

"Not only will Elsa and Nathan have to live under the new rules but if we are going to protect Portia and Henry's children then his children will have to know we are the rulers of this household," Carlisle answered.

Oren leaned back on the sofa, crossed his arms, and peered at his three brothers. "Why do I feel like you three are treating me as a child?"

"We're not, Oren. We are trying to help you. We do this out of love. You have a say in all matters but it will take unanimous vote for any decision to be made. We made a pact, remember?" Carlisle said.

"That pact was to protect our sisters and each other from ever being separated. The town council did not want us to stay together. Our eldest sister and her husband claimed they would care for all of us but in the end it was us who raised the girls and not her. The only thing she ever did was feed our newborn sister. The diapers, schooling, everything that it takes to raise a child we did on our own."

"Now there's a new generation of Garretts to raise," Jesse said.

"Jesse's right. Had my family and I been closer to him and Carlisle, maybe my family would still be together," Moses said.

Oren turned his attention to him. "If you had been there I would have hurt you long ago for what you did to Margaret and

Henry. You're a threat to my wife and children," he snarled.

"Oren, enough. Moses said his peace. Like it or not he's one of us," Carlisle demanded.

Oren gazed at Carlisle. "We are not the same brothers who made that pact."

"No, but the pact was made to protect all the women and children of our family. Our wives and children are included. The disasters that have fallen upon you do not have to continue with Elsa and Nathan. We care about them because they are your children just as we care about Jesse and Moses' children. Now we have no say over how Moses' children conduct their lives but we can have a say on how yours and Jesse's children fare. We can protect our sisters, our wives, and children together just as we protected our sisters when our parents died. Oren, don't you want the best for your children?"

"I do."

"Then retract your permission for the boy to marry Elsa. If he truly loves her he will fight you for it. Then we shall know what the boy is made of. He will have to answer to all of us," Jesse said.

"We're not saying Elsa will never marry Franklin. We're saying we need time to get to know the boy. It would be in Elsa's best interest if we got to know what kind of husband he will make for her," Moses added.

The sound of women's heels echoed off the hardwood floors of the hallway. Jesse, Carlisle, and Moses stared at Oren. Oren watched Margaret enter the room with Elsa. She gasped when she saw the bandage around her husband's chest. "Oren, what happened?" she asked.

"It's nothing. Moses and I got into a disagreement and…"

"It's wasn't a disagreement Ma, it was a fight, just like the one Nathan and I had," Elsa interrupted.

Margaret glared between Moses and her husband. "There was no need for that, Oren."

"So I've heard," Oren answered with a grimace.

Margaret stared at Moses. Moses rose from his seat, tilted his hat, and greeted her, "Margaret, it's good to see you again."

"And you, Moses. Thank you for coming. Have you met, Elsa?"

"I have. She is a sweet girl, Margaret."

"Thank you. Where is my sister? I thought she would have travelled with you."

"We are no longer married. She moved back to Jackson to live with your parents."

"Oh, I am so sorry to hear that."

"Thank you."

"Would you like to meet your grandson?"

"Enough, Margaret," Oren objected.

Margaret and Moses stared at Oren. Oren tapped his foot, glared at Elsa, then said to Carlisle, "I've been thinking about what we have discussed. I agree it would be best for everyone if we get my household affairs in order." Oren rose quickly. "Elsa," he addressed her loudly.

"Pa," she addressed him.

"Stay here with your mother and uncles. I have some words to say to Franklin," he said as he walked towards the stairs. He quickly ascended the stairs, navigated around the landing, and entered Elsa's room. A few moments later, Franklin burst out of her room. He ran down the stairs.

"Frank?" Elsa asked as she began to walk towards him. Jesse rose from his place, grabbed her by the waist and held her back. She looked down at him. "Let go," she struggled.

"It's for your own good, Elsa. Your father knows what he is doing."

"What did he say to him? Frank needs me!"

"He's retracted his permission for Franklin to marry you."

"No! Frank," she pushed harder against him.

"He's not to be alone with you or visit you without our consent."

Elsa huffed with her eyes on Franklin. He turned, looked at her, and then walked out of the house. "Frank," she screamed, pushing against her uncle. She sobbed. Frustrated, confused she didn't understand why her family would allow this. Why wasn't her mother trying to stop them? Jesse grabbed her by the shoulders. "Elsa, stop," he gripped her hard.

"But why? He didn't do anything," she sobbed.

"Because, young lady, there are new rules in this household. If you want something then you will have to have permission not only from your father but also from all of the brothers. If we do not agree unanimously then you will not have what you want."

"That's not fair! You're not my pa! My pa gave Franklin permission to court and marry me. I was doing just fine without any of you! Let go of me," she yelled, trying to push him over.

"You restored the pact," Margaret muttered in astonishment.

Moses nodded. "We're not doing this to be mean to your daughter or to Franklin. We just want to make certain this outsider is right for Elsa."

"Outsider?" Margaret questioned.

Carlisle answered, "Margaret, have you forgotten what life was like when you lived in Vernon Township? We protect our own. You and Elsa belong to our house, not Franklin. If your daughter wants to marry Franklin then he will have to prove to us all that he will not only provide for and protect his wife and any future children but also obey us. Elsa, Nathan, and Henry's family must learn to obey not only Oren but all the brothers as well. It is in their best interest to do so."

"Or what? I remember how you all treated Oren in Vernon Township when we decided to leave the family. You treated him with the utmost contempt for his decision."

"Oren did that to himself. We have always wanted Oren to return to the family. Take care of your daughter, Margaret, and don't question what your husband has chosen to do. He's made the right decision."

Margaret grabbed Elsa by the shoulder and pulled her back. "Stop it. You stop it, right now."

"But ma, I love him," Elsa turned and sobbed into Margaret's chest.

Margaret held her daughter's face then lifted it. "There's nothing you can do to change their minds. What has been done is done. Your father no longer rules this household alone—they all do. Things are going to change. It's going to take some time for you to get used to the new rules." She turned to the brothers as Oren descended the stairs. "Does he have a chance to redeem himself?" she asked them.

"He does," Oren answered, rejoining his brothers. "But first there are matters within our own household that must be addressed. She will not be allowed to visit him until we say so, nor will he be allowed to visit her. I have told him I have revoked my permission for them to marry. If he truly wants to be her husband then he will prove to us that he is capable."

"He won't understand," Elsa cried.

"He must, Elsa, if he is to marry you," Moses said.

"You don't understand. He's different."

"And that is why we are doing this," Jesse countered.

"We have to make certain he won't harm you," Carlisle answered.

"He's not like that at all," she cried.

"How do you know what he is capable of? Courting a man is different from being married to him. Once you are in his household he'll change," Moses said.

"I hate you! I hate all of you," she yelled at them. "I hate this family! Why can't you be happy for me instead of subjecting more hardships and heartaches on me? This! This is why Deborah and Henry left our family. Ugh! I wish I never wanted to know any of you! I wish you were all dead! Dead! Dead! DEAD," she yelled then stormed out the front door. The pouring rain soaked her as she chased Franklin to the barn. "Stop," she cried, running faster to him. Franklin turned at the barn door. She slid several times in the mud then fell as she drew closer to him. Franklin reached out and grabbed her before she landed. The couple stared at each other as he held her.

"Where are you going?" she asked.

"Home."

"Will you ever return to me?"

Franklin stood silent contemplating her question. Return to her? All he wanted in life was to be with her! "Elsa, your pa said…"

"I don't care what my pa said! I want to be with you!"

"And I you."

"Then marry me Franklin! I know you went to my pa for permission. I know he granted it to you. I know you have a ring for me just as I know you were going to ask me at the dance to marry you!"

"How?" he asked in shock.

"I'm not naïve! I found the ring after you collapsed from the diabetes. We never went to Deborah's so I could see my sister. I went there so she could convince Liberty to marry us and so that Aunt Betsy would examine you. I thought if she examined you then she would write an affidavit to the county clerk stating you were of sound mind and body to marry me."

"Why would you do that?"

"Because you had a seizure and your parents feared once word of it spread in Marion the county clerk would question your intentions to marry me. They would say you must have epilepsy and it's against the law for an epileptic to marry let alone someone who is insane or is a drunkard."

"You had no right!" He argued and began to pace. Elsa watched her distraught boyfriend with a broken heart. This was all too much for her beloved. With every step he made the more agitated he became. She walked towards him crying.

"I'm so sorry. Your parents and I just thought you needed help with proposing to me."

"I would have done it," Franklin yelled, waving his arms.

"When Frank? You were so fixated on proposing at the dance then when you missed the dance you couldn't in your mind ever propose to me."

"Elsa," he snarled. "Why would you lie to me?"

"I wasn't lying to you. I was trying to help you. Marry me, Frank, and we can walk away from my family to start our own. We can fix all of this."

"I can't."

"Yes, you can. Your parents will help us. They want us to marry."

"I can't!"

Franklin sighed with a blank look on his face. Elsa swallowed hard, studying him very carefully. The only sound she heard was the pouring rain. Tension filled the area. She could tell by Franklin's reaction his stress level was dangerously rising to a point he wouldn't be able to control himself. She grabbed his face and kissed him on the lips. Franklin stared down at her, returned her kiss and held her close to him. She laid her forehead on his and whispered. "Don't leave me. Speak to me, Franklin. Can you ever forgive me? I was only trying to do what I thought was best for the both of us. I love you."

"I forgive you. What did I do to your family?" Franklin asked.

"Nothing, it was my fault not yours."

"What did you do to them?"

"I shouldn't have ever told Aunt Betsy about you. You remember when I asked her to examine you?"

"Yes."

"That was the day I told her all about your problems. She had wanted to admit you to an asylum."

"Elsa, I'm not insane!"

"I know, Frank. I argued the same thing with her. She must have told Uncle Jesse everything we had talked about then he told his brothers. Oh, God, Frank, I ruined everything."

Franklin grabbed her face and looked her in the eyes. "I don't know what to do, Elsa. I want to be with you but I don't know what to do."

Franklin hugged her tight against his chest. Their soaked clothes clung to their bodies, showing every curve. He kissed her on the forehead then pulled away. "We can run away," she suggested.

"Your father told me never to come near you again."

"He didn't mean it, Franklin."

"Then why say those words if he didn't mean them? I can't marry you, nor am I permitted to be around you. This is the end, Elsa. I am sorry. I don't want it to be so. I don't understand why it has to be but I have to comply with your father's choice."

Elsa lifted her eyes to meet Franklin. "Take me to your house. Your parents will know what to do."

"I don't even know what to do!"

"Franklin, please." She clutched the lapels of his coat and pulled. "Please, don't leave me! Please," she begged.

Franklin pushed her hands down. "I have to go. I do love you, Elsa. But I don't know what to do. Goodbye," he said in a serious tone and went into the barn.

Elsa fell to her knees sobbing. Not only were her siblings dead but now the love of her life had left her too. She bent over her knees, covered her head with her hands, and sobbed in the pouring rain as Franklin rode his horse away from the farm. The rain washed away what little hope she had left.

Cora ran quickly into Franklin's office, closed the door behind her, leaned her back against the door, and closed her eyes thinking about her day at school. At lunch, she had made certain to give Nathan and Sam her condolences of Henry and Deborah's deaths, although she couldn't care less. She pretended to care about their family. Yet all she wanted to know was how upset was their family at Franklin. Franklin had returned home yesterday in a daze. Her parents had asked him several times what had happened but typical upset Franklin never spoke a word. She could hear him pacing back and forth in his room, sobbing. Several times she had peered inside his room to find him in a distraught state. Her father had tried to work with him, but nothing. He wouldn't eat or talk to anyone. Whatever had distressed him had almost pushed her brother over the edge. Maybe if she was able to, she could completely push him over the edge so far her parents would have no choice but to commit him. No, she couldn't do that. He was her brother. As much as she didn't agree with how her parents treated him she couldn't justify destroying what little life her brother had. Besides, what she truly needed was for him to marry Rebekah not Elsa. She decided to leave Franklin alone.

This morning, Franklin hadn't risen from his bed until breakfast was almost over. He came to the table with his pants on and only one suspender hanging over his shoulder. Disheveled, the only words out his mouth were, "Elsa's pa forbids me to marry her," he had grabbed his food then went back to his room. Delighted, it took Cora every ounce of strength she possessed to contain her elations. Life was perfect! Franklin couldn't marry Elsa and there was no way he could try to convince her father otherwise. The Garrett family was in mourning. Franklin couldn't court Elsa for six months; she couldn't attend social functions or receive visitors. If she couldn't socialize then there was no way she and Franklin could ever attend a dance before Rebekah returned from Indiana. Once again, her plans were back in full motion. All she had to do was remind Franklin he loved Rebekah and not Elsa.

"Cora! Where are you?" Isaiah yelled from the entranceway. Cora opened the door and peered into the reception area.

"What do you want?" she snarled at him in front of the secretary. The secretary peered up from her work at both of them. "I mean, how may I help you," Cora politely addressed her younger brother.

"Mrs. Webster said to tell you we are about to leave for our farm."

"I thought pa was going to pick us up."

"He changed his mind. Franklin finally opened up to him and told him what was bothering him. He told Hayden he and ma were going to Elsa's house to speak to her parents about Elsa and Franklin."

"What for? Elsa's pa won't let Franklin marry her."

"I don't know. That's just what pa told Hayden. Are you coming or not? They can't leave until we get there. He wants Hayden to stay with Franklin."

"I'll be along soon. Franklin wanted me to get something from his office."

"Why would he ask you that?"

"He said he wanted his paper and pen to sketch designs on."

"He has a pad and pen at home. We can get it for him there."

"He said he wanted the one in his office. You know how particular he can be."

"Alright. How long will it take?"

"Not very. Go ahead without me. Tell Mrs. Webster I will be along shortly."

Isaiah nodded then looked at the secretary. The slim woman looked back down at her work. Cora swallowed hard. What if Isaiah hadn't believed her lies? What if he knew she was up to no good? Her heart beat hard with anticipation. Isaiah turned and walked towards the door. "Bye, Cora. Don't be too long. Mrs. Webster said she wanted to make dinner for our family and Elsa's. She requires your help."

Cora grimaced. Kitchen work. She hated cooking and cleaning. Why couldn't her family just hire a servant to do all the household duties instead of relegating her to learn about them? There weren't very many households that had servants. An average American worker could earn anywhere between $200 and $400 a year at $.22 an hour. Her father was a businessman who made more than that any year. While they were middle class, they were one of the rare families to own a bathtub and a telephone. Surely they made enough money to hire at least one servant. "I promise," she called out as he walked out the door. Cora turned on her heel and b-lined it straight into her brother's office. She locked the door behind her then ran to the other side of Franklin's desk. She picked up Franklin's 1900 Tampered Shaft Oil-Can Candlestick desk phone with a brass bottomed cylinder made by Stromberg Carleson and placed it next to her ear. Cora lifted her eyes as a female operator's voice came from the other side.

"What city and state, please?" the operator asked.

"Indianapolis, Indiana. Mrs. Gertrude Webster."

"One moment please," the woman instructed then there was silence. Cora tapped her foot with her eyes on Franklin's office door. She just prayed the secretary didn't have the need to make any phone calls. There were three phones in the entire building— her father's, Franklin's, and the secretary's. They all connected to the same line, which meant only one could be on the phone at any given moment. She wasn't supposed to be using the phone, let alone be in her brother's office. She could almost hear Gideon's voice in her head. *"Don't you know how much a telephone call costs? Why just to talk on the phone for three minutes from Denver to New York City costs $11. Never make a phone call without my permission! If you disobey I'll have the telephone removed from our house."*

"Hello," Rebekah's voice lifted into Cora's ear.

"Bekah," Cora replied casting her eyes back to her brother's neat and orderly desk.

"Cora, it's been so long! How are you? How's Franklin?"

"I'm well. Franklin's been ill."

"Oh, no. I miss him, terribly. How ill is he? What did Doctor Riley say he has? Is he contagious? Are you and your family alright?"

"He's not contagious. It's diabetes." Silence fell on the other end of the phone. "Rebekah?" A few moments later she could hear Rebekah speaking to someone in the distance.

"Cora," a deep voice came on the line. Cora immediately recognized it as Rebekah's father.

"Yes, sir."

"Are your parents certain Franklin has diabetes?"

"Yes, sir. He almost died. Doctor Riley verified it. Even if he has diabetes he can still marry Rebekah. It's not that severe. It was only discovered because he was getting lightheaded. Doc put him on bed rest for a few days. He's back to our normal, lovable Franklin," Cora lied, hoping Mr. Webster wouldn't notice her deception. The last thing she ever needed was for Mr. Webster to call off Franklin's engagement with his daughter. A union between their families not only profited her father's business but secured her own financial future.

"Good."

"Are you going to deny him permission to marry Rebekah?"

"No, diabetes is not a reason to deny my daughter's happiness. I trust Doctor Riley has prescribed a procedure to aid Franklin with managing the disease?"

"He has."

"Good. Here's Rebekah. I have to get back to my mother."

"Thank you, Mr. Webster."

"You're welcome."

Cora lowered her head to Franklin's desk during the moment of silence. That was too close! "Cora," Rebekah's voice came back on the line.

Cora placed her left hand on her forehead then answered, "Rebekah, are you alone?"

"Yes. Why?"

"You still plan to return in June?"

"Pa says we should be able to. My grandmother has fully recovered from her fall but Pa wants me to finish out the school year up here. Why? Is something else wrong with Franklin?"

"You could say that," Cora answered, leaning back in his chair as she lowered her hand.

"What's happened to him?"

"Rebekah, he plans to give your engagement ring to Elsa."

"He what?!"

"He's been working with my ma on how to ask Elsa to marry him. He was supposed to ask her at the dance but he was too sick to go. Oh, Rebekah, you should have seen him. We all thought he was going to die."

"Did he ask for me?"

"No, he asked for her and there's more. He lets her touch him."

"No," Rebekah cried. "I should have never left him. I love your brother. He…he can just be too much sometimes."

"I know. Believe me, I want you and Franklin together as much you want to be with him. Look, there still may be a way we can salvage your relationship with him and get Elsa out of the picture for good. She's nothing but a poor vagabond after our family's assets. I know if you marry Franklin, we can control my father's business together, like we had planned. You said you would help me gain control of the company."

"I still want to help you. You deserve that business more than Franklin does. All I want is Franklin. I'll give you the business and make him believe he is the one in charge. I know how to make him believe what I want is what he wants."

"And that is what I need from you, now. I have tried to convince Frank that he doesn't love Elsa but he doesn't listen to me." She moved closer to the desk. "The situation with Franklin is more severe than I led your father to believe. Franklin had a seizure. Ohio Law forbids him to marry if he is epileptic. If anyone learns the truth of his seizure they could deny your marriage."

"Then how am I to marry him?"

"You convince him to go upstate where nobody knows him. You marry then return to Marion County. No one can deny you two if you are already married. Once you have control of the business you can begin to slowly filter the accounts to me."

"True. If Franklin missed the dance because of the seizure does this mean he hasn't asked Elsa yet?"

"Yes. He wants to but doesn't know how. My parents and Elsa had planned to deceive him into believing the dance hadn't occurred yet. Elsa's sister was Deborah Watkins."

"No, the judge's wife? We heard she passed away."

"Yes, she did and not a moment too soon either. My ma and Elsa had planned to tell her sister about what had transpired then ask her brother–in–law to grant a marital license to her and Franklin. She would ask Liberty to host a barn dance to celebrate so he could ask her. But their plans never came to pass. Elsa's brother died and Deborah has as well. Franklin went to both funerals and supported Elsa."

"If the Judge's wife is dead then how is that a problem? Seems to me she has no one to turn to."

"The judge has cut all ties to her and her family. He's acting as if they do not exist."

"All the better."

"Elsa's father has revoked Franklin's permission to marry her and will not allow Franklin to court her without the consent of him and his brothers."

"Cora, if all this has happened then I don't see what the problem is."

"The problem is Franklin!"

"How so?"

"He's had a mental breakdown and now my parents are on their way to Elsa's house to speak to her parents. If they are successful in their meeting then the engagement will be back on. I need something to distract Franklin from her. He needs to remember that he loves you and not her."

"I can't be there for another month. A lot can happen in a month's time."

"Can you call him?"

"I think my pa might allow me to do that. I can hear him talking to my ma right now about Franklin."

"Good. It would be better that way. I don't think he is in the right frame of mind to physically see you but to hear your voice would do him wonders."

"I will try, Cora. Maybe if I send him a couple of letters, too?"

"Yes. That would do nicely. Phone calls and letters. Oh, Rebekah, you are wonderful. I would have never thought about that."

"He responds better with impersonal communication, not personal, Cora. That's the only way we can remind him that I am the woman he loves and not Elsa."

"There is one other way to force his hand if it comes to that."

"How?"

"It should be quite simple for you. If you can get him to get you pregnant before marriage…"

"…Cora, I can't be with him before marriage. It's not right."

"And is it right what he is doing to you? He wants to give Elsa your engagement ring!"

"But what if I get pregnant?"

"You NEED to get pregnant. If you carry his child he has to marry you. Come on, Bekah, I know you want to be underneath him as much as he wants to be inside you! Act upon those desires. Make him suffer if you have to. The only way you are going to win him back to you is if you leave him no choice in the matter. He's already tried to be with Elsa in that manner."

"He...huh…he said I was the only girl he would ever allow in his bed."

"Well, obviously not."

Rebekah grew silent on the other end for a long moment. "Bekah?" Cora question. Nothing. "Rebekah."

"Don't worry Cora I'll be there the first week of June and I'll make certain to make Elsa's life a living hell! No woman steals my man," she yelled then slammed the phone down.

"That's my girl," Cora grinned, lowering the receiver. Everything was perfect. Rebekah was upset and Franklin couldn't propose to Elsa. Now all she had to do was make certain Franklin's heart began to drift away from Elsa long enough so that when Rebekah returned he would be ripe for her picking. But that was going to be easier said than done. At least Rebekah was going to help her with that, using the phone calls and writing love letters to him.

She grabbed the paper and pen on her brother's desk, rose from the chair, pushed it in, grabbed the rest of her belongings, and walked out the door.

14

Raymond Farm
Wyandot County, Ohio

Franklin sat quietly at his desk playing with Elsa's ring box. His heart ached. What had he done to deem himself unworthy to marry Elsa? Every time he tried to figure out a reason for Oren's reaction he came up with nothing. He groaned and lowered his head to the desk. Life was hopeless. How could he show Oren he was right for his daughter when he couldn't even be around her? He couldn't go on without Elsa. There was no life without Elsa.

He lifted his head, feeling something soft hit his back. Thwack. A piece of wadded up paper hit him in the back of the head. He rubbed his hand on the back of his head, lowered it then turned to his door. His best friend from childhood, Hayden Webster, leaned against the doorframe wadding up another piece of paper. "Hayden," Franklin asked. "How long have you been there?"

"Long enough. How long do you plan to stay in your room moping over Elsa?"

"I'm not moping," Franklin answered, turned back to the desk, and then began to fiddle with the ring box. He opened it and stared at Elsa's engagement ring.

Hayden threw his wadded paper at Franklin. Franklin turned in his direction. "Cora and my wife are taking care of your brothers and my children. I promised your pa I'd help with the extra chores since Abraham is unable to leave his bed. Come with me."

Franklin shook his head and began to breathe heavily. He couldn't leave his room! He never left his room after school. After school he and Elsa would…

"Frank!" Franklin pressed his hand to his forehead, leaned his elbow on the desk, and leaned over. His neck grew tight. He lowered his head to his desk and closed his eyes. Hayden closed the door behind him then walked to his friend. "Frank, get up!"

"No. I have to wait for Elsa."

"She's not coming. Get up!"

"Hayden I don't know what to do."

"Well there's always my sister," Hayden sighed, playing with the ring box.

"I don't want her! I want Elsa," he snarled, snatching the box from Hayden and staring at the ring. "I need Elsa. I have to have her. I love her."

"Then don't just sit there, Franklin. Do something."

"Like what? I don't know what I am supposed to do. Her father told me to never come back to his house or visit Elsa again."

"Oh, Frank," Hayden took a deep breath, stared at his best friend then smiled with a light chuckle. "Some days, my friend, I forget how dense you can be when it comes to girls."

"I don't understand."

"I know you don't. Frank, what did you do to make Mr. Garrett upset at you? Think long and hard. Sometimes you can say something that makes people upset and never understand why they are upset with you. What did you say to him?"

"Nothing!"

"Come on, Frank. I know you better than that. Tell me everything that happened between you and Mr. Garrett."

"Nothing happened. I was in Elsa's room preparing a picnic lunch for the two of us. She was downstairs with her uncles. Mr. Garrett stormed into the room, told me he was revoking his permission for me to marry Elsa, then told me to leave and never return."

"He didn't give a reason?"

"No. Elsa was screaming my name when I left so I know it wasn't something she had wanted either. Hayden, I've been racking my brain trying to figure out what I did wrong but can't think of anything. I can't marry Elsa anyway, so what does it matter if her father renounced his blessing or not."

"Can't marry her? You plan on marrying my sister?" Franklin shrugged his shoulders. "Frank, you told me you don't love Rebekah."

"I don't...I don't know what to do."

"What do you want to do?"

"You know what I want to do," he yelled, rising as he swung his hand across his desk. Papers, books and the ring box scattered on the floor. Franklin sighed as he paced his bedroom. Why was everything so difficult? He knew what he wanted in life. Elsa. He knew how to get what he wanted. Marry her. It was all so simple. Then why, oh why, was everyone and everything standing in his way? His mind grew cloudier as his headache spread. His stomach turned. All he wanted to do was cry but he couldn't. All his emotions bottled inside him threatening to erupt. He fell to his knees, leaned over, pounded the floor, and screamed. He just didn't understand! Why couldn't he break through the social codes that had prevented him from being with his beloved? How was he to live his life without her?

Hayden knelt beside his friend and placed his hand on Franklin's back. Franklin twitched. "Sorry," he said, lifting his hand from Franklin's back. Franklin swiped his hands through his hair, rolled into a fetal position, and disconnected from his surroundings. He stared into nothing while the darkness surrounded him. His inner peace. It was nice and quiet in his head. Not a thought, sound, or sight. Just darkness, security, and peace. No one could find him in here.

"Franklin," Hayden yelled, tapping him on the cheek. Franklin jerked out of his dark place and lifted his eyes to his sandy blond friend. "Stop it."

"Leave me alone," Franklin whined.

"No, get up."

"I said…"

"Get up! Even if you withdraw from everything that surrounds you the problem with Elsa will still be here when you come back."

"I don't know what to do!"

"I do and I'll help you get Elsa back."

"Why?"

"Because, Franklin, you may be a little weird but you are and always will be my best friend. Besides, Elsa's a better match for you than Rebekah ever will be. Elsa can handle your differences. Whenever you're with her you are calmer and you're able to handle life much more than you ever were with Rebekah. I hate to say it, Frank, cause she's my sister and all, but Rebekah's too cold-hearted for any man." Someone knocked on the door. Hayden turned his attention to the door as Franklin sat up with his legs crossed. He grabbed his head and leaned over, squinting his eyes. "Headache?" Hayden asked, glancing at him.

Franklin nodded, "Tell whoever it is to go away."

Hayden walked to the door and opened it. His wife stood in front of him, cradling their infant son. "Something wrong with him?" he asked, stroking their son's head.

"Oh, no. He's feeding," she said and glanced to her breasts.

"Oh, why aren't you feeding our son in one of the bedrooms?"

"Because there is a phone call. Cora couldn't answer it because she is putting our daughter to bed and I have Isaiah working with Abraham on some school work."

"Gideon doesn't want Abraham to do any school work while he is recuperating."

"I know but Isaiah needed someone to read to and I thought Abraham would enjoy it."

"Who is the phone call for?"

"Franklin."

Hayden turned to Frank then back to his wife. "He's not well enough to talk yet."

"Who is it?" Franklin demanded.

"Rebek..." Franklin rose from his place and ran down the stairs. Finally! Something familiar! He hadn't heard from Rebekah in months!

"Frank," Hayden yelled, chasing after him. "Frank, this isn't the right time to talk to my sister!"

Franklin waved his hand towards Hayden, stepped onto the kitchen floor, turned then picked up the receiver. "Rebekah," he said with excitement.

"Frank," Rebekah greeted. Franklin smiled. Oh at long last his world had returned too normal. "Frank?"

"I'm here, Bekah. Sorry. I'm glad to hear from you."

"And I you. I miss you."

"I...I...I miss you too."

"How you been, Frank?"

"It's been too long."

"I know, my love. I'll be home soon then we can spend our

days together just like before I left."

"You promise. It's hard without you, Rebekah."

"I promise. Pa says we should be home the first week of June. We'll be taking the train into Marion Depot. I'll make certain to call again with the time so you can meet us if you want to."

"I would like that."

"I thought you would. I have something for you too."

"Oh?"

"I bought you some more books on engineering and a new tool box."

Franklin smiled. "Thank you, Rebekah."

"I want the best for my husband." Franklin's face fell at the sound of the word husband. Husband. It sounded so foreign to him. He stared into nothing, meditating on the word. Hadn't he already tried to be Elsa's husband? Her father had found him unfit to be that. Who was to say Rebekah's father wouldn't do the same thing? He wasn't like most men his age. How could he provide for his wife and children…oh God he was supposed to have children with her! He was supposed to touch her more than he had done with her already. He didn't know if he could do that with Rebekah. He had let her kiss and hug him. Sometimes he would lie down on top of her, but with their clothes off? He wasn't certain if he felt the same way about her anymore. He knew he felt that way with Elsa though. With Elsa nothing else mattered in the world than her. But he couldn't have Elsa. Elsa was his new normal. Rebekah hadn't been here when he needed her the most. Elsa was the normal, not Rebekah. He needed Elsa! He depended on Elsa not Rebekah. Elsa! Rebekah! Elsa! Rebekah! His chest began to tighten as his thoughts ran rampant. The world grew dark around him. He stumbled backwards, gasped, and dropped the receiver. "Frank," Rebekah called to him.

Hayden grabbed the phone and spoke to his sister. "Rebekah, he's having another panic attack. I'll call you later. I need to tend to him."

"What happened? He doesn't get those unless he's been over stimulated."

"I don't know. Just hang up and be sure to tell our parents I love them."

"Alright, Hayden. Love you."

"I love you too. Goodbye."

"Goodbye." Hayden hung up the phone and knelt before Franklin. Franklin sat on the floor leaning against the bottom cupboards with his hand over his heart. Hayden grabbed the side of his friend's face. "Breathe. Focus on your breathing." Franklin nodded and complied.

"Not...huh...the...hu...same."

"What's not?"

Franklin shook his head. "It...changed."

"You and Rebekah?" Franklin nodded. "What do you mean it changed?"

"I...want...Elsa...not...Rebekah... I thought about...Rebekah and me...together...man and wife...ugh," he groaned and leaned over. The pain radiated in his chest. The more pain he felt the more he panicked. Oh, this was the end. It didn't matter which girl he wanted, this was the end. He pounded his fist on the hardwood floor, grunting.

"Frank," Hayden urged him, lifting his head. "We won't talk about my sister or Elsa anymore. Breathe. Relax and breathe. Don't try to talk, just breathe." Franklin nodded and complied. Hayden sat next to Franklin and waited for his friend's panic attack to subside. There was no doubt about it. He had to get Franklin and Elsa back together again or lose his best friend forever to his mind.

**May 15, 1904
First Methodist Church
Harpster
Wyandot County, Ohio**

The congregation's voices lifted high in the air as they sang *Amazing Grace* in perfect harmony. Elsa clutched her hymnal and glanced her eyes around the small crowded chapel. Her family had been attending Franklin's church for a little over a year now. She knew he had to be in here somewhere. But where? Someone nudged her right elbow. She turned to face her older brother. Nathan glared at her with a stern look of disapproval. She sighed with a stern look towards him.

"Pay attention," he whispered to her.

Elsa rolled her eyes at his order as the congregation stopped singing. She was sick and tired of his constant demands on her. Ever since Henry had died Nathan had done nothing but assert himself over her more than usual. He had grown worse when he learned Henry wasn't their father's son. Nathan had always been self-righteous and arrogant. She had expected Henry's death to go to his head. The two brothers had never gotten along to begin with. Now that he was the only son left, Nathan's arrogance had grown even stronger. He was their father's only heir. Nothing could change that.

"You may be seated," the pastor said.

Elsa closed her hymnal and sat in the wooden pew. She glanced down her pew. It felt strange to have her entire family take up the front pew. With the addition of her uncles, Betsy, some of her aunts and cousins, there wasn't enough room for everyone. Elsa ignored the sermon and peered over her shoulder. She smiled as she thought she saw Franklin in the back of the church with his parents, Cora, and Isaiah. She tried to send Franklin a signal that she knew he was there. Oh, who was she kidding? Franklin wouldn't understand any of her movements. Her heart skipped a beat as she saw him softly smile towards her. A smile! That took a lot of effort on his part. At least he knew she was there. Elsa bit her lower lip and smiled back. "I love you," she mouth to him. Franklin nodded then lifted his gaze towards the pastor.

"Elsa," her mother called to her from the left. Elsa turned to face her. "Pay attention to the sermon."

"Yes, ma'am," she complied.

Her mind drifted as she pretended to listen to the preacher. Franklin had acknowledged her. At least that was a start. She had feared by his reaction a few days ago that he wouldn't want to see her again or that his father would have decided it was for the best for Franklin not to think about or be around her as he had been when Deborah and Henry had died. But then again she knew Franklin's parents wanted the marriage to happen despite what her father and uncles thought. For days she had moped in her room thinking all hope was lost. But Franklin had once again restored her hope. Somehow she was going to have to convince her parents to let her marry Franklin, but she wasn't certain how she was going to accomplish that. There were so many people and circumstances standing against them. Elsa wasn't certain she could every marry Franklin but she had to try. She had to be with him and he needed her. No one understood her lovable man like she did.

"Amen," the congregation said in unison.

Elsa pushed her thoughts to the back of her head. She peered around her. The congregation had risen. Families and friends gathered in small groups, talking amongst themselves. Some of the congregation was talking to her father, her uncles, and the rest of the family. When did church end? With the church overcrowded, as it normally was on any given Sunday, it would be the perfect time to slip away to Franklin. She wondered if anyone would notice her. She was still in her mourning clothes but if she could slip through the crowds maybe no one would notice her black dress. Elsa lowered her bible and hymnal to the pew and quietly slipped to the back of the church. Franklin's parents were very popular in the area. She knew they would be talking to someone with Franklin by their side. Suddenly someone grabbed her by the arm. Cora pulled Elsa to the back of the church and pinned her in the corner.

"What do you think you're doing?" Cora threatened, pressing her body next to Elsa's.

"It's none of your business. Leave me alone," Elsa demanded, trying to break free from Cora's grip.

Cora grinned, "He doesn't want you."

"Liar!"

"You'll see. Wait until Rebekah returns in a few weeks. Then you'll know the truth."

"Wh…what?"

"Yeah, that's right, Elsa. You just wait and see." Cora leaned close to Elsa's ear. "He doesn't love you. You're the mistress. She's his fiancée. Leave my family alone, bitch." Cora pushed Elsa then walked away with a smug look on her face.

Elsa looked to her right. Franklin stood by the door, lost and confused. She wiped her hands down her face and leaned her head back. Although he despised his sister, she knew Franklin didn't understand what had just transpired. She was going to have to deal with Cora on her own. First things first. She had to talk to Franklin without getting both of them in trouble. She had to know the truth. If Rebekah was returning in a few weeks to be with him and he accepted her advances then she would know Franklin loved Rebekah more than her. Or did he? Hadn't Gideon said his son preferred structure and hadn't Juliette told her that Franklin and Rebekah had been an item before she came to Marion County? Perhaps Franklin didn't love Rebekah at all, like he had claimed to her. Oh, she was so confused! Elsa wiped her hands down her face again and gathered her thoughts. She walked over to Franklin.

"Hi," she greeted him.

"Hi."

"Can we talk outside?" she asked, touching his fingers. Franklin swallowed hard and peered down at their hands. "Please, Frank. It's important."

"Your father said I wasn't supposed to be around you," he answered, lifting his eyes towards her.

"I know but I need you."

"For what?"

Elsa smiled, "Please Frank? Our parents are busy. No one will notice."

Franklin looked around the crowded church. He exchanged glances with his mother then turned back to Elsa. "Yes," he answered, grabbed her hand and led her out the door.

16

Juliette stood next to her husband with her eyes on the backs of Elsa and Franklin as they walked out the front door. She peered towards the front of the small chapel. Elsa's parents were busy talking to the preacher with the rest of their family. Good. At least they didn't notice Elsa and Franklin had left the church together. The last few days had been horrible for Franklin. Confused and distraught, he had more than one panic attack since he had returned home a few days ago. Despite how much her son craved things to go back to the way they were; life wasn't going to be good for her son until Elsa married him. How much things had changed for the worse since Elsa had decided to seek help from Deborah and Liberty. She wondered if Elsa had another plan or if the young woman was so distraught with a broken heart that she might not be able to think rationally at all.

Juliette watched Margaret interact with Betsy and their sisters-in-law. She exchanged gazes with Margaret, nodded her head, and then returned to her husband's discussion with Hayden. "Would you all excuse me?" she said, tapping her husband's arm.

"Where are you going?" Gideon asked.

"I think it's time I have a heart to heart talk with Elsa's mother."

"Will she listen to you?" Hayden asked.

"I don't know but it's worth a try, isn't it? Franklin needs Elsa and that girl is more in love with him than Rebekah will ever be." Hayden nodded with a long drawn out sigh. "Hayden, I'm…" He held his hand up to her.

"There's no need to apologize, Mrs. Raymond. You're right. Rebekah can find another man but it is next to impossible for Franklin to ever find a woman like Elsa. Besides, Franklin loves Elsa more than Rebekah. He needs her."

"I agree," Gideon answered. Gideon peered over his shoulder to Elsa's family then back to his wife. "It's going to be hard to have a private conversation with Margaret with Oren's brothers surrounding her like the vultures they are."

"Why Gideon Raymond, what is it you always say? Never let two women around each other for more than a minute if you want something done?"

Gideon and Hayden chuckled. "Go," Gideon said with a large grin.

Juliette tapped her hand on her husband's back then meandered her way through the crowd towards the group of women beside the wall. Margaret smiled slightly as she approached.

"Mrs. Raymond," Margaret greeted her.

"I hope I haven't interrupted," Juliette answered.

"Not at all. Have you met my sisters-in-law?"

"No."

Margaret gestured to her right. "This is Dr. Betsy Garrett. She's married to my husband's brother, Jesse."

"It's a pleasure to meet you," Juliette curtseyed.

Betsy nodded with a slight curtsey. Margaret turned to the woman on her left, "Mrs. Hannah Gregory. She is Jesse's twin sister."

"Mrs. Raymond," the raven beauty replied.

"Pleasure to meet you," Juliette answered then turned to Margaret. "How is Portia?"

"Distraught and depressed."

"The poor woman. I can't imagine having to lose one husband let alone a second one. And you?"

Margaret faked a smile; "I have to remain strong for Portia, Elsa, Nathan, Walter and Sam."

"Poor Walter. He's only a year and half old. He'll never know who his father was except for the stories his mother tells him. And the child Portia carries even now." Juliette sighed, shaking her head. "It must be hard upon her to think of such matters."

"It is but Hank's children will have their grandfather and the rest of our family to ensure they know who their father was."

"I'm glad to hear of it. It must be hard for you to be the pillar of the family right now."

"I've done it before, many times."

Juliette exhaled a deep breath and swallowed hard. "Forgive me. I had forgotten you had lost children before."

Margaret nodded. "Is there something we can help you with, Mrs. Raymond?" Betsy asked, stepping in front of Margaret. Juliette peered around the taller woman's shoulder. Margaret clutched Hannah's hand with a stern look towards Juliette. Juliette looked back at Betsy. "I only wanted to offer my condolences and see if there is anything you might need."

Betsy took a step towards her and whispered in her ear. "Our husbands wouldn't approve," she said secretly, handing her a piece of paper then stepping back. Juliette stared at the folded piece of notepaper, lifted her eyes to Betsy then placed it underneath her right glove. "Thank you for your concern but I believe it would be for the best if you left this family alone under the circumstances."

"Of course. It was a pleasure to meet you and Mrs. Gregory. Mrs. Garrett," Juliette curtseyed, pivoted, and rejoined her husband.

"That didn't go well," Hayden said, casting his eyes towards the women.

"Not at all, Hayden. It went perfectly. I believe we should find Isaiah and Cora then go home. Wouldn't you agree, Gideon?" she asked, slowly pulling the note out of her white glove so only Gideon could see. He stared at the note then lifted his eyes to her with a slight smile. Juliette pushed the note back into the glove.

"Of course. Hayden would you gather the children while Juliette and I get the wagon?"

"Yes, sir," Hayden answered.

Gideon placed his hand on his wife's back. The couple walked out of the church and turned silently towards the back of the church. Children ran and played all around them as they worked their way to the barn and entered it. Juliette walked to their horses' stall as Gideon closed the door behind them.

"Who gave it to you?" Gideon asked, walking to her.

"Dr. Betsy Garrett. She said their husbands wouldn't approve," Juliette answered, taking the note out from under the glove and handing it to him.

Gideon opened the note and read it out loud. "We do not agree with our husbands' decision to separate Elsa and Franklin. We want to help. Tell Oren that you are not satisfied with your doctor's treatment for Abraham and that you want a second opinion from Betsy. We will talk at your house. We will bring Elsa with us. Doctor Betsy Garrett and Margaret Garrett."

Gideon folded the note and stared at his smiling bride. "I knew it, Gideon," Juliette beamed.

"No," he bellowed, crumbing the paper with his hand.

Juliette placed her hands on his firm chest. "Gideon, please."

"I will not have a woman examine my son! Women are too irrational and emotional to think logically. You're asking me to risk our son's life for a woman's unsound medical opinion! I won't do it, Juliette." He lifted the wadded paper and placed it in her hands. "You ask too much." Gideon tapped her hands then walked to the back of the barn.

Too much? How could she be asking too much when her son's happiness was in the hands of a woman he couldn't have? "Sometimes you can be the most egotistical man on the planet and I'm ashamed to be your wife for that, Gideon Samson Raymond," she yelled, pivoting on her heel.

Gideon paused for a moment, bent over with a bucket in his hand. He lowered the bucket and turned his face towards her. "Juliette?"

"This is your son we are talking about. You fully admit he needs Elsa but won't do anything to bring them together? What happened to our plan to help Elsa get Franklin to Betsy."

"It was never my intention to have the woman examine him," he said, calmly rising.

Juliette huffed then shook her head. "I don't understand. Don't you want Franklin to marry Elsa?"

"Yes."

"Then?"

"I was going to seek Betsy's father for medical attention when I took Franklin and Elsa to live with Betsy. That cannot occur now that we cannot be around the Garrett family so we will have to find another solution."

"We have one here," Juliette yelled thrusting the paper in her husband's face. Gideon grabbed her wrist and lowered it.

"All of Marion and Wyandot counties know where I stand

when it comes to female physicians. If…" Juliette grinned. *"If,*
Juliette, I'm not saying that I will." She lowered her smile. "If I
decide to allow what the note says to occur everyone will know I
am planning something. You didn't think of that, did you?"

"Oh, I did," she grinned. "The note was given to me not you."

"So? I am your husband. I make the decisions for our family
not you."

"Gideon, things happen when you are at work. Sometimes I
have to make decisions that I do not have time to discuss with you.
Perhaps Abraham turned for the worse and Dr. Riley wasn't
available to treat him. Being the emotional woman that I am I
would want the nearest physician around to examine our son."

Gideon rocked on his heels, placed his hands in his pants
pockets with his thumbs out. "I'm impressed, Juliette."

She rubbed her hands on his chest and stared up into his eyes,
"Not as much as I will be if you allow it to happen."

"You're asking a lot from me."

"I know but deep down in your heart," she started, placing her
hand over his heart, "You know it is the best for our son."

Gideon stood straight, contemplating her words for a moment.
"What of Franklin?" he asked.

"You said it yourself. He's not ready to return to work."

"He needs his routine."

"Gideon, he needs her more. Please, husband, let this happen.
For Franklin's sake?" Gideon took the note from her hand and
studied it. "It took a lot for Betsy and Margaret to write that note. I
wouldn't dismiss it so easily."

Gideon turned his back on his wife and walked towards the
back wall re-reading it several times. Juliette's heart beat strong
with anticipation with every moment of silence between them. The
longer he took the more her thoughts ran rampant in her mind.
Gideon was a strong anti-progressive supporter. He disapproved of
any woman going against her husband or father. Yet here she was
asking him to accept that three women could go behind their
husbands' backs and independently solve the problem with Elsa
and Franklin, let alone that he could trust a female physician. She
could see the wheels turning in his head. Any physician had the
power to commit someone to the asylum. They had worked hard to

ensure Dr. Riley never sent Franklin there, yet if they handed Franklin's medical care over to a different doctor who was to stop that doctor from committing him? He couldn't trust just any doctor with his son, especially a female one whose emotions could get the better of her judgment. Oh, how she wished Oren hadn't taken away his permission for Franklin to marry Elsa.

"And what will you do if she finds Franklin competent but Oren won't change his mind," Gideon asked, pivoting in her direction.

"They can elope."

"To where, Juliette? Everyone in Upper Sandusky knows our son is challenged. That's why we left."

"I don't know, Gideon. But we can figure that out along the way. We still have Judge Watkins?"

"Perhaps not. Franklin told me the judge wants nothing to do with Elsa's family."

"Gideon, please. It must be done for Franklin's sake," she pleaded.

"I don't like going into something without a plan."

"I know but this time you just have to trust."

"Trust? To whom am I to trust the welfare of my eldest son? A female physician? You? Who, Juliette? Who? This is Franklin we're talking about. He hates change. What you are asking him to do will change everything."

"Well, you didn't seem to disagree when Elsa and I first came up with the plan."

"Because he wouldn't have this in his life," he said shaking the note towards her. "Juliette, he's already distraught and you're asking me to bring a stranger into our home to examine him. Did you not think what this might do to him if I'm not there."

"Then be there for your son!"

A thick moment of tension and silence filled the air. Juliette swallowed hard realizing she had said the wrong words.

"Are you…?" Gideon started.

"…no, no. Forget I said anything," she sighed, turning away from him.

Gideon grabbed her wrist and turned her towards him. Tears cascaded down her cheeks. He lightly swept them away. "I realize how hard it has been on you."

"He's always going to be like a child, Gideon. He needs Elsa."

"I know he does but I don't think this is the right way of doing this. It's wrong to go behind her father's back. There must be another way."

"There isn't and you know it. Gideon," she said placing her hand on the side of his face. "You're a good man and an even greater father. We won't always be there for our son. When the day comes and you are no longer there he will need someone strong enough to guide him through his grief, even more so when I die. He needs Elsa and this is the only way we can keep her plan alive. Please, husband. I rarely beg you for anything but I will for this. Franklin…"

"…needs his father beside him when Betsy comes to examine him."

Juliette grinned. "Thank you," she said, lowering her hand.

"Jules, just call me at work after you send for her so I can make it look like there was a family emergency."

"I will. I promise."

17

Rays of sunlight shimmered off the waves of the large lake. Elsa reclined on the grassy shore with her head in Franklin's lap, gazing at his expressionless face. His arm gently rested around her waist. She wondered where his mind was. At least he was allowing her to touch him and he was cradling her. Thankfully, their situation hadn't left him so distraught that he had reverted to his protective state. Yet they had spent more time out here in silence than talking. How much she wanted to come to a reasonable solution to their dilemma with his help. She needed his strength.

"Frank," she softly called to him, gently rubbing her hand on his chest.

Franklin lowered his gaze to her without meeting her eye to eye. Well at least he was trying. That's all she could ask for. Elsa was surprised to see her beloved calm while so much chaos was happening in his life. He was acting as if this was a normal day. Of course he was! What did they always do after church on a normal day? Spend time together! Just her presence must have calmed him down. "Are you upset with me?" she asked.

"Why?"

"The last time we talked you were angry because I knew about your plans. Franklin, I never meant to…"

"Stop Elsa, I can't ask you. It will never happen."

"But it can."

Franklin shook his head. "No. Your father said no. That's the rule. I can't marry you. He said no. No means no."

"Sometimes it is okay to break the rules."

"No, Elsa. To break the rules is wrong. Your father said no," Franklin said, starting to become agitated.

Elsa sat upright with her legs crossed and her elbows on her knees. She rested her head in her hands and stared at the lake. It was always best not to touch Franklin when he started to become agitated. He needed his own space to calm down. She exhaled a deep breath. The walk to the lake had been nice. It was like they had never broken up or had an argument. What was their status anyway? In Franklin's mind he could never marry her but did that mean he never wanted to see her again? If his actions today were any indication, Franklin wanted to be with her. But as long as he knew her father disapproved of their relationship he would never pursue her even though she knew he wanted to. Rules were safe for Franklin. He could understand them better than he could any social situation.

Elsa picked up a few pebbles and threw them into the lake one at a time. There had to be a solution but she couldn't see it. How was she supposed to be with Franklin when her parents wouldn't allow it and Franklin wouldn't budge from his position? The worst part was, no matter how upset she was he couldn't read her body language to see that she was upset. He couldn't comfort her because he had no idea how she felt unless she told him. As much as she wanted to pour out all of her frustrations to him she couldn't. It would only upset him even more.

"Frank," Hayden's voice echoed from behind them. Elsa turned towards the man's voice in unison with Franklin. Although she went to church with Hayden and his family, she didn't know him. Her family rarely interacted with anyone from church except for the preacher's and Franklin's families. "Elsa," he greeted her. He stretched his hand out to her. "I'm Hayden Webster. My wife is your teacher."

Elsa rose and shook his hand. "Nice to meet you, sir."

"What do you want, Hayden?" Franklin asked with a blank stare towards the lake.

Hayden lowered his hand. "Gideon sent me to tell you that we are heading back to the house." Franklin nodded, rose, placed something in Elsa's hand, and turned sharply towards his best friend. "You alright?" Hayden asked.

"No," Franklin answered then walked away from them.

Elsa sighed as she watched him disappear behind the church. She opened her hand to reveal a gold and diamond locket with tulips on the front. Elsa smiled to herself. Her quiet, wonderful man still loved her. She opened the locket. Inside on the right he had engraved, "My love and my life. You are all that I desire." Tears cascaded down her cheeks. On the left side was Franklin's portrait. She wondered how long he had been holding the locket before he had gained the courage to give it to her. "Elsa," Hayden called to her. She sniffed her nose, wiped her tears, and looked up at Franklin's best friend. "Don't give up on him," Hayden told her.

"What?"

"He loves you more than my sister but Franklin doesn't know what to do about that."

"How do you know?"

"He made that for her and gave it to you."

Elsa slammed the locket closed and handed it him. "I don't want it."

Hayden clasped his hands over hers. "Elsa, he would have never given that locket to you if he didn't love you more. It took him weeks to come up with those words for my sister."

"But it's his words for her."

"No, they are for you now."

"But Mr. Webster..."

"Elsa, you say you love my best friend."

"I do."

"But do you understand him?"

"Yes."

"Then think about this. Many times Franklin wants to say something or express how he feels but he can't."

"It's hard on him. He has trouble expressing himself."

"Yes." Hayden lowered his eyes to their hands. "How much harder do you think it is for him to tell you how he feels about you when everyone is telling him he shouldn't?" Hayden asked, lifting his eyes to hers.

"How are we to marry, Mr. Webster? I know Franklin wants to marry me. I want that too but as long as my family stands in the way he will never ask me. Even if my family relented on their position Franklin won't ask me because it's not the right time. Deborah's dead so I can't ask her husband for help and my aunt won't examine Franklin because the family is against him. Tell me, Mr. Webster, just please tell me. What am I supposed to do?"

"You wait."

"What for?"

"Not everyone is against your marriage," Hayden said then

walked away. Elsa watched the mysterious man follow the confused Franklin around the church. Franklin had spoken highly of Hayden several times. If Franklin could trust Hayden enough to share everything about his life with the accountant then why couldn't she trust him too? It was after all harder for Franklin to trust someone than it was for most people. But then again Hayden was Rebekah's older brother and Franklin could be a bit naive about people. Why would Hayden want to help her when his sister loved Franklin too? Oh, her entire life had been thrown upside down and inside out! What she needed more than anything was clarity. She was beginning to understand why her father never trusted anyone outside the family. Yet she couldn't even trust her family at this moment. Why couldn't things just return to normal? Why couldn't her family accept that although Franklin was different he was special to her? Somewhere there had to be an answer to her problem. Someone had to believe in the unconditional love that she and Franklin share. But who? Who would help her see the light at the end of her dark, turbulent tunnel, and could she trust them to save the one thing she needed the most—her engagement.

May 16, 1904
Home of
Henry and Portia Garrett,
Harpster,
Wyandot County, Ohio

Elsa lay on her bed with a headache. Another day of unyielding visitations from family and friends offering their condolences. Worse yet, another day without Franklin. She closed her eyes wishing it would all go away. Sometimes Franklin would escape to his own place, forgetting everyone and everything around him. Oh, how she envied him. Life was hard enough without Deborah and Henry in her life let alone under the new strict regulations her uncles and father had placed her family under, but to not have Franklin around her was almost unbearable. Oh, God what she wouldn't do to run away from this place and elope.

Elope, now there was an idea. Henry and Deborah had eloped and look what that had brought them. Disasters and death despite the happiness they had seemed to glean from their spouses. She exhaled a deep breath contemplating eloping with Franklin. She had never wanted to elope. It wasn't right to turn her back on her family and marry a man without her father's permission, but what else could she do? She thought about the original plan she had concocted with Franklin's parents. As long as everyone in Marion knew about Franklin's seizure he couldn't marry her. Franklin would never lie to the county clerk. He was just too honest. It was a great attribute but also his greatest downfall. In order to gain approval for their marriage she would need a doctor's order. She thought she could get that with her Aunt Betsy but now that the family was against her marriage she doubted her aunt would help her. But what about her aunt's father? If she could just somehow get Franklin to leave with her for Wheelersburg then perhaps Betsy's father could grant them an affidavit claiming Franklin was well enough to marry her. Once she got the affidavit they could ask

Liberty to marry them. But Liberty wanted nothing to do with her family. Perhaps she could convince him to trust her. He knew Deborah had cared deeply for her. Elsa sighed. Who was she kidding? Liberty was suffering hard with his wife's death. Rumors had spread all over Marion that the Progressive judge had slipped into a deep depression and that his parents were raising the children. Perhaps it would be for the best if she married Franklin in Wheelersburg. No one knew him in that large Southern Ohio city. Yes, that's what she would do. She'd run away, tell Franklin's family the plan, then they would elope to Southern Ohio. It seemed like an easy plan but she knew what was easy for a normal person would be hard for Franklin. Franklin wouldn't understand. He couldn't understand. If anything, their conversation yesterday at the lake proved that.

Elsa turned her head towards the window with a long drawn-out sigh. She would need Franklin's father to help him agree with her conclusion. That could take time and time was not something they had. The longer they waited the more chance her family had of leaving this place. She had heard her father talking to his brothers last night about moving back to Vernon. Just how long did she have before her family moved to the mountains of Southern Ohio?

A knock on the door startled her.

"Elsa," her mother called to her from behind the door. Elsa sniffed her nose and wiped the tears from her eyes. She had to remain strong. Wasn't that what the family wanted from her?

"Just a moment, Ma," she yelled, rising from the bed and gathering herself. She wiped her hand down her long black dress and peered out the window. Her father guided Carlisle to the field while Jesse and Moses followed after. She wondered what they were talking about. Whatever it was, it couldn't be good. Ugh, how she wished they would just all leave. Samuel walked out of the barn with Nathan. The two young men joined the others. Elsa stepped closer to the window, placed her hand on the windowsill, and peered over. Her older brother lifted a locket in the air, showing it to their father and uncles. The sun reflected off the golden locket. Elsa gasped, tapping the top of her blouse. "Oh, no," she muttered to herself. She had never noticed it missing. Elsa stared at her precious necklace. She had sworn to herself she would never take it off and it would remain hidden from her family. How could she have been so clumsy as to lose it in the barn? Elsa panicked thinking about her day. Just when did she lose it? The only time she had been in the barn this morning was when she had gone to milk the cow. "Oh, dear, sweet Jesus," she whispered, realizing the clasp must have given way and the locket fell to the hay when she bent down to pick up the bucket of fresh milk. She only hoped it hadn't landed where the cow could have stepped on it. Worse yet, what if her father opened the locket and saw what Franklin had inscribed.

Elsa's heart skipped a beat. She lifted the window, leaned out, and yelled, "That's mine!"

The men turned in her direction as Oren grabbed the locket. "Where did you get it?"

"None of your business, Pa!"

"You will not talk to your father like that, young lady," Jesse corrected her. "Your father asked you a question and you will answer him. Where did you get this?" Jesse asked, taking the locket from her brother.

"Ma gave it to me."

"You're lying, Elsa," her father said. "That's gold and diamonds. We can't afford that. Now where did you get it?"

Elsa swallowed hard.

"Elsa," her mother pounded on the door harder. She turned her attention to the door then back to her father. Elsa didn't know which fate would be worse, ignore her mother or ignore her father. Either way, her uncles would discipline her for her lack of respect.

"Elsa, answer your uncle and father," Carlisle bellowed.

She had about enough of her meddling uncles. Elsa slammed the window closed, pulled the drapes, and answered her door.

Margaret stood in the hall with a plate of cookies and glass of milk. "Sweetheart, what took you so long?"

"Pa…he…uhm…are those for me?"

"Yes, may I come in?"

Elsa opened the door wider with a smile. Muffled sounds of her name echoed off the closed window. She sighed, closing the door. She was going to be in big trouble when her father came back into the house. "What about your father?" Margaret asked, placing the cookies on the nightstand.

"What?" Elsa asked as she closed the door and pivoted towards her mother.

"You avoided my question and said Pa. What are you hiding?"

Elsa faked a smile, "Nothing, Ma."

"You're lying to me."

"Never."

"Elsa, stop it." Margaret sighed as she sat on the edge of her daughter's bed. She quietly glanced at her daughter. Elsa swallowed hard. She recognized that look in her mother's eyes. Margaret wanted the truth and wasn't going to speak until she got it. Yet Elsa wasn't quite sure if she wanted to tell her mother about Franklin's locket. Of course her pa would show it to her mother sometime or another. They didn't keep secrets from each other, but unlike Franklin's parents, her father walked all over her mother. Margaret would never go against her husband let alone speak out against him. In this house, her father ruled everything with a stern hand, yet she wondered just how stern he was with her. Margaret glared even harder at Elsa with the look that said, "I could wait here all day long, young lady."

Elsa twiddled her thumbs then proclaimed with a long, drawn out breathe, "Franklin gave me a locket yesterday that I was hiding but I lost it in the barn this morning while I was milking the cow and Nathan found it. He gave it to Pa. Pa asked me about it but I never told him what it is."

"You have to be more careful, Elsa," Margaret exclaimed, rising from the bed. "Has he opened it yet?"

"No, but..."

Margaret pushed her daughter aside and ran to the window. She quickly pulled the drapes aside, opened the window and leaned out just as Oren began to open the locket.

"Oren!"

Her husband paused and turned to face her. "Margaret," he proclaimed, clutching the locket.

"Oh, thank heavens you found it."

"Is this yours, Margaret?" Moses asked, taking the locket from his brother and holding it up.

"Yes."

"Where did you get it?"

"It was Deborah's. Liberty sent it to me."

"I don't remember anyone sending you anything from the judge," Oren said.

Margaret faked a smile, "Well I was trying to keep it a secret, Oren. I know you have always disapproved of Deborah's marriage to him but she was our daughter. Nothing could ever change that."

Oren nodded. "No, you're right."

"I don't believe you," Carlisle said.

"And why not?"

"I may be blind but I know when someone is scared and lying to me. I could hear it in Elsa's voice just as I hear it in yours."

"And why wouldn't she be? Oren would be upset to know Elsa was the one who retrieved the locket for me from Liberty."

Oren clenched his jaw. "Why did you tell me it was delivered?"

"Well it was, Oren, just not by a messenger."

"She has no right to remain in communication with Liberty and his family, neither do you! We agreed."

"No, you agreed. We have three beautiful grandchildren that we do not know."

"We have Samuel, Walter and Portia's pregnant."

"Those are Moses' grandchildren, not ours! Ours are with Liberty!"

Silence passed between the two of them. Elsa was shocked. She had never heard her mother raise her voice towards her father. "Oren, please do not deny me the satisfaction of having a relationship with all of my grandchildren."

"I'll bring the locket to you and we can discuss this later."

"I promised Liberty I would never open it."

"Don't worry, woman. I want nothing to do with the trinkets he bought her," he said, grabbing the locket from Moses and placing it in his pocket.

"Is it broken?"

"No."

Margaret nodded then closed the window and curtains. Elsa smiled in wonder. "Thank you," she said as her mother grabbed

Elsa's leather-bound travel trunk and opened it. She began to pack Elsa's clothes. "What are you doing?"

"You're leaving," she answered, pulling out Elsa's clothes from the dresser.

Elsa looked at her with confusion. She walked towards her mother asking, "Where am I going?"

"Don't ask. The less you know the better," Margaret replied.

A knock on the door interrupted them. Margaret lowered one of Elsa's skirts into the suitcase and answered the door. Elsa stared at the bundle of clothes in her suitcase. Surely her father hadn't decided to send her away. Perhaps he couldn't stand to be around her and had decided she was to go home with one of his sisters. "No, no, no," she whispered, unpacking her belongings. He couldn't send her away. He just couldn't. She needed to be here with her beloved. Franklin needed her. Tears ran down her cheeks as she quickly unpacked her belongings. She was going to raise hell with her father if he thought of abandoning her with one of his sisters. Oh, hell no, she wasn't about to leave this farm.

"Elsa stop," her mother ordered, placing her hand on top of Elsa's. Elsa lifted her gaze. "What are you doing?"

"I'm not going. I…I…I…don't care what Pa says. I'm not leaving this farm to move to Vernon with one of his sisters."

"Would you leave this farm to live with Franklin?" Betsy asked from behind Margaret.

"Wha…?" Elsa gasped as she sat back on her knees and looked up at her aunt. Had she just heard what she thought she had just heard?

"Would you?" Betsy asked again.

"Yes, of course I would. But…" She peered at both of the women's faces trying to piece together their meaning. It wasn't like Betsy or her mother to go against what their husbands wanted but here they were. Her mother was packing her suitcase and Betsy had implied they were going to send her to the Raymond's house. And why was Betsy carrying her medical bag? She lifted her eyes towards them. "Wh…?" She tried to speak but couldn't find the words. Was this how Franklin felt when he tried to communicate his feelings? She didn't like this feeling at all. Her world had been turned upside down and inside out. She had no idea what was fact and what was fiction but she was beginning to wonder if these two women felt the same way, too. This shouldn't be happening. None of it.

"We don't have time to waste, Margaret. They've already called. I sent my daughter to get the wagon ready."

"What about her suitcase?"

"Leave it. Just pack her a few changes of clothes in here," Betsy said, opening her medical bag.

Elsa watched in bewilderment as her mother complied. Betsy lifted her head. "Get your album and your brother's ring. You'll need them."

Elsa rose, went to her nightstand and grabbed the album Portia had given her. She pushed the falling letters and pictures inside then pressed it close to her chest. She picked up Henry's ring box then placed the items in Betsy's bag. Betsy closed the medical bag. The two women rose quickly. "I'll meet you in the barn," Betsy said, rushing out the door. Elsa stared at her mother, wondering where they were going and why they were in such a hurry. Certainly, they weren't taking her to Franklin, or could they be? But why would her mother and aunt help her?

"Let's go," Margaret ordered, taking Elsa's hand.

"What about my locket?"

"I'll make certain it makes its way to Gideon Raymond next time I'm in town."

"You're really taking me to Franklin? But why?"

"Why?"

"Why are you helping us?"

"We can discuss that on the way. Now let's go before your father comes to his senses and realizes what Betsy and I are doing. Lord, help us all if your father and his brothers figured it out before we got you over there," Margaret said while exiting the room with Elsa. Elsa smiled to herself. Her world may not make any sense but at least there was finally a light at the end of her tunnel. God had answered her prayers. He sent her two angels to aid her. Two angels she would have never suspected would have ever wanted to help her and Franklin. It was wonderful. She only hoped their willingness to go against the family to help her and Franklin would last long enough for her and Franklin to marry. Only time would tell that. She buried her doubts and fears deep within and let herself enjoy this wonderful moment. "Thank you, God," she whispered as they exited the back door and ran towards the barn. This was the best day of her life! Finally someone who understood her plight and wanted to help. Oh, praise God her prayers had been answered.

Raymond Farm
Wyandot County, Ohio

Franklin lay underneath the wagon fixing the brake beam. The simple repair should have been completed hours ago but he couldn't concentrate on the job without thoughts of Elsa entering his mind. He wiped the sweat off his brow, lowered the wrench, and stared at the wooden beam. Franklin traced his hand down the smooth board, slightly lifting his right knee. How many times had he taken Elsa somewhere in this very wagon? He put his hands on his forehead, leaned his head back and closed his eyes. He was so confused and frustrated he couldn't concentrate. He hated that feeling. He had work to do. His father depended on him to do a long list of chores today but he couldn't get past this one. Last night, his father had told him everyone was working hard to return Elsa to his side. All he had to do was to trust his father with whatever plan they were concocting to bring his beloved to him. He didn't understand what that entailed and hated not knowing the details. As much as he pleaded with Gideon to supply them his father would only say he had to trust him and do everything they told him. This morning, at breakfast, Gideon had given him a long list of chores to do and then told him he would return that evening to check on his progress. Franklin liked the long list. Lists were his friend. They brought order where there was chaos. He wondered if there was a list he could use to figure out his life. Why did things have to be so complicated?

"Pa wants you," Cora's voice echoed in the barn. Franklin lowered his hands and opened his eyes. Suddenly, he felt her kick him in the leg. "Did you hear me, stupid?"

"I'm not stupid. Pa says I am too smart for my own good. If that is true then how can you call me stupid?"

Cora crouched on her knees and peered at him from between the floor and wagon. "How's Rebekah?"

Franklin turned his head sharply towards her with a snarl. How dare she ask about her! Why should she bring her up when the woman he desires more than life itself was Elsa? "I don't know," he answered, pulling his body towards the back of the wagon.

"Didn't you speak to her?"

"The other day, yes. Today, no. I don't know how she feels today, Cora. How could I? I have not spoken to her today."

"Ugh, Franklin. I'm not talking about today. I'm talking about in general. How is she?"

"People's moods change all the time. How would I know?" he answered as he stood up next to the back wall.

Cora rose and walked down the side of the wagon to meet her older brother. She watched Franklin wipe his dirty hands on a towel. "Frank, have you ever thought that perhaps Elsa's father did you a favor by denying your marriage to his daughter?"

Franklin paused and stared at his left ring finger. He swallowed hard taking in her words. A favor? How can the denial of something someone wants so badly be a favor. Wasn't a favor something nice that someone did for another?

"Frank," she called to him and touched his back. Her delicate touch felt like several small knives stabbed him in the back. He gasped at her touch. She grabbed him by the arm. Franklin dropped the towel and shrank away from her with a loud cry. More pain. He hated it. Why was she touching him? Why! Why! Why! He fell on his bottom with a deep stare at nothing. Darkness crept closer to him, tempting him to escape from this world. Still she would not let go of him. His face. Oh, God, why was she touching his cheek?

"Cora," he thought he heard his father call out his sister's name. Still she wouldn't stop touching. Franklin lowered his head into his lap and rocked. Pinpricks of pain rolled up his back. Oh, God she was rubbing his back! He rocked back and forth, trying to get rid of the uncomfortable feeling. Oh, why! Why was she touching him when she knew he hated to be touched?

"Enough," Gideon yelled, thrusting Cora's hand away from Franklin's back.

Cora grinned and stepped back as her father sat beside Franklin. "He wouldn't be like this if Rebekah was around," she coaxed.

Had Franklin heard Cora right? Was he a different person with Rebekah than he was without her? No, it couldn't be. It was Elsa who had helped him, not Rebekah. But Rebakah was safe. Rebakah was normal. Elsa was new. "Rebakah, normal, Elsa new. Rebakah right, Elsa wrong," he repeated rocking back and forth.

"That's right, Frank," Cora beamed, kneeling beside their father. "Elsa is wrong for you. You want Rebekah, not Elsa."

Franklin shook his head. He heard his words but couldn't believe they were coming out of his mouth. What was he saying? Why couldn't he tell them the truth? He needed Elsa not Rebekah! Franklin pounded his fists on the floor as he grunted loudly. He had to push it out. He had to push the truth out but it wouldn't come. It just wouldn't come!

"Franklin," Elsa's voice called to him. Was he imagining it? He wanted her so bad but the more Cora pressured him the more he couldn't deny what his sister wanted.

Franklin rolled onto his left side into the fetal position. "Frank," Gideon called to him while the strong darkness tempted him to enter into his secret world. "Don't go there, Frank. Come on, boy, listen to my words," Gideon coaxed him.

"It's her fault, Pa," Cora accused, pointing a finger to Elsa.

"My fault?" Elsa gasped, stepping closer to Cora.

"Everything was perfect until you arrived. You brought these troubles upon my brother. You want to help him? Then leave my family alone," Cora yelled, pushing Elsa to the ground.

Franklin gasped. Was that the sound of his sister beating his Elsa? How could it be? Elsa wasn't allowed to be around him yet he had clearly heard her voice. The sound of fighting entered his mind while the darkness beckoned him to go even further into it. He rolled to his stomach with a deep moan. His head pounded and his heart raced. A part of him wanted to rise up and defend Elsa while another part wanted to stay in this comfortable nothingness. He dug deeper into his pit of despair.

"Girls, stop it. You are both making Franklin's condition worse," Gideon yelled at them. "Cora go in the house and help your mother. Elsa, get your aunt."

"Yes, sir," the girls replied then walked out the door shoving each other.

Gideon turned to his son and leaned over to Franklin's ear. "Frank, they're gone, my boy. Open your eyes."

Somewhere in the distance, Franklin heard his father talk to him. He turned his attention to the sound of his father's baritone voice. For a brief moment he wanted to go towards it yet the solitude felt safe. In here there was peace. Out there, there was only chaos and confusion. It wasn't that he didn't want a relationship with Elsa or Rebekah. No, he had loved both girls equally. He just didn't understand how he could please everyone around him. His parents had loved both girls equally. His sister wanted him to marry Rebekah as did most of the people he knew in both Marion and Wyandot counties. Elsa's parents had wanted to call him their son but now they didn't want him in their daughter's life. Hayden wanted him to be with Elsa, as did his parents and brothers. Seemed to Franklin, it didn't matter who he chose to spend the rest of his life with he was going to hurt someone's feelings. He hated that. Why couldn't he make a decision that would help build people up and not break them down? He was such a failure. An utter disappointment and failure!

"How long has he been like this?" Betsy asked, kneeling beside Franklin, laying her black bag down.

Gideon shook his head and placed his hand on her bag. "Don't do anything. The only one who can pull him out when he is this deep is Elsa."

"Elsa?" Betsy asked, glaring at her niece as Margaret stood behind her daughter with her hands on Elsa's shoulders.

Elsa nodded. "He's done it before. Cora's always mean to him."

Betsy turned to Gideon, "What did his sister do to make him like this."

"She touched him," Gideon said, rising upright. He motioned for Elsa to approach. Elsa looked at her mother. Margaret nodded. she walked to Franklin's side and knelt beside him.

"How can a touch do that?" Betsy asked.

Elsa answered, "He hates to be touched. He told me once it feels like someone is stabbing him with pins."

"If that's true, Elsa, then how will he be able to touch you?"

Elsa shook her head, "I don't know how he does it, Aunt Betsy, but he says he likes my touch." She exhaled a deep breath, and then slowly rubbed his back. Elsa leaned over his ear and whispered, "I love you."

Franklin paused in the darkness. Elsa's angelic voice sung in the air around him. He smiled, taking in every note of her sweet song. He had to return to her. "Frank, I need you, my love," her voice sang again. Joy filled his heart and warmed his soul. She was here. She was actually here! This couldn't be a farce. No one could sing those notes like her. Franklin wet his lips. Now if he could just speak. He was so exhausted. He didn't want to move his body but if he could just push out her name from his lips she would know he heard her.

"Elsa," Franklin muttered.

Gideon grabbed Elsa's wrist. She turned to face him. "He's saying your name. Listen."

"Elsa," Franklin muttered.

Elsa smiled then whispered to Franklin, "I need you. Come back to me, Frank."

Franklin walked towards the long line of bright light that beckoned him out of the darkness. Her sweet, angelic voice grew stronger the closer he walked to the light. Oh, yes. She was by his side. She had to be. He walked through the light, opened his eyes, and stared at the wooden barn wall. He grabbed her hand and turned his head towards her. Elsa smiled at him. "Oh, Frank."

Franklin squeezed her hand and swallowed hard. "What is it, son?" Gideon asked.

Franklin lifted his eyes to the mysterious woman beside him. Gideon and Elsa followed his gaze. "What?" Betsy asked.

"He doesn't like strangers," Gideon answered.

Franklin squeezed Elsa's hand harder and grunted, turning his head towards the wall. "Shh, Frank, she won't hurt you," Elsa pleaded as she lay beside him and wrapped her arm around his back. He shivered then pulled her arm close to his chest. "Shh, my love. It's okay," Elsa coaxed, rubbing his back. A part of him wanted to scream while another part wanted to remain calm under her gentle touch.

Franklin turned his head towards her and looked at her face. He couldn't believe she was here. He exhaled a deep breath. "Tired," he muttered.

Elsa smiled, gently caressing the side of his face. "I know but

I need you to do something important for me."

"Anything."

"Trust me?" she asked, lifting his chin and forcing him to look her in the eyes.

Franklin swallowed hard. Why was she asking him to trust her when she already knew he did? It took a lot of his trust just to allow her to be this close to him. He hated it when people were in his personal space. His body screamed in agitation every time his personal space was compromised. It took a lot for him to be this close to her. Why couldn't she understand that?

"Frank?" she asked again.

"I...I...I," he bit his lower lip and tried again. "I trust you."

Elsa smiled. "Good. The woman beside me. You have seen her before. Don't you remember?" Franklin shook his head. "Think hard, Frank. You first met her at Deborah's house."

Franklin turned his gaze to the right towards Betsy. He studied every one of her features then his eyes fell to her black bag. "Doctor."

"Yes, that's right. I'm a doctor," Betsy replied. "I'm here…"

Franklin suddenly rose from his place and began to walk quickly to the front of the barn, agitated. Why had Elsa brought a doctor to him? He had a doctor. Unless…oh she couldn't have him committed without his parents' permission, or could she? Would she ever betray him like that? Maybe Elsa had asked Cora to help her. Oh, God. Everyone was against him.

"Whoa, slow down, Frank," Gideon said, stepping in front of his son. Franklin breathed heavily, moving side to side. Every step he took, his father met him with his arms out to the side blocking his moves. Franklin crouched over. He turned around, trying to find a way out but there wasn't one. The faces of Elsa, Betsy, and Margaret all blurred together to form one giant female monster. Why was the room spinning? Franklin grabbed his forehead and turned towards his father. "Franklin, we're here to help you." They weren't here to help him. They were here to hurt him. He had to get out of the barn. He had to escape.

"Frank," Elsa called from behind him.

Franklin lowered his hands. How could he trust her? But there was a part of him that told him he had to. Maybe she knew the way out of the barn. Franklin lowered his hands and turned to face her. She reached her hand out. Why was she doing that? What did that mean? Oh, he thought he knew what she was doing. Oh, God! What did she want from him with that gesture? He stomped his feet and crouched over his stomach.

"Franklin, we only want to help," his father said.

Franklin lifted his eyes towards the only man he could ever trust. Gideon moved closer to his son with his arms still out to block him. "You want to be with Elsa?"

Franklin stood up and stared at Elsa. She raised her eyebrow at him. Oh, why another gesture? He shook his head, not understanding what she was silently trying to tell him. Why couldn't she just say what she meant? Elsa stepped towards him as Betsy and Margaret stood around them in a circle, blocking them in a tight circle.

"Frank, I know you were upset that I found out about your proposal."

"Doesn't matter. Can't ask. Won't happen," he answered.

Elsa smiled, "Yes, you can."

Franklin shook his head, "No, your father said no. No means no. My pa taught me that. My pa doesn't lie. Lying is wrong."

"Frank, you have to trust me. Don't you want to be with me?"

"Yes."

"Then trust me."

Franklin looked at Betsy and Margret then took a step back. He tripped over his wrench and stabilized himself on the wagon. Elsa walked towards him. "They won't hurt you."

"Doctor. You brought a doctor to me? I have a doctor."

"Yes, we know. She just wants to examine you."

"No. I told you no before. You don't listen. Why don't you listen to me?"

"Frank," she addressed him, blocking him with his back against the wagon. "Would you let her do it for me?"

"I won't change your doctor, Frank," Gideon offered his support.

"You said no woman doctor would ever touch your children," Franklin retorted his father's previous words.

"I was wrong. People can be wrong."

"Not you. You are never wrong, Pa."

"I'm human, Frank. I make mistakes, too. Please son, let Dr. Garrett examine you."

Franklin shook his head. "It's not normal. She's not my normal doctor. I want my normal doctor."

"Frank, please. Please, do this for me," Elsa pleaded.

"Why?" Franklin asked.

"There are ru…"

"Elsa, don't tell him that," Gideon interrupted, stepping towards them.

Franklin lifted his gaze to his father, "Rules?"

"Do you love her, son?" Gideon abruptly asked, pointing to Elsa.

Franklin turned his gaze to Elsa. Love her? What kind of question was that? "Always," he answered, trying desperately to keep eye contact with her.

"Sometimes when someone loves you they ask you to do things you might not find favorable but you do it anyway because it means something to that other person."

Franklin shook his head. "I don't understand, Pa."

"He means," Elsa started, taking his jaw in her hand and turning his face to hers. "It means you won't always like what I ask of you but you would be wise to give me what I want."

"Why?"

"Frank, I would never ask you to go against someone or something you are familiar with unless it was important to me."

"This is important to you?"

"Yes, please, let my aunt examine you. That is all I ask. Please, Frank. I beg you, please. Do this for me."

Franklin took a deep breath and lifted his eyes to Betsy. "For you, Elsa. Only for you."

20

Elsa paced in the kitchen beside the long cabinets that lined the far wall. She fidgeted her sweaty hands. What was taking so long? She glanced at the staircase leading to Franklin's room. What she wouldn't give to be up there right now with Franklin, Gideon, and her Aunt Betsy, yet no one other than Gideon was allowed in Franklin's room while Betsy examined her boyfriend. She wondered what must have been going through Franklin's mind. It had to be one of the most uncomfortable situations of his life for him. Franklin had always hated unfamiliar surroundings and people. Thank heavens his father was upstairs with him. She couldn't imagine what Franklin would do if his father wasn't by his side throughout the entire stressful ordeal. Franklin wasn't violent. He wouldn't hurt her. In fact, Gideon had agreed to be by his son's side for two reasons. One, he didn't feel it was proper for any woman, married or not, to be alone with his son. Two, Franklin needed the extra support so he would accept Betsy examining him. Franklin often had better control of his emotional state whenever Elsa or Gideon was around him during stressful times. Despite Betsy's willingness to help it was only adding more stress to Franklin's already stressed out life. Elsa worried he might slip into a panic attack any given moment. What was best for Franklin was to leave him alone but that couldn't happen until she married him. Elsa's eyes shifted to the clock on the wall. It had only been forty-five minutes since the three of them had entered Franklin's room but it had felt like an eternity.

"Elsa," Margaret called to her daughter from the table. Elsa nervously pivoted towards her mother. "Mrs. Raymond made you some tea. Why don't you sit down and drink your tea before you wear a hole in her floor?"

Elsa looked to Juliette. Franklin's mother stared into her tea in deep contemplation. Franklin's parents had given so much for their son's happiness and welfare. She wondered if there was ever a time when they wanted to walk away from their son and forget about the troubles he had caused them. It took a stronger person to live with Franklin let alone deal with his peculiar ways. "Mrs. Raymond?" Elsa asked as she approached the table. Juliette silently raised her head towards her. "If my aunt finds favor with my desire to wed your son, how will you convince Franklin to propose to me?"

"Gideon and I have thought much on that matter since we returned home from church."

"And?"

"Elsa," Margaret scorned her daughter. "Show some manners, young lady."

"I'm sorry, Mrs. Raymond, for my ill manners. It's just…" Elsa sighed then sat in her chair. She fiddled with the teabag in her cup and sniffed her nose.

"You love my son and only want what's in his best interest," Juliette finished Elsa's sentence, lightly tapping Elsa's left hand. Elsa lifted her eyes to Franklin's mother with a slight smile. "You'll make him an excellent wife."

"Thank you," Elsa whispered.

"Do you remember what Gideon and I told you about Franklin proposing to you?"

"Yes. But we can still convince him to propose to me. He wants to. I can see it in his eyes."

"Yet you told me he refused to give you the ring and he has made no objection to your father's retraction of his permission," Margaret interrupted.

"Is that what your husband wants, Margaret?" Juliette asked as she leaned back in her chair and looked at her.

"Oren and I want the marriage just as much you and Gideon do."

Juliette scrunched her face, peered at Elsa then turned her attention back to Margaret. "It seems odd that your husband would object if he wants my son to marry your daughter."

"He has no choice in the matter, Juliette. If you want Franklin to marry Elsa then it would be best if they eloped."

"Franklin would never cons…" Elsa began to object. She

stopped as Juliette raised her hand towards her.

"Go on," Juliette asked. Elsa wondered why Franklin's mother would even listen to her mother's nonsense. Franklin would never make the decision to elope. It was too chaotic, rushed, and dishonorable. He needed everything to be perfect. Running away and marrying in secret was not perfect. Unless…

"You plan to tell Franklin it is socially acceptable for us to marry without our parents' permission," Elsa proclaimed, interrupting the woman. Juliette and Margaret glared at her as if she had deduced something that only a baby wouldn't understand. "It won't work," she added.

"Why not?" Margaret asked.

"Because I've told him several times I don't want to marry him like Henry and Deborah married their spouses. He knows how important my family is to me."

"This is the same family who refuses to give you and Franklin consent," Juliette reminded her.

"I tried to get him to propose to me after church yesterday but he won't budge. Franklin believes to do so would go against the rules."

"My son doesn't understand the rules, Elsa."

"No, but he does respect that I cannot make a decision without my father's consent. He thinks by complying with Pa's wishes he is showing my pa that he can be trusted with my care."

Margaret exhaled a deep breath, shaking her head. "And all he is doing is showing your father that he doesn't care enough to win his consent. He needs to speak up against your father, man to man. When Franklin's parents came to speak on his behalf it only strengthened your father and his brothers' stand that Franklin is too weak of a man to be your husband."

"But he's not," Elsa argued.

"It doesn't matter, Elsa. Franklin needs to approach them man to man, not as a boy hiding behind his parents."

"Franklin just doesn't understand," Juliette sighed.

The sound of a woman's heel on the staircase caught their attention. Elsa lifted her eyes to see Betsy walking down the stairs. "Aunt Betsy," Elsa greeted her as her aunt made her way to the middle of the staircase. She turned her gaze to the top then met

Juliette's gaze. Elsa's heart sank at the disappointing expression on her slightly heavyset aunt's face. She swallowed hard, sat in her chair and thought about the situation. Betsy had wanted to suggest Franklin be placed in an asylum when she had first met him. Perhaps her examination of Franklin had only solidified that belief? Maybe she had gleaned more evidence against Franklin that she could hand over to her husband?

"Thank you for granting me permission to enter your home and for convincing Franklin to let me examine him," Betsy said, placing her black bag on the table.

"You're welcome," Juliette answered.

Betsy glanced at Elsa for a long moment, sat down and then turned to Margaret with a nod. Margaret rose from the table and walked out of the house. "Are we leaving?" Elsa asked.

"No," Betsy answered her then turned to Juliette. "He's a remarkable young man."

"Does that mean you will help us?" Elsa asked. Betsy glanced at her then back to Juliette.

"You're the first doctor we have ever heard say those words to describe my son. Every doctor he has seen believes he would do best in an asylum."

"I thought so as well."

"What changed your mind?"

"I don't know, Mrs. Raymond. There is just something about him that intrigues me. I have examined him in a social setting and now in his own home. He seems to do best in surroundings he is familiar with. Franklin was agitated but he calmed down quicker in his own room than when he was agitated at Henry's farm."

"He's always been like that. He doesn't like strangers, change, or new surroundings," Elsa offered.

Betsy turned to her, "Elsa, marriage changes everything. How can he be a husband to you or a father to your children when he can't accept change? Have you thought about that?"

"She may not have but Gideon and I have," Juliette answered.

"And what was your conclusion?" Betsy asked, looking back at her.

"Elsa can move in with Cora. Franklin is already used to that because Elsa has slept over here a time or two. We will gradually move her into his bedroom and then when he marries her he will be used to having her in his bed," Juliette answered.

"You want to place them together when they aren't even married?" Betsy asked in shock.

"I won't let Franklin do anything to me. He's already tried and I turned him away," Elsa answered.

"He what?" Juliette and Betsy asked loudly together.

Elsa swallowed hard. She opened her mouth to speak but couldn't find the words. "Well that changes everything," Juliette proclaimed. "What exactly did he do to you and when?" she asked, leaning towards Elsa.

"It happened when he woke up from his coma. He placed his hand under my skirt. I shoved him away and told him I wouldn't let him be like that to me until we married. He said he wanted me to be his wife but he couldn't propose to me. He had the panic attack after that."

"No wonder. It explains a lot, actually. Gideon and I had wondered how he got into that state so quickly."

"I tried to tell him it wasn't right but I don't think he understood. He told me I should trust that he knows what's best for both of us."

Juliette grinned and leaned back in her chair with her arms crossed. Betsy shook her head. "What am I missing?" she asked.

"We don't have to formulate a plan to get them together. My son has already done so in his mind. It's not socially acceptable but if Elsa was to conceive there would be no way Oren could deny the marriage."

Elsa glanced between Juliette and Betsy. "You…," she bit her lower lip and lifted her gaze to the top of the stairs. An unconventional marriage to a man her family didn't approve of. It was everything she never wanted. Why couldn't she just have a normal wedding where everything was perfect? Was that too much to ask for? But then she had always been the social outcast. Too poor. Too hungry. Clothes tattered and torn. Nobody wanted to be her friend because of her parents' socio-economical position. To marry Franklin would be a step up for her, just like it had been for Deborah when she had married Liberty. She had always admired Deborah but now to follow in her footsteps? She turned to Juliette

"If I do this then Pa will treat me just like he treated Deborah. Why can't we just elope like you were planning with my ma?"

"Elsa, I can't take you to my father for Franklin's treatment without someone telling your pa or one of his brothers," Betsy added. Elsa turned to face her aunt.

"You said you could help us if you thought Franklin's condition could be treated. You said we had a place in your home. That was the plan. You would determine if you could treat him and then if you could treat him you would help us move. You can't change your mind. You just can't."

"I'm not, Elsa. I will help you but even if we followed that plan you would have to marry before you came. I don't think it would be wise for me to approach my husband with the information I have gleaned from my examination of Franklin."

"Why not?"

"Because it will only strengthen Jesse's cause against Franklin. You said your mother and Juliette were talking about elopement. Why hadn't you thought about that?"

"I don't want to dishonor my family by eloping and I don't want to marry Franklin in an unfamiliar environment. Please just write the affidavit and then I will take it to Liberty so he can marry us."

"No."

"She's right, Elsa," Juliette agreed. Elsa turned to the blonde, thin woman. "Franklin already has it in his head that he needs to make you his wife by sleeping with him. It's not a bad idea."

"It's a horrible idea," she yelled, rising as she slammed her hands on the table. "God forbids a woman to sleep with a man before they wed."

Betsy rolled her eyes, "Oh, lord, not this." She leaned close to her niece. "You know who you sound like?" Elsa shook her head. "Your father. That is your father speaking, Elsa. What do you feel in here?" she asked, pointing her finger to Elsa's heart. Elsa looked down at her aunt's finger. Felt there? Oh, if only her aunt knew what she couldn't bring herself to admit. She had wanted Franklin's body as much as Franklin wanted hers. Betsy placed her crooked finger under Elsa's chin and lifted her face. "Elsa, you seem a sensible young woman. You know this young man better than anyone. True, Juliette?"

"Absolutely," Franklin's mother agreed.

"Get your father out of your head and think about what Franklin needs. He's already told you what he needs from you. You denied him his plan and it confused him enough to send him into a panic state. That young man loves you, Elsa, so much he is willing to risk everything to be with you. Can you say the same?"

"But it goes against what the bible says. Pa said whatever the bible says is true and we have to comply with everything God tells us in his holy word."

"Good lord, Elsa. What has your father done to you? The bible isn't God's Rules and Regulations. It's a book about how much God loves us. Elsa, I believe that God knows what Franklin needs more than anyone else on earth. He loves Franklin unconditionally just as He loves you. I don't think God would condemn Franklin and you to hell for eternity for having relations outside of marriage. Besides, if you are blessed with a child out of wedlock then surely would that not show God's approval of the decision you make here tonight'?"

Elsa listened closely to Betsy words and hid them deep in her heart. God is love. It had been one of the descriptions of God that she had clung to for most of her life. When things went wrong, as they often did, she would cling to the hope that God loved her unconditionally and would provide for her. What was it her father had taught her? "The ways of the world are not the ways of God," she muttered the answer.

"What was that?" Juliette asked.

Elsa smiled towards her as Betsy lowered her finger. She tugged on her blouse then silently walked to the stairs. Elsa stopped at the base of the stairs, tapped her fingers on the banister, and studied the ascent to the top floor. Why did it seem longer to her than before?

"Will Franklin's pa let Franklin and me be alone with the door closed?" she asked, never taking her eyes off the stairs.

Juliette exchanged glances with Betsy then rose from her place. "Elsa, what are you doing?" Juliette asked.

"Giving Franklin what he wants," she answered then walked up the stairs.

"Now?" Juliette asked.

"The longer I wait the more agitated he'll become about it. The man has a plan and we all know his plans always work," Elsa beamed from the center of the staircase.

"Elsa, he needs to rest," Betsy objected.

"He can rest after he gets what he wants from me. How long do you think you can keep me away from Pa?" she asked.

Betsy shook her head, "I don't know, Elsa. I'll try to distract him and his brothers but, hmm, I don't know."

Juliette stepped between them, "Gideon and I will do everything we can to help you." She turned back to Elsa, walked up the stairs, and placed her hand on Elsa's back. "Let's go. I'll tell Gideon I need his help with something and we'll leave you two alone."

Elsa smiled and then ran up the stairs to Franklin's room.

21

Elsa nervously knocked on Franklin's closed door, not certain if she could go through with her plans. Why did the silence between her knocks seem so long? Elsa raised her hand to knock again as Juliette wrapped her hand around Elsa's fist. Elsa turned her head towards her. "You don't have to do this today, Elsa," Juliette comforted her.

"But I do."

The door suddenly opened slightly. Gideon stared at the two women with fatherly affection. "How is he?" Juliette asked, lowering Elsa's hand.

"Exhausted. He just fell asleep." Gideon peered at Franklin then back at his wife and Elsa. He stepped into the hallway and closed the door behind him. "What did Doctor Garrett say?" he asked as he leaned his back against Franklin's door with his hand on the doorknob.

"She's willing to help," Juliette answered.

"Good, and Margaret?"

"My ma will help us," Elsa answered.

Gideon nodded his head in deep contemplation. "Franklin has a plan," Juliette interrupted his train of thought.

"What? Since when?" he asked.

"He formulated it when he realized he missed the dance. Elsa rejected it but we all believe it would be in Franklin's best interest if she grants him his...uhm shall we say...desires," Juliette hinted.

Gideon widened his eyes with shock then looked at Elsa. She grinned back with a slight nod towards Franklin's door. Gideon was a good Christian man with a heart devoted to God and his family but unlike her father Gideon wasn't overly religious. Yet she wondered if he would agree to their plan. He had never placed too high a value on anything a woman said or did, believing a woman couldn't think logically because of her emotions. Yet, he had allowed Betsy to examine his son. Perhaps the Victorian man began to see value in the Progressive Era woman after all. Gideon turned back to his wife. "Do you know what her father will do if he learns…?"

"We have no other choice, Gideon. Betsy wants to help but refuses to allow Franklin and Elsa to travel to her father's clinic unmarried," Juliette interrupted. "If she carries his child…"

"…we won't know if she does or doesn't for a few months. What are we supposed to do until then?"

"Franklin will figure it out," Elsa offered.

"Elsa, my son cannot handle change. What makes you think a life on the run will do him any good?" Gideon offered.

"Then we don't run. I spend as much time in Franklin's bed as possible until my father figures out I am here and then I'll return home. If I'm pregnant then my father will have to force my marriage to Franklin."

"And if you don't?"

"I…I haven't thought about that."

Gideon turned to his wife, "This is why women shouldn't make decisions!"

"Gideon, calm down. In Franklin's eyes if he has relations with her then they are married," Juliette answered, tenderly placing her hands on his arms.

"That is hard to prove if she doesn't conceive. You are risking everything on this, Juliette. Franklin won't understand if she is taken away from him, and if she doesn't carry his child then her father will ensure she never returns to his side. How will you explain to our son that under the law they are not married but under God's eyes they are? And if she does conceive what will you do when the baby comes? He doesn't like to be touched. He doesn't like change. He doesn't…"

"I can figure that out when the time comes, Mr. Raymond," Elsa objected. He turned to face her. "Please, I want this as much as he does. Aunt Betsy said she would hide me from my pa as much as she can. We just have to fool my father into thinking I am still there when I am not. Franklin needs me and I need him."

Gideon took a long breath in deep contemplation. Elsa held Juliette's hand as she watched the man think. She could understand Gideon's reluctance to their plan. He was only looking after the welfare of his son. Under normal circumstances she would wholeheartedly agree with his protest. Franklin didn't need any more changes in his life at this given moment. Not when he was under so much stress to begin with. But even if she did become pregnant they had nine months to help him adjust to the changes that would occur once the baby was born.

Gideon silently shook his head, moved to the side, and opened the door. Elsa glanced at Juliette. "You better hurry up, Elsa, before I change my mind," Gideon warned.

Elsa grinned and kissed him on the cheek, "Oh, thank you."

"You're welcome. Don't make me regret this decision."

"I won't. I promise."

"Welcome home, daughter."

"I'll gather your belongings," Juliette said then started down the stairs.

"Belongings?" he asked towards her.

"Margaret and Betsy brought some of her clothes. I told them we would supply whatever else she may require."

"Humpf, you assumed I would agree to this?"

"Not really but I wasn't about to allow Franklin to lose the woman he loves. Would you, Gideon?" She turned then disappeared down the stairs. Gideon turned back to Elsa.

"I need to check on the children."

"Thank you," Elsa whispered.

Gideon nodded then walked down the stairs.

Elsa walked into Franklin's room and closed the door behind her. She stared at Franklin's still body underneath his covers. She bit her lip as she studied his firm back. Years of farming and working on machines had left his upper body strong. His firm chest and back had always been her favorite parts of his body. She wondered how she would feel with him on top of her. Her hands trailing down his back. How would he respond to such sensual touch?

Elsa removed her shawl, laid it down in his chair, rose and examined every aspect of his bedroom. She walked over to his messy desk and sifted through the pile of papers. She smiled reading every new invention he had created. Franklin's mind had always amazed her. His mathematical equations were beyond anything she ever learned in school. Although Franklin had completed his education he had never gone to the university. Yet his work showed the mind of a university trained mathematician and classically trained artist. She flipped through the drawings of his new inventions with a smile. Just when did he create these new mechanisms, and had he shown them to Gideon?

Franklin moaned. She lowered the papers and turned her face towards him. He shifted his body then fell back to sleep. Elsa carefully lowered the papers to his desk, making certain to place them exactly where she had found him. If they were off by an inch Franklin would notice and he would become agitated. Everything had to remain perfect.

She walked to the door and stroked his Sunday suit that hung on the back of the door. How many Sundays had they spent alone together, building on their relationship as they strolled, holding hands? She put her cheek on his coat and sniffed the fabric. It still smelled of flowers from their time together yesterday.

"Hmm, Elsa?" Franklin asked.

Elsa turned towards him and pushed his coat against the door with her hand. She walked to his bedside and sat on the edge of his bed. "You should be sleeping," she suggested as she traced her fingers down his spine.

Franklin swallowed hard and rolled onto his back. "Are you still mad at me?" he asked.

"Mad? Why would you think I'm mad at you?"

"You told your aunt to examine me so she can send me to an asylum."

"Is that what you really believe?"

"Why else?"

Elsa huffed. Franklin had once again jumped to conclusions based on his own perceived evidence and once his mind was made up it was rare for him to change it. Yet somehow she had to convince him of the truth. There was only one way to do that. She was going to have to be forward with him. He didn't understand social games. She could draw this out as much as she wanted but that would just be cruel to him. Elsa unbuttoned her bodice to expose her S-shaped corset. Franklin gasped, rose on his elbows, and stared at her perfectly round breasts. "You were right," she said, leaning closer to him.

"About what?" he asked.

"I'm so sorry. I should have listened to you," Elsa said, removing her bodice and throwing it on the floor. Franklin stared at her in shock and disbelief while Elsa rose from the bed, removed her shoes and shirt, and then threw them on the floor.

"Elsa, I don't understand," Franklin protested.

She grinned, pulling the blanket away from him. Oh, dear God he was only in his drawers. Elsa stared at the bulge in his pants then lifted her eyes to him. "Do you still want to make me your wife?" she asked, as she crawled up to his body.

"You still want to be my wife?"

"Oh, Frank, I'm not a whore."

"I know you're not." He put his hands on his face and slid down his bed with a drawn out groan.

Elsa placed her hands on top of his. "I'm sorry. Can we start over?" she asked tenderly. Franklin opened his hands and stared at the top of her breasts that hovered close to his chest. He lifted his eyes to hers for a moment then adverted his gaze. "You said you wanted to make me your wife. I want that too."

"Your pa said no."

"Forget my father. It's a new century. Make me your wife, Franklin. What God brings together no man can part."

Franklin turned his head back to her with a deep swallow. He lifted his fingers to the bow of her front-laced corset, played with the strings then dropped his hands with the shake of his head. "You don't want this. You said you didn't want this."

"I changed my mind."

Franklin shook his head. "We do this the proper way, Elsa. That's what you said you wanted."

Elsa drew out a long breath and untied the bow in front of her breasts. She unlaced the corset, threw it to the side, and pushed down her chemise to expose her medium sized, perky breasts. Franklin swallowed hard. He turned his head towards the door. She couldn't blame him for his reaction. She could tell from his crotch he was aroused yet mentally he was confused. She grabbed his chin and forced him to look at her. "Do you honestly believe I would whore myself to you if I didn't want to be your wife?"

"I...I...I don... I'm so confused."

"I know you are, Frank. Do you trust me?" Franklin nodded.

"You remember when you tried to touch me under my skirt?"

"You said no. You said it wasn't proper. You said…"

She placed her finger on his plump lips. "I was wrong. You were right, Frank. You know what's best for both of us. Make me your wife."

Franklin glanced up and down her body for a long moment. She wondered what was going through his mind. Was he so thoroughly weighing his options that he had forgotten the urgings he had for her body? Elsa gasped as he pushed her underneath him, removed her drawers and chemise off then threw them on the floor. His tender lips kissed up and down her naked body. She closed her eyes, taking in every warm sensation of his lips on her delicate skin. His hand trailed up her inner thigh. She gasped as he rubbed his fingers between her legs. "Oh, Frank," Elsa whispered, arching her neck. Franklin's lips replaced his fingers. She gasped as his tongue entered her. Damn, this man might not express emotions very well but oh how he knew passion! She wondered just how long he had planned this night. Her lower stomach ached for his attention and he knew it. Franklin crawled up her body as his fingers found their way to her clit. She grabbed the headboard, arched her neck and moaned. Franklin's free hand massaged her breast as his lips found their way to her left nipple. Elsa turned her eyes towards her lover. Never before had she felt such immense pleasure. If foreplay was this intense she wondered how much more would it be when he made love to her. Who knew the sweet, silent, strong man could do such wonderful things to a woman? Franklin lifted his eyes towards her. He grabbed her by the back of her head and kissed her passionately, rubbing his body against hers. Elsa couldn't stand it any longer. She wrapped her arms around his back and kissed him even stronger. They rolled several times in the sheet, groping and kissing. Elsa pulled his drawers off as they rolled and flung them to the floor. Over and over again they rolled. With each turn of their bodies their passion increased until neither of them could stand it any longer. They had to be together. Franklin grunted, pushed Elsa underneath him, and thrust his penis into her.

******

Darkness filled the room as Elsa lay on her back

contemplating the events that had transpired yesterday. She followed her eyes along Franklin's arm over her naked stomach and wondered if she was pregnant already. They had spent the entire night consummating their marriage under God. Five times Franklin had erupted his seed inside her. Her lower body still ached from the experience. The first time they had had sex had been bittersweet. She had never expected to feel pain. It wasn't a bad pain. The more he pushed the more slight pain she had felt, yet she had wanted more. It was quite odd. After their time together she had felt something sticky between her legs. She had rolled over only to notice there was blood on their sheets. It had scared Franklin so much he hadn't even asked if she was all right. Instead he had dressed, disappeared from the room, only to return a few moments later with his parents in a panicked state. Juliette had told them it was normal for Elsa to bleed a little bit after losing her virginity. It had taken Elsa and Franklin's parents quite a while to calm him down, but once they did his parents had left the room and they had made love again.

Elsa moved her hand down her lower stomach. Her stomach ached as if she was menstruating, yet her cycle wasn't due for two weeks. Elsa turned on her side and traced her finger up his long arm. His body was amazing. He was amazing. She would have never imagined Franklin would have been so passionate with her. Franklin squeezed her tighter to his body and slowly opened his eyes.

"Good morning, Mrs. Raymond," he whispered.

"Good morning, Mr. Raymond."

They kissed gently until they heard a knock on the door. Elsa lifted her eyes over his shoulder. Franklin pulled the blanket over her to hide her from view. "Come in," he answered.

The door opened and Juliette stepped in. She closed the door behind her then gathered Elsa's undergarments. "Elsa needs to get ready," Juliette said, handing Franklin the clothes.

"For what?"

"School."

"She's my wife, ma. Married women don't attend school."

"Well yours does. It's 4:30. She has thirty minutes to get dressed and get downstairs. And Elsa," Juliette added.

"Ma?" Elsa couldn't believe the words had escaped from her lips.

"Wear something different today."

"Yes, ma'am," Elsa replied.

June 13, 1904
Linn School
Marion, Ohio

Elsa sat at her desk in the second row as the children exited the schoolhouse. She stared at the phrase on the board: "Have A Great Summer!" Everything had gone perfectly for her since she and Franklin had consummated their relationship under God. She would go home after school, do her chores, then her mother would sneak her off to Franklin's house where she would spent the night with her husband. Early in the morning, Juliette would drive her to the road outside her parent's home, yet not close enough where she would be seen, then would drop Elsa off so she could be seen in the house before school. On Saturdays, Elsa would spend the day with her family and then attend church with them on Sunday morning, where she would disappear with Franklin.

Everything was perfect except for the times Cora belittled or threatened her. She didn't know what she was going to do about that situation. Cora had always been annoying but when Rebekah and her family never arrived in Marion she became even more obnoxious. Rebekah's disappearance from Franklin's life didn't both them anymore. Franklin had become so fixated on her that he constantly wanted her to touch and kiss her. It was amazing at the transformation that had occurred between them just by following his plan. Yet, there was still the problem of making their marriage legal. That problem didn't bother her as much as what today was. Today was the last day of school and she wasn't certain how much longer she was going to be able to keep her relationship a secret from her family.

Elsa lowered her head to her desk and closed her eyes. Franklin had wanted to proclaim to everyone in Marion that she was his wife but she couldn't allow that to happen. She wondered just how long he was going to be able to keep their relationship a secret. He had no idea as to the games his parents and she were playing. It was for the best that he never knew. Franklin would never understand any of it, anyway. Yet deep in her heart she had wanted the same thing too.

"Elsa," Mrs. Webster's called to her. Elsa opened her eyes and turned her face towards the young schoolteacher. "You need to go outside and eat your lunch so no one suspects anything. I don't trust Cora."

"Do you think she told anyone about Franklin and me?"

Mrs. Webster shook her head and stared out the window towards the playground. "I don't know, Elsa. The more freedom you give her the more she's likely to do something to disrupt our plans." Elsa leaned back in her chair as Mrs. Webster turned towards her. "You need to eat lunch and pretend everything is normal."

"But everything isn't normal, Mrs. Webster. I'm so tired and my corset is hurting me."

Mrs. Webster knelt beside her student. "Where does it hurt?"

Elsa shook her head. "Someplace I shouldn't be talking about. Forget it," Elsa protested, grabbing her lunch pail from beneath her chair. Mrs. Webster grabbed Elsa's wrist. Elsa paused and stared back at Franklin's best friend's wife.

"Elsa, how long has it been since you and Frank became man and wife?"

"Four weeks …" Elsa dropped her lunch pail with a gasp of realization. "Four weeks," she whispered, placing her hand on her lower stomach. She swallowed hard and stared at the phrase on the board. Everything had changed more than she could ever realize.

"Elsa, what's wrong?" Mrs. Webster asked.

"My cycles are predictable." She turned to face her teacher. "I…," she shook her head. "I should had one two weeks ago but I never bled."

"When did the exhaustion and tenderness begin?"

"I've been tired since last Wednesday but it has grown worse since. The tenderness started this morning."

"Have you told anyone?"

"No. Do you think…?," she began then stopped as Hayden barged into the schoolroom and ran towards them.

"Hayden," his wife proclaimed, rising from beside Elsa.

He looked at Elsa then back to his wife. "Frank's been arrested," he proclaimed, rushing towards his wife's desk. He rummaged through the drawers.

"For what?" Elsa asked.

"I don't have time, Elsa. Your father's on his way here to pick you and Nathan up."

"But school hasn't ended," Mrs. Webster said, approaching her husband.

"Doesn't matter, Bess. Cora told Nathan about Franklin and Elsa yesterday at church. Nathan told his father and Oren pressed charges of kidnapping, rape and molestation against Franklin. He's relocating his children to Wheelersburg."

"But he's innocent," Elsa protested.

Hayden closed a drawer then rose, stuffing a stack of money into his coat. "That doesn't matter, Elsa. He's already in an agitated state because he doesn't understand the circumstances he's in. Now that he's in the system he could very likely end up at the Central Ohio Asylum."

"He doesn't belong there."

"Don't you think I know that, Elsa!?"

Elsa jumped back. She had never known Hayden Webster to yell at anyone. The usually calm accountant had been one of the strongest men she had ever looked up to, yet she had always doubted just how much this man cared about Franklin. He had every right to support Cora's accusations against Franklin. It would be easier for Franklin to be left to rot in prison until Rebekah arrived, then Hayden could persuade Franklin to marry his sister. But Hayden's outburst of anger had shook Elsa's belief about the man. Perhaps Hayden truly cared about Franklin.

Mrs. Webster placed her hands on her husband's chest. "Hayden, she's pregnant," she whispered. Hayden glanced at Elsa then back at his wife.

"Are you certain?"

"No, but she is starting to show signs of being with child."

Hayden pushed his wife aside and approached Elsa. "You have to run, Elsa."

"Run? To where?" she asked in confusion.

"Our house," Mrs. Webster answered.

"How is that going to solve anything?"

"Because it will show the courts that you are acting on your own and Franklin is not...," Hayden paused at the sound of a carriage approaching the school. He stepped around Elsa and went to the door. Elsa walked to her teacher and took her hand. Hayden peered out the door for a long moment then turned back to his wife. "Her parents and uncles just arrived."

"I can't go back," Elsa pleaded.

"Hayden, what are you going to do?" his wife asked as her husband paced. Elsa's heart beat hard as she clutched her teacher's hand tighter. She couldn't go back to that horrible house. She hated her uncles' strict rules and she didn't want to even imagine what her punishment would be if they learned the truth of her situation. Blaming Franklin was just a ruse to get him out of her life so her family could control her. She wasn't about to let them tell her what she could or couldn't do. "Hayden, they will come in here soon," Mrs. Webster urged.

"Elsa, come with me," Hayden said, reaching his hand out.

"Where are we going?" Elsa asked.

"Not we, you. You're going to hide."

"Where?"

Hayden pulled her to the back of the school and walked into the small storage room behind the front of the classroom. "No one will suspect you are back here. I want you to hide in the shadows until I come for you. Understood?"

"Yes, sir," Elsa answered then crawled through the crowded storage room filled with chairs, desks, and boxes until she reached the back wall.

Hayden grabbed a couple of blank slates from one of the boxes, left the room and closed the door behind him.

Hayden stepped out of the storage closet and closed the door behind him. If only Franklin hadn't fallen in love with Elsa, his best friend wouldn't be in this predicament. Yet he had never seen Franklin happier then when he was with Elsa. There was something about the girl that calmed Franklin like no other person could. Sure he had his own effect on the inventor. They had been close friends since childhood. That unto itself was something of a miracle. Franklin had a hard time making and keeping friends. Come to think of it, aside from the late Henry Garrett, he was Franklin's only friend.

"Hayden," Mrs. Webster said from the middle of the schoolroom.

Hayden looked up at his wife and swallowed hard. Oren, Margaret, Nathan, Jesse, and Moses Garrett stood before her.

"Here's the slates you needed," he said, stepping forward.

"Oh, thank you," his wife responded. "You can place them on my desk."

Hayden nodded, never taking his eyes off their guests as he placed the slates on her desk.

"Mr. Webster," Oren commanded his attention.

Hayden gathered his strength with hopes the men would believe whatever he decided to tell them. The young man walked to his wife. "Mr. Garrett," he greeted Elsa's father.

"Where's my daughter?"

Hayden looked to his wife then back at the stern man. "I do not know. Bess sent Cora to tell me she couldn't find Elsa."

"That's not true," Nathan protested next to his mother. Jesse looked at his nephew. "Cora ate lunch with me. She never left the yard. He's lying because he's Franklin's best friend."

Jesse stepped in front of his younger brother. "Is this true, Mr. Webster?" Hayden swallowed hard as the one-legged man stared sternly into his eyes. How could he lie to this man without giving away their deception? He needed to protect Elsa for Franklin more than anything in the world at this very moment, but he was outnumbered. Jesse stepped closer to the shorter accountant. "I would think long and hard before you answer me, boy. You don't want to stand against my brothers and me. You hear me?"

"Yes, Mr. Garrett."

"Now, where's my niece?"

"I have no idea, sir. I was about to search for her myself."

"Why?"

"Why?"

"Yes, why do you want to find her? I very much doubt she will be of any use to Franklin anymore. By the sounds of it he'll be transported to the asylum by the end of the day. He's been causing trouble for the prison guards."

Hayden swallowed hard. This was all happening too fast. Franklin had been arrested only an hour ago. He wondered how the sheriff was able to get a court order to transport Franklin so quickly. What kind of pull did the Garrett family have with the Marion County courts? Perhaps it wasn't the family who had the pull but… "Where's your wife?" Hayden asked.

"Does it matter?" Hayden clenched his jaw. Jesse grinned with a slight huff. "You are so naive, boy. Do you honestly believe my brothers and I didn't know what Margaret and my wife were planning? It didn't take a week for us to figure out what kind of game our wives were playing. My wife told me everything after she had examined Franklin. We had hoped Margaret would have made her daughter come to her senses with this nonsense but this has gone on far too long."

Hayden took a better look at the group before him. Margaret wasn't simply standing there. They were holding her against her will! Margaret's hands were bound behind her back and Moses held her tight by the arm. Elsa's mother stood still with her head lowered. No wonder Elsa didn't want to return to her family. These men were monsters. How could Oren stand by and let his brothers treat his wife with such disrespect? He looked back at Jesse. "You sent your wife to testify against Franklin to the courts."

"No, I sent her to Judge Watkins' father, who has been quite helpful in persuading his son to write the court order to have

Franklin committed. It seems since Judge Watkins lost his wife he's become even stricter on underage marriages. The union between Franklin and Elsa isn't legal because they never married according to the court records. But what is clear to the judge is just how dangerous Franklin is to society. Raping, molestation, kidnapping…just a few charges that are evident. I'm quite certain we can find more. My wife knows better than to cross me. Margaret, on the other. Well, that's a different story. Now! I want Elsa!"

"I don't know where she is, Mr. Garrett."

Jesse grabbed Hayden's vest and pulled him closer with a threatening growl. "Don't lie to me, boy. You think Franklin's fate is bad, wait until you see what I do to you if you continue to cross me. Give me Elsa," Jesse threatened, pulling out his revolver and placing it against the accountant's heart. Mrs. Webster gasped.

"Please, we have children," she pleaded.

Jesse grimaced and turned his face to her as Oren held a gun at her head.

"Bess, don't," Hayden whispered.

"Where's my daughter?" Oren commanded with the click of his gun.

Mrs. Webster turned her eyes at Elsa's father and raised her hands. "I don't know. She was here for school and when the children went outside. I…I…I turned for just a moment. She was gone."

"Nathan?" Oren asked.

"It's true, Pa. Elsa was here this morning. I haven't seen her since lunch," Nathan confirmed.

"Please, Mr. Garrett. You're a father. I have two small children. I know how upset you must be at the disappearance of your daughter. I would be if something happened to my children. I care about your daughter very much. Please, I beg of you. Let my husband and me go. We'll help you find her."

"Jesse?" Oren asked.

"Hmm, I don't believe them," Jesse answered. "What about you, Moses?"

Hayden and his wife lifted their eyes towards the youngest Garrett brother. Jesse didn't believe them but perhaps Moses and

Oren did. Maybe they could cause a disagreement between the brothers or perhaps if that didn't work they could persuade them Elsa was somewhere else. That would give them enough time to get Elsa to a safe place. Moses moved his gaze between the young couple then shook his head. "I don't…"

"Wait," Hayden interrupted in desperation. All eyes turned to him.

"Well, well, you do know something?" Jesse smirked, pushing the gun.

"Elsa's at the Miller's farm."

"How did she get out there? Old Miller's farm is close to Upper Sandusky," Oren asked.

"I took her. She ran to Franklin's office and told me she was supposed to meet Franklin in the old farmhouse."

"Margaret, is that true?" Jesse asked.

Margaret lifted her head with tears coming down her eyes.

"Answer him," Moses urged with the pull of her arm.

"I don't know. Elsa never spoke to me of it."

"Then it's another lie," Jesse grimaced.

"Jesse, Elsa wouldn't have told me. She…well…she's Franklin's wife now."

"She is not his wife under the law unless there is something else you are hiding from us!"

"No, nothing. I swear."

Jesse nodded his head. "Old Miller Farm, huh?"

"Old Miller Farm," Hayden whispered.

"You better not have lied to me, boy," Jesse said with a shove then turned towards his family. He silently walked towards the door. Oren lowered his gun then joined his family.
Hayden grabbed his wife and held her close to this chest as he watched Owen lead Nathan and Margaret out the door. He turned his eyes to his wife, ignoring Jesse and Moses. "It's over," he whispered in her ear, comforting her.

"Mr. Webster," Jesse yelled from the back door. Hayden turned his gaze to the door. His heart skipped a beat at the sight of Moses with his rifle drawn. Hayden pushed his wife, protectively behind his back. "I don't like liars."

"We told you the truth, Mr. Garrett. Elsa's at the Old Miller

Farm," Hayden said, eyeing Moses as he moved in position.

"Yeah, that may be the truth but I don't appreciate liars. I'm certain Elsa and Nathan have told you my brothers and I all served in the Civil War."

"Yes, sir."

"You know what Moses did in the war?"

"No, sir..."

Suddenly Moses pulled the trigger of his long rifle. Hayden turned to push his wife out of the way but it was too late. She fell to the ground with the bullet in her head. "No," Hayden yelled in a panic state. He was so consumed with his grief he never noticed the second shot. Hayden fell beside his beloved wife with a bullet in his chest. The pain. Oh, God, the pain. Why couldn't the bullet have hit his heart? He gasped for breath and turned his eyes to his dead wife. Slowly, he moved his hands to hers. If he was going to die then this was the only place he wanted to be. Sharp pain radiated through his chest. He groaned and turned his head to face the man's foot, holding him down. Jesse leaned over with a grimace.

"Moses was a sharpshooter. Don't think he missed his target." Jesse chuckled. "Hell, he never misses. I want you to think long and hard about your decision to lie to me as you die a slow and painful death. Goodbye. Mr. Webster. It's been a pleasure," Jesse said, emphasizing the last part with the push of his foot. He turned, walked to his brother. "Good job, Moses. Let's get our niece."

"With pleasure," Moses replied, with an eye on Hayden. He tipped his hat then walked out of the school with Jesse. The door slammed hard behind them.

Hayden closed his eyes and cried.

24

Elsa rocked on her bottom with her head in her lap and her arms across her knees. Gunshots. Oh, God, gunshots. Terrified, chaotic thoughts ran through her mind. Over and over she replayed the sounds she had heard. The scuffling of feet, disconnected pieces of conversation and then gunshots. Just how long had it been since the gunshots had gone off? How long had it been since she heard her family leave? Was her father involved? Of course he was involved. She had heard his voice. But why? Why would her father and uncles do this? Her mother had tried to warn her not to cross her uncles. Hadn't her uncles told her, Nathan, and Samuel they had to comply with the new orders? Samuel!

Samuel wasn't at school today. He had stayed home to help his mother with the household chores, packing and taking care of Walter. Oh, God, what had they done with her nephew? Was Portia alright? She was under the same dictatorship she and her brother were under. If her family could be so cruel to them who was to say they hadn't made life unbearable for the pregnant widow and her children? Oh, if only Henry was still alive. He wouldn't allow their family to step in and take over like this. Was this why Henry didn't want the family involved in his life?

Elsa leaned her head against the wall and cried. She had to get out of here without anyone suspecting she was still in the schoolhouse, but where was she to go? The children. Oh, no. What of the children? Had Cora and her friends had the commonsense to get the children to safety once they heard the gunshots? Linn School was on the outskirts of Marion. It was at least a fifteen-minute ride by horse to get to town and a half hour walk. Her family, aside from Hayden and his wife, were the only adults around, and then there were the railroad tracks that ran in front of the school. If a train had come by and there was a young child who had disappeared from the group… She couldn't bear to think of the disaster that could have befallen the children. She had to do something.

Elsa wiped the tears from her eyes, gathered her strength, and crawled through the mess of desks, chairs, and boxes to the door. She stood up, placed her hand on the doorknob, and then paused with her eyes on the box where Hayden had taken the extra slates. How much she had underestimated the handsome accountant. She wondered what had befallen him and his wife. Was it even safe for her to enter the room? The sound of a woman's heel caught her attention. She was alive! Mrs. Webster was alive! Elsa turned the knob on the door, threw it open, and ran into the room. "Mrs. Web…," she paused, seeing Cora stop in the middle of the schoolroom with the children crowded outside, peering in.

"What do you want?" Elsa yelled, storming towards her. She had had about enough of Cora.

"Elsa," Cora pleaded, pointing to the bodies.

Elsa slammed her fist into Cora's face. Cora stumbled back and tripped over a desk. She struggled to her feet. Elsa grabbed her by the front of her dress and hit her again. "Stop," Cora cried with a bloody nose.

"Why should I? Just tell me why, Cora. I have been nothing but respectful to you and your family yet you continue to ruin my life!"

"Hayden needs our help."

Elsa lowered her fist, recalling the sound of gunshots. She thrust Cora to the ground and turned towards the bodies. Cora rose to her feet and slammed her fist into Elsa's jaw then pushed her back. "Don't you ever think you have bested me, Miss Elsa Beatrice Garrett. If we weren't in this situation I would gladly fight you, bitch."

Elsa huffed as Cora ran to Hayden's side. Dazed and confused, Elsa stared at Franklin's sister. She had known better than to start a fight with Cora. What had she been thinking? This woman was dangerous and yet she didn't care. All that mattered was Franklin's welfare. Yet she couldn't understand why Cora would place her brother in such a predicament if she loved him. "Why did you do it?" Elsa asked, nursing her jaw.

"Do what?"

"Tell my brother what Franklin and I were doing."

Cora turned her head to Elsa while applying pressure to

Hayden's wounds. "You don't deserve him, Elsa. Franklin needs to marry Hayden's sister, and he will."

"But how is he supposed to do that when he's been placed in an asylum."

"What are you talking about?"

"I heard my uncle tell Hayden that Franklin was being transported to an asylum today."

"I...," Cora rose to her feet with a look of shock. "I didn't. I mean it wasn't... I only wanted you and Franklin apart so Rebekah could convince him to marry her."

Elsa groaned and ran to Hayden's side. She placed her hands over Hayden's wound as Cora stood speechless. "You killed the teacher, committed Franklin, and now Hayden might die all because of your selfishness."

"My selfishness!" Cora burst, connecting back to reality. "Who are you to claim I've been selfish? You're the one who ruined everything! You and your family. Our lives were perfect until the day you came into Franklin's life. Now all he cares about is you."

"He loves me."

"No, he loves Rebekah. You're the reason he's confused. You're the new normal for him but what happens when Rebekah returns next week and Franklin's forced to face his old reality."

"He'll be fine. He has me."

"Ha, more like he'll be in a more confused state than he already is, assuming we can release him from the asylum. You know what, forget that. It's for the best he's in there. At least it keeps him away from you..."

"...and our child."

"What!?"

"I'm pregnant, Cora!"

"Hmm," Hayden moaned, arching his neck back.

"Hayden," Elsa called to him, placing her bloody hand on the side of his face. "Tell me, Cora, that someone sent for the doctor."

"Isaiah ran to Hayden's farm to call our parents as soon we heard the gunshots."

"How far is their farm?"

"Half a mile from the schoolhouse."

"Half a mile!"

"My brother runs it all the time. He can make it there in about four minutes."

"But it takes twenty minutes for your parents to get here from the store."

"He's a fast runner, Elsa, and my pa can run our team faster than anyone in the county. Franklin has this thing with horses…"

"Yeah, I know. He and Henry were breeding their horses together. How long has it been since Isaiah left?"

"Thirty minutes." Thirty minutes? Had it only been thirty minutes since… "My family," Elsa gasped.

"What?"

"What if they run into my family? I have to do something."

"There's nothing you can do. We have to save Hayden. My parents will think of something. They're not ignorant like yours are."

Hayden grabbed the side of Elsa's arm and stared deep into her eyes. He stared between Cora and Elsa then motioned for Cora to come closer. Cora knelt beside him and listened. "Take her to my house. Hide her."

"No, we're staying here with you," Cora refused, placing her hands over Elsa's.

Hayden grabbed Cora's wrists with a low growl. "Cora, please. She means the world to Franklin."

"So does your sister," she snarled in his face.

Hayden shook his head, closed his eyes and turned his head towards his wife. "No, Hayden," Cora yelled, turning his head towards them. "Stay awake, Hayden. Hayden," Cora cried with tears streaming down her cheeks.

"Elsa, Cora, let him through," Gideon's voice echoed from behind them as he ran down the aisle with Doctor Riley.

The girls rose as Doctor Riley knelt beside them and began to work on Hayden. Cora pushed Elsa, yelling, "If he dies I swear I'll kill you, too!"

"Cora," her father disciplined.

"I'd like to see you try," Elsa yelled, pushing her back.

"Elsa, that's enough," Gideon said, stepping between the two girls. If looks could kill they'd both be dead.

"You're nothing but trash, Elsa. Our lives were fine without you. I hope your family finds you and hurts you bad for what you did."

"That's enough, Cora," Gideon yelled, pulling his daughter away from Elsa.

"Why is everyone defending her? I'm your daughter not her."

"She's Frank's wife under the eyes of God and you will respect her."

"Absolutely not, Pa! It's all her fault. All of this! I hate her, Pa, even if she is carrying Franklin's child. I hate her," Cora yelled then ran out of the schoolroom as her mother entered.

"Cora?" Juliette asked.

"Leave her, Juls," Gideon replied, staring at Elsa. "Is it true?" he asked, calmly taking her by the arms.

Elsa nodded with a sniff of her nose. "Mrs. Webs…" she gasped, replaying the event in her mind and the image of her poor teacher's bloody head. Elsa embraced her father-in-law and sobbed. Gideon wrapped his arms around her in the loving embrace only a father could give. He was everything she needed right now. Never before had she known so much love until the day Franklin's parents accepted her as one of their own. She needed their strength now more than ever. Her entire world had fallen apart all around her and yet one thing remained constant, their love for her.

"Doc?" Gideon asked, tenderly stroking Elsa's back.

"He's lost a lot of blood. We need to move him but I dare not take him to Marion," Dr. Riley answered.

"Why not?" Juliette asked, approaching them.

"He won't make it. I can operate here and then take him home. But I will need help and someone will have to ensure the children are distracted while I do so. I don't need any surprises."

"We should hide Elsa. She doesn't need to be under any more stress, especially since she is carrying our grandchild," Gideon said.

"Cora and her friends can take care of the children. I told Isaiah to stay at Hayden's house. I'll take Abraham and Elsa home while you help the doc."

"Not our house, Jules. Her family are looking for her and they might suspect she's on our farm."

"They're heading in the opposite direction," Elsa said.

Gideon and Juliette lowered their gaze to her. She turned her head to meet Juliette's gaze. "What do you mean?" Franklin's mother asked.

"I didn't hear much of the conversation but I did hear Hayden tell my family I'm at the Old Miller Farm."

Gideon replied, "I still don't think it's a good idea for anyone to be at our farm."

"Abraham," Juliette gasped then grabbed Gideon's arm. "The preacher's wife is with our son at the house. What if they come to our house, hurt her and our son? Abraham can't move, Gideon. His leg is still healing."

Gideon asked, "Doc, it's been seven weeks since my boy broke his leg. You said the bone is healing nicely."

"It takes a normal break to fully heal between four and eight weeks. Abraham's bone was severally broken, Gideon, in three places. He's fortunate I was able to save the leg. It might take him anywhere between fourteen to twenty weeks to fully heal and that's not even counting the rehabilitation period afterwards."

"Do you think we can safely move him?" Gideon asked in the direction of Doctor Riley.

"Normally, I would tell you no. But under these circumstances, do what you have to do to save the boy, Gideon," Doctor Riley answered.

Gideon peered down at Elsa and pulled her away from him. "Elsa, go with my wife. She is going to take you somewhere safe."

"What about Franklin?" she asked.

"We'll deal with my son's situation later."

"But…"

"No, buts, Elsa. My main concern right now is you, the baby, my children, my wife, and Hayden. Go, child. We'll protect you," he explained, cupping her face in his hands.

Elsa nodded with a sniff of her nose. "Okay," she whispered.

Gideon released her face and turned to his wife. "Get the children and head to my parents' house."

"Gideon, they won't help us with Frank."

"Probably not but they will protect my family. They love us,

Juliette, and I think in this situation it would be for the best if we moved back to Upper Sandusky. When Franklin is released he can marry Elsa up there. I'll make certain no one denies the marriage."

"They'll object. We have family members on the bench up there."

Gideon placed his arms around Juliette, "They can't deny Franklin's child, now can they?"

Juliette turned her gaze to Elsa, "No, they can't."

"Go, hurry, Juliette. There is much that needs to be done if we are going to save our son and his family."

25

The wagon bounced up and down the rocky road as Elsa held Franklin's thirteen-year-old brother in her arms. Abraham clung to Elsa's sleeves and screamed with each bump. Tears ran down Elsa's cheek as she pulled him closer to her chest. "Hold onto him, Elsa, and keep your head down. We're not far from Upper Sandusky. The sooner we get to Gideon's parents' house the better," Juliette ordered from the bench as she moved the reins.

"Yes, ma'am," Elsa complied and lowered her body.

"Ma," Abraham screamed.

"I'm trying, Abraham. Muffle those screams," Juliette ordered.

Abraham peered up at Elsa, sobbing with pain. She pulled his face closer to her chest and lifted her eyes towards Isaiah and Cora. Cora held her nine-year-old brother next to her body and glared at Elsa. "This is all your fault," Cora mouthed to her. Elsa rolled her eyes and turned her face upwards. Thick, dark storm clouds threatened to pour heaven's wrath upon the earth. Elsa swallowed hard. She had traded one family for another yet even in a family full of love she couldn't escape hate and destruction. The farther north they went the more her heart ached to be by Franklin's side and defend the man she held dear to her heart. Every roll of the wheel brought more heartache. She worried about Hayden, Gideon, Doctor Riley, and Gideon's children, but most of all she worried about Franklin. At least Franklin's parents were God centered people who loved their children unconditionally. She could find rest and comfort in their home as long as Cora didn't ruin that for her as well.

Abraham screamed as the wagon went over a large bump. Elsa shifted her attention to the young man then up at Cora. As much as she hated it she needed Cora's help. "Cora," Elsa called to her sister-in-law.

"What?" Cora huffed.

"Like it or not I'm a member of this family."

"Not legally."

"She's Frank's wife, Cora," Isaiah objected.

"Shut up," Cora growled at her younger brother, pushed him aside and then lifted her eyes to Elsa.

Elsa leaned over Abraham as he screamed in her chest, clutching her arm. "We can have this argument later. I....I....Abraham needs your help."

Cora grinned and leaned closer to Elsa so their faces were only a few inches from each other. She chuckled, looked down at her brother then up at Elsa. "Are you asking for my help?"

Elsa clutched her jaw. "His leg needs to be stabilized. If we work together we can ease his agony."

Cora lowered her eyes to Abraham's broken leg and stared at her brother's injury for a long time. Elsa wondered if Franklin's sister even cared about her brothers or if she was so self-centered that she gleaned enjoyment from their pain. "Cora," Elsa yelled.

Cora turned her head towards her enemy. "Tell me what to do but don't you dare think I will ever take orders from you again, Elsa."

"Deal. Hold his legs." Cora complied as Elsa turned her attention to Isaiah. "Get on the other side and help her, Isaiah."

Isaiah nodded and followed her instructions. "Elsa," Abraham cried as his siblings grabbed his legs and immobilized him.

"Shh," Elsa tenderly comforted him. She stroked his back and closed her eyes. How could her entire life have gone entirely wrong in just a few short months? Everyone she had ever depended on had either died, been captured, or betrayed her. Yet she had gained what she had wanted the most. Marriage. It wasn't a legal marriage, not yet anyway. She smiled to herself as she recalled the night she had given her body to Franklin. He had been the most passionate, wonderful lover any woman could ask for. She could easily accept her marriage to Franklin under God's law and despite how much she had objected to the union in such a manner, God had blessed their union with a child. The child was the key. Now her family had to accept Franklin as her husband and force him to marry her. Yet that was easier said than done. As long as her family believed Franklin was unfit to be her husband they would continue to hunt her down and have Franklin imprisoned in the asylum. It seemed to Elsa that by solving her desire to be Franklin's wife she had caused even more problems for their union. There was only one thing to do.

26

June 27, 1904
Home of
Howard and Lila Jacobs
Upper Sandusky, Ohio

Elsa vomited into the toilet as Juliette held back her long, brown hair. She grasped the sides of the porcelain bowl and stared at the bits of her breakfast, with her hand on her lower stomach. Her heartache for the life she dreamed of with Franklin. Her plan had been simple enough. She's stay by Franklin's side as his wife and when she started showing they would legally marry in Marion. Her parents couldn't and wouldn't deny the marriage. Hadn't they allowed Deborah and Liberty to marry because he had gotten her pregnant out of wedlock? Her father would be more concerned for their family's honor than some petty argument between his brothers and Franklin. She wondered if her mother, brother, Portia, Sam, and Walter were still alive. No matter how much she had hated her life before her uncles had arrived, things were now far worse than she could ever imagine. She just hoped they didn't try to look for her in Upper Sandusky. She was safe as long as she remained with Franklin's family.

Franklin.

Elsa sniffed and pushed aside the thoughts of her lover. Two long weeks had passed since Franklin had been arrested. It hadn't taken her family very long to convince Liberty to commit Franklin to the Central Ohio Psychiatric Hospital in Columbus, Ohio. The police had placed him in a paddy wagon and drove the one-hour trip to Columbus where Franklin was secured behind the massive hospital's doors all while her family had shot Hayden and his wife then went to look for her. Her poor Franklin had been left alone in solitary confinement with his hands and feet chained for days.

Tears rolled down her face. Cora had caused the death of

their teacher and the incarceration of her brother. She just couldn't forgive Franklin's sister for placing them in this predicament. She worried about Franklin and didn't completely trust Cora. What if Cora ever decided to tell her family where she was? Oh, God, she couldn't even imagine the horrors that would further bring upon Franklin's family. Thankfully, Cora had been so shocked at what happened in the schoolhouse that she didn't, that Elsa knew of, wanted anything to do with Nathan or the rest of Elsa's family.

Elsa took a deep breath, pushing thoughts of Cora aside. She was safe. All she had to do was stay with Juliette and Gideon. Gideon's parents had warmly welcomed Juliette and her children into their home, along with Elsa. Their family doctor had tended to Abraham while Juliette had called Hayden's parents to inform them of his condition. The Webster family had arrived in Upper Sandusky along with Rebekah four days later. Elated, her best friend was back, Cora became even more determined to make Elsa's life miserable. The trip had made Abraham's leg worse, and now he faced the possibility of never being able to walk. Elsa could only lay blame for her brother-in-law's misfortunate upon Cora. If Cora had just left her and Franklin alone, they wouldn't be in this mess.

The night of their arrival, Juliette and Elsa had explained their situation to Gideon's mother and stepfather, telling them the entire story. Mrs. Jacobs had been delighted to know that Elsa carried her first great grandchild, and the couple had done everything they could to make Elsa feel right at home. The greater attention they gave Elsa only made Cora even more upset with her. She should have suspected that Cora would do something else to ruin her life, but Elsa was so exhausted from the entire ordeal that all she wanted to do was sleep. She fell asleep that night only to wake up two days later!

"Oh, sweetheart." Juliette comforted her as she wiped Elsa's mouth with a cloth, and then held her close to her chest. "Things are going to get better."

"I'm sorry. I shouldn't cry. I...I have to be strong for him. I can't be acting like a child. Not when I am going to be a mother," Elsa said as she tried to pull herself together.

Juliette wiped the tears from Elsa's eyes and then cupped Elsa's face with her hands. "It's alright to cry, Elsa. You've been through an emotional ordeal and you're with child. No one expects you not to have mood swings."

"When can we see Frank, again?"

"I don't know, Elsa. Everything is different since Rebekah and her family returned. Rebekah's father..."

Elsa huffed, rose sharply and turned to Juliette, "He chose me, not her! I should be the one with the visitation rights, not her."

"It's not that simple, Elsa. Franklin has a legal agreement with Mr. Webster that he would propose to Rebekah in two years. By seeking your hand in marriage he could be charged with bigotry."

Elsa paced, gesturing with each argument she presented. "I'm carrying his child. It's not her he cries out for when he's distraught. It's me. Rebekah only agitates him even more."

"Elsa, we need the Webster family support. Gideon's family is not going to help us as we had thought except allow us to remain in this house."

"Cora," she snarled.

"Elsa, I know she has done some terrible things to you and Franklin, but..."

"...This family has always protected her," she accused pointing sharply to the floor.

Juliette rose and placed her hands on the side of Elsa's arms. "Elsa, we love you and Cora equally."

"That's not true," she cried, pulling away from her mother-in-law. Elsa paced the small room, sobbing.

How could Franklin's mother be so blind? Her body quaked with each tear she shed. She placed her hand on her lower stomach as it pushed its contents up her throat. Elsa knelt at the toilet and vomited. She was an emotional and physical mess, but she had to pull herself together. If not for her, then for Franklin. She wasn't about to let Cora destroy her chances of being with him.

"Elsa, perhaps we should delay the hearing."

"No. The longer we wait, the more she wins."

"This isn't a game."

"It is in your daughter's eyes," Elsa said, glaring at the taller woman.

Juliette sighed as she knelt next to her. "Elsa, I will do anything to fight for my son."

"You didn't stand up for us when Mr. Raymond's stepfather retracted his position to help Franklin and me. He only did that because Cora convinced him that I'm a whore who manipulated Franklin into leaving Rebekah and marrying me. I'm not a whore."

"I know that, sweetheart. But you have to understand his reasoning. Your parents are so poor that their farm is in foreclosure. Your brother is dead and the creditors are coming for his farm. Gideon's stepfather believes you know Franklin's weaknesses and are using them so you can rise in money and position, just as your sister had done with Liberty."

Elsa shook her head, "No, Deborah loved him just like I love Franklin."

"Men don't marry for love, Elsa. They marry to secure their wealth and social standing."

"Franklin loves me," she begged.

"I know he does, and I know you will make him a good wife. You're fortunate that his stepfather allows you to remain in this house. The only reason he does so is because you carry Franklin's child."

"What happens after I give birth?"

"Don't worry about that now."

"What about your family or …. or…or Mrs. Webster's family?"

"Bess' parents buried her last week. They need time to heal their hearts. As for my family, I have spoken to them concerning the matter. My brother may be persuaded to help."

"He's a judge. He presides of the family courts in Wyandot County."

"How is that supposed to help me?"

"He's agreed to hear your case. But I must warn you. He can't do much with the charges that were placed upon Franklin in Marion County but if he deems Franklin's sane then he can have Franklin released."

"The only thing saving him from serving in prison for the charges that stand against him is his insanity plea but if that's taken from him then he'll be ...."

"There may be a way to dismiss those charges. Liberty presides over family court. The charges against Franklin are of a nature that presumes you were ineligible to give your consent due to your age. But if we can prove you two were married at the time then it would be legal for you to carry Franklin's child."

"You have to prove my parents gave consent to the marriage."

"I have a solution but I need my brother's help."

"Cora will change his mind, too."

"Not if you stand against her."

"I've stood against her this entire time, but all it brings me is even more grief. No one believes me, not even Franklin."

"Elsa, I know my daughter."

Elsa stared at Juliette for a long time. She knew her daughter? It seemed odd for Juliette to tell her that. She wondered if she had heard her correctly. "Are you saying you believe me?"

"Cora can be quite cruel sometimes, but she has a good heart. She loves her brothers and me. In a way, I can't blame her for what she does."

"Can't blame her!"

"You don't understand, Elsa. Franklin and Cora don't have too many years between them. I couldn't give her all the attention I should have because Franklin required more of my attention than she did. She's been angry with Franklin for a long time because of it, and I think she believes we don't care about her. I've tried so many times to convince her otherwise, but she won't believe anything Gideon and I tell her."

"If you know this, then why don't you punish her?"

"If I punish her, she will take it as if I love you more than I love her."

"So you let her get away with everything she has done," Elsa yelled.

"No, Elsa. I want you to teach her a lesson, and today you will have that chance. My brother isn't a stupid man. He can't be easily swayed. He's only going to make a decision based on the facts and not out of emotion. You need to present a just argument to him today without letting the frustrations you have with Cora and Rebekah get in the way. They have a strong case against you."

"You said as long as I carried his child, then no one could deny the marriage."

"You can't marry my son as long as he's been declared a lunatic."

"We can change that today, can't we?"

"It's going to be a hard fight. Everyone who knows my son has always believed he belongs in the Central Ohio Asylum."

"But he doesn't. He belongs with me. I can help him more than they can."

"I know you can, sweetheart, and you just need to prove it."

"If we could just convince Liberty...."

"No."

"No?"

"It's not safe for you to return to Marion while your family is still looking for you. It's best that we depend upon the Webster family to help us."

"They won't help me. Rebekah's parents side with her."

Elsa huffed and turned away from Juliette. Hayden had survived the operation in the schoolhouse and had been transported to his home to recuperate, but Gideon had felt conflicted about leaving the young accountant in his own home with a gang of murderers hunting Elsa. After Juliette had arrived to Hayden's farm, Gideon had arrived two days later with Hayden and his young children. His parents and sister had arrived last Monday to care for Hayden and the children. It seemed to Elsa, that ever since Rebekah had arrived, the raven-haired beauty was bound and determined to steal her man from her. Cora was more than willing to do whatever it took to make that happen.

Elsa weighed the situation in her head. The more she thought about it, the more hopeless it all seemed. She couldn't stop crying. Her heart yearned for Franklin. Today was her last hope. If she couldn't prove Franklin had acted out of his own will, then he would be forced to remain in the asylum until he agreed to marry Rebekah. She knew Franklin would never agree to it as long as he believed he was Elsa's husband. It was stupid for Elsa to think her man would ever abandon her and the baby. She never told him about their child, and hoped it wouldn't come out in court. The thought of being a father would scare Franklin. Wasn't he under enough pressure?

"Elsa." Juliette again held her close to her chest.

How many times had she cried in her arms? Juliette was safe and warm.

"Sh, sh, sweet child," Juliette coaxed, as she rubbed Elsa's back. "You can't be under a lot of stress, Elsa."

"I was under a lot of stress before that harlot arrived. You know what she's doing to Franklin, and yet you do nothing about it," Elsa sobbed.

"The ring was Rebekah's, not yours. Can't you understand how this works against Franklin? Rebekah's father expects Franklin to deliver on his word or pay him back. We just don't have the funds to return what he borrowed in full."

"What if your brother sides with me? Even if I give the ring back to the Webster family, that doesn't mean they won't try to sue us. Franklin won't understand why I had to give it back. He doesn't understand social situations. So how is he supposed to understand why I gave the ring back?"

"Elsa, don't overthink this. It will just drive you insane. Let Gideon and me take care of the Websters. You just need to focus on this hearing. It's our last chance to grant you and Franklin a life together."

Elsa clutched her jaw and shook her head. "He's been in

the asylum for a month, and when we went to visit him a few days ago, he was agitated. It took the entire hour we had with him just for me to calm him down, and when he was finally calm we were forced to leave him. The longer he stays in there, the more he will struggle. Franklin doesn't understand what's going on. If your brother wants to present him..."

"Sh, Thaddeus understands about Franklin's condition. He won't do something that will upset him."

"Then he should have had him released and marry us."

"He doesn't quite trust you, Elsa. He's very protective of Franklin, and one of the few family members who supported Gideon and my decision raise our son away from our families."

"But...,"

Juliette placed her finger on Elsa's lips. "Trust Gideon and me. That is all I ask from you. We know what is in the best interest of our son."

Elsa sniffed her nose with a nod. Despite her internal need to free Franklin from the situation they found themselves, in she knew Juliette meant her words. They had cared for Franklin his entire life and had fought hard to keep him out of the asylum. Yet here they were faced with their worst fears, and Franklin was living in his own personal hell. Labeled as a lunatic, he could never marry her, and without her Franklin became the monster everyone thought he was. Elsa swallowed hard as Juliette lowered her finger, and embraced the older woman. Juliette held her close.

"I'm so sorry. I don't doubt you. Not at all," Elsa pleaded.

"I know, Elsa."

Someone knocked on the door. "Juls, they're ready," Gideon's voice called to his wife from the hallways with a slight tap of his knuckles on the door bathroom door.

"We're coming," Juliette answered. She flushed the toilet, wiped Elsa's face, and then led her out of the bathroom.

27

Hayden Webster lay on his bed in a daze. He couldn't remember much about his ordeal, except that his wife was dead, Franklin had been committed to an asylum, Elsa was with child, and he had been shot in the chest. He remembered briefly waking up in this strange room and his parents were by his side. His father had told him Dr. Riley had removed the bullet from his chest and part of his lung. He had almost died several times during the operation due to shock and blood loss. Gideon had given his blood to Hayden during the operation. The emergency blood transfusion had worked, but he was very weak when they moved him to Upper Sandusky. The only reason Gideon had moved him was for his and his children's safety.

He had been in and out of consciousness for three days. It had been hard to breathe with half his lung missing and a few broken ribs. A part of him wished he had died. At least he would be in heaven with his wife.

But another part reminded him that he needed to be there for their young children. It was bad enough that his children wouldn't remember their mother. He wasn't about to let Elsa's family steal both their parents from them. He mourned for his wife but didn't let it consume him. He needed to get stronger for them.

"Hayden." His father voice entered his ears.

Hayden slowly lifted his eyes to his father and swallowed hard. Deep emotional scars echoed the searing pain in his chest.

"Hmm, what time is it," Hayden whispered as sunlight from the window fell upon his face.

"Eleven o'clock"

Hayden pushed the thick, warm blankets off and sat upright. He held on to the bedframe as a wave of dizziness overcame him. He struggled to stay upright on the edge of the bed.

"Hayden," his father said, tapping the side of his son's leg.

"Dizzy," he mumbled.

"You don't need to rise. The judge brought everyone to you."

Hayden opened his eyes and stared at his father with a grateful heart. Last week had been the first time he had risen out of his bed since he'd been shot. His broken ribs were healing nicely and his chest was getting stronger, but he had a lot more healing to do if he was to completely recover. Dr. Riley had wanted the young accountant to walk two times a day so his legs wouldn't lose their strength. Hayden looked forward to those moments of his day the most. It was hard to walk without the support of his father, but he tried his hardest. His children were too young to understand what had happened to their parents.

He spent most of his walks with his parents, Rebekah, and his two children. He loved spending time with them, his little ones, and hated that he was too weak to give them a hug. His daughter was three and his son only one. All he wanted to do was hug them close and reassure them that he was never going to leave them.

"Where are the children?" Hayden asked, seeing his mother and sister behind his father.

"Juliette's mother is tending to them."

Hayden nodded as he placed his hand over the bandage stabilizing his ribs. He lay back down with a deep groan. Every move he made seem to radiate pain somewhere in his chest. His father gently placed his legs on the bed and pulled the warm blankets over his chest. "Do you need something for the pain?"

"Please."

Hayden's mother walked to the side of the bed with a glass of water and two aspirins, as his father helped him sit upright against his pillows. He reached his hand out, took the aspirins, placed them in his mouth, and then swallowed them down with the water.

"Are you certain you are capable of giving testimony?" his mother asked with a slight British accent.

He turned to his parents. "I need to do this for Frank."

His mother exchanged a look with her husband, and then joined Rebekah and Cora beside the window, as his father sat in a chair beside the bed.

Hayden turned his attention to the small crowd that filled one end of the room.

Elsa stood next to Franklin's parents at the foot of his bed, with Franklin's locket around her neck. He smiled softly to himself. She had his sister's ring and locket, but they were where they rightfully belonged. He could tell by the look on her face that she didn't quite trust him yet. Why would she? He was, after all, Rebekah's' older brother, and her family had killed his wife.

"Mr. Webster."

A middle-aged, well-dressed man called his name from the foot of his bed. Hayden turned his attention to the unfamiliar man.

"My name is Judge Thaddeus Maxim. I believe you know my older sister, Mrs. Juliette Raymond," the handsome judge said, pointing to his sister.

"Yes, sir."

"Good," he answered as he lowered his hand and walked to the end of the bed. "My sister has asked me to determine whether or not the claims against her son are valid."

"He was charged with kidnapping, molestation, and rape in Marion. I don't understand what you can do in this county while the charges stand against him in Marion."

"I can't remove the charges that stand against him, but if I find in his favor I will post his bail and have him removed from the asylum into my custody. He will still have to stand trial in Marion."

"What of Elsa?"

"Ah, well, if I determine that she is in the best interest for Franklin, then I will marry them. Now, I have heard testimony from your parents and Franklin's parents this morning concerning the matter. I have yet to hear from the girls. Before I do so, I have a few questions for you."

"May I ask you a question?"

"Certainly, Mr. Webster."

"If you find in favor of your nephew, won't that seem as if you're being biased towards someone in your family?"

"That is a most excellent question, and something I want to know myself," Hayden's father said.

Elsa's heart skipped beat at hearing the men's conversation. She glared over at Cora and Rebekah. The two young women smiled coldly towards her. She could feel her knees give way.

How could she have trusted Hayden? He was a Webster. How could she have thought that this man, who only pretended to care about her, would actually help her?

"Elsa," Juliette asked as she wrapped her arm around her waist.

Elsa lifted her eyes to Juliette's face. Why had everyone stopped talking?

She glanced around the room. Everyone was staring at her.

"Gideon, the baby is making her weak. She needs to sit down," Juliette said to her husband.

"No, no. I'll stand. I'm alright," Elsa protested, regaining her composure.

"Are you certain you are well enough to attend to this hearing?" Thaddeus asked her. "You are in a delicate condition, Mrs. Garrett."

"I am, Judge Maxim. I'm carrying Franklin's child, sir. This hearing isn't just about Franklin. It's about the future of our child and the woman he calls his wife," she stated, with her eyes focused on Rebekah.

Rebekah huffed and crossed her arms over her chest. "The only reason you have his child in your stomach is because you're a manipulating whore."

"That's enough, Mrs. Webster," the judged ordered her.

Elsa caught Hayden's slight grin out of the corner of her

eye. She wondered if he was happy because his sister had finally said what he felt, or because the judge had disciplined her. She turned her attention to the injured man.

Hayden placed his finger below his neck and tapped it a few times, with his eyes on her locket. Elsa peered down at the silver locket with understanding. He wasn't smiling at Rebekah. He had asked the judge that question because he wanted to make sure that whatever judgment was passed, it was in favor of Elsa.

Oh, what a fool she had been not to trust him. She lifted her eyes and nodded to him. Hayden lowered his finger and turned his attention back to the judge.

"Mr. Webster," Thaddeus said, with an air of authority. "I am an impartial judge. I will not come to a decision that brings more harm to society. Rest assured I am considering all sides, while I determine what is in the best interest of my nephew."

"That is what we all want, sir. Isn't it, Father?" Hayden asked, turning his head to his parents.

"Yes, I like the boy but he has problems," his father reluctantly answered.

"As his uncle, I know all about Franklin's problems," Thaddeus reassured Mr. Webster.

"Then you know the harm he causes because of his condition," Hayden's father stated sharply to the judge.

"I do. But as a judge, and that is who I am in this room, I must not stand here with biased beliefs about the boy."

"He stole from me."

"Then presses charges for theft against him, Mr. Webster."

"Can you not take that into consideration?"

"I will not. The matter at hand is whether he kidnapped, raped, and molested Elsa Garrett," Thaddeus said, turning to face Elsa.

"He didn't!" Elsa protested.

Thaddeus raised his finger at her and turned back to Hayden.

"Mr. Webster, how long have you known Mr. Franklin Raymond?"

"All my life, sir. He's my best friend," Hayden answered.

"Good. Can you tell me about him?"

"He's a good man, sir. Franklin's always been strange, though. He prefers to be alone and make inventions rather than be with anyone."

"Even girls?"

"He doesn't understand them. His sister, Cora, thought it would be a great idea if Franklin married Rebekah and she married me."

"Because?"

"Well, because my sister is her best friend and Frank's mine. But I never saw Cora in that. I.." He closed his eyes and pushed back the tears. Hayden rubbed his hands down his face with a drawn-out breath.

"I understand, Mr. Webster. My condolences. Take your time."

He lowered his hands, and tears ran down his face. He shook his head and turned to Cora. "You never liked my wife because I loved her. And, Cora, I will never forget what you did. She would be alive today if you hadn't told Elsa's brother what Franklin and Elsa did."

"Hayden," Cora pleaded as she approached his bed.

"Get away from me!" Hayden yelled.

Cora stepped back, took Rebekah's hand, and lifted her gaze to Elsa with a deathly glare.

Hayden growled at Cora and then regained his composure. He lifted his gaze to the judge. "If you ask my opinion as to which woman is best for Franklin, I would tell you it's Elsa."

"No, that's not what you're supposed to say! I'm your sister! We had it all planned out!" Rebekah yelled, charging towards his bed. Her mother pushed her daughter back.

"No, you had it all planned out, Rebekah! You never loved Franklin, but she does!" Hayden shouted at her, pointing to Elsa. "You don't deserve him, Rebekah. You call her the manipulating whore, but you've tugged at Franklin's heart for years. You treat him like your personal toy, and when you're tired playing with his heart you...,"

Hayden groaned and leaned his head back as pain radiated throughout his chest. He closed his eyes.

"Hayden?" Elsa asked in concern, with a step forward.

"Perhaps we should continue this discussion at another time," Thaddeus said.

"No," Hayden whispered, opening his eyes. He slowly lowered his gaze to the judge. "I want to speak. Franklin doesn't belong in the asylum. My parents and sister are angry because Franklin made a decision that they neither consented to nor can control. I love my family, but they are wrong, sir. Elsa is good for Franklin. He's become a better man since she entered his life. He's more independent and can handle more in life than he ever could with my sister. Rebekah seems to think he is a child that she must control. Elsa sees the wonderful man he truly is. You came here for my honest opinion because you value what I have to say about my best friend?"

"Yes, Mr. Webster, I do."

"Marry Franklin and Elsa. "

"No!" Rebekah cried, as her mother held her away from her brother.

Elsa stood in front of the tall mirror in her bedroom, nervously pushing the fabric of her new Lane Bryant dress. She had never had a store-bought dress before. She turned and studied her image carefully. How could she still look so thin when she felt so fat? She felt full in her lower stomach, but it didn't show. Juliette had told her she wouldn't show for quite awhile because this was her first child. She would show earlier with her later pregnancies.

"Elsa," Hayden called from behind the closed door as he knocked.

Elsa walked quickly to the door, opened it slightly, and peered out. She carefully looked to see who had accompanied Hayden up the stairs, but could only see the well-dressed accountant.

"Looking for someone?" Hayden asked.

"Your family."

"My parents are with my children, and Rebekah went to Marion with Cora."

"Marion? What for?" Elsa gasped, opening the door wider. Juliette stood behind Hayden.

"The girls said they wanted to do some shopping. They would much rather shop in the city than this small town," Juliette explained with her hand behind Hayden' back. "May we come in?"

Elsa nodded, then silently stepped back to let them in. It didn't sit well with her that Cora and Rebekah had gone to Marion, especially today of all days.

Hayden's testimony and Rebekah's reaction had changed everything at the hearing. Thaddeus had interviewed both her and Rebekah separately, and then had disappeared for a few days. Those days were the worst days of her life. Not knowing what the judge would decide, she began to work out an exit strategy, but couldn't think of a single way to survive. She didn't know what would happen to her if she returned to her family, only that it had to be a fate worse than death. That, along with the broken heart she would have, knowing she would never be able to see her Franklin again.

The longer they all waited on a judgment, the more Cora and Rebekah had been convinced that they had won the case. All they needed was Elsa out of the way, and they could do whatever they wanted to with Franklin and their families. The girls endlessly taunted her during those long, trying days. She was already a hormonal mess because of the child, and all Elsa could do was cry for most of that long wait.

Her reprieve had finally come the previous Friday, when Thaddeus returned to the house with a verdict and a warning. He had visited with Liberty, only to find out that the judge was an emotional mess and Elsa's family was still in the county. Liberty was as much of a victim of the Garrett brothers as Elsa was, and they still had control over his friend.

Liberty had felt conflicted. He hated Deborah's family, but his father was partial to the men and had been the one who persuaded him to press charges on Franklin. Liberty never forgot the love Deborah had for Elsa but he was too weak to stand against his father.

Thaddeus, for his part, never gave up on Franklin and Elsa. He visited upon his friend every day until Liberty finally made a deal with him. He couldn't drop the charges, but he could declare Franklin sane and allow his friend to post Franklin's bail.

"Franklin should arrive soon," Juliette said, closing the door behind her, as Hayden sat on the bed with his hand protectively on his chest.

Elsa gazed at Hayden. "Thank you for defending us. I didn't think you would."

"Why wouldn't I?" Hayden asked.

"You're Rebekah's brother."

"So?"

Elsa shrugged, "Brothers are supposed to protect their sisters and make certain she honors the family name."

"Henry never did that."

"How do you know, Henry?"

"I met with him a few times when Franklin talked about going into business with him. I couldn't believe he was your brother. He loved his parents but never agreed with the way they treated you, Deborah, Nathan or Sam. He didn't want to raise Sam or Walter the same way his parents had raised him and he struggled with the fact that he needed your family support."

"He was like a father to me. I miss him, Hayden."

"I'm so sorry my wife and I never made it to the funeral. My children were sick."

Elsa nodded her head with a slight smile. She took a deep breath. "Are you parents upset with you?"

"I'm a grown man, Elsa. They can't tell me what to do."

"Parents can tell you what to do even after you're an adult. You still have to comply with their instructions even if you don't agree with them."

"That's not always true, Elsa. You've been sheltered and overly protected by your parents you entire life. You don't understand what it means to live in a household with parents who respect you."

"He's right, Elsa," Juliette said. She turned to face her mother-in-law. "Gideon and I see the fear you have in your eyes whenever you even think about your parents. You don't trust us."

"I do. It's...it's just so hard, Mrs. Raymond. I want to be the best wife and daughter but I can't live up to the expectations everyone has for me."

"What scares you the most?"

"I want to give Franklin the life he wanted for us. I don't want a marriage that starts in debt. I know what poverty does to a family and that's not the life I want for our child. I don't know how we are going to pay for the cost of the ring. But we will."

"Don't worry about it," Hayden reassured her. She turned her attention to him.

"How can I not? Frank borrowed money from your father to buy the engagement ring. He told me he had to work extra hours to earn the money to buy it...."

Juliette interrupted, "Gideon asked him about that, Elsa. It seems Franklin was once again one step ahead of us in his thinking."

"I don't understand."

"One thing about, Frank," Hayden started, "he knows his numbers. He may not know how to balance a checkbook be he knows how to save. He knew he would have to pay off my father because it was debt. What he didn't understand was that the longer the debt remained, the more my father controlled him. "

"He doesn't understand social situations."

"Exactly. To Frank, a debt is a debt. He didn't want to enter into a marriage with any debts."

Elsa grinned with understanding. "He was working extra jobs so he could pay off the debt and start a fresh life with me."

"Yes," Juliette answered.

"No wonder he was so agitated this entire time. He had our marriage already planned, but we pushed him to go against what he knew to be normal. Everything fell apart when he had the seizure and he couldn't control the circumstances surrounding us. The conditions he had placed for our marriage were ruined, and he couldn't change fast enough. When he came up with a plan, I was foolish enough to deny him until it was too late. The 'normal' he conceived in his head was ruined when my family interfered. Now he has a new situation and ...."

She looked up into Juliette's eyes. "He's going to panic, Mother. This is a new setting, and he doesn't know the people around him because he's never met your family before. He's had a routine in the hospital, but we are changing his routine by bringing him here."

"It's worse that that," Hayden said.

She turned to him. "What do you mean?"

"His 'normal' was Rebekah, Elsa. I don't know how he will react when he sees her."

"He loves me. He's told me several times she means nothing to him."

"And she doesn't," Juliette said. She placed her hands on the side of Elsa's arms. "He loves you. I can guarantee that." Juliette paused. "I'm going to tell you something that may hurt your feelings, but don't take it personally." She glanced at Hayden and continued, "He didn't do so because he loves her."

"Wha...,?" she closed her mouth, afraid to ask.

"You won his heart, but you have to win his mind," Hayden proclaimed bluntly.

"I...."

Tears cascaded down Elsa's cheeks. Win his mind? What had that bitch done to her Franklin? She embraced Juliette and sobbed. She knew what Hayden meant by those words, but she didn't want to admit them. No wonder Rebekah had been granted more time with Franklin, and he was distraught. Rebekah and her family had been plotting to turn Franklin against her.

"All hope is not lost, Elsa," Juliette said, taking the sides of her face and staring deeply into her eyes. "Franklin was saving his money to pay off the debt he owed."

"How much money did he save?"

"Not enough. Hayden has agreed to pay off his debt, but Franklin won't take it, because in his eyes he will think he owes Hayden money."

"Will we?"

"No," Hayden said as Juliette lowered her hands. "Consider it one of your wedding gifts. Elsa, my sister and Cora will be gone all day. We need to act quickly if you are going to marry Franklin."

"He already thinks I'm his wife. He won't understand that we need to be married by a judge."

"I know, but we can convince him otherwise. It's a long drive from Columbus to Upper Sandusky. That gives Gideon plenty of time to talk to Frank about the wedding. It won't be a large ordeal. I don't know how you feel about that."

"I don't care. I just want a life with Frank and our baby," she said, wiping the tears from her eyes with one hand on her stomach.

Hayden nodded, and then rose. He groaned, placed his hand on her headboard and stabilized his body.

"Hayden?" Juliette asked, concern on her face.

"I need to rest," he said with his head lowered.

"You can rest here," Elsa offered as she walked towards him.

Hayden lifted his head towards her with a smile. "I appreciate the offer, Elsa, but I would rather do so in my own bed. Franklin doesn't know what happened at the schoolhouse, and I don't think he needs to know, not yet. He won't take it well."

"I agree. We have to take things slow with him. Too much has happened, and he doesn't understand what is going on."

"Elsa," Hayden said, placing his arm on her shoulder. He looked her squarely in the eye. "Don't think for a second that, just because his uncle marries the two of you, that Rebekah will stop fighting to control him. You think Cora is mean? You haven't seen what my sister can do. My parents let her get away with anything because she is their only daughter. My family will make your lives miserable because Franklin chose you and not Rebekah."

"Frank is nice to Rebekah..." Juliette interrupted, and Elsa turned to face her... "only because she is 'normal' to him."

"He wouldn't cheat on me," Elsa said.

"He already has, but not because he wanted to."

Elsa stepped back, shaking her head. "No, he wouldn't," she muttered, glancing between the two of them. "He....he...he couldn't...He..."

"He doesn't understand, Elsa," Hayden explained, with a step in her direction. "Do you remember when your father told Franklin he couldn't marry you?"

"Yes. Frank didn't understand why it had happened. I could tell he was confused. I told him all I wanted was to be with him, but he left in such a state. I knew he wasn't sound enough to drive home."

"Oh, Elsa, you should have seen him after that. He was in that state for days, and he was so inconsolable that even Gideon couldn't calm him," Juliette said. "We went to your parents' house to ask what could be done to remedy the situation. Hayden and his wife stayed with Franklin and the children."

Hayden continued, "Franklin was so deep, Elsa, I didn't think I would be able to pull him out."

"But you did," she said.

"No, Rebekah called."

"Rebekah! He…," She clenched her jaw and glanced swiftly between them.

"Don't get upset, quite yet," Hayden said. She glared sharply at Franklin's best friend with a look that could kill. "I warned him against talking to her, Elsa. I really did."

"Then why did he do it?"

"Think about it, Elsa. She was with him for years before he met you," Juliette answered. Elsa turned in her direction. "You know how my son reacts when life becomes too stressful."

"He needs stability and …," Elsa swallowed hard, releasing the tension. "Isaiah told me Rebekah and Franklin have an off-and-on relationship. Cora told me Franklin dates other women when Rebekah isn't around, and when she returns he dumps them to run back into her arms."

She paused as she stared at the locket. Then she lifted her eyes to Hayden, "You said this locket was to be your sister's."

"I did, and do you remember what I told you after he gave it to you?"

"You said it took a lot of effort for Franklin to give it to me, and I should cherish it." She gasped with realization. "Oh, God, I'm not his wife. I'm 'the other woman'!"

Elsa stumbled back and sat in a chair by her vanity. She pulled the locket off, opened it, laid it aside, and held her hand to her stomach, her heart broken.

Hayden painfully knelt before her and pushed her chin up

with the crook of his finger.

"Listen to me, Elsa. If that were all you were to Franklin, we would not be having this discussion. You've done something to Franklin none of us ever expected another woman to do. We just assumed my sister would control him. We all knew what she was planning to do, but we couldn't stop it because Franklin followed Rebekah like a puppy follows its owner. She doesn't love him."

"Then why does she fight for him?"

Juliette answered, "For Cora. Cora believes she should have a share in the company, but my husband won't allow it because she's a woman. If Franklin marries Rebekah, she could control the company through Franklin. My husband's will states that the company is to be divided equally between our sons. Rebekah doesn't care about our family's business, but Cora does."

"Rebekah can have Franklin committed after her father dies," Hayden continued. "That would leave everything in the hands of his wife, and then she can hand his inheritance over to Cora."

"Gideon and I tried to convince Franklin that the match wasn't a good one when he told us he wanted to marry Rebekah. We saw it for what it was, a scam. But Franklin had his mind made up and, well, you know my son…"

"…once his mind is made up it's impossible to get him to change it," Elsa finished for her.

"You changed that, Elsa," Hayden said. Elsa turned to her eyes to the handsome man. "Frank loves you. That's what makes you different than all the other women he has dated."

"Cora said he falls in love all the time."

"He says he loves any woman he's dated, because he doesn't understand what that means. But that all changed when you came into his life, and he's confused by it. Elsa, you have power over Frank that threatens my sister. Rebekah knows it. So does Cora. That's why the girls hate you. Don't sit there and think you are just 'the other woman'. Franklin doesn't see you like that," he said, and lowered his hand.

"I love him, Hayden."

"I know you do. The problem is, in Franklin's eyes, he thinks he loves both of you equally. If he had a choice, he would marry both of you."

"Polygamy? That's illegal."

"He doesn't understand, Elsa," Hayden repeated firmly.

"You told me I won his heart, but if he loves both of us equally, then how can that be so?"

Juliette answered, "Because he doesn't understand the difference between true love and lust. I won't lie to you, Elsa. Franklin hasn't had sex with Rebekah, but he has touched her."

"But he doesn't like to be touched."

"No, but he'll let Rebekah. The only thing that keeps them apart in that matter is marriage and you. Rebekah wants his child because it will ensure her control over the company, especially if she has a son. You're an even greater threat to her now because you carry Franklin's child."

"Franklin won't give me his heart completely, will he?" Elsa whispered, playing with her engagement ring.

"He can't, not right now," Hayden answered. "But you can change that."

"You have a lot of faith in my abilities, Hayden. If Rebekah is around him, I might lose him."

"Elsa, look at me," Hayden ordered.

Elsa lifted her eyes to him. "You are the only woman, other than his mother, that I have ever seen have an effect on my best friend. He'll listen to you. Please don't give up on him, because if you do, Rebekah and Cora will stop at nothing to destroy him!"

"All I want is to be with him for the rest of my life."

"Marry him, and fight my sister on his behalf."

"What if she gets my family involved? I don't want any more bloodshed."

"Don't worry about that, Elsa," Hayden said, gently placing his hand on the side of her face. "You need to be strong. Gideon, Juliette, our families, and I will do everything we can to protect you. But we can't protect Franklin from Cora and Rebekah. You need to do that. Can you?"

Elsa nodded with a sniff of her nose. "Yes."

"Good. Rebekah told me she had some errands to run in Marion for my parents. She and Cora plan to return by tonight. The wedding needs to happen while they are gone, and I don't trust my sister to have given me the right time of her arrival. I wouldn't put it past her to come home earlier so she can try to persuade Franklin against the union. Therefore, Franklin won't be coming to this house."

"But…"

"We're going someplace that I know will be safe, where your family won't look for you, and that has a special meaning for Franklin. But we need to leave now."

Raymond Farm
Wyandot County, Ohio

Elsa sat on the end of Franklin's bed and swiped her hand down his quilt.

"Someplace special to Franklin". How could she had have been so naïve as to not think about his room when Hayden had told her of their journey? It was here Franklin had made her his wife.

Wife. The four-letter word had a bittersweet taste to it after everything she had been told today. But she loved this man more than life itself, and would do anything to have a life with him. That was far more than she could ever say about Rebekah Webster's attitude toward him.

Elsa crawled onto the bed, laid her head on Franklin's pillow, and closed her eyes. Warm memories of their time together in this room swarmed through her mind. She knew it was dangerous for her to have left Upper Sandusky only to return to Gideon's farm, but she didn't care. Hayden had vowed to protect her, and the community had sided with the Raymonds to keep her family away from the farm. To that end, the farm was under constant surveillance by the Wyandot sheriff's office.

Elsa rolled on her back, opened her eyes, and placed her hands behind her head. She stared up at the ceiling, recalling the time when Franklin had taken her as his wife.

The doorknob of his bedroom suddenly turned. She rose from the bed in anticipation as the door opened.

"Frank!" she cried, seeing her beloved enter the room. She ran and embraced him. Franklin kissed her deeply and closed the door behind him with his foot. He suddenly picked her up in his arms.

"Careful, Frank. I'm with child."

Franklin lowered her to her feet with a startled look on his face. "You're...uhm..," he glanced at her stomach then back to her face.

Elsa placed his hand on her stomach and held it there, "You're going to be a father," she told him, her eyes shining.

He pulled his hand away and shook his head. "We..I.."

Elsa could see it in his eyes. She had spoken too soon. He had just lived a life of hell in an asylum without her, and now she had told him this? What kind of fool was she? She needed him to think, not retract into his mind.

She walked over to him and gently took his hand. Franklin stared at her hand for a moment, and then silently raised his eyes to meet hers.

"It's alright. You don't have to change for the baby, Frank. I'll take care of everything."

"Where did you get the dress?" he asked, fidgeting with one of the buttons on her bodice.

Elsa smiled. Her typical Frank was trying to figure everything out. "Don't worry about the dress, my love. We have more important matters to attend to today."

"We can't afford a new dress. I haven't worked for a month, and..."

"Shh, Frank, it's alright. We don't owe anyone for my dress. Your mother said my clothes wouldn't fit in a few months. She promised to buy me maternity clothes from the store. This is just one of the dresses she bought me. I gained a few pounds, but not enough that I have begun to show. My clothes were already too small for me and I needed new ones anyways."

Franklin nodded, then walked to the bed. He sat down and pulled off his shoe.

Elsa turned to face him. At least he was settling back into his normal routine. Hayden's plan had worked. Her quiet man had returned to a place he felt comfortable with, and was somewhat at ease, but she could tell a piece of him wasn't with her in that room. The asylum and Rebekah had stolen the man she had worked so hard to bring to the surface. She picked up his shoe, knelt before him, and placed her hand on his leg.

"Stop," she told him in a soft voice.

"I'm tired."

"I know you are, Frank, but I need you to do something for me."

Franklin paused and stared blankly at the wall behind her, avoiding eye contact.

Elsa sighed to herself. They had worked so hard on maintaining eye contact, and now it was gone. "Look at me, Frank," she instructed him.

"I am looking at you."

"No, look me in the eyes."

Franklin slowly turned his eyes towards her. "Ask me."

"*Ask* you?"

Elsa huffed as she placed his shoe back on. Franklin had regressed terribly from his month of confinement and limited visitations with her. She had thought that her husband would return to her as the same man who had left her, but now her wonderful husband was trapped in the recesses of his mind. She wondered just how long he had been back there.

"We are going to get through this together, Frank. I know you are in there, and I know you love me," she said as she tied his shoe. "You wouldn't have kissed me if ..."

She paused as his fingers reached for her locket. Elsa grabbed the locket and stood. She stared at his longing face. "Frank," she whispered, removing the locket from around her neck.

"I gave that to you," he said, staring at his hand.

"Yes, at the church, remember?"

"I remember everything, Elsa. I'm not a fool."

"I never said you were," she said, and sat down next to him. She handed the locket to him. Franklin fidgeted with it, and then laid on his back.

"I'm so confused."

"How much did your father tell you?"

"What don't I know?"

"Frank, it's for the best I don't tell you everything," she said, gently stroking his chest.

"My father told me our pastor is coming over today to

marry us. I thought we were already married," he said, turning his eyes to face her.

Elsa lowered her body next to his and stared him deep in the eyes. "Under God we are united as man and wife, but man's law says we are not. Frank, I need to make this legal so no one can deny that the child is yours."

"I am your husband. You are pregnant. It should be simple enough. I will claim the child."

"Frank, it's not simple and, well, I never wanted it this way."

"You said you were wrong and I was right. I made you my wife under God and you agreed."

Elsa straddled her husband and sat upright as she stroked his chest. "I do not deny that what we did under God united us as man and wife." She placed his hand on her lower stomach. "You may recognize this child as your own, but society won't. They will call me a whore."

"You're not a whore."

"This child will be called a bastard."

"I am its father. It's not a bastard."

"Frank, you don't understand. I know you are my husband, and I freely accept that, but I want to carry your name. I can't change my name until we exchange vows."

Franklin moved his hand around her stomach. "A baby, Elsa," he reflected, lowering his hand and staring into her eyes. "I wanted to make you my wife, not start a family. I don't know how to be a father. I don't know what to do. I don't...." He paused as she leaned over him and placed her hand on his mouth.

"Frank, don't think about the baby. You are the husband. Your job is to work and provide for us. I am the wife. My job is to care for you, our children and our home. Stop. Don't go down that path in your mind. The baby is here, and there's nothing we can do about it except prepare for the inevitable. We need to marry, today."

"Today," he mumbled under her hand.

"Yes, today. It won't be a large wedding and you don't have

to worry about my family. They won't be in attendance. It'll just be you, me, your parents, and Hayden."

"What about his wife and children? Where's Rebekah? I know she's back. She visited me more than you ever did."

Elsa lowered her hand, clenched her jaw, and rose off of him.

"Where were you? She told me you didn't love me anymore."

"Shut up, Frank," she snarled at his accusation.

"I know I love you, Elsa but I love her, too. She wants to be my wife." He glared at Elsa. "I think I made a mistake."

"No, no, you didn't," Elsa exclaimed with tears in her eyes. "Please, Frank, don't believe her lies."

"I don't know what to believe. She told me you're a whore. But I know you aren't a whore. I have feelings for you, but I have feelings for her, too. Elsa, I don't know what to do. We are married under God, but you tell me that I have to marry you today. Rebekah's upset because she knows the ring on your finger...never mind." He sprang off the bed and headed for the door.

Elsa grabbed him by his coat and turned him to face her. She grabbed the back of his head and pulled him down. Then she kissed him.

Franklin slowly placed his hands around her body and returned her kiss.

She pressed her forehead to his. "Frank, you want me and you know it. Can you honestly tell me you have the same reaction with her?"

"Yes."

"Alright, but can you talk to her like you talk to me?"

"No." He rubbed his eyes. " Oh, Elsa, I'm so confused."

"I'll tell you what. I'll make you a deal."

"What?"

"Marry me for the sake of our child. If you fall in love with me..."

"...I'm already in love with you...."

"....I will not force my way into your heart, Frank. You're a grown man and should be treated as such. I would expect if you do ever decide to divorce me ..."

"I would never leave you."

"You can't have the both of us. You chose me once over her. Choose me again, Frank."

Elsa grinned from ear to ear as she fastened the last button of her dress. She never imagined things would turn out the way they did.

Franklin had made his choice between her and Rebekah the only way he could express it to her. Her wonderful handsome man had picked her up, placed her on their bed, and made passionate love to her. Her heart fluttered at the very thought of their encounter. He may be a man of few words, but oh, could he express himself. She was quite certain he was going to give her more than one child in this union.

Franklin was so exhausted from his entire ordeal that he had quickly fallen asleep after spilling his seed inside her. Elsa spent most of the early afternoon with her head on his chest, thinking about their future. There was no denying that Rebekah still had a grip on him, and she was going to have to do something about that, especially since Franklin had begun a physical relationship with her. Thankfully, he had never had sex with Rebekah, as far as anyone knew. She was able to see glimpses of Franklin today, but the man who lay beside her was more distant with her than usual. But the small glimpses of his personality that she had seen were worth more than gold. Her Franklin was still in there.

Elsa fixed her hair. She took one last look at her dress. Franklin was already downstairs, waiting for her next to the preacher. How odd it seemed that he had already opened his package before they'd said their vows. Normally, women wouldn't allow their future husband to have relations with them before the wedding, but Franklin wasn't normal. Nor were their circumstances.

She picked up her locket from the floor, placed it around her neck, and walked out the door.

Hayden stood in the hallway, dressed in his best suit, with a bouquet in his hands.

"I...."

He swallowed hard, and then handed it to her. "My wife carried it on our wedding day. I know she would want you to have it."

Elsa glanced at the beautiful arrangement of roses and tulips, and then gently took it from him. "Thank you," she replied, so overcome that she couldn't think of anything else to say.

"It's old, and I know the flowers are dead, but..."

She placed her hand on his arm. "Hayden, it's lovely. Really, it is. I would be honored to carry it. How did you get it from your house?"

"I didn't. Cora caught it on our wedding day. I was surprised she still had it, knowing how much she hated my wife."

"Oh."

"If you don't...."

"Hayden, I didn't mean it in a bad way. I just find it quite odd, like you do, that Cora would have retained it. Perhaps she did so because of Rebekah."

"Probably," he said, taking her arm in his. "I've saved all my energy to do this for you."

"Do what?"

"You need a man to give you to Franklin, don't you? I don't quite think your father would be someone we should ask, do you?"

"Absolutely not." Hayden nodded, and then slowly escorted her down the stairs to the parlor. "I never told Franklin about the schoolhouse or your injuries."

"I told him my wife and children are with Rebekah. I appreciate your kindness in the matter."

"You're welcome." She sighed. " He's not the same man, Hayden."

"I know. I see that in him as well, and I don't like it."

He paused in mid step and gripped the banister with a

grunt of pain. He moved Elsa's hand from his arm and clutched his rib cage.

"Hayden, what's wrong?" Franklin asked from below, as his best friend hunched over with a long groan.

"It's nothing, Frank. Go stand by the preacher," Gideon directed his son, as he ran across the room and up the stairs.

Elsa stared at Franklin while she held Hayden. She knew that look on Franklin's face. He wasn't a fool. Everyone was pretending nothing had happened while Franklin had been committed, but Franklin wasn't buying it. She wondered what pack of lies Rebekah had told him, and what he believed had happened to Hayden's family.

She couldn't stand it any longer. Franklin needed to know the truth.

She watched Gideon help Hayden, then looked down at her beloved. Then she picked up the skirt of her dress and walked down the stairs.

"He can rest in our room, Mr. Raymond. There's no sense having him climb down the stairs when he has obviously overexerted himself," Elsa said with authority.

"Elsa, what are you doing?" Gideon asked.

"Something that needs to be done."

She walked to Franklin and pointed to Hayden. "Hayden came to the schoolhouse after you were arrested so he could get money to bail you out. He also wanted to tell me what had happened. But it was too late. My parents, Uncle Moses and Uncle Jesse came to the schoolhouse to get me. Hayden saw them and hid me in the storage room. Then he confronted my family. They asked for my location and he lied to them. Then Uncle Moses killed his wife and shot him in the chest. They left him for dead."

"Wha..," Franklin started to ask, then stopped as she placed her finger on his lips.

"There's more, Frank." She closed her eyes and prayed for the strength to continue.

"When Cora and I came upon the scene, Hayden had lost too much blood. Isaiah had called your father and the doctor from Hayden's house. Your family and I have been hiding out in Upper Sandusky ever since. Dr. Riley operated on Hayden, but he was so weak from the loss of blood that he almost died. Your father gave a blood transfusion to him during the operation. Hayden has several broken ribs, and half his lung was removed. He's not strong enough to return to his normal life yet because of the complications from the lack of oxygen, blood loss, and the shock he had after he was shot. That man," she strongly said taking her finger from his lips and pointing to Hayden, "believes in our union so much that he testified against his sister to the judge. He's the reason you are free." She lowered her hand. Franklin stared up at Hayden and his father. "Frank, I know you are confused. I know you love me and you think you love Rebekah the same way. You proved your love for me in our bedroom this afternoon, but I know you still can't let Rebekah go." She reached up and turned his head, forcing him to look at her. "I didn't visit you in the asylum not out of choice. I was pushed out of the way by Rebekah and Cora."

"Your family did that to Hayden," Franklin asked, clearly not understanding the entire situation.

"That's not the point, Frank," Hayden cried, then coughed.

Franklin pushed Elsa aside and turned to face his friend.

"Marry her!" Hayden sat down on the stairs and coughed. He heard a footfall, and looked up to see that Franklin had climbed the first few steps. Hayden huffed and shook his head while Gideon rubbed his back.

"I don't understand, Hayden."

Hayden pushed through his pain, "I know you don't. She's good for you, Frank, and I think you know that. Don't ruin her life, Frank. Do the right thing and make her your wife."

"I made her my wife. She carries my child."

"Ugh," Hayden moaned, lowering his head between his legs.

"Franklin," Gideon said to his son, his voice soft.

Franklin turned his attention to his father.

"In your mind, she is your wife," Gideon continued.

"Yes."

"Remember when I told you that sometimes what is in your head is not what other people around you perceive as the truth?"

"Yes, sir."

"You did wrong to Elsa, and perhaps we all did wrong to the both of you by allowing it to happen. When a man makes a mistake, he admits he did wrong and he rectifies the situation, no matter the cost."

"She told me she wanted to be my wife. She seduced me."

"It was your plan to begin with!" Elsa argued.

Franklin turned to her, then back to his father. "I... made a promise. I always keep my word. You taught me that, father. I can't marry Elsa because I promised Rebekah I would marry her. I love both women. I don't know what to do."

"You already married Elsa," Hayden growled. "How the hell do you think you can marry my sister when Elsa carries your child? Do the right thing and marry Elsa. Forget my sister."

"I stood next to the preacher. I'm ready to marry her under the law."

"You stood there because everyone is telling you what to do, Frank. Be honest. What do you want?"

"I want both women."

"You can't have both of them! It's either Rebekah or Elsa. Choose one, and don't choose Elsa because you think that's what everyone wants from you. Choose her because you love her."

"I love both..."

Hayden lunged at Franklin and pulled him towards him. "Frank, you've never lied to me before, so don't start now. Close your eyes."

"What?"

"Just do it."

Franklin complied with Hayden's instructions.

"Alright, I want you to imagine that you are in your workshop. Not the one everyone knows about. The one your father built for you underneath his own shop."

"That's my secret, Hayden," Franklin replied in a whisper, opening his eyes. "I haven't even told Elsa about it. She thinks I work in my office."

"Trust me, Frank. Close your eyes and go there in your head."

Franklin reluctantly closed his eyes and focused on the subterranean workshop he loved the most.

Hayden continued, "Imagine there was a disaster."

"What kind of disaster?"

"It doesn't matter."

"Yes, it does, because the interior of my workshop might be compromised in several different ways, depending upon the severity of the disaster and the...."

"Franklin, stop thinking and focus on my words."

"Fine, but I still..."

"Frank!"

Franklin closed his mouth and refocused his attention on the workshop. Hayden took a deep breath and coughed.

"Hayden?"

He cleared his throat. "I'm fine. I can't get used to not having half of my left lung. Ugh, where were we?"

"I'm in my workshop and a disaster happened. We were discus..."

"We weren't discussing anything, Frank. I want you to imagine something has happened to Marion. You can only survive in the workshop and you can only choose one woman to live with you in the workshop. Who would you choose, Elsa or Rebekah?"

"That's easy, Hayden."

"Who is it, Frank?"

"Elsa."

Hayden released Franklin with a nod. "Open your eyes." Franklin complied. "You chose Elsa because you not only love her, but you trust her."

"With all my heart, Hayden."

"You only want to marry Rebekah out of duty, not from in here," he said, holding his hand over Franklin's heart. "Don't lose Elsa, Frank. You don't know what it's like to lose the woman you love and know that you'll never get her back. I do. My wife is gone, Frank. Gone," Hayden said with a tear running down his cheek. "I tried so hard to protect her, but there was nothing I could do to save her. I don't want you to feel the pain I bear. Give your entire heart to Elsa and forget my sister. Please."

Franklin rose from the stairs and peered toward his beloved Elsa with a fresh look. Hayden had been right. He hadn't fully committed to his union with Elsa. He was only marrying her because everyone had told him it was the right thing to do.

He tugged at his vest and turned to Hayden. "Thank you."

"You're welcome. You wouldn't mind if I use your bed?"

"Elsa already said you could. Besides we already used it."

"You know you're supposed to have sex after the ceremony and not before."

"Is that another rule I missed?"

"Frank. Go get married."

Franklin ran down the stairs. Hayden had been right. Although he loved Elsa, he hadn't been fully committed to this idea of a private wedding in their home. Hadn't he already married her? He had tried so hard to make this day come true, but not like this.

Elsa deserved better than this. She deserved the big church wedding with lots of family surrounding them. The kind of wedding she had always dreamed of. But here she was standing in his living room with a new dress and his child in her stomach. Why couldn't things just happen the way he had planned them?

He took Elsa's hand in his own and tried to look her in the eyes, like she had always wanted him to do. He wanted to tell her how much he loved her and what she meant to him. He opened his mouth to speak and closed it.

"It's alright, Frank. I know," she gently told him.

She knew? Of course she knew, but he still wanted to be able to say the words.

"Don't get frustrated. I'll help you through the ceremony, alright?"

Franklin nodded. It was all he could do. She guided him to the preacher with a gentle smile. Thank heavens the person marrying them was someone he knew and admired. He watched the preacher's mouth move but didn't hear any of the words. The words didn't make much sense to him anyway. It was a lot like sitting in church and hearing some of the sermons. He loved his pastor, but didn't understand why people would be so cruel to each other and why the pastor needed to remind them to act out of love instead of selfishness. It was as if he was lost in this world.

Juliette was suddenly there. She placed her hand on the preacher's shoulder.

Where had his mother come from, and why did she appear so distressed?

The preacher stopped and listened as she whispered something in his ear.

"The rings?" he asked, Hayden, who was still sitting on the stairs.

"I almost forgot," Hayden said, standing up. He handed a ring box to Gideon. Franklin watched his father leave his best friend's side and approach the pastor with the strange looking box.

Rings? Where did the rings come from? He mentally ran through a list of things he had bought before he was arrested. He had planned to buy a set of rings but he couldn't afford them. Franklin stared at the preacher's hands. The man opened the box and ...oh, God, it was those rings!

His heart plunged at the sight of the rings that had been chosen for his wedding. They were too expensive. He didn't have the funds. He didn't.....

"Frank," Elsa's voice entered his ears. He turned to face her. "They're a gift from Hayden. He said he knew which rings you had planned to buy for us, and wanted us to have them."

"Gift?"

"Yes, my love. Shh, it's ok. Shh."

He closed his eyes and took in the sweet feel of her soft hands stoking his cheeks. He loved the way she touched. There was no one in this world that could calm him down like her.

"Frank?"

Franklin opened his eyes. "I'm okay."

"You sure?"

He nodded as he exhaled a deep breath.

"Good."

The pastor turned to Franklin and handed him Elsa's ring. "Put it on my finger," Elsa whispered. Franklin gently placed the ring on her finger as the pastor asked him, "Franklin Thaddeus Raymond, do you take Elsa Beatrice Garrett to be your wife? Will you love her, comfort her, honor and keep her, in sickness and in health, for richer, for poorer, for better, for worse, in sadness and in joy, to cherish and continually bestow upon her your heart's deepest devotion, forsaking all others, keeping yourself only unto her as long as you both shall live?"

"I will."

The preacher looked sternly in his direction.

Elsa mouthed to him, "I do."

"I mean I do," he answered to the preacher.

"Now let go of my hand and give me your left hand," Elsa guided him.

The preacher handed a ring to Elsa just as Franklin gave her his left hand. She took his left ring finger and gently slid his ring on as the preacher asked, "Elsa Beatrice Garrett, do you take Franklin Thaddeus Raymond to be your husband? Will you love him, comfort him, honor and keep him, in sickness and in health, for richer, for poorer, for better, for worse, in sadness and in joy, to cherish and continually bestow upon him your heart's deepest devotion, forsaking all others, keeping yourself only unto him as long as you both shall live?"

"I do," she answered.

"And so, by the power vested in me by the State of Ohio and Almighty God, I now pronounce you man and wife. You may now kiss the bride."

Franklin placed his hand on the back of Elsa's head and

kissed her passionately. She embraced him tightly. Never before had he felt so much passion for her. What was it about this ceremony that made him want her even more?

He picked Elsa up in his arms. She laughed as she wrapped her arms around his neck. "Hayden, go rest in my sister's room," he blurted out as he climbed the stairs.

"Ladies and gentlemen, may I present Mr. and Mrs. Franklin Raymond," the pastor said, as the newlyweds headed up. Everyone laughed.

Suddenly the front door opened. Franklin turned to see who had entered his home.

Rebekah and Cora stood in the living room with a look of shock and horror. He ignored the girls, carried Elsa into his bedroom, and slammed the door behind them.

Don't miss out on the next installment of THE
SECRET HERITAGE series

Something New,

Something Old

Read on for a preview ...

Chapter One

July 23, 1904
Raymond's Farm
Wyandot County, Ohio

Midmorning sunlight shown brightly through Frank and Elsa Raymond's small, second story bedroom window. Elsa grimaced, with her eyes closed. Her stomach turned. "Oh, not again," she complained with a hand over her nine week pregnant belly. Elsa slowly sat upright with her feet on the floor. Her head pounded from the sounds of hammering outside. She could hear Cora and Rebekah's voices across the hall. Seemed everyone was awake, active and alert, except for her. All she wanted to do is go back to bed but that was out of the question.

Elsa rose, grabbed her robe from the back of Franklin's chair, placed it on and walked to the open window. The light nearly blinded her half awake eyes. She shielded her eyes, adjusted to the light then peered down at the lawn

"Frank," Elsa cupped her hands and yelled out their second story bedroom window.

Franklin turned to face her. "Good morning," he yelled to her as he stepped towards the house with a hammer in his right hand.

"Ugh, I don't know if it's such a good morning or not. What time is it?"

"Eleven thirty. You still sick?"

"Stupid question, Frank!"

"I'm sorry," he pleaded, lifting his hands in the air and stepping backwards.

Elsa sighed. It wasn't his fault. Her poor husband didn't understand what he should and should not say to her in her condition. Thing was, even though he didn't understand social cues and he didn't communicate very well, he wasn't unlike most men in the area of being a new father. Most men didn't know how to talk to a woman during her pregnancy or while she was menstruating.

"Apology accepted, Frank. I'm sorry for my foul mood. I don't feel well."

"I left the aspirin on the nightstand. Ma left some soup for you on the stove. She said you need that instead of the food we eat."

"Where is she?"

"Oh, she went to take food over to Hayden's house. Pa said he should be ready to come back to work next week."

"Oh, Hayden's healing nicely then?"

"Physically, but emotionally he still mourns his wife."

"He will for sometime, Frank. It hasn't been that long since he lost her." Elsa placed her hand on her stomach, lifted a finger to him then ran to the metal basin next to their bed and vomited. She heaved several times then slowly rose from over it, wiping her mouth with her sleeve. Elsa walked slowly to the window.

"You alright," Franklin asked.

Elsa nodded. "I don't think I'll be in the mood to socialize tonight. I just don't know why you agreed to have the festival at our farm when I'm with child," she groaned, lowering her head to the windowsill.

"No one has ever asked me to do something for them like this before."

"You don't even like to be around people."

"I don't like being around you or people. You I have to live with them I don't," he snarled at her.

"Ugh," she grunted, stood up and slammed the window hard. How dare he talk to her in that manner! She closed the drapes. Elsa pulled her long brunette hair from behind the robe and brushed her hair while she looked into the mirror. Tears ran down her face. Oh, great, she was crying, again. She was angry with Franklin for disrespecting her, upset that they had gotten into a fight and sadness from the harmful words he had sad. She was an emotionally mess. She only hoped that she would emotionally stable when it came time for his trial. That last thing the courts needed to see was a husband without emotion and a wife with too much emotion.

Elsa placed her brush on the vanity, washed her face in the basin of water, wiped her face off with a towel and dressed for the day. Today was Summer Barn Dance. She might as well make the best of the rest of the day. Franklin was determined to show the county he could be as normal as they are. Problem was, Franklin was never going to be normal.

"Diabetes," she gasped, realizing she didn't see Gideon out there with him. It wasn't like Gideon or Hayden not to be constantly by his side. Her husband needed constant attention when dealing with people. He didn't interact well with others. Franklin said it was 11:30 and he had been known to work all day without eating anything. It was a hot day out today. Her mind began to swarm with terrible thoughts. She rushed to the window, opened it and yelled towards him. "Frank!"

"What do you want," he yelled from the stage, holding a plank of wood in place.

"When was the last time you ate anything?"

Franklin sighed and lifted his head towards the window. "It's been awhile, Elsa. We got so busy I forgot my mid-morning meal. Pa went in to get me something to eat."

"When was that? You're in a fool mood and that usually happens when you're starting to have a diabetic attack."

"He just went inside! Elsa, please. I need to finish this."

"No, you need to come inside and eat something."

"I'm fine."

"Then why are your hands shaking?"

Franklin lowered his eyes and stared at his hands for a long time. "Elsa," he called to her then swallowed hard.

ABOUT THE AUTHOR

Bestselling author Allison Bruning has always had a passion for the literary arts. She originally hails from Marion, Ohio but lives in Marfa, Texas with her husband and their Australian Cattle Dog, Lakota Sioux..

The Secret Heritage series is a very personal series to Allison because it is deeply rooted in her family history. Asperger's Syndrome is very prevalent in her mother's side of the family and her father's side of the family is bipolar. She knows what it means to be a caregiver and one who has difficulties in life. The relationship between Franklin and Elsa was inspired by the relationship of her aunt and uncle who taught her that no matter what difficulties you go through in life a real marriage is all about commitment and unconditional love.

Allison's educational background includes a BA in Theatre Arts with a minor in Anthropology and a Texas Elementary Teaching certificate, both acquired at Sul Ross State University in Alpine, Texas. Allison received National Honor Society memberships in both Theatre Arts and Communication. She was also honored her sophomore year with admission into the All American Scholars register. She holds graduate hours in Cultural Anthropology and Education. In 2007, Allison was named Who's Who Among America's Educators. She is also the recipient of the Girl Scout Silver and Gold Awards. Allison received her Masters of Fine Arts in Creative Writing at Full Sail University on June 28, 2013, and currently pursuing her PhD in Gifted Education from Walden University. She is an educator, writer, speaker, screenwriter, film director, and publisher.

Allison's interests include Ohio Valley history, anthropology, travel, culture, history, camping, hiking, backpacking, spending time with her family, and genealogy. She can be found on Facebook at https://www.facebook.com/AllisonBruning. She is also on twitter @emeraldkell. Her blog can be found at http://allisonbruning.blogspot.com. Her author page on Goodreads is http://www.goodreads.com/emeraldkell and her Amazon author page may be found at http://amzn.to/LZ0UsT.

www.ingramcontent.com/pod-product-compliance
Lightning Source LLC
Chambersburg PA
CBHW070914260626
47162CB00007B/2668